O Lambe

GIDEON'S LONDON
OMNIBUS

This is the first Gideon Omnibus to appear in
paperback, and it contains three full-length
stories from the best-selling Gideon series.

Gideon's London
Omnibus

John Creasey
writing as
J. J. Marric

CORONET BOOKS
Hodder Paperbacks Ltd., London

Printed in Great Britain for Coronet Books,
Hodder Paperbacks, Ltd.,
St Paul's House, Warwick Lane, London, E.C.4,
by Richard Clay (The Chaucer Press), Ltd.,
Bungay, Suffolk

ISBN 0 340 16653 3

Contents

Introduction

INTRODUCTION

Maurice Richardson said in *The Observer* that 'George Gideon has done more than any other character in fiction to maintain the reading public's faith in Scotland Yard.' It is equally true that no other author since Dickens has done more to show London in all its many-sided aspects than John Creasey in this unique series. The books are far more than police procedurals. In each there are slices of London life presented so vividly and with such telling accuracy that those who know and love London revel in them, and strangers have pictures of the great city and its teeming millions clearer than any they could get from guide, descriptive, or even illustrated, books of any kind.

In each book there is one main theme dealing with an aspect of London crime, which Gideon—Commander of the Criminal Investigation Department—investigates through the actions of one of his chief superintendents. Other cases—some of great significance, some almost trifling—are handled by different detectives of various rank, but all of their work passes over Gideon's desk and through his mind.

The main themes are in themselves absorbing studies of different features of London life.

In GIDEON'S MARCH the reader is taken behind the scenes in the preparations for a State Visit, when the Queen rides with her distinguished guest from overseas. The throbbing life of the crowd, the pageantry, the thoroughness of the police in trying to make sure nothing goes wrong, while at the same time an assassin plans to strike, comes home with tremendous impact.

GIDEON'S RIVER has the Thames as its main theme; the busy, bustling, dangerous life of the river, and of the remarkable men who police this great artery of London—an artery, too, for desperate criminals who plan the coup of a lifetime.

In GIDEON'S WRATH the main theme is of vandalism in London's beloved cathedrals as well as in some parish churches; of hatred for religion as well as deep love and respect for it. And all the time there is an impending sense of danger, of menace, not only to these historic buildings, but to men and women going about their daily lives.

These are stories not only of the police and of people but of London. . . . Gideon's London.

BOOK ONE

Gideon's March

CONTENTS

1

LONDON'S PAVEMENTS

THE old and the young wives' tale about the pavements of London being harder than pavements anywhere else had never impressed George Gideon, partly because he had long been aware of the usefulness of thick leather soles. In his schooldays and early adolescence, home-made soles had been hammered on to the shiny surface of new boots and shoes by his father, who had been hard put to it to make ends meet, yet determined that no son of his should ever go ill-shod. Soon after he had been accepted by the Metropolitan Police as a constable, and stationed in Hampstead—just about as far away from his home in Fulham as one could get in the Metropolitan area—Gideon had realized the importance of boots, shoes and feet which could stand up to a lot of use. His first extravagance had been to have boots made for him, with specially padded soles; his second had been to pay hard-earned money for the monthly attention of a chiropodist. To Gideon, always a man of down-to-earth common sense, this had been the same kind of thing as making sure that the tyres of his bicycle were inflated properly, and that the tread was never smooth.

A consequence of this was that today, in his fifty-third year, he could pound the pavements of London as solidly and purposefully as any newly appointed constable. Sometimes his legs ached; his feet, never.

In those early days a glow of romanticism had seemed to turn the smooth paving stones to gold, or the promise of gold, and in a way he had never stopped looking for it, although there was no more rational man in London. Few things gave him more satisfaction than a walk through his own Square Mile, with Piccadilly Circus its heart. London had the comfortable familiarity of a good wife, and gave him just as much satisfaction.

On a morning in May, just after nine-thirty, Gideon got off a bus half-way along Victoria Street and walked towards Westminster Abbey; there were few approaches to London which he liked better. He was on foot because his car was being serviced. A squad car would have picked him up, but he preferred to go by bus, even though it had meant queuing for ten minutes, then standing for another fifteen. Now he strode along, watching the late arrival office workers darting into gloomy doorways and disappearing up narrow staircases or crowding round old-fashioned lifts. This part of London had changed very little in fifty years, none of the rectangular modern blocks of offices and flats yet gashed the skyline. Gideon strode along, head and sometimes head and shoulders above most of the people whom he passed, big powerful shoulders slightly rounded, thick iron-grey hair brushed straight back from his forehead, head thrust forward—he walked as he lived, always knowing where he wanted to go, and finding the shortest way. He had a look of almost aggressive power. Every policeman on the route stiffened when he recognized the Commander of the Criminal Investigation Department.

Two sergeants met at the approach to Parliament Square just after he passed.

"Old Gee-Gee looks as if he'll be on the rampage this morning," one man said.

"I was just thinking about him," said the other. "I've known him for twenty years, and except that he's a bit greyer he hasn't changed at all."

"Dunno that I want him to change," the first man reflected. "Do you remember the time when he said if we didn't get more men on the force, he'd throw his hand in?"

"Who doesn't? Wonder why he's walking this morning?" the second man mused aloud, and grinned. "Probably come to keep an eye on us, although we wouldn't know it!"

Gideon kept to the right of Parliament Square, passing the statue of Abraham Lincoln, so that he could see the courtyard of the Houses of Parliament, Big Ben, all the recently cleaned gothic stonework, the intricacy of the carving, the satisfying, harmonious whole. Then he reached the corner of Parliament Square, glanced along Whitehall towards Trafalgar Square, and made a pick-pocket who was having an early session dodge quickly out of sight; there were many habitual criminals in London prepared to swear that Gideon had eyes at the back of his head.

He turned along the Embankment, glanced across at the London County Hall, heard a moaning note from a tug on the river, was saluted by two uniformed men on duty as he turned into the Yard, and up the stairs to the front hall. The duty sergeant said "Good morning," and smiled. A dozen strapping, youngish men were waiting in the hall, and Gideon remembered that a party of Australian policemen from the Criminal Investigation Bureaux of five states were going to be shown round the Yard. The grey-haired sergeant opened the door leading to the C.I.D. section of the building, but Gideon turned round to look at the visitors.

"Is Detective-Inspector Wall here?" he inquired.

A man with a rather big head, and a very brown face, took a half-step forward.

"I'm Detective-Inspector Wall, from Brisbane."

"I'm Gideon," said Gideon, knowing quite well that they had been told who he was as he had walked up the steps. "Glad to see you, Inspector. Your father was a Superintendent here when I was a flatfoot." He shook hands with Wall, and acknowledged the others with a wave of the hand. "Enjoy the tour."

He went through the passage door, leaving a gratified and murmuring group behind him, and strode along to his own office. He knew that from the moment he had stepped into the Yard, old Joe Bell had been warned. Joe, his personal *aide*, was only a few years off retirement, and there were those who said that he should have retired at sixty, not waited until he was sixty-five. He was the best personal assistant Gideon had ever had. Already he would have all the morning's reports looked over and placed in order of importance.

He was sitting at his desk, square behind the door; Gideon's desk was slant-wise across the wide window, so that he could get full advantage of the light from the Embankment. The office had pale green walls, dark brown furniture, a carpet, two filing cabinets, several telephones and a couple of rows of books—from police manuals to bound copies of the *Police Gazette*, Gross on *Criminal Investigation*, Glaister's *Medical Jurisprudence*, a dog-eared dictionary, and a current edition of *Whittaker's Almanac*, as well as of the New York *World Telegram's World Almanac*. This last was a regular Christmas gift from a friend in New York Police Headquarters.

"'Morning, Joe."

"'Morning, George."

Gideon eased his collar, then took off his coat; it was warm, and the sun was gilding the windows.

"How have the bad men been behaving?" inquired Gideon, and glanced out. The Thames' boats were gay with striped awnings on the smooth water, for the up-river and down-river trips had already begun.

"About average," said Bell. He was a smaller man than Gideon, rather plump, round-faced, a little untidy, nearly bald, always apparently in need of a haircut. "You'd better have a talk to Abbott. He's got a bit mixed up over the Carraway job, can't make up his mind whether we ought to charge Carraway or just watch him. Apart from that, there's nothing you need worry about until you've seen the A.C."

Gideon, glancing down at some reports on his desk, said absently: "Eh?" and then looked up. "What was that about the A.C.?"

"I had a call put out over the air for you. Didn't you get it?"

"I walked."

"Oh, lor'," said Bell, in dismay. "I thought you'd be

all ready for the conference." He was obviously perturbed. "Something's up. I tried to get an inkling out of the A.C.'s secretary, but the bitch says she doesn't know what it's all about. Can't we do anything about that woman, George? Ever since she got that job, she's been—"

"When's the meeting due?"

"Rogerson says will you go in as soon as you can."

"Where's Abbott?"

"Waiting next door."

"I'll talk to him." Gideon picked up a telephone, said : "Mr. Rogerson, please," and held on. After a moment, he heard Rogerson's secretary. "Mr. Rogerson there?"

"Who wants him, please?"

This was what Bell meant; the newly appointed but fairly long-in-the-tooth secretary who had been wished upon the Assistant Commissioner knew perfectly well who was calling. Gideon was tempted to raise his voice, but instead said mildly :

"Commander Gideon."

"Just one moment, Commander." There was a pause, and during it the door opened and Abbott came in. Abbott was a comparative newcomer to the Chief Superintendents' ranks, and wasn't yet sure of himself. Gideon had a feeling that he might never make the grade; he was too often afraid that he might do the wrong thing.

"Take a pew, Abbott," Gideon said, and Rogerson came on the line.

"Yes?"

"How long can I have?" Gideon asked.

"Can't you come right away?"

"I'd rather be ten minutes."

"All right," said Rogerson. "We'll turn up a bit late. Don't be a minute longer than you can help."

"I won't," promised Gideon, and put the telephone receiver down and pushed his chair back. He knew that to Abbott, as to many men who did not know him well, he was something of an ogre; certainly a man to be wary and chary of.

Abbott was shorter than many at the Yard, and that

put him at a disadvantage. To look at, he was the ideal strong man of the boys' adventure books; his chin was square, his brown eyes deep-set, his eyebrows thick, well defined, and slightly blacker than his hair, which was beginning to turn from chestnut brown to grey. He moistened his lips.

"'Morning, Abbott," said Gideon. "Carraway playing you up?"

"I can't make up my mind whether we have enough evidence against him to justify an arrest," said Abbott. "Mind you, I'm pretty sure he's our man. But his alibi for the night when Arthur Rawson was murdered might stand up. And if it does—" he broke off.

"Seen Carraway himself since yesterday morning?"

"Only for five minutes."

"What did he say?"

"He's as bland as ever, Mr. Gideon—seems to enjoy pretending that he doesn't know that he is under suspicion of murdering his partner. The fact remains that he inherits the business, and he was in serious financial difficulty before his partner's death. Apart from this alibi, we could make a good case," Abbott said. "There's another angle I'm following up. Carraway's living with a young girl named Belman, Marjorie Belman. I thought she would turn out to be a hard-bitten bitch, but she seems a nice enough kid. I'm going to see if I can work on her to break the alibi."

"Go over it again, every aspect of it. Interview the three men who make the alibi for Carraway, then talk to that girl. Be here at six o'clock sharp this evening, and we'll go over it together."

"I'll be here on the dot," Abbott promised. "Thank you very much, Mr. Gideon."

He backed out.

"If you ever make him worth a Chief Super's pension, I'll buy you a dinner," said Bell. "You going to leave the rest to me?"

"Yes—but keep a check on that Australian party, make sure no one skimps with them in the *Information Room* and in *Records*. Send a personal note—no, wait a minute, I'll do that myself." Gideon lifted his telephone as he got up, and said: "Get me Mr. King-Hadden, of *Finger-prints*." He stood looking across at Bell, saying: "You have a word with the Black Museum, and make sure that they don't overdo the sex and sadism stuff. Hallo, Nick— George here. You know we've an Australian party on the way round?" He grinned. "I know what you think about Cooks' tours! Make sure they get a complete story on those prints you dug out of the pot-hole in Derbyshire, will you? Show 'em that the Yard can solve a forty-years-old murder when it feels like it. And tidy your place up a bit. . . . You know damned well what I mean! Show one of your chaps a duster, clear away some of the junk in the corner, and don't have too many dirty tea cups around." He paused, chuckled, and went on: "All right, Nick, all right, I'll look in myself and see whether you've had a spring cleaning or not." He rang off, took his jacket off the back of his chair and went to the door. "Now I'll go and see what all the trouble's about," he said to Bell. "I can't think of anything that would need a special con-ference, unless the Home Secretary's latest pronounce-ment on the state of crime in the country has stung questions out of the Opposition. We haven't got any big job outstanding."

"Nothing I know of," Bell said.

"I'll get back as soon as I can," promised Gideon, and went out, thinking of the summons and, a little uneasily, about Carraway.

"And it's got to be done as soon as possible," Carraway was saying, about that time. He was a man of medium height, smooth haired, smooth shaven, with very dark brown eyes. He looked into the scared face of Eric Little, one of his car salesmen, and took a packet of five-pound notes out of the side pocket of his beautifully tailored tan-coloured suit. He slapped the wad on to the palm of his left hand. "Here's five hundred of the best, Eric. You get the other five hundred when she's dead."

"Bruce, how do you know she'll talk? How do you know—?"

"She'll talk because she hasn't got the guts to stand up to police questioning," Carraway declared. "You know it as well as I do."

"Listen, I—"

"Now you listen to me," interrupted Carraway sharply. "You take her down to Brighton, and drown her. I don't want any more argument. You're getting a thousand quid for the job, you've got nothing to worry about."

"Bruce, Jorrie's a nice kid—"

"So what? There are thousands of nice kids. There was one you strangled, remember? You choked the life out of her because she was in the family way, and going to make trouble with your wife and kids. You got away with that, thanks to me. Now you'll kill this other *nice* kid—my way. Because if you don't, an anonymous telephone call to the police will make them ask a lot of awkward questions. Don't give me that line about conscience."

Little muttered: "Okay, Bruce, okay." He put his hand out and took the wad of notes. Soon, his eyes brightened. "Don't you worry," he went on. "I'll put her down with the fishes." He moved away and looked through the glass walls of Carraway's office, to the rows of used cars, all marked *For Sale*, and at the big sign which read: *Car Hire—Lowest Terms*. There was a slump in second-hand car sales, and it would take him six months to earn five hundred pounds in commission.

Carraway, who knew him well, could almost read his thoughts.

2

SPECIAL CAUSE

THE office of Rogerson, the Assistant Commissioner for Crime, was on the same floor but round a corner from Gideon's. Rogerson was sitting on the corner of his desk, dictating to the middle-aged secretary, a Miss Timson, who had recently taken over from another middle-aged secretary who had unexpectedly decided to get married. Miss Timson was rather tall, slightly angular, always neatly and simply dressed, always freshly coiffeured; except for her manner, there was no way she could be faulted. Her manner now said that even the Commander should have knocked. Rogerson held up a hand to Gideon, and finished dictating:

". . . and in my considered view the Home Secretary's statement to the House of Commons that crime in London is showing marked signs of a decrease is ill-advised and ill-timed, as the decrease in the period under review is almost certainly due to the extremely hard winter. That's all, Miss Timson." He stood up. "Good morning, George."

"'Morning," said Gideon, and waited for Miss Timson to disappear. Her skirts were short; she had nice legs, and from behind looked ten years less than her age. The door closed on her. "What's the rush?"

"Don't know much about it myself," said Rogerson. He was tall, and running to fat, although when Gideon had first known him he had been lean and hardy-looking. A coronary had pulled him down, and he was no longer allowed to play golf or take much exercise. "Might be this Home Secretary nonsense in the House yesterday. You heard what I think of it."

"Heard an echo of what the Opposition thinks of it," said Gideon, mildly. "That all you've got?"

"Scott-Marle's secretary said something about the Permanent Under-Secretary of the Home Office being with the Commissioner. Let's go."

Gideon opened the door, and they walked out of the Criminal Investigation Department Section, through long, bare passages and past long windows of frosted glass, until they reached that section of the Yard given over to administration. The Commissioner's office was very nearly luxurious, but the Commissioner himself, Sir Reginald Scott-Marle, did not like ostentation. For years, Gideon had regarded him as a very good man at his job, but cold as a fish. Recently he had come to know him better as a person, to like as well as to appreciate him. He had held two Colonial posts before coming to the Yard, and was known as a man who would make no concessions for the sake of peace and quiet.

His secretary was smaller, younger, bigger-bosomed and untidier than Miss Timson.

"You're to go straight in, gentlemen—the Commissioner is here already." She opened the door of the Commissioner's office, and this told Gideon that it was to be a small-scale conference; a large one would be held in the main conference room.

Scott-Marle was sitting behind his large flat-topped desk, looking a little aloof. Charlie Ripple was perched rather awkwardly on a wooden armchair noticeably too small for him. Ripple, the Commander of the Special Branch of the C.I.D. and an old friend of Gideon's, was broader across the beam than most chair makers allowed for. He always dressed in brown, he was more muscular than fleshy, and he had a large bald spot although his hair remained a dark brown; the uncharitable said that he had it dyed. Sitting next to him was Sir Thomas Barkett, the Permanent Under-Secretary at the Home Office, a formal man, a clever man, one who believed in the conventions, in tradition, in propriety—and yet could slash red tape.

"Good morning," Scott-Marle nodded, almost coldly.

"Sit down, please." Gideon waited for Rogerson, then sat well back in a chair the same size as Ripple's; the fit was fairly tight. He nodded across at Barkett. As he did so, the door opened again and Mullivany, the Secretary of the Metropolitan Police, came in, bustling; he was always inclined to hurry, always inclined to bemoan the fact that he never had time to do his job properly. He took the one vacant chair.

"This is a preliminary conference about a task which could give us all some awkward problems," Scott-Marle announced, and looked at Barkett invitingly. "Would you care to give us the details, Sir Thomas?"

Barkett was dressed in a well-cut black jacket, grey striped trousers, a silver-grey tie.

"That's what I am here for," he said. "I needn't take long. The meeting of Foreign Ministers of the main Western States has recommended an early Western Summit, to prepare for early proposals to the Soviet Union. It is to be held in London, and they aren't wasting any time—they want to get it in before the next Russo-Chinese Conference. So there will be a visit to London from the Heads of Governments of the United States, France and Western Germany. It has been arranged for the first week in June—in exactly four weeks' time." He had a rather casual way of speaking, as if he were really thinking of something else.

"The Government has decided that invitations should also go to Heads of States, so as to make the meetings more impressive. The State Visit will be in addition to the political meetings between the Heads of Governments. There will be a State Procession to the Houses of Parliament, where the Heads of States will make speeches at a joint meeting of the House of Lords and the House of Commons." Barkett sounded almost bored.

"The Procession Route will be from the Palace, along the Mall, Whitehall, Horse Guards Parade, the Embankment and Parliament Square, and on the way back will go round Parliament Square, enter Parliament Street, proceed along Whitehall and then through Admiralty Arch

17

and back to the Palace." Barkett paused for a moment, his pale hands resting on a thin, black brief-case on his knees.

"This procession will follow a luncheon at the Palace, and will take place on Wednesday, June 2nd. The Heads of States will arrive in London by air on the Monday or Tuesday preceding. On the Tuesday evening there will be a French Reception ; on the Wednesday they will address a joint meeting of the Houses of Parliament at midday and there will be an American Reception in the evening. The State Visit will end on the Thursday evening, following luncheon with the Lord Mayor of London, and the politicians will then get down to their job."

Barkett stopped.

"Such short notice," Mullivany complained.

"Nice to know someone is getting a move on," Ripple said.

Rogerson remarked, *sotto voce* : "Well, when they're at the House and the Guildhall, we'll have a breather."

It was the kind of inane remark which Rogerson was liable to make occasionally. Ripple glanced at Gideon, and wriggled his rear to get further back in the chair. He had a heavy chin, a rather broad nose, unexpectedly mild brown eyes. He was probably as puzzled as Gideon because Grimshaw, the Commander of the Uniformed Branch, wasn't present.

Scott-Marle looked at Gideon, but seemed to address them all :

"How much of a problem does this give us ?"

Rogerson hesitated, and then said : "The usual main one, I suppose—moving enough men from the Divisions into the West End for the occasion. It always means stretching things a bit." Sensing that Gideon wasn't yet ready for comment, Rogerson went on : "What do you think, Ripple ?"

Gideon was still puzzling over Grimshaw's absence.

"I can't envisage any serious trouble, but you can never tell on a job like this," Ripple said. "Apart from the lunatic fringe, we're bound to get some hot air from the Ban the Bomb boys and girls. Eh, George?"

"Bound to," agreed Gideon.

"I've got reasonable time to get in touch with the people overseas," said Ripple. He rubbed his chin; everyone could hear the rasping. "Have to get cracking, though. Got to check up with the Security chaps in Washington, Paris and Berlin—know what I'd like to do, sir?"

Scott-Marle asked: "What would you like to do?"

"Nip over and see these chaps," answered Ripple airily. "Find out at first hand what kind of precautions they want us to take. Then they can come over a couple of days before the big show and check that everything's the way they want it."

"Is this *really* necessary?" Mullivany wanted to know.

"What I mean," went on Ripple eagerly, "is that if I can have a talk with the chief security chaps who'll be coming with the nobs—I mean the Heads of States—it will enable me to look after my side of the problem properly." He sounded almost smug as he glanced at Barkett. "Don't you think that would make the other States realize we were taking every possible precaution?"

Barkett didn't waste words. "Yes," he said.

Mullivany frowned, but made no further comment.

"When I get back I'll be able to make sure we're on top of the job," Ripple said. Then he allowed himself a grumble, as if realizing that he mustn't show too much pleasure at the prospect of the visits aboard. "Been much better if we'd had one Head of State at a time to deal with, though. These big conferences are hell."

"I think you would be wise to consult with the Security authorities in each of the three capitals," said Scott-Marle. "See to the arrangements, will you?" That was to Mullivany. Then he went on: "Gideon?"

"First thing I'd better do is find out who's out and about the first week in June," Gideon responded slowly. He didn't need to explain that certain kinds of criminals thrive on crowds: the pickpockets, the bag-snatchers, the shop-lifters, the touts, the confidence tricksters, the dealers in forged notes and counterfeit coins. The whole of the Criminal Investigation Department in the Metropolitan area would have to be alerted, and the County and Borough forces, too. The brunt of the arrangements would really fall on Uniform, however, and it remained a puzzle that Grimshaw wasn't here.

They were all waiting for Gideon to go on.

"I'll have to get as much leave stopped in that week as I can, and I'll get busy with all the Divisions." He grinned at Ripple. "As a matter of fact, I think I ought to go and see them all!"

Even Scott-Marle chuckled.

"Going to fly?" inquired Mullivany, half-sourly.

Gideon didn't retort. He had a feeling that the Commissioner still had something important to say.

"Sir Thomas?" invited Scott-Marle.

"I was with the Home Secretary himself last night," announced Barkett, "and he made it clear that he hopes very much that the improvement discernible in the figures for crime throughout the country, particularly in the Metropolitan area, will be maintained during this visit period. You will have all possible co-operation from the Chief of Immigration to keep undesirables out of the country. The Minister asked me whether it might not be possible to use the June visits as a kind of morale booster," went on Barkett. "They were his actual words. If the exemplary behaviour of London crowds when welcoming overseas guests were emphasized, and—"

"See what he means," said Gideon, hardly realizing that he was interrupting. "Prove that the relationship between the police and the public has got right back to normal, and that this relationship is a big factor in the improvement of the crime situation. Is that it?"

"Yes."

"Might not be a bad idea at all," conceded Gideon. He ventured another grin and said: "These politicians occasionally have a good idea, don't they? When I see the Divisional chaps I'll put it to them that we've been given the chance we've been waiting for. There will be a few Jonahs, but there always are. The only thing I can't understand, sir, is—where is Commander Grimshaw? This is largely a uniform job."

"Grimshaw's going to be on sick leave," Scott-Marle announced, and everyone in the room reacted with surprise and near-dismay. "He has had some chest trouble, and the doctors have found a spot on one lung. He should be back in three months, and I don't propose to fill his position. He has a young deputy who should not be faced with the responsibility of such an occasion, so I want you to take charge of both C.I.D. and the Uniform arrangements for the State Visits, Gideon. I know it will mean a lot of extra work for a few weeks, but I hope you'll find that it's worth it."

Everyone was looking at Gideon.

Gideon pursed his lips, smiled wryly, and said : "I hope you find it worth it, sir."

"We must compare notes when all the Heads of States are safely out of the country," Scott-Marle retorted drily.

Gideon left the Commissioner's office, half an hour later, with Rogerson on one side and Ripple on the other. They had left Barkett obviously pleased, Scott-Marle in a better-than-usual mood, and Mullivany silent.

Gideon himself had mixed emotions. A "lot of extra work for a few weeks" was a considerable understatement. He was going to be run off his feet. That prospect could only make him feel uneasy, for ordinary crime would not stop while he got ready for the big show.

His greatest cause for misgiving, however, was nothing to do with the work involved. He wondered what Ray Cox, the Deputy Commander of the Uniformed Branch, would feel. He knew Cox slightly, and agreed with Scott-Marle that he hadn't sufficient experience for the job. If anything went wrong, the Commissioner would be held to blame for having too young a man in charge of the Uniformed Branch. He had made the right decision, but Cox would probably disagree.

"Better let Scott-Marle brief him first, then I'll go and see him," Gideon decided.

He wished very much that he knew Uniform's Deputy Commander better.

Ray Cox said: "I quite understand, sir." He stood stiffly at attention in front of the Assistant Commissioner of the Uniformed Branch of the Metropolitan Police Force, who was an elderly, rather vague-mannered individual with a keen administrative mind.

"That's good," said the A.C. "Doesn't make your job any less important, of course."

"No, sir."

"And I'm sure you'll get along well with Mr. Gideon."

"Thank you, sir."

"Let me know if you run into any problems," the A.C. said, in a tone of dismissal.

Cox said: "Yes, sir," formally, and went out. He was tall and lean, with black hair and an unexpected bald spot which showed up very white, with square, almost angular shoulders, and a long neck. His features were thin, his nose too long and pointed, but his mouth was full and he could smile easily. His eyes were piercingly blue.

He was not smiling as he shut the door, or when he went back to his own office. He was glad that it was empty; he did not feel like talking to anyone. He went across to the window overlooking the courtyard, his hands clenched, his eyes very narrow, even his lips set tightly.

"My God, what do they think I need? A watchdog?" He took out cigarettes, lit one, blew smoke out in a long streamer, and stared down at a squad car moving out on some urgent errand, an errand for Gideon. "Goddam Mr. Bloody Commander Gideon!" he said explosively.

He knew Gideon as a kind of legendary father figure at the Yard, but had had very little to do with him. He knew that most C.I.D. men would go all the way with their Commander, and the Uniformed men felt much the same. There was talk that Gideon would one day be Assistant Commissioner for Crime as a stepping-stone to the Commissioner's job when Scott-Marle retired. This might be part of the plan for him.

It certainly wasn't part of his, Cox's, plans or hopes.

Cox was not able to see the situation objectively enough, at that moment, to know that he was angry because it was the first real slowing down in his career. At thirty-nine, he was by seven years the youngest Deputy Commander of the five at the Yard, and at thirty-nine he believed that he should have been in charge of his branch for this big job. Instead, he was passed over—in fact put aside—for Gideon.

"He doesn't know a thing about Uniform," Cox said in a hard whisper. The telephone bell rang. "You sure you don't want Gideon?" he growled, and then he gave a short, amused laugh at himself, strode over, and picked up the receiver. "Deputy Commander," he announced.

"Mr. Cox?" asked a man with a deep, penetrating voice.

"Yes."

"This is George Gideon," the latter said, and Cox thought: *Of course, this couldn't be anyone else's voice.* "Will you be in if I come over and see you in about twenty minutes?"

Cox paused.

Gideon began: "If it's a bad time—"

"No, it's as good a time as any," Cox said. "I will expect you, Commander."

"Right, then. I'll be there," said Gideon, and rang off.

3

THE OTHER SIDE OF THE LAW

When the evening newspapers came out with their headlines :

WESTERN SUMMIT FOR LONDON
BIG FOUR MEET IN JUNE

and gave details already released by the Home Office
about the procession route for the State Visits, some men's
eyes sparkled at the thought of the illegal profit likely to
come their way as a result.

One of these was a little, perky man named Alec
Sonnley. He had bright green-grey eyes, a shiny little
pink-and-red face, and was always smartly dressed. When
the sun shone on him he looked rather like an apple half
hidden by leaves, for he wore a green hat, and his clothes
were always green, grey-green or browny-green. The most
noticeable things about him, apart from his rosy, shiny
complexion, were his hands and feet, which were much
larger than average, making a man of five feet six look a
little ridiculous.

Everyone called him Sonny Boy, partly because of his
name, partly because of his habit of whistling popular
songs—like an errand boy. Actually there was nothing at
all boyish about Sonny Boy. He had carefully and very
skilfully organized a business in London which had all the
outward appearance of being legitimate. He ran a large
wholesale warehouse in the Petticoat Lane district of the
East End, from which he supplied street traders and
hawkers, as well as small shopkeepers from the Greater
London area.

In addition to this, he owned thirty shops, all in popular
shopping areas, all dealing in what he called "*Fancy*

Goods, Jewellery, Gold and Silver Articles". In each shop he had a manageress and two or three assistants, and each member of the staff was strictly honest—none of them knew that he or she was dealing in stolen goods.

To make discovery much less likely, Alec Sonnley bought up a great deal of bankrupt stocks, salvaged goods, and low-priced ornaments, in all of which he did good business. No single item in any of his stores cost over five pounds, and he had a series of "special advertising offers" at five shillings and ten shillings each. At least half his stocks were stolen goods.

He also had the third aspect of the business worked out just as carefully as the retail and wholesale angles. He used six steady shop-lifters and eight steady handbag and pocket pickers, or snatchers and dips. This team operated in big shopping areas, especially in the West End of London or in the bigger surburban districts. These thieves concentrated on stealing branded goods, which were taken to the retail outlets and sold quickly.

Sonnley paid his pickpockets a retainer all the year round.

Every now and again, especially when he believed that the police suspected one of them, he "rested" these operatives, but because of the retainer they were ready to work again the moment he felt it safe.

The great simplicity of his system helped Sonnley to success. Quick-selling goods stolen from one part of London were often on sale in another part on the same day, for he had a plain van driven by his chief operative, a man named Benny Klein, who made the rounds regularly, collecting and delivering. Anything of real value, Sonnley disposed of through ordinary receivers.

No one knew quite how much he was worth, but it probably approached a quarter of a million pounds.

Any attraction which drew the crowds to the heart of London would set Sonny Boy whistling chirpily. His pickpockets, bag-snatchers and shop-lifters often quadrupled their takings, and his wholesale warehouse supplied hundreds of street traders with souvenirs.

That Tuesday, he drove from the small suite of offices in a narrow street near Baker Street Station, and out of the corner of his eye saw a newspaper placard : WESTERN SUMMIT FOR LONDON. He slowed down by the next news boy, and kept a dozen cars waiting behind him while he bought a newspaper. Very soon he began to whistle, and the whistle became gayer while he drove to St. John's Wood, where he had an apartment near Regent's Park. He turned into the underground garage, then whistled his way across to the lift which would take him up to the seventh floor, and his wife. He was married to a plump, good-natured woman with thin, metallic-looking reddish-yellow hair. She loved expensive clothes, loved her Sonny Boy and, rather unexpectedly, loved cooking. So Sonnley went home to lunch whenever he could.

His tune was rounded and full as he stepped out opposite his apartment, Number 71, and let himself in. There was a faint aroma of frying onions, which suggested a steak or mixed grill. When he went into the spotless tiled kitchen, the steaks were sizzling and the onions seemed to be clucking. Rosie glanced round, saw him, and immediately plunged a basket of newly sliced chips into a saucepan of boiling fat. A great hiss and a cloud of steam came.

Sonnley went across and slid his arm round his wife's comfortable bosom, squeezed, gave her neck a peck of a kiss, and said :

"I hope it's good. We've got a lot to celebrate."

"Oh, have we, Sonny dear?" said Rosie. "What is it?"

"Believe it or not, sweetie-pie, we're going to have a State Procession for a great big Western Four Power Summit meeting in li'l old London Town," declared Sonnley, and held the newspaper up.

Reading, Rosie looked more and more puzzled.

"I'm sure it will be very nice, dear. Can I have a seat?"

"A what?"

"There are bound to be some wonderful stands put up for the Procession. In the Mall, I shouldn't wonder, or perhaps near the Abbey. You know, where the Houses of Parliament are." Rosie prodded a steak. "It's a pity it

26

isn't a wedding, really. I do love to see them coming out of the Abbey with their lovely dresses. There will be stands, won't there?"

"You can bet your life there will!"

"And can I have a seat?"

"Front row, dead centre, the best there is," Sonnley promised. "Rosie, that steak smells wonderful. How long will it be?"

"About ten minutes."

"Just time for me to make a phone call," said Sonnley. He went out in the hallway, rubbing his hands, turned into a big drawing-room which overlooked the park, beyond the gardens of the building. The drawing-room had been furnished by a large London store, and although Sonnley was never sure why, he realized that it was as nearly perfect as it could be. The colourings were wine-red and pale blue. The furniture was mid-nineteenth century French. He sat at the end of a long couch, dialled a Whitehall number, and was answered almost at once by a man with a slightly foreign accent.

"Benny, you seen the papers?" Sonnley asked.

"Sure, I've seen the papers," answered Benny Klein.

"You getting ready to throw your hat in the air?"

"I'm getting ready all right," said the man with the accent. "I thought I'd be hearing from you."

"Just have a word with all the boys and girls, and tell them to have a week or two off," said Sonnley. "I don't want anyone in trouble between now and you-know-when. All okay?"

"Holiday with pay, is it?"

"You've got it in one, Benny," Sonnley agreed. "And I've got a little vacation planned for you, too."

"*Me?* I'm going to the Riviera, Sonny Boy. You know that."

"Not now you're not," Sonnley declared. "Buy your lay a nice diamond bracelet, and tell her to stay home and be a good girl. You know what's going to happen, don't you?"

"I'm not going to alter my plans for anybody." Klein was suddenly harsh-voiced.

"Now take it easy, Benny, take it easy! No one said anything about altering your plans. It's just a little postponement, that's all. You can take the girl with you if she loves you so much! You're going up to Glasgow, Liverpool, Manchester and Birmingham, and you're going to tell the boys up there to keep out of the Big Smoke when the V.I.P.s are here. We don't want any of those provincials muscling in on our London, do we?" When Klein didn't answer, Sonnley repeated sharply. "Do we?"

Klein said gruffly : "No, we don't."

"And I don't know anyone who can tell them so better than Benny Klein," said Sonnley. "Just make them understand that they keep out. See? If they don't, they'll run into a lot of trouble. Can you make them understand, Benny?"

"They'll understand," Klein asserted in a stronger voice.

"That's more like it," Sonnley approved. "Tell them I'll organize every gang of razor and chain-boys in London if provincials come down here. And when you've warned them good and proper, Benny, you can come down here and talk to the London gangs."

After a pause, Klein said : "The London gangs will want some dough."

"They'll get it, don't you worry. The same terms as for Maggie's wedding—they'll be okay. And tell your lady friend you'll buy her a mink stole as well, if she gives you a good time in England and forgets all about the Contingong." Sonnley chuckled. "Okay, Benny?"

"I suppose so."

"I thought it would be," Sonnley said. "See you, boy."

He rang off, stood for a moment by the telephone, and frowned. He had far too much on Benny Klein for Benny to be rebellious, but if he should get awkward, it would make a lot of difficulties.

"But he won't get awkward," Sonnley reassured himself, and began to whistle, but on a slightly subdued note.

After a few minutes he joined Rosie, who had now laid the table. A steak which looked juicy and tender teased Sonnley from its silver dish. The chips were a golden brown, and there were peas and broad beans as well as deep-fried onion rings.

"What's the matter, Sonny? Doesn't it look nice?" inquired Rosie.

"Blimey, it looks as if it's sitting up and begging to be eaten! Don't worry about me, I was just thinking about a business acquaintance who might need a little watching. Now, let's go!"

Sitting in a small Chelsea café and tucking into a plate of bacon, sausages, eggs and chips, was Michael Lumati, well known to Alec Sonnley, and also well known to the police, although it was now three years since he had been under suspicion of any crime, and five since he had been in prison.

On that occasion he had earned full remission after a three-year sentence for issuing forged banknotes. According to his own story, he now earned a reasonable living by selling lightning portraits at fairs and race-courses, for ten shillings a time. He also designed calendars and programmes, and did a few catalogues—including Sonnley's.

Lumati had a small studio at the top of one of the old, condemned buildings of Chelsea, not far from the river, and he spent a lot of time in the studio, usually cooking his own breakfast and evening meal, but going out for lunch. Today he sat in a corner of the café, a man nearing fifty, rather thin, with a healthy looking, tanned complexion, very clear grey eyes, and a small Van Dyck beard. That, and the faded beret which he always wore at the back of his head, made him look the part of an artist.

Some of his craftsmanship, at its best in copies of currency notes, was unbelievably good. When he had been caught, experts had agreed that it was almost impossible to tell the difference between his work and the real thing.

He had a copy of the London *Standard* propped up against the wall at his side, and kept reading the story of the coming State Procession. There was a calculating expression in his eyes. The police did not know that, after years of experiment and error, Lumati had succeeded in drawing a line which looked as if it were a tiny thread through the paper—making detection nearly impossible—nor did the police know that he had tens of thousands of these one-pound and ten-shilling notes printed and ready for distribution.

He knew a man who would want plenty of paper money at the time of the visit, too. Sonny Boy Sonnley.

One other man, an almost pathetic, elderly clerk in a shipping office, earning only twelve pounds ten a week, was preparing to make hay in a very different way. Money itself did not greatly interest him. When he first read of the coming visit, his heart had leapt because of the fact that the next time the Head of the French Republic appeared in London he, Matthew Smith, was to act as assassin. He was by no means matter-of-fact about it, but was very sure of success. It had been planned so carefully.

The police and the security forces would be watching all the likely sources of danger in London, of course, and airports and railway terminals would be closely watched to make sure that no terrorists arrived there. Probably all possible suspects would be rounded up before the visit—but that would make no difference at all.

No one would suspect such a mild little Englishman as Matthew Smith of hating France so bitterly, or of having so much power in his hands.

Still less would they suspect that he also hated his wife, simply because she had always tried to soften his attitude towards the French, and so had drawn some of his venom upon herself.

At that time, however, the thought of murdering his wife had not crossed his mind. He exulted only because he would soon be the man—perhaps the martyr—who had killed the leader of France.

4

CONFLICT?

"Very good, Commander," Cox said formally.

"If we get started early it shouldn't be much trouble," Gideon said.

"No."

"I shouldn't think we'll need any U.B. men from the Provinces. Do you?" asked Gideon. He felt strangely uneasy. The interview with Cox hadn't gone right, largely because of Cox's stiffness—not really obstructiveness, but next-door to it. In a way he reminded Gideon of workers who would not come out on strike, but worked strictly to rule. He wished that he knew the man better, then he could judge whether Cox was simply resentful of the situation, or whether he was often like this. Instead of saying, "I shouldn't think we'll need any U.B. men from the Provinces," it would have been better to say : "Do you think we'll need any?"

"I have had no experience of a situation like this," Cox answered. "I can hardly advise."

The manner in which the words were uttered annoyed Gideon, and for the first time, he thought : *I'm going to have to watch him.* He stared into Cox's very bright dark blue eyes, and read the defiance in them. If he used the wrong tactics now he might make co-operation extremely difficult, and he had plenty to do without adding a kind of departmental feud.

So he ignored Cox's retort.

"Have a closer look at the figures of Uniform Branch men used for the Coronation," he said. "That's the guide the C.I.D.'s working on."

"Very well," said Cox.

"Give me a ring when you've checked, will you?" asked Gideon, and went out.

He was subdued as well as uneasy, not at all sure that he had been wise to ignore that retort; had it been one of his own men he would have reacted sharply. He simply didn't yet know how best to handle Cox, but already the dangers as well as the difficulties inherent in taking over another branch were threatenng.

Joe Bell was at his desk, coat off and collar and tie loose, because it was so warm. In a different mood Gideon might have asked Bell's opinion about Cox, but, in any case, Bell was obviously preoccupied.

"What have you got there?" Gideon demanded.

"Just running over that list of the chaps we ought to watch for the Visit," said Bell. "When are you going out to the Divisions?"

"I'll make a start next week," said Gideon. "I'll do a memo for them first, and warn 'em I'm coming. Heard anything from Lemaitre?"

"No."

"Write to him, and write to the Chief Constables of the big provincial cities—Glasgow, Manchester, Liverpool, Birmingham, Bristol, and any others where they might plan to send raiding parties to pick up as much loot as they can for the Visit. Ask for reports on all gangs, all pick-pockets, shop-lifters and con-men—you know, the usual. If any of them start planning a little holiday in London, we want to know."

"Right," said Bell.

"If you get the letters off today they'll have 'em in the morning. Tomorrow afternoon you can telephone the Superintendents and ask them to play."

"They'll play," said Bell, confidently.

"I hope you're right," said Gideon. "Now I've got to go along and have a cuppa with those Aussies. The A.C.'s putting on a bun fight for them." He went out, thinking about Cox, looking almost ponderous as he walked along the passages. He rounded the corner to Rogerson's office, and found a grey-haired sergeant on duty outside; some

32

of the elderly men became little more than messengers in their last year or so of service. "Hallo, Charlie," said Gideon. "How's that ankle of yours?"

"Could be worse, Mr. Gideon, but it's been dry lately. In wet weather it's something cruel. You going in?"

"Think they'll let me?"

"Wouldn't be surprised," said the sergeant. He pushed the door open, and a babble of voices came from twenty men and two women—women whom Gideon hadn't expected, who had been tacked on to the Australian touring party.

The doorway between Miss Timson's office and the A.C.'s showed thick with tobacco smoke. In the smaller office a long table had been set with cups and saucers, sandwiches and cakes, and Gideon espied Miss Timson carrying two cups of tea to men standing a little on their own in a corner. They brightened up at sight of her. Not a bad-looking woman, Gideon thought, as another girl in the secretarial pool came with tea and sandwiches. He was swept into the talk, had a few minutes' chat with young Wall, sensed that everyone had enjoyed themselves, discovered that one of the women was an Australian newspaper reporter, and the other an American publisher of crime stories, who had come with an introduction from Police Headquarters in New York.

At a quarter past five the Australians went off. In the littered room, Miss Timson and some canteen helpers were busy packing dirty crockery on to trays. Rogerson was looking out of the window.

"Glad that's over?" asked Gideon.

"Very," said Rogerson. "It wasn't my day for making pretty speeches. Miss Timson, how soon can I have my office free?"

"In five minutes, sir."

Rogerson said. "Try and make it four. Is Bell in your room, George?"

"Yes."

"I've been like a bear with a sore head all day," said

Rogerson, under his breath. "Scott-Marle annoyed me by putting that lot on your shoulders. How did Cox take it?"

"He'll do."

"Hope you're right," said Rogerson. "Ripple's going to start his flying vacation on Friday, just as soon as he's got all the Algerian nationalists in London checked. He thinks that the Algerians are as likely a source of trouble as any. Some anti-American lunatic might take a pot at the President of the United States, of course, and the country's still full of people who think the Germans are all Nazis. No special reason to expect trouble, though, is there?"

"Shouldn't think so," Gideon said, but was more acutely conscious of a sense of disquiet, almost certainly due to Cox. He saw Miss Timson coming out of Rogerson's office, looking very prim.

"Your room is in order, sir."

"Thanks," grunted Rogerson. He and Gideon went into the office, and Miss Timson closed the door on them.

All trace of the invasion had gone. Ash-trays had been emptied, the windows were wide open, there was little odour of smoke, and the place had a new-pin look.

Rogerson said lugubriously : "She's so damned efficient it's almost a crime to grumble at her."

"Are you worried about the German Group?" Rogerson wanted to know, next morning. Obviously he had been preoccupied by this overnight.

"There's always the lunatic fringe of anti-Germans," Gideon said. "And the really bitter people who lost sons or—" he paused, as Rogerson looked at him steadily. "What I mean is, if anyone had a crack at the German President, it wouldn't necessarily be any organized group, more likely some individual, brooding by himself over some war-time grief. We caught three of them on the 1956 visit, remember?"

"Yes. Anyone in mind?"

"We can't have."

"Suppose not," conceded Rogerson.

34

Just before six o'clock the evening before, Gideon entered his office. He wasn't surprised to see Abbott standing by Joe Bell's desk. Abbott had that strong-man look about him, but was clenching his hands, as if keenly aware of tensions. His voice was a little too hearty.

"I hope I'm not too early, Commander."

"No, it's about right," said Gideon. "Did you get those letters off, Joe?"

"I'm just going along to the typing pool, to sign 'em for you," said Bell. "Anything else for me tonight?"

"No, thanks."

Bell went out, nodding good-night. Abbott was sitting on an upright chair, unable to relax. Gideon pushed his chair back against the wall, loosened his collar and tie again, and pushed cigarettes across the desk ; when Abbott took one, his fingers were unsteady.

Gideon asked bluntly : "What's the trouble, Abb ? Anything wrong anywhere ?"

Abbott echoed : "Wrong ?"

"I can't see Carraway worrying you as much as you're worried," said Gideon. "If we don't charge him now, we can later—it isn't a matter of life and death, is it ?"

Abbott echoed : "Life and death." He drew deeply at the cigarette, and then said : "George, I'm in a hell of a spot. I really am. I ought to have brought Carraway in forty-eight hours ago. You remember I told you about the Belman girl? I've checked closely, and there isn't any doubt that Carraway spent the night of the murder with her. If he was with her, he wasn't playing cards with the men. So they lied."

"They might say they lied to save her reputation. We can work on them, but it looks like a switch from one alibi to a better one. That doesn't help us much."

"Don't I know it!" said Abbott. "Anyway, I questioned her yesterday morning, then put a couple of detective constables on to watching her—thought I might be able to wear her nerves down. Now she's disappeared. I can't help wondering if Carraway's got her. If she knows

35

anything, she might crack under pressure, and—well, she's vanished."

Gideon said : "Carraway might have paid her to go away somewhere." He lifted a telephone which had a direct line to Information, and when a man answered he said : "Gideon here. I want a general call out, London, Home Counties, ports and airports, for a girl whom Superintendent Abbott will tell you all about. He'll be along in five minutes. Put a call out saying that this girl's wanted for questioning—what's her name, do you say?"

"Marjorie Belman."

"One L or two?"

"One."

"Marjorie Belman," Gideon repeated into the telephone, and added. "One L," before ringing off. "Let's get the full description, her address, everything you know about her." His tone belied the urgency of his actions, he knew that he would have to be very careful if he was not to drive Abbott into a nervous flap. "Can you give it to me straight?"

"Yes," said Abbott. He seemed clearer voiced and steadier, as if the vigour of Gideon's reaction had already done him good. "Marjorie Belman, aged twenty or so, height five-five or six, weight about eight stone, size 32, 27 or so, 36—"

"Flat chested?"

"Not big and busty anyway," Abbott said. "Nut brown hair, like a feather mop, dark blue eyes, slightly olive complexion, rosebud mouth . . ."

A picture of the girl etched itself on his mind as he talked.

5

THE FEARS OF MARJORIE BELMAN

Bruce Carraway had always been able to make Marjorie Belman do what he wanted.

She could never really recall what had happened on the first night they had met, but she remembered waking, naked body next to his naked body, and remembered the sense of shock and even of shame, until he had wakened, and looked at her through his dark lashes, and then caressed her, kissed her, possessed her. She would never forget the ecstasy, and yet she could never be wholly without shame. The awful moment had been when she had gone home after work next evening, and had a violent quarrel with her father when he had accused her of lying to him. The scene with her mother, who had begged her to tell the truth, had been nearly as bad. Only her elder sister, Beryl, had shown any understanding or sympathy.

She had left home for the tiny two-roomed flat, everything she needed paid for by Bruce. She had television, better clothes, a luxurious bathroom—and she did not need to work. Since then happiness and ecstasy had been her bedfellows, and apart from the shadow of the dismay of her parents, she had known nothing but contentment. Beryl had been to see her three times, and the last time had tried to make her go back home, but her first real anxiety had been over Arthur Rawson's murder.

Had Bruce killed him?

She wasn't really sure, only feared that he had—because she had heard him saying to Eric Little that "dear old Arthur would be better out of the way". She was to meet Bruce at six o'clock on the Swan & Edgar corner of Piccadilly, and already her heart was beating fast at the prospect—partly excitement, partly fear. She had to find out the truth about that murder, because the police kept on questioning her. They had, only that day. (It was the day when Abbott had talked to Gideon.)

Marjorie was ready to leave, and actually closing the door of her flat, when she heard footsteps downstairs, and then her older sister's voice. "Is Miss Belman in, do you know?" Beryl was talking to the liftman. Tight-lipped, Marjorie went forward, and Beryl caught sight of her.

"Jorrie!" she exclaimed.

"Beryl, it's no use talking, I'm not coming home," Marjorie said thinly. "I've told you before—"

"Jorrie, *please* listen to me," Beryl pleaded. She was slightly taller, had a fuller figure than Marjorie, and was quite as attractive. Now tension and desperation made her eyes shine. "I've simply got to make you understand that Mum's terribly ill. If you don't come back—"

The liftman was very near them.

"For heaven's sake, don't talk so loudly," Marjorie said angrily. "Everyone will hear you. Anyhow, I can't wait now."

"You've got to listen to me!" Beryl put a hand on her sister's arm. "If you don't leave that man, it will kill Mum. She's like a ghost walking, she's terrible. And Dad's nearly as bad."

"They'll get over it, like thousands of strait-laced parents before them," Marjorie said. "You're the real fool, for getting so worked up about it. If you can't mind your own business, I don't want to see you again, either."

"Jorrie, you don't know what you're doing."

Marjorie said thinly: "Let go of my arm, and if you can't be friendly, stay away from me." She wrenched herself free and half-ran out of the hallway into the street. The door swung to behind her.

Half-way along the street toward Piccadilly she glanced round, but there was no sign of Beryl. She was breathing heavily, still angry, but now partly with herself. Why had Beryl chosen such an awkward time? Why wouldn't she leave her alone? Parents were always the same anyhow—

why, her father had practically driven her away from home.

When she reached Piccadilly Circus, she watched every well-dressed man in the distance, longing to see Bruce. The bustle of traffic and of people was all around her. The pavements seemed hot, the petrol fumes smelly. A coloured couple came walking along, arm-in-arm, oblivious of the heart of London. Marjorie kept looking across at the tiny statue of Eros.

A middle-aged man sauntered up to her. "Would you care for a drink, my dear?" She glared at him. "Now come on—" the man began, and then broke off and moved away quickly. Marjorie saw a youthful-looking policeman staring at her; he had frightened the man off, but her heart began to pound. She was so scared of the police.

Why didn't Bruce come? She felt as if everyone was staring at her, saw a youngish man with a bushy moustache bearing down on her, with a beaming smile. She turned and walked away.

"Now, come, darling—"

It was beastly.

The policeman walked towards her and the man with the bushy black moustache marched past. She thought the policeman was going to speak, but he did not. She had no idea how pretty and lonely she looked, how many men glanced at her, almost wistfully.

She kept looking round for Beryl but did not see her; that was one good thing.

When at last she heard a familiar voice, it wasn't Bruce's.

"Waiting for someone, Jorrie?"

She turned quickly, to see Eric Little. He was short and stocky, his black hair was curly, and he had a very bright smile. He wouldn't have been so bad, except for the fact that whenever Bruce was out of the way, he was likely to slide his arm round her waist, or nuzzle her neck.

"I—I thought Bruce would be here by now," she said, acutely disappointed.

39

"He got held up," said Eric, "so he asked me to come and collect you. Had to go down to Brighton, you see. Be a nice night for the drive, won't it!" He put his hand on her arm and led her towards Piccadilly; his black Austin Cambridge was parked near the hotel. His grasp was firm, but with no hint of impudence of familiarity. She got into the car beside him. Soon, the cool evening air swept in through both windows, caressing her.

She had a final look round but saw no sign of Beryl.

Eric chose the Fulham and Putney Road, which was slightly longer but less busy. Marjorie noticed that he kept glancing at her, which puzzled her. Usually, even if she felt his fingers at her knees, she would look at him angrily, and find him staring straight ahead. This evening, he kept stabbing those strange glances at her. He drove very fast once they were on the open road, especially after turning off towards Guildford; as if he had something on his mind.

"Eric, why did Bruce have to go to Brighton tonight?" Marjorie asked suddenly.

"Big bizz, old girl."

"He didn't tell me about it."

"Can't tell the little lady everything."

"Eric—"

"Yes, sweetie?"

"Is everything all right?"

He looked at her sharply.

"What's that?"

"Is everything all right?"

"Why shouldn't it be?"

"I—I thought Bruce's been rather—rather worried lately."

"Old Bruce? Not on your life!"

After a few minutes' silence, she moistened her lips and said:

"Eric?"

"Yes?"

"It isn't any use lying to me."

"As if I would."

"Eric, Bruce is frightened of the police, I know he is. So am I. I—I'm afraid of what I'll say if that man comes again."

"What man?"

"The detective."

"That man Abbott you told Bruce about?"

"Yes."

"Forget him, honey bun."

"Don't be ridiculous," Marjorie said.

"Listen, Jorrie," said Eric in that rather high-pitched voice, "I tell you there's no need to worry. Bruce is fixing things. We're going to smuggle you out of the country." When Marjorie caught her breath, his left hand gripped her firmly just above the knee. "Bruce knows that it worries you when the police ask questions. He didn't have anything to do with the murder of his partner, it's only a matter of time before we prove it, but meanwhile—well, he doesn't want you worried by the police and he's fed up with them, too. He's on board a big motor yacht, off Brighton. You and Bruce are going to have a nice little holiday, going all the way to the Riviera. I'm going to take you out to the yacht as soon as it's dark."

Marjorie felt quite sure that Bruce was running away, and it scared her. But she loved him so, she *had* to be with him. And—the Riviera was wonderful.

They had dinner at Horsham, and night had fallen by the time they reached Brighton. Eric kept joking about a Riviera "honeymoon". She would not let herself think about the probability that Bruce was really running away. She could hardly wait to see him. A small motor-boat was waiting on the beach some distance from the main piers; the fact that it was a quiet spot didn't surprise Marjorie at all.

When they were some distance out to sea, with the lights of the two piers and the promenade like diamonds and emeralds, rubies and sapphires, reflecting on the calm water, she had a creepy feeling. She couldn't understand

41

why Bruce hadn't turned up by now. Why was Eric taking her so far in this small motor-boat? It was cold, too.

Eric moved away from the wheel.

"We'll let Oswald the automatic pilot take over," he said jocularly. "Listen, Jorrie—" He slid his arm round her. "Old Bruce won't be long . . ."

Soon she felt the boat slowing down, and realized that Eric had cut out the engine; they were going round and round in circles. She tried to push Eric away, but he was too strong for her. Suddenly fear came over her like a great wave. He was holding her in a peculiar way; he was lifting her from her seat, he—

She realized suddenly what he was going to do, and with a surge of terror, she kicked and struck out at him. But he just swung her over the edge of the boat, and dropped her into the sea. She tried to scream, made a funny gurgling sound, and took in a mouthful of water. It made her retch and choke. She struggled wildly to reach the surface, but as she did so a weight pressed against her shoulders.

She felt a sharp pain, on her right shoulder, as her head went under.

Eric was kneeling on the edge of the boat, pressing her down, down, down.

Undressing Marjorie when she was dead made Little feel sick. Dragging on the bikini pants, tying the bikini top about her little soft breasts, was horrible. Pushing her body into the sea again was a relief. He started the engine almost at once, and the pale blur that had been Marjorie Belman sank slowly out of sight.

Now all he had to do was to get rid of her clothes.

Beryl Belman got off the bus at the end of Carmody Street, Clapham, and walked quickly towards her home, Number 43. The long street had three-storey houses of red brick on either side, and each house looked very like the next. A few people were walking along, a motorcyclist passed, a woman from next-door-but-one came hurrying, stopped, and said :

"Beryl, dear, I do hope your mother's feeling better. She's been looking so ill lately."

"She's a bit run down," Beryl said, and thought : *The nosey old bitch, she knows what's happened.* "I must hurry, Mrs. Lee."

Actually, she did not want to hurry, for she hated what she would find. She squared her shoulders, put on a bright smile, and knocked at the front door. Her father opened it, looked at her searchingly, and then half-closed his eyes as if he knew she had failed. As she went in, he said :

"So you didn't see her."

"Yes, I saw her," Beryl said. "She wouldn't listen, that's all." Suddenly all her courage died away, and tears stung her eyes. "It's no use, Dad. It's no use at all."

"Don't tell your mother you saw her," her father ordered. He was a short, thin, harassed-looking man. His lack of a son had always hurt him, and too often driven him to outbursts of spiteful bad temper. Now, Beryl knew, he reproached himself dreadfully because he was partly responsible for driving Jorrie away. "Don't tell her, Bee. She's—she's a little bit better, I think. Don't tell her, just say that Jorrie was out."

From the kitchen along the hall, his wife called :

"Is that Beryl?"

"Yes, Mum !"

"Well, don't stand there whispering to your father. Have you seen Jorrie?"

Beryl lied : "No, Mum. She wasn't in."

Her mother stared at her as if with doubt and suspicion. Eyes which for so long had been gentle with love for her daughters, and pride in their appearance, were lack-lustre, red-rimmed, far too prominent. A soft voice had become harsh, a mild manner had become impatient and sharp.

"Don't lie to me, Beryl !"

"But, Mum, I—"

"It's bad enough to have a daughter go off and live in

43

sin, without having another who lies to me. Did you see Jorrie?"

Slowly, helplessly, Beryl said. "Yes."

"And she won't come home?"

"She—she won't yet, Mum. She—"

"She won't ever come home, I know that," said Mrs. Belman, in a strangled voice. "I've lost her. I've lost my Jorrie. I've lost . . ."

Quite suddenly, she crumpled up. As she fell, Belman pushed past Beryl, thrust her mother towards a chair and saved her from falling heavily, then stood looking down at her ashen face and at her slack mouth. Watching them, twenty-two-year-old Beryl Belman dedicated herself to a task which she did not dream was impossible of achievement.

"I'll make her come home," she pledged silently. "I'll make her realize what Carraway really is, and what she's done."

It was easy enough to tell her parents, after supper, that she was going out to a dance club. At half past eight she walked briskly and determinedly along the street, caught a bus at the end of the road, and went straight to Piccadilly. It was dark, but the lights flashed in a dozen colours, the Circus and the streets leading off were thronged. She saw a young constable stare at her, ignored him, and walked quickly, angrily, towards Alden Street, where Jorrie had her flat. The street door was open, and a small lift was at the end of a narrow passage. A light showed at the door of the caretaker's room, down in the sub-basement, but no one opened the door. Now her heart began to thump, for Marjorie was probably here, with Carraway. Even if they were together, she had to talk to Marjorie, and she could tell Carraway to his face what she thought of him.

The man must have *some* decency.

Beryl pressed the fifth and top floor button of the lift, stepped out, and stood in front of Marjorie's door. A light was on inside, so she was in. Beryl clenched her hands,

44

and her teeth, feeling a tension greater than ever she had known.

She *had* to talk to Jorrie, whether Carraway was there or not.

She pressed the bell, heard it ring, and stood back a pace, her teeth still clenched, words churning over and over in her mind : she must shock Jorrie into listening, had to make her pay attention.

Jorrie did not answer.

Tension and anxiety and a kind of fear began to melt together into anger. Carraway was in there with her sister, of course. They were probably in bed together. The last thing they would want was an interruption ! Beryl stabbed at the bell again; nothing would make her go away until she had talked to Jorrie.

There was no answer.

"Jorrie!" she called out in a sharp voice. "I know you're in there. Come and open the door."

There was only silence.

Beryl put her finger on the bell-push, pressed hard, and kept it there, hearing the long, harsh, ringing sound. Surely no one could fail to answer it. It must be getting on their nerves.

"If you don't answer I'll go for the police!" she cried.

It was a threat drawn out of her by desperation, the only threat she could now imagine which might make Jorrie open the door. When the last word quivered on the stuffy air of the tiny landing, she felt that she had tried everything she knew, and lost. Tears of mortification and disappointment filled her eyes, and she turned away, not knowing what to do. The lift gates were open, behind her ; and by the side of the lift was a narrow staircase. She stepped forward, and then heard a click of sound behind her. Her heart leapt. *Jorrie!* She spun round. The door of the flat was opening, but no light was on there. Only the light here showed that it wasn't Jorrie, it was a man.

He flung himself at her.

A cloth was pulled over his face and she could only just

see his eyes, dark, bright, glittering. She uttered a scream, but he struck her across the face, sending her reeling against the wall, silencing her. She slipped on the top step, and fell, banging her head painfully. Terror as great as her sister's welled up in her.

Then she heard a voice from below, loud and clear :

"What's going on up there?"

She heard other sounds, including a whining, and realized that the lift was going down. Through the iron trellis-work of the shaft she saw the man who had attacked her. The cloth had been pulled to one side, and she caught a glimpse of his profile before he disappeared below the level of the floor. The man from below called again :

"What's going on?"

Panic-stricken, she realized that she mustn't cause a scandal, for her mother would never stand it. She was dazed, frightened, unsure of herself, unable to grasp what had happened—but she must not cause a scandal. It would kill her mother, and Jorrie would never forgive her.

Beryl got up, slowly, awkwardly, and called : "It's all right, I slipped." She leaned against the wall, listening to the whine of the lift, hoping that the man on the floor below would not come up to investigate. She listened for the sound of footsteps, and believed that she heard him coming. She swayed away from the wall, and noticed that the door of Jorrie's apartment was open. She stepped inside quickly, and closed the door; it slammed. She stood in the darkness, heart thumping, eyes strained as they tried to accustom themselves to gloom broken only by a glow of light at the door.

No one called out.

At last, Beryl groped for the light switch, and found it. Blinking against the bright light, she went into the flat, with its furniture which to her seemed luxurious. Light in the big living-room came from a lamp with a monster shade. The television stared with square, vacant eye. Thick carpet cushioned her feet.

The bathroom, jade green in colour, made her gasp.

Everything here seemed all right, but Jorrie wasn't here; at least she hadn't refused to open the door.

But who had the man been? Who would come here alone by night, if it wasn't Carraway? And why should a man behave like that unless he was frightened?

Soon, Beryl went out, and down in the lift, and back home by bus. The next step, she told herself, was to find out where Carraway lived, and go and see him.

Bruce Carraway was not thinking about Marjorie or about Eric Little just then. He was busy making telephone calls in quick succession to private hire car dealers in the Home Counties, on the perimeter of London. He was obtaining options on cars and drivers at normal rates for the week of the Visit. Rental cars would be in great demand, whatever the weather.

In between calls, his telephone bell rang.

He hesitated, wondering who it was. Eric Little had already reported that the job at Brighton had been finished, so it wouldn't be Eric. It might be the police. Carraway lifted the receiver and said briskly:

"Bruce Carraway speaking."

"Bruce." It was Little again, and something in the way his name was uttered warned Carraway of trouble. "Bruce, I—I went round to—to her flat to get her things." There was a long, alarming pause. "I—I went to make it look as if she'd moved, like you told me, and—" Little was breathing very hard, and Carraway gripped the receiver tightly, but he did not speak. "Her sister called. She—she threatened to go to the police if the door wasn't opened. I got away all right, she didn't see me, but I had to leave the clothes and everything there."

Carraway said softly, slowly: "Keep away from that place until we know which way the police are going to jump. And keep away from me, except at the showrooms. Understand?"

Before Little had a chance to answer, Carraway rang off. He sat there, scowling, and it was a long time before he made his next call. Even then, he wasn't concentrating on business, but on this new danger. Supposing this sister had seen Little, after all? Supposing she could identify him?

That could make the difference between being safe, and being caught for a murder.

6

RIPPLE

AFTER the general call had gone out for Marjorie Belman, earlier that evening, Gideon studied Abbott's reports, and listened to everything the man said to amplify them. He could understand what had driven Abbott to make his decisions, and there was nothing in the preparation or the carrying out of the investigations which Gideon could fault. Abbott was sitting opposite him, still tense.

Gideon pushed the reports aside, bent down, opened a drawer in his desk, and took out a bottle of Scotch, two glasses, and a syphon.

"Like a nip?"

"Be glad of one."

"Say when," said Gideon, and in fact mixed Abbott's fairly strong, his own half-and-half. He pushed it across the desk, put his own glass to his lips, and said : "Here's to the end of crime," and sipped. He wouldn't have had a whisky, then, but for the need to give Abbott one. "Now," he went on, "if you'd come in yesterday morning and told me about the girl Belman, I would almost certainly have advised you to leave Carraway for a few days, and concentrate on the girl. I would also have told you to have her followed, and added the usual 'don't lose her'."

Abbott's eyes were brightening.

"You're not just saying this, George?"

"No," Gideon assured him. "I don't know how the case will work out, but I hardly think Carraway will kill the girl—he must know that it would be asking for trouble. Can't be sure, of course, but apart from that risk, there's only one thing I don't like."

Abbott went taut. "What's that?"

49

"The fact that you've dithered," Gideon said. He had a strange feeling, one which came every now and again and which he never liked but which had to be accepted for what it was. He was the headmaster, Abbott was the pupil in trouble; the relationship between two grown men was temporarily suspended. "Nothing wrong in the handling of the case, but there will be in future ones if you have the same approach. When did you last have a holiday with your wife?"

"Last year, but—" Abbott hesitated.

"Yes?"

"Well, we didn't go away," said Abbott. "Haven't been away for four years, as a matter of fact. Just messed around the house, going out for odd days. We have a bit of a problem at home."

Gideon thought: *Why didn't I know? Is this wife trouble?* "Sorry about that," he said. "Serious?"

"In itself it's not," replied Abbott, hesitantly. "It gets on my nerves, though. The wife's, too. We've got her mother living with us. The old soul's practically bedridden, and there's no one else to take over. Ties my wife all the time, and I can't very well go off on a holiday without her."

Normally Gideon would have told Abbott to fix a holiday of some kind, soon, and taken him off the job whether he liked it or not. But it simply couldn't be done. Every man on the Force would be needed until after the Visit.

"No sisters, brothers or relatives to take over for a week or so?" he asked.

"No one who will, George. You know how it is. My wife's always been the Martha in her family, and—" Abbott broke off.

"As soon as the V.I.P.s have gone home, you've got to take a few weeks off," Gideon compromised. "That's an order."

"Oh, sure," said Abbott.

After Abbott had gone, Gideon sat back, frowning. He had the frustrated feeling which often came to him, because he could not go out and tackle this job himself; that

50

feeling would probably come frequently in the next few weeks. But it was no use sitting and brooding. He did up his collar, tightened the knot of his tie, jumped up, and went out. He put his head round the corner of the office where the night duty Inspector was, said : "Nothing much to worry about, Mac, except this Marjorie Belman job. Seen that call?"

"Yep."

"Watch it. And in your spare time, check all duty rosters, holidays and special leaves, will you? Get as many holidays over as you can, before May 23rd, and postpone all of 'em after that a while, June 4th or 5th, say."

"Big Visit blues," the other man said. "Okay."

Gideon strode on, nodding good-nights right and left, until he reached the courtyard and saw someone standing by the side of his car, back from its check-up. When he drew nearer, he recognized Ripple. He frowned because he hadn't recognized the other at once. Usually his long sight was fairly good ; he needed glasses only for continuous close work.

"Hallo, Rip."

"Going to be busy tonight, George?"

"Not specially," Gideon said.

"Think Kate will want to throw me out if I come round for an hour?"

"Come and have a meal with us," invited Gideon.

"Can't do that—I've a lot of odds and ends to clear up before I pack it in for tonight. I'll have a snack at the canteen. Okay if I come round about nine?"

"We'll have a drink anyhow."

"Good man," said Ripple.

There was something curiously secretive about him. In appearance he was much too heavy, almost coarse, and his face was badly pitted, probably from severe chicken pox as a child, although he had never said anything about it. He looked both tough and rough, but his voice was gentle, and whenever he was pleased he could not repress high spirits ; whenever preoccupied, he seemed to brood.

Gideon reached Parliament Square, saw many more

cars there than usual at seven o'clock in the evening, then noticed that a car was on its side, blocking part of the road to Victoria Street. How could any driver manage to do that with a car on a perfectly dry road in a thirty miles an hour limit area in broad daylight? A constable came up.

"I'd filter through to the right if I were you, sir, and go through St. James's Park. Nasty business over there."

"How nasty?"

"Two stone dead, I'd say—pedestrians. And the driver of the car's a hell of a mess. He side-swiped a lorry— oh, there's the ambulance. Shall I see you through, sir?"

"Please," said Gideon. "Thanks." The constable moved on a dozen pedestrians from the middle of the square, and Gideon crawled past them. He saw a middle-aged woman being led away from the scene by a man; the woman looked greenish-yellow, as if she would be sick. As Gideon passed, she muttered : "Terrible, terrible."

He moved along with a line of traffic into St. James's Park, thinking of Cox, because Cox was in charge of Uniform except over the Visit, and accidents like these were handled by his Department. It was a hell of a job. For the first time, Gideon found himself wondering whether Cox was the right man to take the brunt of public and newspaper criticism about motoring and motorists. Whenever there was a big traffic jam the police were always blamed; the Visit would cause some of the biggest jams ever.

Gideon was half-way along Birdcage Walk when he caught sight of a man and a woman strolling along on the far side of the road, arm-in-arm. The woman was tall, had a nice figure and slim legs, and kept her shoulders straight. As he drew level he saw that it was Miss Timson —and, good God! Young Wall from Sydney. Thirty-five-year-old man and forty-five-year-old woman, if Gideon was any judge. The coincidence made him forget both the accident and Cox.

It was half past seven when he put the car into his garage round the corner from his house in Harrington

Street, Fulham, and locked the shutters and strolled round to the house. It hadn't been painted on the outside for three years, and ought to have a coat this year. Three or four years ago he would have taken that in his stride; it would be three week-ends' work at the most, if he could get three off duty in a row. He could forget that this summer—after the Visit he would be so involved with a backlog of normal work that week-ends off would be skimpy, to say the least.

He opened the iron gate, passed the neatly trimmed privet hedge and the trim, postage-stamp sized lawn, and as he did so, the door opened and his wife appeared.

"Hallo, dear! I was in the bedroom. I thought I saw the car pass."

She had been making-up for him; not too heavily, just enough to look fresh and appealing. She made up more these days than she had when she was young. She was tall, in fact a big woman, deep-breasted but with a well-defined waist, nice legs, rather large feet, narrow enough for shoes of fashion. Her hair was a lighter grey than Gideon's, and she'd had a set today. It was good to see the way her face lit up, good to feel the satisfaction which he felt; yet their kiss was light and almost casual.

"You look as if you're expecting visitors," Gideon said.

She looked pleased. "According to the news, you're expecting the visitors."

Gideon laughed, then told her all that had happened. Kate was quiet and thoughtful until they were sitting at the table. Gideon had a huge plate of meat pie in front of him, knife and fork at the ready. "Isn't it going to be rather a lot?" Kate asked.

"What?"

"Your ordinary job, *and* Uniform."

"It'll break my back!"

Kate gave a little laugh, and started to eat; five minutes later, she looked across at his empty plate, shook her head, and said:

"I suppose it's no use saying you'll ruin your digestion. You haven't improved in thirty years. George."

"Hm-hm?" Gideon was helping himself to more pie.

"Do you think you could get me a seat on the balcony of the Ministry?"

"Wouldn't be surprised," said Gideon. "I'll put in the request tomorrow."

He helped Kate to wash up, and at half past eight switched on the television. There was a news telecast at 8.45 to make time for a two-hour Shakespeare performance. Kate took out some of their son Malcolm's socks, drew them over her hand, found a small hole in one heel, and began to darn.

The news announcer reported the forthcoming Western Summit as if it were fresh and epoch-making. There were a few Russian comments, some African news, some home oddments, and finally :

"In reply to questions in the House of Commons today following his speech about the reduction in overall crime figures the Home Secretary said he fully realized that the improvement might be short term, and the police would certainly not relax their efforts in any degree. His speech was not intended to suggest that there were any grounds for complacency. In reply to Mr. Lubbock, Labour, West Ferry, he said that the improvement was certainly due to improved police methods in which scientific aids to the investigation of crime were being used to the full. There had been no material increase in police manpower. In reply to Mr. Ventry, Conservative, Lushden, he said that some measure of the improvement was undoubtedly due to the spell of severe cold weather in the month of March but he did not believe that this was a major cause. The major cause was undoubtedly the unceasing vigilance of the police, and the use of new methods of crime detection. In reply to Mr. Goss, Liberal, Ockney, he said that it was Government policy to put as much emphasis as possible on the prevention as distinct from the detection of crime, and that in the long run this would undoubtedly be the deciding factor. The Home Secretary added that he did not think that a long-term policy of

*crime prevention would really enable anyone to sleep
more easily in his bed tonight or for many nights to come
—detective work by the Criminal Investigation Department and patrolling by the uniformed policemen were
still the main weapons used against modern crime.*"

The announcer turned to some racing news.

"The Home Secretary sounds almost as if he's got some
sense, doesn't he?" remarked Kate.

"Scott-Marle had a go at him," said Gideon. "We had
a conference this morning . . ." He was half-way through
a recital of what had happened at the conference when
the front door bell rang. "That'll be Rip," he said. "I'll
go." He had a queer little thought as he went to open the
door. He wished this was Cox, come to discuss their joint
problem, instead of Ripple.

Mildred Cox knew that Ray was in a gloomy mood
almost as soon as he got home, just before seven o'clock.
He was sharp with Tom, their only child, nine years old,
whom he usually spoiled. Mildred's problem was to prevent a scene with the nine-year-old without making her
intervention too obvious.

Everything she did to help Ray had to be unostenta-
tious. Outwardly, he was the hub of the little family, and
Mildred cheerfully went along with that. For one thing,
she was so small and he so tall and rangy; seen from
behind, they looked like father and daughter, for the top
of her blonde head barely came up to his angular shoulders. She wore her soft, golden-blonde hair in a feather-
like cluster. Her grey eyes were big and round with an
expression of constant wonder. She had a button of a nose,
and, like Ray, nice full lips and a little pointed chin.

Tom took after her in features and colouring, and
promised to take after his father in height.

"Now you go along to your room and get your homework done," Cox ordered his son. 'Don't let's hear another
squeak out of you until it's finished."

"Okay, Dad."

"And don't say 'okay'. Use the English language."

"All right, Dad." Tom was always subdued when his father picked on him.

The boy went out of the long, narrow living-room, and closed the door quietly. In the corner, the 21-inch television screen was blank. This was a four-roomed apartment in Lambeth, just across the river from the Yard, in a square, squat new apartment building. The window overlooked the Thames, the Embankment, the training ships moored alongside, the passenger jetties, the Thames side jetty and the launches, the Victorian buildings cheek-by-jowl with modern blocks—and New Scotland Yard.

That was why they had moved here, five years ago.

When the boy had gone, Cox stood staring out of the window. A few lights were on, although there was another hour of daylight. The river was calm and beautiful. Boats skimming along it looked almost unreal. Cox kept looking at the C.I.D. block, grey and fairly modern; he could see Gideon's office window.

Suddenly, he said aloud : "We'll have to watch the river. Be a hell of a lot of extra traffic on it."

"When, dear?" asked Mildred, although she knew very well.

"During the next State Visit. Haven't you heard about it ?"

"There *was* something on the television."

"It's going to be a very big show."

"I suppose so, with all those Presidents. There's one good thing, it won't interfere with our holiday this time, as we're not going until August. Will it mean a lot of extra work for you ?"

"Not as much as it should."

"What a funny thing to say," murmured Mildred. She put down some of Tom's stockings, and smiled up. "You don't *want* more work, do you ?"

"I wanted this," growled Cox.

"I think I must be extra dumb tonight," said Mildred, apologetically. "I don't know what you mean."

"Well, it doesn't take much explaining. I've been given

a kick in the pants, and . . ." He talked slowly at first, and then with increasing vigour, so that both bitterness and injured pride showed all too clearly. He walked about the room as he told her how Gideon had actually come to see him, to lay down the law and show his authority. By the time he had finished, it was nearly eight o'clock. More lights were on across the river, and a pleasure craft with festoons of coloured bulbs went swinging down-water.

"I think it's shameful," Mildred said hotly.

"Shameful's *one* word !"

"I always thought Commander Gideon was a good sort."

"There can be a big difference between a man and his reputation," Cox said sourly.

"I suppose there can," said Mildred, as if that was a new and profound reflection. After a pause, while she looked up at her husband's face, she went on : "I know what I would do."

"Do you ?" asked Cox. When his wife made a pro-nouncement like that he was always mildly amused. Talk-ing had helped a great deal, already, although he did not realize it. "And what would Mildred the miracle-worker do ?"

"I'd do the job so well that it would teach Gideon a thing or two," declared Mildred. "I'd make sure I didn't put a foot wrong. *I'd* show them !"

Cox actually laughed. . . .

He was more his usual self with Tom, after homework and before bed ; and after Mildred had gone to bed he sat at a desk, outlining his plans for the Visit.

Mildred had something there, all right. He'd show Gideon.

Ripple stayed at Gideon's place until after midnight, long after Kate had gone to bed.

His chief worry was the tight time schedule. He knew that Gideon had plenty on his shoulders, and his own chief *aide* would be right on top of the job—but would he,

Gideon, keep an eye on anything which developed in the next week or ten days, especially in the next two or three days? If there were an influx of Algerians, for instance, they ought to be watched closely, and there was always the risk that they would work through some other groups.

"They might send a group of Algerian colonists over to distract us, and use someone we least expect to make an attempt on the French President," Ripple said. "Don't know why it is, George, but I've got a nasty feeling about this show. There isn't enough time to prepare properly. Can't very well tell Rogerson this, certainly not the Commissioner, but I thought you ought to know."

"Thanks," said Gideon. "I appreciate it." When he saw that Ripple had said all he wanted to say, he chatted idly for a few minutes, then went on: "What do you think of our Timson?"

"Vi?"

"That her name? I didn't think she was human enough to have one," Gideon said, with laboured humour.

"If you ask me," said Ripple, "Vi Timson's a bit of a dark horse. Why?"

"Just wondered," said Gideon, and had a mental picture of "Vi" walking along with the Australian detective inspector, at least ten years her junior. He added, as if casually: "Didn't you work at JK Division with Cox once?"

"Ray Cox?"

"Yes."

"Touched him on the raw, has it?" Ripple inquired shrewdly.

"Oh, I wouldn't say that. I just want to make sure it doesn't."

"Ray's all right," pronounced Ripple, judicially, "but he's gone ahead too fast. He ought to have had another two years on the beat, way back. Just the man I'd like beside me in a big job, though, provided I didn't rub him up the wrong way."

"So working with him should be easy—is that it?"

"Could be," corrected Ripple. "You'll either have to slap him down, or give him his head."

Ripple was often over-confident, whereas Abbott was not confident enough. Gideon thought a lot about Abbott —more, ironically enough, than he did of the Belman girl, or of Carraway.

7

THE BOMB

"DON'T look now," said Ricky Wall, "but when you get a chance, tell me what you think of the man dancing with the blonde with the Edwardian hair style. He's like a big-time criminal who was murdered in Australia two years ago. We never caught the killer."

"I thought the Sydney police were *so* much better than ours."

"Cut that out," said Wall, with a grin. "Those boys at the Yard really know their job. You could try you well-known charm to find out what they think of the Australian party."

"Sometimes what I would like to use on the Yard men is *not* my well-known charm," said Violet. "Oh, they're so *smug*!"

"None of them pinched your bottom yet?" demanded Wall. "Vi, you're my girl. How about getting shot of this place, and seeing how well we can get to know each other between now and eight o'clock in the morning?"

"I have to be at the office at nine o'clock, so I've got to be up by half past seven," said Violet. "I'll think about your kind offer at the week-end."

Wall complained: "And I thought I was on a safe bet."

"Nothing about me is safe," said Violet, looking at him through her lashes. She wore a cocktail dress, high at the neck, but her arms were bare; she might be nearer fifty than forty, but she looked in the late thirties, and her skin was smooth and without blemish. "When does your party go back, Ricky?"

"We leave London on Tuesday, go over to Paris for three days, Berlin for three days, spend a week in Scandinavia, three days in Milan and another two in Rome, and then fly back here for a final few days in London. Just in time for the big Visit," he went on, and his eyes kindled. "I've always wanted to see what London puts on for these occasions."

"Where would you rather be posted—at the Palace, or at the Houses of Parliament?" asked Violet.

"Which do you recommend?"

"For a Colonial," said Violet, wickedly, "I would think the Palace."

"We hicks from the Dominions are great royalists but we are also true democrats," retorted Wall solemnly. "I'll be at the Houses of Parliament. Can you fix it?"

"Yes," said Violet, simply.

They went up the narrow stairs to the street, a turning off Bond Street. It was quite chilly. The doorman asked : "Cab, sir?" "No, thanks," said Wall. He slid his arm round Violet's waist, and raised his hand to cup her breast. "Change your mind," he pleaded.

She closed her hand over his.

"We'll have a wonderful week-end," she said. "But I have a lot to do in the morning, and I won't be in bed until nearly two o'clock as it is."

"Now who takes work to bed?" demanded Wall, but he laughed, squeezed, and lowered his hand. "I want you to know something," he said. "I think you're quite a girl." After a moment, he went on : "Do we need a cab?"

"It's only five minutes' walk," said the Assistant Commissioner's new secretary.

They walked, slowly.

Without knowing it, they passed the house where there was a small, empty flat, with Marjorie Belman's clothes still hanging in the wardrobe, her make-up things still on the dressing-table, food intended for that day still in the refrigerator.

Wall saw Violet to the front door of her flatlet in South Audley Street, and then strolled towards Piccadilly, smiling, half dissatisfied, half pleased with himself. He hailed a cab, gave his hotel address, and sat back.

As he got out of the taxi and glanced across the Thames, which he could hear lapping gently against the embankment, momentarily he looked straight in the direction of the little house in Streatham, not far from the common, where Matthew Smith was lying next to his wife in the big double bed, thinking of his bomb.

Smith was restless and on edge that night, filled with repressed excitement and impatience. He kept his thin, bony body as still as he could, for he believed his wife was asleep. She stirred unexpectedly and asked in a clear voice :

"Can't you sleep, dear?"

So she was restless, too—almost as if she sensed his excitement and his tension.

"I'm all right," Smith answered gruffly.

"But I honestly don't think you are," his wife said. "You looked peaky all the evening. Matt, dear, what is it? If I don't know, I can't help, can I?"

He felt like striking her fat face, felt like shouting : "I tell you it's nothing!" Instead, he kept silent.

"Matt, is—is it because of the French—the Frenchman coming? If it is, you mustn't let it upset you. It's so long ago, now, it—"

"I don't want to talk about it," he said in a hard voice. "If you can't go to sleep, keep quiet."

He woke early on Saturday morning, in spite of the bad night. He did not go to the office on Saturdays, and usually spent the morning in the small garden, with some fuchsias, his favourite flowers, or weeding the small herbaceous border, or pottering in his little workshop at the end of the garden.

In this workshop he had a carpenter's bench, a good selection of tools in two wall racks, and always some repairs waiting to be done. It was surprising how skilful he was with his thin, bony hands—which looked almost too frail to hold tools firmly. He was a good carpenter, and could French polish as well as most professionals. Any work with wood soothed him. All the furniture in the house was in perfect condition; as a handyman, no one could be more efficient. His married daughter often called upon him to do odd jobs.

It was a long, long time since his son had died—the eager-eyed, fresh-faced lad of nineteen who had gone out to France so happily for a three-months' training course in Grasse, the French perfume centre in the mountains behind the Riviera. His son—he always thought of the lad as "my son", hardly ever as Robert—had been keen on chemistry, and had got a job in the research department of a firm of cosmetic manufacturers on the Great West Road. His future had seemed very bright, and would have been but for the awful thing which had followed.

A girl had been murdered, and the French police had accused the boy.

Even today, twenty-five years afterwards, at the thought of the trial, at the thought of that awful slicing smash of the guillotine, Smith would feel his blood going hot and his hands clenching and unclenching, and sometimes he would break out into cold sweat. Ever since that awful day, Smith had hated France and the French with unreasoning, venomous hatred. Whenever the French were in trouble, Smith was elated; the political crises, the economic crises, the damaging strikes, the Algerian revolts— all of these were simply a vengeful fate. Years ago, when France had collapsed under the Panzer divisions and the Stukas, he had screamed aloud that the English were fools for ever trusting Frenchmen. He hated, hated, hated them.

His wife knew this.

From the beginning, she had tried to soothe him, saying that it wasn't just the French, it was the law everywhere. Anyone could make mistakes, and this had been an awful one; that was the way to look at it.

Smith had soon learned that she had no hatred in her heart for the French murderers, and that had been the beginning of his antipathy towards her, a slowly increasingly, deepening, bitter dislike.

Only when driven by physical need, did he touch her. Sometimes he wished her dead. He did not fully realize that his hatred had swollen to hideous size and shape.

One day a dark-skinned Frenchman had got into conversation with him on a bus, and started to damn his own country folk as colonialist aggressors, sadistic brutes, decadent morons in sex and art. Before long, Smith had been talking more freely to the dark-skinned man than to anyone he knew. All his hatred for France and the French had come out.

The man had asked if he would do anything to help the Algerian Colonists' cause. In his work as a shipping clerk Smith handled bills of lading, invoices, all kinds of things to do with imports and exports, and he often went on board ships in London docks, with these papers. Would Smith act as a messenger? the man asked. Sometimes it was useful to pass small packages, letters and secret information—it would be invaluable to the nationalist cause if Mr. Smith would help. And of course he would be paid for taking risks.

It wasn't very much money; just five pounds a week, every week. But it increased Smith's income by nearly a half. He told his wife that he had been given a rise, with a more important job, and as far as he knew, she believed it.

It was three years since the suggestion that he should take another, this time drastic, step; that of assassinating General de Gaulle on a state visit in 1960. For:

"... no one in Algeria believes that he wants to end the war and make peace ... His spies are everywhere ... He will cheat us, like all the other leaders ... See what happened to the real friends of the Nationalists ... See how slow he is in redeeming his promises ... We must shock the French nation and strike a great blow for the freedom of Algeria."

Matthew Smith had grown into the acceptance of the fact that this was exactly what he should do. It would be the ultimate act of vengeance for his dead son.

". . . and the best way is to throw a bomb, which we will provide for you. In London it is easy for you to be at the front of a crowd during a procession, and you can be within a few metres of the carriage in which de Gaulle will ride."

Smith went along to his workshop, on that Saturday morning, remembering that the great chance had been lost in 1959. Everything had been ready, the bomb had been in his possession, he had known exactly where he was to stand, and a few white sympathizers with the Algerian nationalist cause had been primed to help him to get away, by causing confusion in the ranks. Then on the day before the great opportunity he had woken with a terrible headache, aches and pains all over, and a matter-of-fact wife had called the doctor. His temperature had been a hundred and four. He had not even been able to stagger across the room. Luckily, he had been able to satisfy the others that it had not been last-minute fright.

He had never really recovered from the disappointment. He ate very little, and was terribly thin; the knowing ones among his fellow workers murmured : "T.B. or cancer." But there was surprising strength in his frail-looking body; it was his hatred which burned up his flesh.

He went into his tiny workshop. It had a brick floor, and underneath four loose bricks, deep in a little cavity close to the wall, was the bomb. The Algerians had assured him that it would keep for ever.

He stared at the spot, and planned how he would take up the bricks, and put the bomb in his pocket. He began to wonder where he would stand during the procession. Suddenly, he heard a sound and glanced round. His wife was in the doorway, staring, and he saw fear in her eyes.

"Matt—" she began chokily.

"What the devil are you doing here?"

"Matt, I—I saw you come out before breakfast. I didn't want you to catch cold. I—"

"You lying fool, you're spying on me! Go back into the house, put some clothes on, and stay there until I come back. Stay indoors! Do you understand?"

"I—I didn't meant to upset you, dear," his wife muttered, but she continued to stare. He did not realize how glittering his eyes were, or how his lips were drawn back over his teeth.

That had convinced her beyond doubt that something was hidden in this workshop. She had suspected it for a long time.

And she was more frightened than ever of her husband.

Beryl Belman was not frightened for herself. She had no idea that she had need to be. But she had.

8

SATURDAY ROLL-CALL

On that same Saturday morning, Gideon was in his office a little after eight o'clock. Saturday was always the odds-and-ends day, a kind of roll-call of unsolved crimes. Gideon liked to go over all the jobs on which there had been no progress during the week, to see if he or the men in charge had missed anything obvious.

"Did you get hold of all the Provincial Supers I asked you to?" he asked Bell.

"Yes, George." Bell put his hand on a sheaf of letters. "They'll all play. They want someone to go and brief them on our bad boys, though, and I said we'd send someone up. Our chap can pick up a lot of information, too."

"Let me see the reports," Gideon said.

He read them closely, and by the time that and the morning briefing was done, it was ten o'clock.

"Going to have a breather for five minutes?" suggested Bell. "Lemaitre's coming at a quarter past, Evans is due from London Airport, and Abbott said he'd like to see you at half past eleven."

"Anything from Cox?"

"Not a squeak."

"Hmm," said Gideon. "All right, Joe, send for a cuppa." He got up, went to the window, and looked out, stretching himself and yawning. His collar was done up and his tie in position, for it was chilly. The windows were closed against a wind which seemed to have come in mistake for March, and was whipping up the surface of the Thames. He had been wrong as a weather prophet.

At a quarter past ten exactly there was a bang at the door, and Superintendent Lemaitre came in. For years Lemaitre had sat where Joe Bell did now. He was an old friend of Gideon's, a senior detective with one big fault, which somehow showed in his alert, thin-featured face and sounded in his Cockney voice, with its overtone of slick confidence.

"Hiyah, George!" He came in briskly, waved to Bell and added: "Joe," and shook Gideon's hand. "Just thought I'd come and put you out of your misery."

"What misery?"

"You won't have to come to Cornwall to do my job for me," announced Lemaitre. He sat on a corner of Gideon's desk, bony hands clenched, a confident and happy-looking man given to taking too much for granted and jumping to conclusions. "All three deaths were natural causes—I mean, all accidental drownings, George."

"Sure?"

"Yep. And I'm back full of the joys and ready for anything. Just had ten days down by the briny, all expenses paid—got in a couple of dips every day. My wife's so brown you wouldn't think she'd been decent! She wants to know if you and Kate can come round to tea or supper tomorrow."

"If Kate hasn't booked anything, we'd like to," said Gideon. "Then you can make your wife a police widow for a week or so."

"What's all this? I'm just the man you want for the Big Visit."

"So you are. Visits to Glasgow, Liverpool, Manchester, and the rest, to check whether any of their boys are planning an offensive in London during the Visit."

"Okay, okay," said Lemaitre, without a moment's hesitation. "I'll go. Heard anything about Sonnley, or Benny Klein?"

"Dimble of Manchester said he'd heard that Klein was up there," Bell put in.

"Buying the Manchester mobs off," Lemaitre guessed. "When do you want me to go?"

"Tuesday."

"Right-i-ho!" Lemaitre slapped his hands together.

"Won't be sorry to get out of this den of vice again. Don't forget to ask Kate about tomorrow."

As he went out, Abbott came in, looking rather over-eager; quite obviously he thought he had something to report, and couldn't wait. Lemaitre's footsteps clap-clapped down the corridor, as the door closed.

"Well, Abby?" Gideon asked.

"Eric Little was seen to pick up a girl at Swan and Edgar's on Tuesday night, just before the call went out for Marjorie Belman," Abbott said. "The girl answered Marjorie Belman's description. It's a belated report from a uniformed man, and I'm having the story checked. Might be the angle we're looking for."

If he had come in simply to report this, it was a bad sign. Gideon waited, concealing his disappointment, and then Abbott glanced at Bell, as if he wished the Chief Inspector wasn't there.

"Joe, nip along and get those letters from the typing pool for me," urged Gideon and winked.

Nothing flustered Joe Bell, who was not only self-effacing and competent, but a first-class second-in-command. As he went out, Gideon wondered, not for the first time, who would replace him, and shrugged the thought off.

"Something on your mind, Abby?"

"Yes," said Abbott. "Wasn't sure whether you'd want Joe in on it. Er—did you know I used to play a lot of tennis with Ray Cox?"

Gideon sat up, surprised.

"That's news to me."

"Well, I did. We were out at JI together for years. I—er—happen to know Ray's nose has been put out of joint. None of my business," Abbott went on hastily, "but he's been giving his Department hell this last day or two. He always was a bit tense. Thought you ought to know."

"That's a big help," said Gideon warmly. "Thanks."

"You won't let Ray know that I—er—warned you?"

"No one warned me."

"Thanks, George," Abbott said. "Well, I'll be on my way."

When he had gone, Gideon stared at the rain on the window, glad that Abbott's mind was working well, and wondering how he could get round Cox's antagonism. Warnings from Ripple and from Abbott must not be ignored. Before he reached any kind of conclusion, Bell came back, and at the same instant the telephone bell rang. Gideon picked up the telephone.

"That's probably Rip," said Bell. "He was due to call from Paris."

"Gideon speaking . . . yes, put him through." Gideon looked up at Bell. "Yes, it's him." He waited until Ripple's voice came. "Hallo, Rip. How's Paris?"

"They've put a bit of paint on since I was here last," said Ripple. "The Sûreté's got things laid on pretty well over here, too. Specially trained men will come with de Gaulle's party, and they'd like to send over about thirty of their chaps familiar with Algerian Colonists and Nationalists to have a look round. Have we any objections?"

"No. How will they come over? As tourists?"

"That's the idea. All unofficial."

"I'll fix it with Rogerson," promised Gideon. He talked for another couple of minutes, without learning any more, and replaced the receiver slowly.

"He expecting trouble?" asked Bell.

Gideon explained.

"Be a bit of a load off our backs," said Bell practically. "Better make sure how many will want accommodation, we don't want to have to give 'em bed and board here. They say that there's hardly a hotel room left in London for the week of the Visit. The Yanks are coming over in shiploads."

"Why not ask Miss Timson to book a hotel for these French chaps? That place over at Chelsea won't be any good, the Aussies will be back by then."

"Okay," said Bell, and immediately called Rogerson's

secretary. Gideon heard him draw in his breath, and for once Bell raised his voice.

"When the Assistant Commissioner's not in, you'll take your orders from the Commander. I don't care if it keeps you here all day." He rang off as angry as Gideon could remember seeing him. "The impertinent bitch."

"May be trouble between her and her boy-friend." Bell was the one man whom Gideon had told about the Australian and "Vi". To give Bell time to recover his temper, Gideon went on : "Joe, I'd forgotten the hotels and bars. There will be more con-men at work at the big hotels than we've had for a long time. Who've we got spare?"

Bell recovered and considered.

"Parsons," he came up with, at last. "He knows London hotels as well as anyone."

"See if he's in," ordered Gideon.

Parsons was a chubby, jolly, happy-looking man, with a smooth skin and a ready tongue. He listened to Gideon for ten minutes before he said :

"I've got it, skipper. We want every hotel detective on the look out for suspect con-men, and we want a few of our chaps spread around pretty thin, because we can't spare many. Mind if I make a suggestion?"

"Go ahead."

"Might be a good idea to have New York, Washington, Paris and Bonn send over photographs of any of their missing con-men, so we can distribute the pictures to the hotels."

"Do that," approved Gideon.

It was half past six in London, and in New York the time was about half past one. The door of the Police Commissioner's office at Headquarters opened and a tall, slim man in a pale grey suit came in, without any of Lemaitre's kind of bustle.

The Commissioner looked up.

"You heard anything new?" he demanded.

"I've heard enough to make me think that O'Hara's flown to London, and that could mean he's going to try to kill the President there," the young man answered. "I think it's time we informed Washington."

"That's exactly what I'll do, Jed," the Commissioner said.

Gideon still had that restless feeling, and wished that he could go out on a job himself instead of leaving them all to others. Abbott and Cox between them were on his mind, and he was uneasy in case concentration on the plans for the Visit should make him slip up on one of the more immediate jobs.

There was no doubt that Abbott was seriously worried about the Belman girl, and it would be easy to put that down to Abbot's lack of confidence. But supposing he was right? Should Gideon have made a great effort to trace the girl? He was still brooding about Marjorie Belman when he heard footsteps outside, and looked up at once : for these were the footsteps of a man in a hurry. There was a perfunctory tap at the door before it opened, and Abbott stood dramatically on the threshold. Abbott's news showed in his over-bright eyes and his pale cheeks. It was almost an anti-climax when he said :

"They've found Marjorie Belman, drowned off Sandown in the Isle of Wight. That swine got her."

Gideon said very slowly : "Have we got Carraway?"

"He's over at his main showrooms. I've sent a Q car to watch him."

"Come on," Gideon said, and stood up. "Let's go and see him."

9

KILLER?

IT was like being released from solitary confinement.

Gideon strode along the passages of the Yard with Abbott a pace behind him, and men saw him and stood hasily aside, or watched covertly from half-open doors. The word went round : "Gee-Gee's on the rampage." There were sighs of relief when he headed for the lift, and the main door. His car, with a chauffeur at the wheel, was pulling up at the foot of the steps : Bell had lost no time.

"Hop in," Gideon said to Abbott. "Tell me about it on the way."

All there was to tell were the bare facts, reported by the police from Sandown. Abbott hardly knew whether to blame himself for the girl's death, or to feel vindicated. The chauffeur, slowing down as lights changed to amber, felt the back of his seat move as Gideon gripped it, and boomed :

"Get a move on."

"Right, sir."

Traffic seemed to fall aside for them. Policemen who recognized Gideon's car kept the evening crowds at bay. They swept along Whitehall, along Haymarket to Piccadilly, and round to Regent Street, then to Portman Place. Five minutes before he had expected Gideon saw the big new garage, painted a pale pink, with the name *Carraway Car Sales and Rentals*.

Thirty or forty new-looking cars with price labels were parked alongside the petrol pumps, where two boys were busy with petrol. The car pulled up near the showrooms, in which new cars were standing, with *Immediate Delivery* signs over the windscreens. Gideon got out of one door and Abbott the other, on the instant. Gideon caught sight of a glossy-haired, stocky little man talking to a tall woman—and saw the way this man stared at Abbott, and how he looked across at a door marked: *Office*. Gideon did not know it then, but this man was Eric Little. He had no time to warn Carraway before Gideon and Abbott reached the door, which Gideon pushed wider open. Carraway was sitting at a flat-topped desk, in his shirt sleeves, cigarette dangling from his lips. He looked immaculate.

"What the hell—" he began, and then appeared to see Abbott for the first time. His lips tightened, his eyes narrowed.

Gideon growled: "Mr. Carraway?"

"I'm busy. Can't you—?"

A telephone bell rang on his desk. Carraway stretched out for it, but Abbott moved swftly, took it first, and said into the telephone:

"I'm afraid he's busy. Will you call him back?" and rang off.

"You've got a nerve," Carraway said roughly. His eyes were still narrowed, but he had shown no outward signs of fright. "Who are you?"

"I'm Commander Gideon of New Scotland Yard. When did you last see Marjorie Belman?"

"What the hell's that got to do with you?" Carraway demanded.

He certainly wasn't going to be easy; in fact he was going to be a hard man to beat. It was already easy to understand why Abbott was unsure of himself. Gideon glanced out of the window and saw the glossy-haired man driving off in a car, with the woman beside him. The couple would be followed, and if he was demonstrating a car it would make no difference. Two more Yard men were in sight already.

"Answer my question, please," Gideon said.

"Why the devil should I?"

"Try answering it."

"Now you listen to me," Carraway said coldly. He pushed his chair back from the desk, squashed out his cigarette, and stood up. He spared a glance almost of derision for Abbott, then looked back to Gideon. "I don't care if you're the Commissioner of the Metropolitan Police himself, no one's going to burst into my office like that and get away with it. I had enough trouble with Abbott over the murder of my partner. I don't want any more over a skirt."

"When did you last see her?"

"I tell you—"

"All right, Abby," Gideon said roughly. "Let's take him along to the Yard. Call the others—"

Abbott stepped to the window, and raised his right hand. A man standing at the far end of the rows of cars came forward; another followed him. Gideon saw Carraway lose a little colour, and moisten his lips momentarily, but that was his only sign of weakness.

"I can't waste time going to the Yard. I've got a lot of work to do. I haven't seen Marjorie Belman for days."

"How many days?"

Carraway said: "Three or four."

"How about Tuesday night?"

"I didn't see her Tuesday night," declared Carraway. The other two Yard men were at the window, waiting for a signal from Gideon. "I was working late. Ever since Rawson died I've worked late every night. I'm trying to do two men's work."

"Can you prove you didn't see Marjorie Belman that night?"

Carraway exploded: "Why the hell should I? Why—?" he broke off, paled again, hesitated, and then stared at Gideon as if worried for the first time: he was very, very clever. "What's happened to her? What's the matter?"

"Sure you don't know?"

"Just tell me what it's all about, and I'll tell you what I can."

Gideon did not know why he evaded the question as he did; there was something of a sixth sense in his move, that sense which made him so much more able than most detectives. He knew that Abbott would not interrupt or give him away, and he said :

"She's been missing since Wednesday evening."

"Missing," echoed Carraway. "Didn't she go home?"

"You didn't exactly encourage her to, did you?"

"Listen, Mr. Gideon," Carraway said, "this isn't an inquiry into my morals, is it? The kid wanted a gay life, so I gave her one. If she'd known what was good for her she would have stayed with me. But her family nagged at her, and finally she gave up. She told me she was going back to them."

"Did you quarrel with her?"

"I don't quarrel with hysterical kids," Carraway sneered. "While she was sensible, she was okay." He moistened his lips again. "Er—didn't she go back home?"

"She's not been seen for three and a half days. Unless you've seen her."

"I haven't set eyes on her," Carraway insisted. "The last time I saw her was Monday. She'd had a talk with a sister, who'd been sent round by Ma and Pa, and the session upset her. I tried to calm her down, but she wasn't having any, so I told her if she preferred living like a nun, it was okay by me. I walked out of the flat I rented for her when she said she was going back home." He frowned. "Are you sure—?"

After a pause, Gideon said : "I'm sure." He stood looking at Carraway intently, twice as powerful as the motorcar salesman, and then nodded and said : "If you hear from her, let us know at once."

He turned and led the way out, Abbott nearly stumbling over his heels, and then looked round sharply ; but Carraway's expression hadn't changed.

The man with the glossy black hair, an Italian type, was driving back into the garage with the woman still by his side.

"That's Eric Little," Abbott volunteered. "Want to talk to him?"

"Not now," Gideon said, and climbed into his car. He waited for Abbott to join him, and the doors slammed.

"He's going to be a tough nut," he declared. "Don't let up on him, Abby."

"Believe me I won't," said Abbott. "But, George—"

He was getting bold.

"Hmm?"

"He didn't bat an eyelid."

"He didn't bat enough eyelids," Gideon growled. "He put on his poker face too soon."

He knew that a weaker man than Carraway would probably have given himself away under the weight of that sudden pressure; and he felt quite sure, as Abbott did, that Carraway knew exactly what he was about. It would probably be best to attack him through one of his salesmen, now—Little, for instance; and he must be followed wherever he went in an effort to break his nerve.

In spite of the failure to make Carraway give anything away, Gideon felt better; the little flurry of action had done him good. It would also do Abbott good, in the long run, to know that he wasn't failing on an easy job.

Abbott already seemed rather more confident of himself.

"Don't you worry," he said, quietly. "I'll make sure he's watched. Why didn't you tell him she was dead?"

"Let's keep him on the hook a bit," Gideon advised. "His defences were up too soon. We need a bit more evidence."

"I'll get some evidence," Abbott said grimly. "I'll keep Little and the others on the hook, too, and try to make them squirm."

Soon after Gideon and Abbott left the office, Eric Little brought the middle-aged woman back to sign a hire purchase agreement. The woman was rather too self-confident and loud-voiced. Carraway let her take control of the situation, witnessed the agreement, took her cheque, and watched her drive out of the garage. She was seen off by Little. Then he shrugged his arms into his coat, went out and met Little between the roadway and the office. He hardly moved his lips as he said:

77

"They don't know she's dead. Watch yourself, they might be tailing you." In a loud voice, he went on: "If I don't get a drink, I'll break a blood vessel. You take over."

He walked on.

On the Saturday evening, about the same time, Eric Little shook hands with a plump man who had just signed a hire purchase agreement for an Austin Cambridge, and escorted him to the door of the showrooms. Then he went back, and picked up each of the two London evening papers, early editions, which were on his desk. Each had advertisements for the company's rental and for sale, but he was much more interested in news about Marjorie's body. The body of "a young woman in her early twenties" had been found off Sandown on the Isle of Wight, but the police, according to the report, hadn't yet been able to identify it.

"It's as safe as houses," he told himself, and remembered how the two Yard men had been rebuffed. Carraway certainly kept his nerve, and that was all there was to it. Strong nerves. If that damned sister hadn't come round —

He saw a girl walking past the petrol pumps towards the door. At first, he felt as if someone had stuck a knife into him, it was such a shock. That walk. That hair. He stood by the desk, white-faced and with his hands shaking as he lit a cigarette; then the girl stepped out of the shadow of the cover over the pumps, and he saw that the likeness was only a passing one.

But for that moment he had thought that this was Marjorie Belman, come back to life.

The girl hesitated outside the door, looking in. Little was placed in such a position that he could see out, but could not be seen — he always liked to make sure that he could vet callers first. When standing still, as when walking, this girl was uncannily like Marjorie. The cigarette burned Little's tongue because he drew in the smoke so deeply.

78

It must be the sister. He hadn't seen her clearly the other night, but—who else could it be?

She came in, looking round. Near her was a bell-push marked *Inquiries*. Little moistened his lips, stubbed out the cigarette in a large ash-tray, and stood up. The girl saw him. Her eyes were very like Marjorie's, too, but her complexion was much fairer—and now that she was closer he saw that her hair was dark brown. There was another difference ; she had more of a figure than the dead girl— was much fuller at the breast.

"Good afternoon," Little said, as breezily as he could. "Can I help you ?"

She looked at him appraisingly. His heart was thumping, he still felt the effect of that uncanny likeness, and he knew cold fear ; but she showed no sign of recognition.

"I'm Beryl Belman," she announced.

He played dumb.

"Who ?"

"Marjorie Belman's sister," the girl said flatly.

He had to say something, he had to recover from the shock.

"Good Lord," he exclaimed. "Jorrie's sister !"

"That's right," said Beryl Belman, solemnly. "Her older sister."

"I didn't even know she had one."

"Will you please tell me where she is ?"

Little was feeling better now, and beginning to think clearly. If she had seen him the other night she would have said something about it by now, so there was no emergency—yet.

"Isn't she at her flat ?"

"No. I've just come from there."

"Well—*I* don't know where she is," Little declared. "No—no idea. I know she is a friend of my managing director, but he's not at this branch today. I'll ask him to let you know if he has any idea where Jorrie is, shall I ? Eh ? Can I—can I get in touch with you ?"

He offered cigarettes. When Beryl Belman didn't appear to notice them, Little took one himself, his fingers unsteady.

"Sure you won't have a cigarette?"

"I don't smoke," she said flatly.

Now she was staring at him even more intently. It was almost as if she was wondering where she had seen him before, as if she was accusing him.

"Well, er, if you'll tell me where I can get in touch with you, I'll ask my boss if he can help," Little offered.

"Where can I see him?"

"He travels about so much that you can never be sure."

"I want to talk to him. I've telephoned him twice, but he's been out each time. I want to talk to him about my sister."

Little replied calmly: "Your sister was quite old enough to look after herself, you know. She—" He realized suddenly that he had said "*your sister was*", and for a terrible moment thought that this girl would realize the significance of the slip, but she did not seem to be alarmed. "I mean, she's over twenty-one, she can do what she likes."

"I don't want to argue with you," said Beryl, "but I intend to see Bruce Carraway. He may not realize it, but he's broken my mother's heart, and my father's terribly upset, too. I've got to see Marjorie and make her come back home. I've been along to her flat twice a day since last Tuesday, and there's no answer. One of the cleaners said that a man was there last night, but that she hasn't seen Marjorie, and—I want to know if Carraway *has* cast her aside."

The words came out so quietly that they carried tragedy, not pathos, even when she went on:

"Has he? If he has, she's got to realize that Mum and Dad will forgive her. All they want is for her to come back."

Little was feeling much better, virtually certain that she hadn't recognized him, confident that he could handle the situation.

"I don't think there's been any trouble between Jorrie

80

and my boss," he said. "But I haven't seen her for a couple of weeks or more."

Beryl Belman looked astonished: "Of course you have!"

"Now look here, young lady," said Little almost playfully, "are you calling me a liar?"

"You saw her last Tuesday evening, and took her off in a car," asserted Beryl sharply. "I'd been to her flat, and followed her to Piccadilly. I saw her go off with you."

The words sounded like a death-knell to Eric Little, each one booming sonorously inside his head. It was an awful sound, with a terrible significance which he could not fail to see. If this girl ever talked to the police, he would be caught for murder.

He thought: *I've got to get rid of her.*

Beryl thought: *He's lying to me.*

And she thought: *He looks like the man I saw at Jorrie's place, but I can't be sure.*

Her heart was beating very fast as she waited for him to make some comment, for no man liked being called a liar. Other thoughts passed rapidly through her mind, the most important that she had to find out where Jorrie was, and that this man might be able to help her. She was scared, and yet determined, as she stared defiantly into the man's sallow but rather good-looking face. He kept moving his lips without opening his mouth, and she assumed that he was trying to keep a hold on his temper.

Before he spoke, Beryl said:

"It's no use pretending. I *did* see you."

"All—all right," said Little, and his lips parted in a tense smile; she did not notice that there was no smile in his eyes. "I can't fool you, I can see." He rubbed his nose with a sharp, vigorous action. "As a matter of fact—"

A car turned in from the main road, and moved fast towards him; it was one of the other salesmen. He glanced round. He saw no policeman, so apparently they had gone after Carraway. He waved to the newcomer, a kind of "keep off" gesture, and the other grinned and went jauntily into the saleroom. Heavy traffic was passing along the road, often very fast.

"Listen," said Little. "We can't talk here, we're bound to be interrupted, and I've got a customer coming in five minutes' time. How about meeting me later?"

"I want to know where my sister is," Beryl said firmly. "I'm not going to be put off."

"Don't you worry, I'll tell you all I can," he assured her. She could not make up her mind whether he was lying or telling the truth. "It's a bit complicated, and—well, Carraway's my boss, see, I've got to watch myself." She saw sweat on his forehead. "We close at half past eight. How about meeting me at Hampstead Heath at nine o'clock?"

"I don't know Hampstead Heath very well," Beryl objected quickly.

"That's all right, we can meet somewhere central," said Little hastily. "How about by the pond? You can get there by bus. The easy way is to go to Swiss Cottage and walk. We can have a talk, and—"

"*Do* you know where Jorrie is?"

Little said : "As a matter of fact, I'm a bit worried about her. I don't think Carraway's playing the game by her. But—listen, I can't talk here, my customer's just arrived."

A scarlet MG car swung off the road, a young man with snowy fair hair driving, and a girl with a mop of shiny black hair sitting beside him. They looked handsome and attractive. The driver raised a hand in greeting to the man with Beryl, and she realized that there was no chance to talk now ; all that mattered was making this man tell her where to find Jorrie.

"Will you be there?" the man demanded.

"I—yes, all right, but you'd better have news for me."

"I'll have news," he assured her. He gripped her hand, and gave a forced smile. "Don't worry, I'll have news for you." He turned away and walked hurriedly towards the snowy-haired driver and his companion. The girl was sitting at ease with an arm stretched along the back of the bench seat. "Good evening, Mr. Armstrong," the salesman said, his voice carrying clearly. "I've got that Bristol ready..."

It was half past seven, so there was plenty of time—too much time. With a sense of eagerness and excitement which she had not known before, Beryl left the showroom. It looked as if she was going to get what she wanted. It wouldn't be long now.

"I tell you she saw me, she can put a finger on me," Little said huskily. He was in the office, just before half past eight, and Carraway was sitting at his desk, his jacket on now, looking as if he had just come from his tailor. "We've got to keep her quiet, can't you see?"

"We haven't got to keep anyone quiet," Carraway said.

"What the hell do you mean?"

"Listen, Eric," Carraway said, and leaned forward, staring up into the other's eyes. "You're in trouble. *I'm* not. The only witness who could have caught me out on the Rawson job is dead, and you killed her. You laid it all on. *I* didn't touch her. I hadn't seen her for days. I wasn't anywhere near Brighton or the South coast, and I can prove it. Don't get anything wrong. I'm not in any trouble."

Little stood, half crouching, his body so rigid that it was almost as if it had turned to stone. The only vivid sign of life was in his burning eyes.

"I was playing poker with you and the others on the night Rawson was murdered, and the others will stick to that story," Carraway went on. "Understand that? If you try to back out now, I'll say that you're trying to frame me. The police might question me, they might even charge me, but they couldn't make the charge stick. You could talk till you're blue in the face and it wouldn't be any use to them as evidence."

Little said, in a queer, grating voice : "You paid me—a thousand quid."

"For commission, Eric, for commission! We've had a damned good season, in spite of the slump. I paid the others a thousand quid each, too. After all, fair's fair. You're in trouble all right, but you can get yourself out. Don't try to drag me into it, that's all." He gave a short, high-pitched laugh. "Why, it was you who went to Jorrie's apartment and started getting her clothes together! I was right out at Wimbledon at the time, and can prove it. Just get yourself out of trouble, Eric, and don't expect any help from me."

"Why, you — you *swine*."

"You don't have to worry," Carraway said, smoothly. "You've got a good job, and you'll always get a fat bonus while you work for me. All you have to do is keep yourself out of trouble — like you have before. Just think what your wife and kids would feel like if you got topped for killing — "

"*Keep your bloody mouth shut!*" Little screeched.

"I'm only telling you," said Carraway. Then he leaned forward and went on earnestly : "You've got a lot to thank me for, Eric. The cops are after me, not you. They're not interested in you yet. You've got plenty of time to do what you want to do. Why don't you use that time? I'm going to have a nice little drive out to Watford. That will keep them busy, radio patrol cars and all. While I'm leading them up the garden, you've got plenty of time to shut that little bitch's mouth."

10

SHADOW

ERIC LITTLE stepped out of Carraway's office, almost blinded with rage, but as he walked across to the cars, his heels smacking against the macadam, fear began to creep up on him : fear of what that girl's evidence could do. By the time he reached his car, he realized beyond doubt that Carraway was right. The slimy, cunning swine had fixed things so that nothing could be proved against him ; he had swung the whole load on to Little's shoulders.

Little almost choked.

He had to get rid of that girl.

He sat in the car for a few minutes, drawing fiercely at a cigarette. It was twenty-five to nine. The other salesmen had gone home, only Carraway and the petrol pump attendants were on the premises, and he did not think that Carraway would come out yet.

He was a devil.

One sentence he had uttered burned itself into Little's mind : "*Just think what your wife and kids would feel like if you got topped for killing—*"

Nora and the kids, the triplets, Beth, Jane and Bob. He had killed once to save his home and his family, and Carraway knew that it was the one all-consuming love of his life. Somehow he couldn't help playing around with other girls, but he was never serious and Nora never knew. Nora mustn't know.

Why the hell had he allowed Carraway to make him kill Jorrie?

It did not matter how often he asked the question, the answer was always the same : not for money, at least not only for the money, not because of the earlier murder, because he would do anything to save his home.

Now he had to go and see—*now he had to go and kill*—Beryl Belman.

He tossed the cigarette out of the window, started the engine, and drove with more than usual care on to the main road, where the traffic had slackened. Then he turned towards Swiss Cottage. He could be at the Pond in ten minutes, and might arrive before the girl. He didn't want that, he wanted to draw up alongside her, tell her to step in, and make sure that no one standing around could identify him. He could change the number plates on the car in the morning; there was no danger from that.

He drove slowly as far as Swiss Cottage and up the hill towards the Heath to the Pond.

A few children were still playing with boats in the dusk, and the lights of a dozen cars were reflected in the water. Several adults were standing around, idly. A man went hurrying up to a girl, and they flung their arms round each other, as if life depended on their meeting.

Beryl wasn't here.

Little drove down towards the village, and it was then that he noticed the Rover. Shocked, he remembered that the police often drove Rovers. It was fairly close behind him, and although he gave it two chances to pass, the driver preferred to lag behind. Now Little's heart began to pound. He peered into his mirror, and made out the heads and shoulders of two men in the front of the car; both big men who might be from the Yard. He could not see them well enough to be sure, but who else would follow him? He turned a corner without giving a signal; and the Rover came after him but made no attempt to catch up.

Words burst from his lips: "They're after me."

He was in a panic for several minutes, wanting to pull up and to give himself a chance to think, wanting to make sure that these men were detectives. He slowed down to ten miles an hour—so did the other car. There was no reasonable doubt that they were detectives.

That girl would be waiting for him by now.

The police mustn't see him with her; if they once saw him with her they would start asking questions and she would talk, just as Jorrie would have. He was sweating and half choking as he drove on, fighting for self-control, trying to make himself think clearly.

If he didn't turn up at the Pond, the girl would probably go to the police. The danger was acute. He must stop her somehow—oh, God, what should he do? And what would the police think of him, driving around like this? He had to fool them. It could be life and death. As he began to reason with himself, he felt better, and slowly evolved a practical plan. He must drive to a corner fairly close to the Pond, park the car, give the impression that he was waiting for someone, then make a rush for the Pond and the girl. He must put her off somehow, without being seen with her; that was the only chance.

He waited until five past nine, then pulled up near the gates of a big private house. He parked for a few minutes before getting out and walking up and down. The men sat and waited for him, without troubling to get out, as if they believed that he would be all right while near his car. He strolled as far as the corner of the street, turned as if casually, then swung round again and made a rush for the Pond. He did not see whether he was followed, just raced towards the spot itself. He saw Beryl waiting, looking about her. She saw him coming. He rushed up to her, now walking very fast, and before she could speak he burst out :

"I can't wait now, Carraway's following me. Call me at the garage, Monday. I'm on Jorrie's trail. Ask for Eric Little."

Then he left her standing.

An hour later, the Rover turned into the street where Little lived, in Hendon, a street of modern houses, with the lamps alight and windows aglow. He turned his car into the garage and got out. He had decided what to say to Nora if the police came to ask him questions; he would put all the blame on to Carraway. He felt better, as he always did when he had time to think.

87

He let himself in, and the living-room door opened. Nora, tall, fair, willowy, appeared against the light.

"Is that you, Eric?"

"Yes, pet, I'm sorry—"

"Don't make a sound, they've only just got off to sleep."

"I won't make a sound," Little promised.

He felt much, much better an hour later, for the police had not called on him, and the Rover had disappeared from the street. He had won another chance to make sure that Beryl Belman could never give evidence against him.

Beryl knew only that the black-haired man had looked scared, and that frightened her, too. She took it for granted that he was frightened by Carraway, and if Carraway could have that effect on a man, what could he do to Jorrie?

She could wait until Monday, anyhow, ask for Eric Little, and see what he had to say. If she got no results she would have to make herself confront Carraway. But it would be far better if she could find out from the other man where Jorrie was.

The fear which entered her head about Jorrie, the obvious explanation of her disappearance, did not really shock Beryl, but just made her feel miserable because of the effect it would have on her mother and father.

Supposing Jorrie was going to have a baby?

11

TWO MEN WALK

JUST after ten o'clock next morning, Sunday, the telephone bell rang in Gideon's house. Two of his daughters were in the kitchen, finishing the washing-up, and young Malcolm was scurrying through his week-end task of peeling the potatoes and apples for lunch, not exactly resentful of the chore, but with a thirteen-year-old's impatience. Kate was bustling about upstairs, making the beds. It was a heavy, muggy day. The grass was dripping with moisture, the windows were streaked, and unless the sun broke through there would be no chance of working in the garden. Gideon was sitting in the front room, a Sunday custom, with the newspapers. He turned to the gardening notes of the *Express* as the bell rang.

Sleeves rolled up, shirt collar undone, Gideon strolled into the hall, where one of the telephones was.

It was Abbott to report fully on the pathologist's report on Marjorie Belman. Abbott was much more incisive than usual; he had taken the girl's death hard, and blamed himself for letting her disappear. The consequence seemed to be an even greater determination to catch her killer.

"Yes, it was murder all right. There's a scratch on her shoulder, probably where she was held under water. Her bikini was put on after death—scratch marks make that clear. That's official."

"What do you want me to do?" asked Gideon.

"I need to know whether Carraway or one of his three stooges has a big ring on either hand," said Abbott. "Shall I call the Yard about it?"

"I'll call 'em," Gideon said. "I want to check whether anything's in, anyhow."

Information told him that there had been no major

89

crimes during the night, and that there should be no difficulty about getting the information about any of Carraway's men who wore a ring. As Gideon finished, Kate came downstairs briskly, turning at the foot of the stairs with an unconscious grace which Gideon noticed much more these days.

"You haven't got to go to the office, have you?" She looked anxious.

"Day off, I should say," said Gideon. "Kate, I'd like to go up to town this afternoon. Have you anything fixed, or will you come?"

Kate's eyes lit up.

"No, do you want an early lunch?"

"One-ish."

"I'll go and see how those girls are getting on," said Kate, and hurried along to the kitchen.

Gideon heard the three of them talking, then laughing. There was something reassuring and satisfying about a happy family, and these days his could hardly be happier, although ten years ago the marriage could have gone on the rocks. Rocks. He thought of the three drowned girls in Cornwall, and now the drowned Marjorie Belman, whom he had never seen, but who had been eager and alive on Tuesday—certainly as recently as last Tuesday.

He thought, as he so often did, of the impenetrable fog of London; of the secrets it held; the horrors it could cover; the fear that lurked in many places; the death that threatened. For four days Marjorie Belman had been dead, and there had been a moment when she had realized that she was about to be murdered, an awful moment of dread and horror and pain.

How many others had suffered?

How many had died? How many bodies would be found, this week, next week, even in a few weeks' or a few months' time? Too many. And how many men were sitting in a pub, or at their own breakfast table, or reading the newspapers, and plotting the crimes for next week and next month? How many were cashing in on the Visit, for instance, or planning to?

He left with Kate soon after two o'clock, well fed on roast beef. Kate was wearing a summer weight suit of small black and white check, black shoes, white gloves and black handbag. She looked fresh and contented.

"I thought we'd have a drive along the procession route, and walk back," said Gideon. "We can pick up a cab back to the car if we feel like it. Then how about tea at the Dorchester?"

"Sounds lovely and expensive," said Kate.

She watched him when they reached Buckingham Palace, approaching it from Victoria and Birdcage Walk. His large hands were very square and firm on the wheel. He anticipated where other cars would go, and what they would do, so well that no other vehicle drew too close. He had to crawl round Trafalgar Square, where a band was playing. When it stopped, a man's voice came over the loud-speaker.

"What's happening here today?" asked Kate.

"Some kind of drive to help refugees," Gideon said. "Haven't got a thousand, have they? Give them a Ban the Bomb meeting, or an anti-something hate campaign, and we wouldn't be able to move. Like to stretch your legs for a minute?"

A few people were sitting by the bronze lions. There was a thick crowd near the Strand, beseiged by the pigeons. The man was still talking; a dozen banners were being held high, as the Gideons listened.

Kate felt Gideon's hand tighten on hers. "Look straight ahead," he whispered, but before she could stop herself she glanced around, and noticed a tall, lean man with angular square shoulders, walking with an absurdly short woman by his side, and a boy of nine or ten. Gideon stared straight ahead. Kate saw the man glance round, too, and saw him react, much as her husband had done. She caught his eye, and because she had no idea who it was, and suspected a man on the Yard's blacklist, she looked away.

"See that man in the green hat and brown suit?" asked Gideon, when they were back in the car.

"With the tiny woman and the boy?"

"That's Ray Cox," said Gideon. "I pretended not to notice him. Last thing I want is to make him think I'm watching him all the time."

"You're a bit worried about Cox, aren't you, George?"

"I suppose I am a bit."

Had Kate pressed the subject he would not really have been able to say why.

"Did you see that?" demanded Cox.

"What, dear?" asked Mildred.

"Gideon."

"Commander Gideon?"

"Yes, Mr. Commander Gideon," said Cox in a hard voice. "He cut me dead, and his wife snubbed me, too."

"Ray!" Mildred glanced down at their son, who was looking up with keen interest. Then she went on : "Perhaps he didn't notice you, dear. He's probably doing the same as you, spying out the ground."

"Spying," Cox echoed, and laughed without humour. "That's about it."

On that beautiful Sunday afternoon, half London seemed to be patrolling the route for the Visit. Gideon did not see them, but Alec Sonnley and his Rosie walked the length of the route, Rosie sighing about her poor feet, Sonnley whistling softly. Lumati had a stand near Trafalgar Square—outside the National Gallery—where he did his lightning portraits for ten shillings each, and was seen earning this honest living by at least a dozen men from the Yard, including Cox. Matthew Smith walked the route with his wife, who was willing to do anything to placate him; he was desperately anxious to select the perfect spot for throwing his bomb. Now and again the realization that he would soon strike the final blow for the memory of his son affected him so that his eyes took on that glittering frightening expression. He did not realize this physical change : but Grace, his wife, did.

Carraway wasn't in the heart of London, but Little, his wife, and three children were, and actually passed the Belmans, father and mother. Belman had persuaded "mother" to come with him, in another effort to shake her out of herself, but she walked along as if in a daze, saying "Yes," and "No," and "Really!" whenever he tried to spark her interest. Beryl was at home doing her smalls and washing her hair.

Gideon and Kate were back at their car when a plain-clothes man came up, gave a half-timid grin at Kate, and reported :

"There's a message for you, sir. Will you telephone the Commissioner at his house when convenient ?"

That was a rare request.

"I'll call as soon as I can," Gideon promised, and a few minutes later pulled up near Westminster Bridge Station. He left Kate in the car, and called Scott-Marle's home number from a call-box.

"Oh, Gideon. Thank you for calling." Scott-Marle paused for a moment, then went on, in his clear, precise way : "I have had an urgent call from Washington. A man named O'Hara is known to have flown from New York to London yesterday morning, and Washington thinks he might try to harm the President when he is here next month. Will you start a search for this O'Hara ?"

"I'll get it started at once," Gideon promised. His voice gave no indication of the way his heart lurched; this was the kind of development he most feared.

"I'll be glad if you will," said Scott-Marle.

Gideon still covered his feelings when he went back, said : "Sorry, Kate. You'd better sit here and watch the river. I've got a job that will take twenty minutes or so."

"I'll be all right, dear," Kate assured him.

In fact, it took Gideon half an hour to brief some of Ripple's men, and to start inquiries at the London airport. Once it was done, he felt better. At least they were forewarned. The Special Branch men would get a dossier on this O'Hara from Washington, probably from the Federal Bureau of Investigation, and the airport police would start the long, painstaking and often futile task of checking back on passengers. Washington would always fuss over the President, but by naming the man O'Hara, they showed how worried they were.

Gideon went back to the car and tried to put this new anxiety out of his mind.

Kate looked inquiringly, and he said : "Washington wants some special precautions," and left it at that.

He drove back to a street leading from Birdcage Walk to Victoria Street, and parked. It was still warm, but the sun was dodging behind clouds as they walked along to Parliament Square, then up to Whitehall. At Trafalgar Square they crossed the road and walked on the other side, towards the Houses of Parliament, passed the little street leading to the Yard, and stopped at the corner approaching the Houses of Parliament.

"Here's another danger spot," he said. "Just imagine what could happen if a lunatic threw a bomb from here."

"It might kill a dozen people !" Kate sounded shocked.

"That's the second big worry," said Gideon. "We can be reasonably sure of saving anyone in the procession, but a man with a nitro-glycerine bomb, or even dynamite, could injure a lot of bystanders."

Deep down in his mind, that worry was as great as any ; the consequences of any attempt at assassination among the crowd could be dreadful. It was a half-formed fear, a dread which drove him to even greater precautions, greater thoroughness. More than ever he wished that he could cut through the barrier which seemed to him to have become erected between him and Cox.

"Very well, as we've come this far, let's go into the Abbey," said Matthew Smith to his wife. He was smiling to himself, calmer now because he had selected the exact place from which he was going to stand and throw his bomb—from the pavement in front of a big stand, already being erected. Grace felt momentarily happier, too, because he seemed more content, but her underlying anxiety remained.

Abbott came up from Brighton but did not go near the crowds that Sunday. He spent his time at the Yard.

In the afternoon, he learned that Donald Atkinson, one of Carraway's salesmen, habitually wore a ring. At twenty past four, he was told that Eric Little, the chief salesman, also wore one. Carraway himself did not.

Before long, Abbott knew, the fact that Marjorie Belman had been found drowned would have to be released, but he believed that the right tactics were to play cat-and-mouse with Carraway, Little and the man Atkinson. It would make little if any difference to the girl's parents; they would endure another day or two of uncertainty, that was all. From all he heard, the sister was a nice kid, but the young were seldom affected so much as the old.

If Gideon would agree, Abbott decided to stall a while longer.

On that Sunday, in Glasgow, another and very different kind of crime was being considered, one which made Benny Klein and Jock Gorra, of the Glasgow Blacks, feel very pleased with themselves. They had hatched out the plot together—one man who had been adopted by Great Britain and given its nationality, the other the leader of one of the most vicious of the gangs north of the Tweed. Their plan was simple, and depended entirely on perfect timing. Instead of Sonny Boy Sonnley's pickpockets and bag snatchers being busy during the Visit, the Glasgow Blacks would descend on London in strength.

Whenever they had done this in the past there had been a clash with the London crooks, often a pitched battle. Each side had brought its gangs as reinforcements, and usually the fights were broken up by the police.

Klein had said, and Gorra had agreed, that this was a crazy way to go on.

"All you want to do is put Sonny Boy's artists out of

action for a few days," Klein had said. "Then London's wide open."

"You're telling me what to do, now just tell me how." Gorra was a thickset man with a small, round head covered with a gingery bristle. His short, pale eyelashes and stubby eyebrows made him look almost like an albino ; his pale blue eyes seemed to stare all the time.

"You ever seen a dip or a bagman work with burned fingers ?" Klein had inquired smoothly.

At first that had not made sense to Gorra, but the light had soon dawned. They were working out a way to burn the fingers of Sonnley's artists, and Klein was on a winner : acid would do the trick, a nice hot, corrosive acid.

The only question was how to get it on to the right fingers.

12

EFFICIENCY

ON Monday morning, there was a thick file on Gideon's desk, marked: *"Proposals for Special Occasion—Uniformed Branch."* Bell was on the telephone, and the report was on the top of a pile. Gideon leafed through it. In a small, meticulous handwriting were detailed proposals for the whole of the State Procession. With it was a sketch map of the area, taken from previous processions, and marked in red were those points which Cox suggested should be barricaded off. Wooden fences with small doors would be erected; the Office of Works would require details soon. Cox was right on the ball.

Gideon took out his own files, and checked.

"Victoria Street, police cordon." On the map, police cordons were marked in broken blue lines. *"Whitehall approach from Great Scotland Yard—barricades both sides."* Good. Gideon's lips moved as he checked, until at last he came to the last entry: *"To regulate traffic more effectively, it is recommended that the approaches to Westminster and Lambeth Bridges be cordoned off."* This was new, but at first sight wise; every big occasion brought more and more traffic into the city.

Bell stopped talking into the telephone and put it down.

" 'Morning, George."

" 'Morning, Joe. When did this thing come in from Cox?"

"It was here when I arrived."

"He must have been at it all the week-end."

"And couldn't wait to show you how good he was."

Gideon looked at Bell sharply.

"He been needling you?"

"I met him in the corridor. He just acknowledged that I exist."

"Can't see what else has rubbed him up the wrong way," Gideon said, and rubbed the shiny bowl of the big pipe in his pocket. He seldom smoked it, but it was a kind of touchstone. "Have you seen this?"

"Seems a good job."

Gideon didn't answer.

"Isn't it?" asked Bell.

"As far as it goes, yes."

"Where doesn't it go?"

"Far enough. He's forgotten the plans at the airport on arrival, the routes to the embassies and hotels, and the periods before and after the actual Procession."

Bell rubbed a stubbly chin.

"I missed them, too," he admitted, ruefully. "Couldn't see the trees for the wood. Think he'll come up with it later?"

"We can't wait too long," Gideon said. "I'd better see him." He had already decided what to do with Cox today. "Get him on the line for me, will you?" He glanced through other reports as Bell called Cox's office. Abbott was waiting for an interview. There were several other jobs on which the men in charge needed briefing; an hour altogether. "Make it eleven o'clock," Gideon called across, and Bell wiggled a finger. Then he said:

"When you find him, ask him to come along to Mr. Gideon's office at eleven o'clock, will you?"

Abbott had nothing new to report, but his new mood and determination reported itself. Gideon decided to let him defer an announcement of the finding of Marjorie Belman's body for another forty-eight hours. It seemed so harmless and so right. Quite unaware of what the decision could mean to the murdered girl's sister, Gideon soon forgot Abbott and Carraway. Parsons came in, a clerical cherub, to report full co-operation from all hotels.

Bell said that all big stores had been asked to draw up special plans for watching for shop-lifters.

London Airport reported that they could not trace the

arrival of anyone named O'Hara. Washington cabled full description and a dossier of O'Hara, adding : *You can expect officers Webron and Donnelly to arrive London early tomorrow Tuesday.*

Glasgow telephoned, to say that Benny Klein had spent the week-end with Jock Gorra, of the Black Boys. Gideon noted this, and also that there was a negative report on Alec Sonnley.

By the time Gideon had been through all of this, given instructions and made suggestions, cabled the negative report to Washington, and glanced through Cox's report again, it was nearly eleven. Big Ben was striking the hour when there was a sharp tap at the door.

"Come in," called Gideon.

Cox was as spruce as any new pin, immaculate in a medium grey suit, handkerchief showing in his breast pocket, tie to match it. He came in with almost military precision, and closed the door smartly.

"Good morning, Commander."

"Take a pew," Gideon invited, exerting himself to be affable. "You've been busy over the week-end, I see." He pushed a black lacquer box of cigarettes across the desk. "Smoke?"

"No, thank you."

Stiff as a board, Gideon thought gloomily. That might not matter much if Cox did his job really well, but it could create the conditions for serious mistakes or omissions.

Cox sat down, and kept silent.

"Can't see any big problems in this," said Gideon. If he congratulated the other it would seem patronizing, and he was sure that would be the wrong tactics. "We'll need to check with the Commissioner and Traffic about blocking off the two bridges, but I think they'll take your advice. Will you check with Traffic?"

"Very well."

"You've asked for a thousand uniformed men to be drafted in from the other divisions. Sure it will be enough?"

"I think so—together with the eight hundred special constables we can call on."

"How many will we want for the days preceding the Procession?" asked Gideon, almost casually.

He sensed on the instant that Cox had in fact overlooked that, and was suddenly acutely aware of the omission. He went pale, and his lips set more tightly. It seemed a long time before he said:

"I understood that you required only the Procession details."

"Until we know what men we want before and after, we can't tell how many we'll have to spare on the day itself," Gideon said reasonably. "We might need to draft some in from the County forces, and they always want a lot of notice." When Cox didn't respond, he went on: "Will you get the total figures out, allow for rest periods, and then let's have a look at the whole picture again?"

"Very well."

"Thanks," said Gideon, and now his manner was as stiff as Cox's.

When Cox had gone, Bell said caustically: "That's what comes from putting jumped-up louts in big positions."

It wasn't often that Bell sounded bitter about his comparatively low rank, and Gideon let the remark pass. It was half past eleven. He wanted to check a lot of things with Rogerson before lunch so that he could go out and see some of the London Divisions. Each one would have its problems for the Visit, and he knew from experience that if he went to see each Division on its own ground he could get a better view of the situation.

There was little time to worry too much about Cox.

Cox left Gideon's office pale-faced and hard-eyed. He knew that Gideon had had to make his point, but in his highly sensitive mood, Cox told himself that Gideon had talked to him as if to a junior official, had given him "orders".

He hadn't said a word about the perfection of detail of

the proposals, but took that for granted; his only interest seemed to be in finding fault.

Just before twelve noon Gideon went along to Rogerson's office, gave a perfunctory knock, and strode in. Miss Timson was sitting at her desk, with a typewriter in front of her. There was no mistaking the impatience with which she looked at him above the paper in the machine.

"Mr. Rogerson in?" demanded Gideon.

"No," said Miss Timson.

"Where is he?"

"I don't know."

Gideon said: "Well, find out and let me know, and be quick about it." He went out, and the door slipped from his grip as he closed it, and slammed. He was annoyed with himself the moment he heard it bang, still annoyed when he got back to his office. There was no need to behave as Cox wanted to. As he opened the door, one of the telephones on his desk rang, and Bell started to get out of his chair. "I'll take it," said Gideon. He lifted the receiver and growled: "Gideon."

"This is the Assistant Commissioner's Deputy Secretary," announced Miss Timson. "I would like to speak to Commander Gideon."

No "please".

"Speaking," Gideon said.

"I have ascertained that Colonel Rogerson is confined to his bed with a temperature, Commander, and is not likely to be in the office for three days," said Miss Timson. "I am instructed to give you all the assistance you may require."

Gideon managed to say quite mildly: "Thanks. Have you made a start on the hotel arrangements for the French security men?"

"Arrangements have been finalized, Commander. Some men will stay at the Embassy, most at hotels. All the German officials will stay at the Embassy, so will the American security men who come with the President, but the two men coming in advance wish to stay at a hotel."

Gideon found himself smiling.

"Thanks," he said. "Fix up for those two American security officers for tomorrow. Better have about four double bedrooms in reserve, too, or eight singles. We might get others who don't want to stay at the embassies. Have you got access to the Assistant Commissioner's files for the last State Visit?"

"They are in front of me."

"Familiarize yourself with all arrangements," Gideon instructed. "And for the Procession itself, arrange fifty places at least to be available for our senior officers and members of their families at the Ministry building on the corner of Whitehall and Parliament Square."

"Very well, Commander."

"Also in the file you'll find details of what help we received from the Divisions—number of men in uniform, number of C.I.D. personnel, number of women police constables. Have details for each Division tele-typed to every Division, marked provisional. Let me have several copies with good margins for notes and alterations, and let Mr. Cox of Uniform have three copies."

"Very good."

"Get what help you need from the typing pool."

"Very well."

"Report to me when it's all done, will you?" Gideon rang off, and Bell grinned across. "That'll keep her out of mischief for a while! Joe, I'm going over to N.E., and then I want to double back to K.L. Tell them I'm on the way."

"I'll warn 'em," promised Bell.

Gideon went out of the office and down the stairs as Big Ben struck twelve. The sun was breaking through heavy cloud again, and striking hot. Traffic was fairly heavy, with a great deal of truck and trailer movement heading for Lambeth Bridge, and for the New Kent Road, when he reached Blackfriars. He took a short cut towards Billingsgate, passing out of his own area into the district covered by the City of London Police. Once through the traffic at the London Bridge bottleneck, he was able to move faster, for the day's market sales were nearly finished. A few lorries were still being loaded with huge, slimy-looking boxes all marked *Grimsby*, and the stink of fish was very high.

The cobbles on Tower Hill were fairly clear, although soon there would be the throng of office workers eating out, the usual orators on the spot where the gibbet had once stood. It was hard to realize that festive crowds had gathered with their oranges and apples, their knitting and their scandal sheets and ballads of condemned men, to watch the public hangings. Where today political speakers droned, the tumbrils had passed only a hundred and fifty years ago. The grey mass of the Tower of London gave the curious impression that it had been built last year, the stone was so clean. Beefeaters in red and black uniforms were answering questions at the gates, some youths in battle-dress trousers and shirts were kicking a football about in a moat which had once been the Tower's shield against enemies from the rest of London and the surrounding countryside.

Gideon drove past the Mint, reflecting that hordes of people would come here during the Visit; he must soon have a word with the City Police, who would be in charge here.

He turned into Aldgate, where London seemed suddenly to become a working-class suburb, where traffic was moving at a crawl, diesel fumes were stinking, motors had a sullen note. He worked his way round the mean streets to N.E. Divisional Police Headquarters, and it was a quarter to one when he entered Christy's office.

Hugh Christy was fairly new at N.E. Division, which was the toughest in London. He was in his middle-forties, military in appearance and manner, brisk in movement and in speech, with rather a big head, and a manner which often seemed aggressive. Bighead was the nickname most often applied to him at the Yard and in his own Division, but it was no longer as harsh and censorious.

Christy had proved in two years that he was able and shrewd.

As he shook hands, and showed Gideon a chair, all in one movement, he said :

"I've got a couple of big steaks on order. They're ready to go under the grill when I press the button."

"Suits me fine," said Gideon.

Christy's finger prodded a bell-push, twice. Then he squared his shoulders and sat very erect behind his flat-topped desk. "They'll come in and get the table ready ten minutes before we start to eat. Any complaints, George?"

"Lot of worry," replied Gideon mildly. "I'll need all the men you can spare, uniformed and C.I.D., for the big show, and a lot of spade-work between now and then."

"As per memo," said Christy.

"What memo?"

"Yours."

"I haven't sent round any memo yet."

"Came through on the teletype ten minutes ago—here it is," said Christy. He pushed a sheet of foolscap-sized paper across the desk, and Gideon saw the instructions for the Divisions exactly as he had told Miss Timson to send them. Beneath his amusement was annoyance, even re-sentment. "Don't tell me your memory's slipping," Christy quipped.

"No," said Gideon. In fact, Miss Timson was simply setting out to prove her efficiency, like Cox. "I'm using a secretary who keeps beating the gun."

"Pleasant change to have a quick one," said Christy. "Any special angles?"

"I'm told that Benny Klein, Alec Sonnley's right-hand man, is away."

"That's right. He went off north with the blonde he's living with, and didn't tell anyone where he was going. But I know the mob he works with," said Christy. Then he began to frown, and rubbed the bridge of his nose. "Come to think, a lot of them have gone off on holiday. I noticed that earlier in the week, and didn't think anything of it, just thought they were taking advantage of the weather. Think Sonny Boy Sonnley is preparing for the big show?"

"Probably."

"I'll keep an eye on him," promised Christy grimly. "Don't you worry."

"How many shops has Sonny Boy got in your manor?"

"Three."

"Concentrate on them," said Gideon. "I'll have all his other shops closely watched, too. With luck, we'll get him on this job. But don't have any of Sonnley's or Klein's boys followed unless Lemaitre asks you to. He's gone to find out where Klein's been."

"Everyone on the ball," Christy approved.

"Did you get a memo from Rip, before he left?"

"Yes, and we're watching for French and Muslim Algerians and known agitators."

Gideon was satisfied that nothing would be missed in N.E. Division, and after a good lunch he made two telephone calls to Superintendents of Divisions on the perimeter of the Metropolitan area. He left the N.E. station at ten past two, and drove straight to K.L., where Superintendent Jackson was in charge, the district where Alec Sonnley and Bruce Carraway lived. Four of Carraway's five garages and showrooms were in this area.

Jackson, big, blond and bluff, had received his memo by teleprinter, and everything was in hand. From his office, Gideon telephoned the Yard.

"Joe," he said to Bell, "tell Timson to prepare a memo asking for a special check on all goods sold from Sonnley's shops and warehouses during the three days of the Visit. And tell her without comment not to send it off until I've seen it."

"So you've picked up that teleprint notice she sent out."

"Yes."

"You ought to talk to that woman," said Bell.

"When the time comes," promised Gideon. "Anything new in?"

"Abbott wants to release the identification of Marjorie Belman to the Press. He plans to have Carraway, Little and Atkinson trailed all today, and break the news in the papers tomorrow morning. He thinks that one would be bound to crack."

"Tell him I'll talk to him this evening."

"Right," said Bell. "By the way, that telephoto of O'Hara's in. I've sent it over to Special Branch, and they're going to check with the Airport right away. He's a pretty nondescript type."

"Pity," grunted Gideon. "Get copies round to the Divisions, will you?"

Later, Gideon drove past the big, flashy looking garage slowly, and saw Little talking to a small man by the side of a big American car; there was no sign of Carraway.

A few minutes after the customer interested in the American car had gone, a girl from the office called Little to the telephone. He wiped the palms of his hands as he went to take the call. Every time the bell rang for him he thought it was Beryl Belman, but she hadn't called yet. Had she changed her mind? If she knew he had been at Jorrie's flat, would she go to the police?

"Eric Little speaking," he said.

"You know who this is, don't you?" It was Beryl, with her clear, slightly Cockney voice. "I hope you've got some news for me, Mister Little."

"Yes, I have," said Little eagerly. "You needn't worry, I've got plenty. Meet me tonight, at the Pond, at nine o'clock . . ."

Marjorie Belman was dead. Beryl Belman was walking with death. Other people were unaware of it, but were also moving towards danger. Two of these were in grave danger indeed : a girl of seventeen named Doris Green, who lived in Whitby, and a middle-aged man, named Arthur Ritter, who lived in Worcester.

Both planned, that very day, to come to London for the Visit. They did not know of each other's existence. The girl had decided to come as cheaply as possible, by motor coach ; the man intended to come by train, first class, and to hire a car in London.

Grace Smith was in the shadows, too—like everyone who would be near the spot when her husband threw his bomb.

13

CLOSING SHADOWS

"He'd better come tonight," Beryl said to herself. "If he doesn't, I'm not going to be put off any longer. I'm going straight to Carraway."

It was dark near the Pond, and there were fewer people about tonight. Two men with dogs on leashes were standing together and talking, not far away, and the dogs were sniffing at each other. Cars passed slowly, engines whispering. It was a quiet, balmy night, and even footsteps disturbed the stillness. An owl screeched from the trees in a garden nearby.

"He'd *better* come," Beryl repeated.

She did not really know what to do if Eric Little failed her again. The week-end had been one long worry, for the more she had thought of Carraway, and his effect on Little, the more scared she had become. On the other hand, her mother was listless and sick, her father irritable, and there was little doubt that it would take them a long time to recover—unless Jorrie came back soon.

But suppose Jorrie did have a baby?

"She couldn't have!" Beryl exclaimed, *sotto voce*. "She couldn't have been such a fool. She would know how to make sure she was all right."

Then Beryl thought : *Would she?*

A car turned off the road and drew fairly close to her. She stared at it ; this had *better* be Little. It was a quarter past nine already, and if he was standing her up, she would let him know all about it. The absurdity of the thought passed her by.

The car crawled closer.

It might be someone trying a pick-up, Beryl reminded herself ; men were all the same, the beasts. If it was, she would give him a piece of her mind. Her heart beat fast as the car drew nearer; it was an old Austin, not the kind of car she would expect Little to drive. If this was some old beast—

"Beryl?" a man whispered.

It was Little!

She went forward quickly, as the car slowed down, and at last she recognized him. He sat rather far back in his seat, away from the window, but she was so pleased that he had come that she did not notice anything peculiar about this. She believed that her sister was alive, and still had no reason at all to suspect the awful danger which was closing in on her.

"Yes, I'm here." She sounded eager.

"Hop in," said Little. He leaned farther away from her and opened the far door; to get in she had to go round the other side, but she did not worry about that. In a few seconds she was sitting by his side, and almost before the door had closed, the car was moving off. She sensed his nervousness, and looked round.

"What are you looking round for?" Little demanded harshly.

"Well, I—"

"Has someone been following you?"

"No, of course not. I—I thought *you* were scared. Is Carraway—?" she broke off.

"No need to worry about Carraway tonight," said Little, in a lower voice. "I'll look after that swine in future, don't you worry."

Beryl sat absolutely still, her hands in her lap, worried by the venom in this man's voice and by the implication in what he said. She was almost too nervous to ask questions. He drove more quickly once he was away from the Pond, heading for the Heath itself. She saw the lights from distant houses and the far-off streets. It was true that she did not know the Heath well, but she was aware that it was a big stretch of common land, several miles across, that roads led over it, and that in places it was unlit and eerie. On Bank Holidays the whole place became alive and alight with all the fun of the fair. She had twice been here for a night of furious excitement, but now the dipped headlights of Little's car seemed hardly to make any impression on the darkness.

Yet she was thinking mostly about Jorrie.

"What—what have you found out?" she made herself ask at last.

"Found out?"

"About—about Jorrie."

"Oh, *Jorrie*!" His manner was peculiar, and she could not understand it, but she was not yet frightened. "Well, Carraway turned her out—that's what the swine did. He let her down flat. Got tired of her, and turned her out."

Beryl gasped: "No!"

"Yes, he did. Boasted about it, too—I made him talk to me this afternoon," Little went on. He spoke as if he were under the stress of some great emotion, but there was nothing to tell Beryl that it was the outward manifestation of his intention to kill. He was talking just to keep her quiet until they reached the spot where he planned to kill her. He knew it well; it was just off the road, hidden by shrubs and trees, exactly where he had once strangled another girl because she might break up his family life. "I told you he was a swine, didn't I?" he went on.

"But—where *is* Jorrie?" When Little didn't answer, fear clutched at Beryl like a cold hand at her heart. "Where is she? She's all right, isn't she? She didn't—she didn't *do* anything to herself?"

Little shot a glance at her as they passed beneath one of the last lamps.

"No," he said, "—she's okay."

"Are you sure?"

"Yes, she's okay."

"Where is she?"

"She's—well, there's a little place on the Heath, that's where she is."

"A place?"

"Little house," he said. His voice seemed to be getting

hoarse. "Over on the heath—she's staying there with a friend. That's where we're going."

"Is she all *right*?" repeated Beryl shrilly.

"I tell you she's okay," Little said sharply. "Stop worrying. I'm taking you to her, aren't I?" He turned off the road along a rough track which led to a copse and to shrubs; ahead of them were the stars and in the distance a haze of light over the fringes of Greater London. "Won't be long," he added. He moved his hand to the instrument panel, and something clicked; it was even darker outside, and the lights did not seem to be working at all. For the first time, a twinge of fear caught Beryl, but she took no notice of it. She did not know that they were moving along in darkness, now, and could not be seen from the road.

"How—how far is it?"

"Just over there," Little said. His voice had become hoarse. His emotion or excitement seemed to be getting greater. "Don't you worry, I know where it is." He turned the wheel of the car and then slowed down; and the next moment, he stopped.

It was a moment of sudden dread for Beryl Belman.

In that instant she realized that there was no house near by, that they were here in darkness, remote from other people; she was alone with this man. She heard him breathing hard. She had read about men like him; sex maniacs, that's what they called them, sex maniacs. She sensed the truth in a tiny flash of time, as his hands left the wheel.

"What—?" she began.

She felt his hands against her, one thrusting hard across her breast without lingering, the other scraping across her shoulders. Next she felt pressure at the back of her neck and at the front, the awful pressure of this man's hands. Outside there was blackness; inside, the dark horror, and his gasping breath, and those fingers, squeezing with savage strength, as if he couldn't wait to choke the life out of her.

She believed she was going to die.

She felt an awful explosion of terror and pain as if her

very heart was splitting. She heard herself gasping for breath in great hawking noises which drowned those of the man's heavy breathing, noises which seemed to get louder and louder and to be inside her head. She could not struggle. He had trapped her so that she could not move. There was tightness round her chest, becoming closer and closer, and pain like a stabbing knife.

Then, suddenly, the nightmare vanished. Lights blazed, men shouted, Little squealed, the doors opened. Half conscious, Beryl was aware of moving figures, of heads and shoulders blotting out the stars, of Little being dragged out, of a man putting an arm round her shoulder, and speaking with a kind of gentle urgency :

"It's all right, don't worry. You'll be all right."

That was the first time for a week that she had forgotten her sister.

"I thought I'd better call you at home," Abbott said into Gideon's telephone just before midnight. "I thought you'd like to know that we got one swine, even if we haven't got Carraway yet. The worst thing about it is what nearly happened to the sister." Abbott was talking very fast, and Gideon did not attempt to stop him. "If I'd released the news of the murder earlier, it would never have happened. That's what worries me. Hell of an experience the kid had. She'll be all right, though. I've talked to the hospital doctor. Shock and bruising, that's about all—she should be all right in a couple of days."

"That's good," said Gideon, at last. "That's fine."

"Damn lucky we had Little shadowed. If it hadn't been for you I would have concentrated on Carraway," said Abbott. "Don't know, though, after I knew that Little wore a ring . . . It was Little who went off with the other sister, from Piccadilly . . ."

Abbott told the story in the next five minutes, gradually getting more order into his mind and into his sentences. He would be bitterly angry with himself because his tactics had turned sour on him, and it was no use Gideon saying that he was at least as much to blame. That was the worst part about his job ; the consequence of failure, or of doing the wrong thing.

The consequences, for instance, that would follow any failure over the Visit.

". . . well, good night, George. Oh, I meant to tell you, I've seen the Belman parents. They're badly cut up, but they've got some neighbours in. They'll be all right. It's been quite a night."

"I bet it has," said Gideon. "What's Little's wife like?"

Abbott said, as if surprised : "Didn't I tell you? She looked struck dumb. She did really, George—struck dumb. The only time I felt sorry for Little was when he kept crying out about his wife, begging me not to tell her until the morning, to let her have a good night's sleep. He's got triplets, aged seven, you know. Two girls and a boy."

Gideon rang off, but stood by the telephone for a few minutes, letting the whole story run through his mind, relieved because of what had been avoided, glad that one case was partly solved, although there was as yet no proof that Carraway was involved. This strange oblivion was at once the frightening and the compelling factor in his life : this complete unawareness of what evil other people were doing and planning.

Was *anyone* planning trouble for the Visit?

In Glasgow, Benny Klein was experimenting with a little water pistol, using corrosive acid instead of water in the rubber holder. Tomorrow morning he would know how the rubber stood up to the acid. If it burned through, he would have to think of something else. Jock Gorra was watching—staring—fascinated.

A little farther south, and on the east coast of England, little Dorris Green, a pretty girl who worked in a coal order office, lay in her single bed, lonely and yet happy. She was deciding what clothes she would take with her to London for the holiday she longed for.

And in a London suburb, Matthew Smith was dreaming of throwing a bomb into the air—a bomb meant to

113

kill one man, but which could also kill dozens or might injure hundreds in or near the big new stand.

In that strange, half-realized world of the mind, Gideon was aware of such dangers as these, and felt helpless because of them. He lay wide awake, next to Kate, fighting the shadows which the Visit cast over London.

14

INVASION

"COMMANDER," said Miss Timson, early on the Wednesday morning.

"Yes?"

"F.B.I. Agent Webron and Secret Service Agent Donnelly are now due at London Airport at eleven-fifteen this morning, and the latest information is that the flight will be on time. Visibility is good. Superintendent Abbott will be at the airport in connection with the Carraway investigation, making arrangements for a watch on all passengers answering the descriptions of Carraway or any of his salesmen. So I have asked him to meet Lieutenant Webron and Mr. Donnelly. Accommodation has been booked for them at the Piccadilly Hotel, which is very central. Have you any further instructions?"

"What time are they due at the hotel?"

"There should be no delay at the customs shed," said Miss Timson. "I imagine that they will be at the hotel at twelve noon."

"Be there to meet them," ordered Gideon. "Have lunch with them and bring them over here for two-thirty."

Miss Timson seemed too startled to respond.

"Good-bye," said Gideon, and rang off. Bell was leaning back in his chair, pencil poised, shaking his head slowly.

"You crafty old so-and-so."

"No woman as efficient as our Miss Timson can be bitchy all the time," said Gideon. "Anything in about O'Hara?"

"Not a thing," replied Bell. "No one at the airport can say for sure that a man answering his description came in this week."

"Did you get plenty of prints of his photograph done?"

"A hundred and fifty."

"That's enough. Send one to each Divisional station and sub-station, with an instruction to report to me if the man's seen."

Bell nodded, but before he spoke, Gideon's telephone rang again, and he lifted the receiver: "Gideon."

"I have made a note of your instructions about the reception of the two American security officials," said Miss Timson, in a rather less acrid voice, "but there is another matter, Commander."

"What is it?"

"The usual space allotted to us on the roof and balconies of the Ministry Corner Building will not be available on this occasion, as special requests have been made for extra space by the Foreign Secretary and the Home Secretary for official guests."

"Oh," said Gideon, and thought how disappointed Kate would be. "Well, see what you can do on the route."

"The official accommodation is limited because of repairs being carried out on the façades of other buildings," reported Miss Timson. "However, permission has been granted to Public Utilities Limited to erect a public stand with a thousand seats, at the corner of Old Scotland Yard. I have been in touch with Public Utilities Limited and they are perfectly willing to allot us twelve complimentary seats, and we may have a further twenty at half price."

Gideon said: "Nice of them. We'll have 'em all for emergency use, and remember my wife wants one."

"Very good, Commander."

"That the lot?"

"I am a little puzzled by the use of the term 'Secret Service' to describe the second American, a Mr. Donnelly."

"It's the title they use for the security branch which looks after the President—nothing really secret about it. Webron is from the Federal Bureau of Investigation in

Washington, to liaise with the C.I.D. itself. Donnelly's the liaison with Special Branch."

"Thank you," said Miss Timson.

"Right." Gideon rang off, and immediately lifted the receiver again. "Mr. Cox, Uniform," he said, and then in an aside to Bell: "Anything in from Lemaitre?"

"He's going to telephone at eleven o'clock."

"Parsons?"

"He's waiting to see you."

"We haven't detailed anyone to cover Soho yet," remarked Gideon, and then heard Cox say:

"Deputy Commander speaking."

"'Morning," said Gideon, gruffly. "Gideon here. Can you spare me half an hour?"

"Yes, Commander."

"Come over, will you?" asked Gideon.

He rang off, frowning, thinking suddenly of the girl who had so nearly died on Hampstead Heath. It seemed a long time ago, although only yesterday a pale, frightened Little had been remanded for eight days. He had talked wildly about Carraway, but so far there was no real evidence against his employer. "I'll see Parsons," Gideon decided, and was standing up when Parsons came in briskly, face round and chubby. "'Morning," said Gideon. "What's on your mind?"

"Not enough," Parsons declared. "I wondered if—" he paused, deliberately, with that innocent expression which made him so like a rubicund cleric.

"Go on."

"I've got a hundred per cent response from the hotels, so the rest is routine," said Parsons. "And as I'm to be around the West End most of the time, I wondered if you'd like me to try Soho."

"Ho-ho," Bell said, almost inaudibly.

"Why?" asked Gideon.

"For the strip-clubs and the gambling clubs, the whore-shops and the innocents," answered Parsons. Gideon had never known a man more sure of himself. "Bound to get a lot of out-of-town visitors. London wouldn't be London without its haunts of vice. But we ought to have the clubs watched for con-men, and . . ."

There was a tap at the door.

"Come in," Gideon called, and Cox entered with his now familiar precision. He looked startled at sight of Parsons, but closed the door and came forward. "'Morning, Mr. Cox," said Gideon, formally. "Do you know Superintendent Parsons?"

"We have met," Cox said.

"Several times," said Parsons.

"Good. Superintendent Parsons is going to be in charge of the watch on the hotels, the clubs, the strip-clubs and disorderly houses," explained Gideon. "I think it would help if he sat in on this discussion."

"Yes," said Cox.

"Of course," Parsons said, but looked puzzled.

"Any luck with those estimates of men required?" Gideon asked, and Cox handed him a file. "Thanks." Gideon opened the folder, spread it out on his desk, then spread out a similar list of men required from the C.I.D., said : "Pull your chairs round," and began to check.

He was completely objective, and gradually Cox thawed. They checked the men required at the various points, with special concentration at the airport, the embassies and hotels, as well as the Procession route. Parsons made occasional succinct suggestions. Gideon made notes about men required at the check-points in eight-hour shifts. Gradually a comprehensive picture was formed.

After an hour, Gideon said : "We need three hundred men more than we've got, each day, and five hundred more on the Procession day."

"Have to work on overtime." Parsons placed the tips of his fingers together.

"I've allowed for two hours' overtime for each of my men," said Cox.

"Good idea. I haven't for mine," Gideon said. He looked across at Bell. "Fix it, Joe, will you?" Before Bell answered, a telephone rang on Gideon's desk, and he picked up the receiver. "Gideon."

It was Lemaitre, calling from Liverpool; he sounded brisk and bright.

"Having a nice quiet time down there, George?" he inquired. "That's good. While I think of it, save Soho for me. That's my beat when I get back."

"It's sold," Gideon said.

"Lecherous old devil," jeered Lemaitre. "But I can't stay here talking . . . I've done Glasgow, Manchester and Liverpool, already. None of the top coppers has heard of any exodus for the Visit; all the local boys seem to have decided to stay at home."

"Any idea why?"

"Benny Klein's left Glasgow, and seen a lot of the mob leaders," answered Lemaitre. "There have been two squeaks. Benny's paying each leader five hundred quid to keep his boys at home, and threatened to use razor and coshboys if they don't. It's a wicked shame, George — Sonny Boy's trying to establish a monopoly."

In spite of himself, Gideon laughed.

"So Sonnley and Klein want the field to themselves."

"Looks like it."

"Any word from Birmingham or Bristol?"

"No one gave me any wings."

"Hire some," urged Gideon. "Okay, Lem. That the lot?"

"Picked up a funny little thing," said Lemaitre.

"How funny?"

"Some of the car hire firms up in these wild parts are getting letters from Carraway, offering to take orders for cars for hire in London during the Visit."

"Cheap?"

"Not on your life! Double the usual price. That's how it was found out — one of the Glasgow chaps moaned about it to a pal of his in the Force."

"So it's business as usual with Carraway," Gideon mused. "Thanks, Lem, that might come in useful." He rang off, and after a moment looked across at Bell, and went on: "Get the drift of that, Joe?"

"Yes."

"Send another chit out to all our Divisions for a special watch on Klein's boys, and on Sonnley's shops."

"Right."

"Looks as if we're going to have the crooks in our own back yard to worry about," remarked Parsons. "Not many strangers."

"Could be a good thing. You could help us a lot there, Cox," Gideon went on. "Will you brief your chaps to keep a special watch on—"

"Klein, Sonnley, and Company?"

"Yes."

"I will."

"Ta. Now, let's go over the day of the Procession again, shall we? First, lining the route." That job took twenty minutes. "Now, the cordons." That took ten. "Barriers next," said Gideon.

Bell, looking across at the three men, wondered whether Cox and Parsons realized that they were having an object lesson in the power of concentration, plus wide experience, plus an inexhaustible knowledge of London's pomp and circumstance. Gideon said just what was necessary, co-related facts and situations, and did sums in his head by some kind of arithmetical shorthand. He did not let up until, at half past twelve, he leaned back and said :

"Now, all we've got left is the big Public Utilities stand." He got up, and went to a big wall map which had been brought up from the Map Room only that morning. "Come and have a look," he urged, and Cox and Parsons joined him.

He found the spot on the map, and made a red line at the street on the east side of Whitehall, nearly opposite the Horse Guards sentries. His red mark showed exactly where the big temporary stand, of the kind erected for all great occasions, was to be. He showed how this would block the view of some Ministry windows from the street, but these could be covered from the roofs of buildings opposite. No man-holes—the other main source of danger, where an assassin could hide—were hidden. It was safely away from the danger spot where the procession would have to slow down ; by the time it arrived here, it would be going at a normal pace. Moreover, allowing only a limited number of spectators to stand in front of the stand, the area would not be too crowded ; the essential thing was to keep enough space for free police movement in case of emergency. He did not think of bomb-throwing.

"Make a note not to allow spectators more than two deep in front of the P.U. stand, will you?" he asked.

"Yes," Cox promised.

"And that's about all," Gideon said. "Hope I haven't kept you too long. Wish we could have lunch, but I've got to go down and see those French and German chaps." Gideon fastened his collar, shrugged his coat into position, and smiled at Cox. "Any bright ideas about getting those extra men will be welcome," he said.

"Commander," said Parsons.

"Yes?"

"You forgot Soho."

"You have another look," said Gideon. "Cox's allowed for an extra thirty uniformed men to be around, and we'll need as many from the C.I.D. Will you two work together on this?"

"Sure," said Parsons.

"Very well," said Cox.

Gideon nodded, and went out. He left a silent office behind him, until Parsons held his hands up in a mock gesture of surrender, and said :

"Human atomic power in action. Ever seen anything like it?"

"There isn't anything like it," said Bell.

"*Very* impressive," contributed Cox. It wasn't exactly a sneer, but it certainly wasn't a reflection of the other's mood. "I've one or two urgent jobs, Mr. Parsons. Can we meet after lunch?"

After a pause, Parsons said : "Two-thirty?"

"If you'll come to my office."

"Okay," agreed Parsons. He waited until Cox had gone, then turned round, looked at Bell and let out a long, slow breath.

"Who put his nose out of joint?"

"I give him two more days before Gee-Gee explodes," Bell said.

Cox, hurrying along to his office, was staring straight ahead. He felt as if he had been out in a heavy storm, which had taken all the strength out of him. He was anxious to make notes, copious notes, so as to be sure he missed nothing.

In a peculiar way, Gideon scared him.

Gideon went along to the lift, and downstairs to the larger of the Yard's two cinemas, later than he had meant to be, and with much more to think about than Cox. In the cinema, there were seats for a hundred men, an 8-mm. and a 16-mm. movie projector, and a projector for 35-mm. stills.

The room was only half-filled, with the French security mission in the centre block of seats, the Yard men who would be liaising with them around the perimeter, and four German officers by themselves at the back. A senior from the Uniformed Branch was present; so was Ripple's deputy. The German security officers had come over from Berlin after Ripple's visit. Gideon wished that the two Americans were here, but their plane had been delayed, after all, although arrangements for this session had been left to the last minute. Gideon felt the gaze of nearly every one of the Frenchmen as he took up a position at the screen end of the theatre. Mollet, the man in charge of the French mission, came and joined him.

"Gentlemen," said Gideon, in passable French. "I am very glad to welcome you to London, and I regret only that the average Englishman's French is so poor. Consequently I shall have to speak mostly in English, and so will our chief lecturer. I hope you'll forgive us."

There was a dutiful laugh.

"I don't believe there is one of you who doesn't understand and speak English well," said Gideon. "Is there?" He looked round the men, noticing the difference in the cut of their clothes and the cut of their hair; hardly one of the Frenchmen could be mistaken for an Englishman, and *vice versa*. "Thanks. I suggest that you sit one and one— one overseas officer next to one English. If there are any points of clarification needed, it will be easier." He waited for the men to shift positions, and Mollet, a grey-haired, smooth-faced man in his fifties, with a drooping mouth and rather heavy-lidded eyes, nodded approval.

"What we're going to do," said Gideon, "is flash on to the screen in the 35-mm. pictures some enlarged maps of the routes from the airport to London, and also of all the other official journeys, as well as the State Procession. We shall explain the normal precautions taken, and the special precautions planned for the State Procession, when all Heads of States will be vulnerable at the same time. The State Procession route will be marked into sections, and after that each section will be shown separately, and on a much larger scale. All understood?"

There were murmurs of agreement.

"In front of every seat is a booklet showing these same maps, and at the end of the session you will be able to make notes of anything you want to discuss at another meeting. After we have studied the maps on the screen, we shall see two moving pictures of earlier processions. Here you will see not only the places where the crowds are thickest, but how the Metropolitan Police and different regiments of the Army, Navy and Air Force, line the route, making a break through by an individual from the crowds difficult if not impossible. We will then show the moving pictures in slow motion. The whole procedure this afternoon will take about two hours, after we shall break up for half an hour for that peculiarly English institution, afternoon tea. After tea, preliminary questions will be asked and answered. Is that all understood."

There was a chorus of agreement.

"Right," said Gideon. "Let's go." He signalled to the operator, then went down to a front seat, with Mollet, to see the whole thing through.

There were a dozen questions afterwards, and it was Bayer, one of the Germans, who asked the last.

"The stand for spectators, Herr Commander—how will that be guarded?"

"We will have seats on the middle gangway of every fourth row," Gideon answered, and after a moment a diagram of the proposed stand was flashed on to the screen. He pointed to small pencilled numerals which showed in outline. "Here—here—here." He stabbed at a dozen figures. "Then at the side gangways we shall have four men—one at each side of the top of the stand, another at the bottom. We shall have men at the one entrance—there will only be one entrance although there is the emergency exit. A diagram like this is included in the book in front of you."

"Thank you, Herr Commander," said the German. "I ask one more question?"

"As many as you like."

"Is it possible for each nation, the French, the Americans and we ourselves, the Germans, to be represented in this stand, as well as in the streets?"

"Yes. Are you worried about the stand?"

"A little, Herr Commander," the German said, and sat down. They were all worried, of course.

Gideon left the theatre ahead of the others, went back to his office, and found Bell anxious to see him. Webron and Donnelly had been in, and gone off almost at once; there was a rumour that a man answering O'Hara's description had been seen in a hotel in the Strand.

"And they've gone to watch," Bell said. "They've taken all the files we had for them, to study at the hotel."

"So they're bang on the ball," Gideon remarked.

"They're on the ball all right," Bell said. "I've sent Chann over with them. He'll phone if they have any luck."

At half past six, when Gideon left the office, no word had come through, and the two Americans were still at the hotel in the Strand.

In fact, the man O'Hara was in a private hotel, a kind of glorified boarding-house, in Kensington. He was officially here on vacation, spent a lot of time out of doors with his movie camera, and was no trouble to anybody. That afternoon, while the two men from Washington were on the false trail, O'Hara, who had a passport under the name of Hann, was putting a new magazine of film into his 16-mm. movie camera. At least, that was what it looked like. The magazine of film was in fact a .22 automatic pistol, operated by the press-button of the camera. O'Hara *alias* Hann practised putting it in every day, so that it would give him no trouble when the right moment came.

O'Hara did more than practise; he prayed.

He was nondescript only in appearance; emotionally he was a man of tremendous power and conviction, and he was convinced, within the narrow limits of his religious bigotry, that Roman Catholicism was an evil thing. During the election campaign he had preached this gospel, fighting desperately against the more liberal-minded, and when the President had been elected on a desperately narrow margin, bitterness had turned to hatred.

O'Hara was a kindly man by nature, a good man by training and conviction, but deeply rooted in him was the belief that men of dark skin were inferior to men of white skin. He had no doubts about this in his own mind, just as he had none about the wrongness of Roman Catholicism.

Then the new President had acted—as well as preached —to give full rights to Negroes. O'Hara, already poised on the delicate balance between religious fervour and religious mania, began to pray and plan for the death of the President.

He knew what would happen to him if he succeeded, and did not care. He believed that he had been privileged by the Almighty to strike the fateful blow.

As the moment drew nearer, his prayers grew more fervent and his handling of the camera-gun more skilful.

"Now we've got to get a move on with this job," said Reggie Simpson, managing director and chief shareholder in Public Utilities and Car Parks. It was the same afternoon, and getting late. "The stand had got to meet the usual London County Council specifications, and if you think you can get away with anything on that, you're making the mistake of your life, chums." He was talking with two foremen who would be in charge of the erection of the stands. "I've worked out the quantity of tubular scaffolding we need, the unions, the boards, the stairs, and the coconut matting. We want twenty men on the job by Monday morning, that's the earliest we can start. Gives us just time to get the job done."

"It'll be a cakewalk," one foreman said.

"When I see it sold out, I'll tell you whether it will be a cakewalk," said Simpson. He was small, perky, and thin-faced, and his Cockney voice could hardly be more nasal. "If you get it done by Saturday night without overtime for the men, there'll be a fifty-quid bonus for each of you. It's blue ruin if the men have to work on Sunday."

"It'll be finished Saturday week," the "cakewalk" foreman assured him.

"Rosie, ducks," said Alec Sonnley when he went in to his evening meal that day, "I've got a little present for you."

"What is it, Sonny?" asked Rosie, mildly. "It won't take too long just now, will it? I've got a pheasant in the oven, and if I don't go and look at it, it'll be overdone, and I know you don't like that."

"And game chips and peas?"

"Yes, dear."

"Okay, then," said Alec Sonnley. "There's a stand going up at the corner of Old Scotland Yard and Whitehall. I've got two of the best seats for you, bang in the front row!"

Rosie's eyes lit up, and her husband was fully satisfied. At that time he had not the slightest inkling of Klein's experiments with corrosive acid.

"Of course we're going to buy the seat," said Gideon. "If I start getting free seats and using them for my family there'll be a screech about corruption the first time anyone hears. You worry too much about money."

"I must admit that I've always wanted to see a big procession," said Kate.

Michael Lumati, reading in the evening paper that Wednesday of the stands which would be available, wondered whether he would treat himself to a good seat, or whether he would stand in the crowd. London's ceremonial occasions had been part of his life since he could remember, and he was looking forward to this particular show for its own sake, as well as for the great opportunity it would give him.

Lumati was sitting pretty with fifteen thousand pounds of near-perfect currency notes, and still his only worry was how to get them distributed.

What he needed, he had to admit, was someone with a lot of shops, or a lot of barrows, and someone with a big turnover during the Visit. The real truth was that he ought to use Sonnley, who had already ordered artwork for special *Souvenir Programmes* for the occasion.

"Mr. Sonnley, I've got an idea for a special Visit Sovenir Catalogue, and another way of making a bit of quick dough," Lumati said on the telephone. "Could you spare me half an hour? I don't think we ought to talk about it on the telephone."

"Let's have a drink," said Sonnley. He prided himself that he never missed a chance. "How about the Woodcock? You know it?"

He knew quite well that Lumati knew it, and that Lumati was eager for the meeting.

Matthew Smith left his desk in the city, not far from the Tower of London, an hour earlier than usual that day, pleading a headache. There was no specific purpose in his mind. He was on edge, and concentration was very difficult. He thought of that buried bomb as a miser thought of a hoard of gold.

He resisted a temptation to go and see how the stand was progressing, for he did not want to be seen at his chosen spot too often, and travelled by Underground, before the rush hour crammed Londoners in like placid flies clinging to every available piece of floor or seating space, and had the rare luxury of a seat. On the windows of the train were coldly printed green notices :

CERTAIN STATIONS WILL BE CLOSED BETWEEN MIDNIGHT ON JUNE 1st AND SIX O'CLOCK (P.M.) ON JUNE 2nd, THE OCCASION OF THE STATE VISITS. TIME TABLES WILL BE VARIED DURING THAT SAME PERIOD. EXTRA LATE TRAINS WILL BE RUN.   LONDON TRANSPORT SERVICE

Smith thought : *I'll have to get out at Charing Cross. It makes no difference.*

He kept picturing the Queen's carriage, kept wondering who would come next, kept seeing the picture of the President of France sitting proud and erect in his gilded carriage. He clenched his right hand as if the bomb were in it, and his mind went through the motions of tossing it through the air. He could even picture the scene—the panic, the cries, the rush of people. For some reason he did not see the blood or the smashed faces, and he did not hear the screams of the innocent people there to watch the colourful pageantry.

He had never given a thought to escaping, either, and it did not occur to him now. He simply had to throw that bomb.

There was no sign of Grace at home and he was glad ; Grace was intolerable these days, always watching him, always asking if he felt all right. It was almost as if she suspected what was in his mind.

Nonsense !

He put on the kettle for some tea, and while waiting for it to boil was drawn as if by irresistible force towards the workshop in the garden. He smoothed down his hair as he went towards it, more relaxed than he had been for hours.

Then he reached the window, and glanced in.

His wife was on one knee, and bricks were out of the floor at the spot where his bomb was buried.

Grace Smith had never been so worried in her life.

She was sure that something serious was the matter with Matthew; she had known it for a long time. She feared for his mind. Ever since the death of their son there had been moments, sometimes whole hours, when his eyes had glazed over and an expression of incalculable pain had tightened his features, drawing them up in a kind of contorted mass of nerves—as if he hated.

His eyes had become feverish for days on end, his manner jumpy, he had shouted at her, had sunk into long periods of silence—and spent a lot of time in his workshop. When this strange manifestation had reappeared, she had tried to remember the exact circumstances of the first occasion, and one thing had been easy to recall. It had been on a great day in London, when some big pot from the Continent had visited the Queen. Grace Smith never failed to go and watch the great processions; the displays of England's pageantry fascinated her. For royal weddings, she would wait all night to get a good view of the happy couple—a view lasting twenty or thirty seconds or so.

On the morning when Matthew had turned on her so furiously, Grace Smith had feared the truth with a great and terrible fear.

She had to help Matthew, but she could not allow a terrible thing to happen.

She ought to tell the police . . .

But she might be wrong, she reminded herself; she was only guessing.

It would be a *terrible* thing if Matthew . . .

She had to find out for sure, and it dawned on her that if she did, if she confronted Matthew with her knowledge, it would be enough to deter him. That was the all-important thing. He would need a weapon, a gun or—or even a bomb. The obvious place to hide it was in the workshop.

And there *was* something.

It looked like a small vacuum flask, but was lying in a bed of cotton wool, and the bricks she had discovered loose had cotton wool stuck on them, too. Only a high explosive would be so well protected. She knelt by the side of the little hole, staring down, horrified, terrified.

The she heard a sound, glancing around in alarm, and saw Matthew.

He was coming in. His eyes were staring. His hands were clenched, and held some distance in front of him. Sight of him like this should have terrified her, but in fact it did not. She rose from her knees, and spoke quite calmly.

"Is this a bomb, Matthew?"

He didn't answer.

"Are you planning some terrible crime?" She was still calm.

Matthew stopped two yards away from her, staring, lips parted now, breath hissing through them.

"Matthew, answer me." When he did not answer, she went on as if she were talking to their lost son, in those days when he had been changing from boy to adolescent; when she, not Matthew, had realized there was a bad streak in him. She had always believed that he had killed that French girl, although she had never breathed a word of that to Matthew. "Matthew," she declared, "you're not well. You're not well, I tell you. We've got to go away together, at once. We—"

Then, only then, did she realize her awful danger. A shimmering brightness such as she had never seen made his eyes hideous. His lips twisted, his hands seemed to writhe in front of her.

"Matthew!" he gasped. "Matt—"

He sprang at her, and carried her back against the bench, then got his hands about her throat and squeezed and squeezed.

It was a long, back-breaking task to pull up more bricks, dig a deep hole, put his wife's body in it, then replace the bricks and fill all the cavities between them with dirt. It took almost as long to load a wheelbarrow, after dark, and carry the displaced soil out into the garden.

But the bomb was safe.

15

VICE-MAN

PARSONS was a funny chap, thought Gideon. He gave the impression of being a bit flabby in body and mind, a bit too facile with words, everything to all men; but he absorbed work like a sponge, did it quickly and efficiently, and came up smiling, asking for more. He also absorbed knowledge about London's vice spots, and it had been said that he knew every prostitute by name—much as an earnest curate might, when he saw each as a soul to win. There was nothing even slightly sanctimonious about him when he came into Gideon's office at nine o'clock next morning, even though he wore a pre-sermon kind of smile.

"'Morning, skipper."

"What's making you so happy?"

"Just being my natural self," replied Parsons. "Like the Deputy Commander, U.B."

"What's that?"

"He's bending over backwards to be Mr. Efficiency but he's got some bee in his bonnet. None of my business, but—may I go on?"

"Yes."

"He's not sure whether to hate himself or Commander Gideon," said Parsons. "He's got Uniform at his finger-tips, though. Joe Bell was saying that he's asking for trouble. I know, so am I. Will you leave Cox to me for a bit?"

There weren't two other men at the Yard who would go this far with Gideon. Gideon stared at the half-smiling face for a long time, before he said:

"Yes."

"Thanks, skipper," said Parsons. "Mucho gracias. I've been over the Soho district with him, and I think everything's laid on. In the big clubs we'll have two men and a woman, and Uniform will have regular quarter-hour street patrols, in pairs. We won't stop the vice that way, but we can stop it from becoming too blatant. I drifted in on the strip-club kings and queens, too."

Gideon was smiling.

"Warned them that we wanted no extravaganzas, no special private exhibitions of sexual peculiarities, a firm bar against all under-ages—they're to keep 'em out—and no doorway soliciting. If they'd play, I said we'd play. Okay?"

"Yes."

"Thanks," Parsons said again. "I gave the gaming houses a miss."

"Why?"

"If we try to cover them, too, we'll be stretched too tight. Better a man lost his bank balance than a boy his virginity."

"Don't let the gamblers know."

"No."

"Anything else?" asked Gideon.

"One thing that wants a bit of deep thought," Parsons answered. "At least a dozen Italian prostitutes have come in during the past week, all very high class. You might think about trying for wholesale extradition orders. They're organized by a man called Sapelli, Luigi Sapelli. He's taken over a couple of houses in Green Street, all one-room apartments."

"We'd never get wholesale extradition," objected Gideon.

Parson's grin was more devil's than Christian.

"Sapelli doesn't know that."

"You want to warn him?"

"Just tell him we don't like vice in London organized by outsiders; we prefer the home product. But I don't think *we* should tell him."

Gideon thought : *Now what's he up to?* and he asked :

"Who should?"

"Our native Soho boys," replied Parsons, smoothly.

133

"A few threats from them would do a lot of good. If Sapelli thinks his ladies aren't going to get many customers, he may send some of them home."

"No," decided Gideon, promptly. "That could lead to a lot of trouble. Is Sapelli from Milan or Rome?"

"Milan."

"Try to get enough on him to extradite him," Gideon said. "Let me know what we're doing, too."

Parsons rubbed his fleshy hands together.

"Okay, skipper," he said. "I'll do just that."

Gideon had a sneaking feeling that "just that" was exactly what Parsons had wanted to do, but had preferred it to come as an order.

Parsons went off, leaving Gideon alone in the office. He put Parsons out of his mind—Parsons could be left to his job all right. Joe Bell was with Miss Timson, sending out reports and instructions. There were two telephone calls from Divisions and five minutes' breather before the operator told him that Lemaitre was on the line, from Birmingham.

"Hallo, Lem."

"You up already?" Lemaitre could seldom resist being facetious. "George," he went on, "there is a fishy smell."

"In Birmingham?"

"No, Glasgow. I got a squeal."

"What is it?" asked Gideon.

"Benny Klein's been here in Birmingham, and talked to all the big boys," Lemaitre announced. "Now he's going back to Glasgow. The word is that the Glasgow group will be in London for the Visit, but the others will stay home."

"You mean Gorra of Glasgow is going to defy Klein?" Gideon could see the inevitable consequences of such an invasion. It would almost certainly lead to warfare between gangs of pickpockets and shop-lifters; it might bring out the razors and the bicycle chains, the coshes and the flick-knives. If that happened, police urgently needed for normal crowd control would have to be diverted, which would create a lot of difficulties.

"That's the fishy smell," Lemaitre told him, sounding really puzzled. "Klein and Jock Gorra are like old buddies."

"Does that mean that Klein's fooled him?"

"I don't know what it means. I just don't like it."

"I'll warn the Divisions," Gideon said. "Lem, while you're on—ask Birmingham if they could spare us a hundred men, say, if their gangs do move out. Just see how the wind blows. If they'll play, I'll get an official request sent up from the Commissioner, but we don't want to ask and be refused."

"Right," said Lemaitre. "I'm going on to Bristol tonight, and should be back on Saturday. Okay?"

"Fine."

"Take care of London for me," Lemaitre quipped, and rang off.

Gideon was pondering over this unexpected and puzzling news from Birmingham when his telephone bell rang. He lifted it, said: "Gideon," gruffly, and heard a man speak in an American accent. From one aspect of London during the Visit, he switched instantly to another.

"Is that Commander Gideon?"

"Yes it is."

"Commander, can you spare me and Agent Donnelly a little time?" It was Webron, of the F.B.I.

"Yes, of course."

"We'll be right along," said Webron, and Gideon rang off. He took out the file on O'Hara, mostly consisting of the dossier which had been brought over from Washington. It was pretty thin. The man had been suspected of plotting against the President, and was known to be a religious bigot—an anti-Catholic. He had made threats against the President soon after the election, and the F.B.I. had discovered that he was an expert in firearms, especially small weapons. There was a note saying: *Ideal for assassinations in crowded places.*

Gideon checked the physical description of O'Hara: five feet seven inches high, sallow complexion, blue-grey eyes, no outstanding feature, no visible distinguishing

135

marks when dressed, although he had an appendectomy scar.

There was a tap at the door.

"Come in," called Gideon, and stood and rounded the desk to greet the Americans.

Webron was short, swarthy, probably Jewish, with thin black hair brushed over his white pate so that it looked streaky; a man with big eyes and a constant half-smile. Donnelly was tall and lean, dressed immaculately, wore his black hair in a crew cut, and wore glasses.

"I've been recapping on O'Hara," Gideon said. "If you could find a single distinguishing facial mark it would help a lot."

"Sure, his looks are as nondescript as they can be," said Webron. He did most of the talking for the pair, and now sat back in an easy-chair, while Donnelly leaned against the mantelpiece. "Commander, we want you to know that we are very satisfied about the efforts you are making, and the precautions you're taking, but we are worried as hell."

"Any particular reason?" Gideon asked.

Webron said: "Yes, there is," and glanced at Donnelly.

"A very good reason," Donnelly said.

"Commander, the Bureau in Washington has dug up more information about O'Hara. They caught an old friend of his, also a good religious hater. This friend says that O'Hara is in England, but that's not all. He says that, before he left, O'Hara perfected an automatic pistol with a fifty-yard range which can be used from a movie camera." After a long pause, Webron added: "How about that?"

Donnelly shifted his position.

"From now on, every time I see a movie camera I'm going to get the shakes," he stated.

Gideon thought bleakly: *So there's real danger.* He looked from one man to the other, and spoke after a long pause: "I'll put more men on to the search. I'll send reminders to all stations. And I'll have reports made on every American or Canadian we can find who has a movie camera. What size is this one?"

"Sixteen millimetre," answered Webron. "And that's some job you're planning."

"It's got to be tried," Gideon said.

When the Americans had gone, he roughed out the order for all London and Home Counties police stations, knowing what a groan would go up when the station chiefs saw it. He sent for Violet Timson, told her to rush it, and then forced himself to read other reports. It wasn't easy at first; it couldn't be done, but he wanted to be out on O'Hara's trail. Soon, however, a report gained his full attention.

Carraway flatly denied everything, and his other salesmen stood by their earlier statements. The truth was that Gideon could not concentrate on Carraway, because problems of the Visit kept obtruding, and he felt a return of the sense of restlessness, the urge to go out and take an active part in a case. He hadn't done much good the last time he'd gone out, but next time—he grinned to himself.

Benny Klein was grinning, too. His sharp-featured sallow face was twisted in an expression of beastly delight as he watched the mouse squirming. It was stuck to a small chromium plated tube which he had smeared with vitriol overnight, and left to dry. Only it hadn't dried; the squeals and antics of the mouse proved that.

Klein sent a postcard to Jock Gorra which read : *"I've got it."*

Fussy Mrs. Benedict, who lived two doors away from the Smiths, wasn't grinning. She was frowning because she was puzzled and a little worried. When her husband came home that evening, he was welcomed with a gusty :

"She still isn't back, Jim. I've been there four times, and there isn't a sign of her. I'm sure if she'd intended to go away she would have told me."

"Oh, you worry too much," said Benedict, a plump, easy-going man, who was already kicking off his shoes. "Matthew Smith is home. I saw him in the garden as I came by. If you're so worried about Grace, why don't you ask him where she's gone?"

"All he'd do is tell me to mind my own business," said Mrs. Benedict.

"I see what you mean," said her husband, solemnly, and glanced out of the window. He saw Matthew Smith locking the door of his workshop before strolling back to the house, but didn't think twice about it.

"I asked my dad, and he said there isn't any need to book a hotel. If you book a place in advance, they'll charge you the earth," said a girl who worked with Doris Green, and envied her the coming visit to London to see the Procession. "He says there are hundreds and hundreds of places in London where you can get bed and breakfast real cheap, but you have to go and seek them out. You've got your money out of the Post Office, haven't you?"

"I took it all out today," Doris told her.

"Well," said the other girl, "take my dad's advice, and don't go throwing any away."

16

COINCIDENCE

GIDEON was in his office at a quarter to eight on Saturday morning, a week later, and Bell was already there. Only the night staff was at the Yard, and Gideon had the usual Saturday morning feeling, that everyone was anxious to get through his job as soon as possible.

A messenger came through with a huge bundle of mail, and envelopes of all shapes and sizes were piled high in front of Bell. He groaned. It was too early for the secretarial staff to be in. Gideon was about to speak when one of his telephone bells rang. He picked up the receiver.

"Gideon."

"Good morning, Commander," said Miss Timson. "I understand that this morning's mail delivery is very heavy."

Gideon had his first relaxed moment so far.

"Mountainous," he said. "If I send it in, will you get it opened?"

"Yes, Commander."

"Eating out of your hand," jeered Bell. "Like to know why our Violet is so chirpy?"

"Why?" asked Gideon, as he rang off.

"She's had a postcard from Ricky Wall, from Berlin," Bell reported. "Couldn't mistake his handwriting, and couldn't mistake the Brandenburg Gate, either."

Gideon said: "Good luck to them. Has Lemaitre been in?"

"No."

"I'm puzzled about that Glasgow business," Gideon said. "Telephone Glasgow and ask for the latest on Jock Gorra, will you? Before I get the post back, I'll go and have a word with Mollet and the German, Bayer. Those two start work at seven every morning. They seem surprised when we don't."

"Who's surprised?" asked Bell. "They sleep all night."

Mollet, the droll-looking Frenchman, and Bayer, big, bullet-headed, almost like a caricature of his race, were proving good friends and good collaborators. They shared an office which had been cleared for them by putting senior Yard men in rooms which were already occupied. They were in fine humour, and Gideon saw their notes, their marked maps, their files, kept in a methodical order which did him good to see. As he turned to go, the door opened, and Webron and Donnelly entered.

"Good morning, Commander. Glad to see you," Donnelly said.

"Everyone is getting here earlier in the morning," Webron remarked. His voice had a trace of mid-European guttural. "Do you consider that a good thing, Commander?"

"Very good indeed," Gideon said. "It allows you plenty of time for sightseeing." He was rewarded with a burst of laughter.

"Anything new in about O'Hara?"

"I'm beginning to wonder if that guy really is in London," Webron said.

Gideon went out, reflecting that for an early morning session it had been remarkably good-humoured. As the door closed, he heard Webron say: "*Gee-Gee's quite a guy.*" Instead of raising Gideon's spirits and keeping them high, that brought about a return of the earlier mood of dissatisfaction with himself.

O'Hara had disappeared among London's millions, adding to general anxiety. The Glasgow situation was a worry. Cox was still an unknown quantity, too. Would it be a good idea to do the rounds with Cox? Or was that simply an excuse to get out of the office? Gideon wondered which job he would go out on, if he could, and unhesitatingly decided that he would join the hunt for O'Hara, who seemed the greatest menace.

A young police constable, named Kemp, strolled past the little private hotel in Kensington, near the High Street, at a time when O'Hara was looking out of the window down into the busy street, and picturing how busy the Procession route would be. O'Hara turned away from the window, went for his camera, brought it forward and trained it on the back of P.C. Kemp. No one saw O'Hara doing it, but had anyone done so it would have looked a perfectly innocent action.

O'Hara, a man in his forties, turned away from the window, sat in a shadowy corner, closed his eyes, and unlocked the camera, then took out the magazine of film, put it in his pocket, took out the other, deadly type of magazine, and placed that into position. His fingers were thin, long, and precise in their movements. When he locked the camera again, he opened his eyes, checked that everything was as it should be, levelled the camera, and pressed the button. The usual whirring sound came, punctuated by little snapping noises : *zpp, zpp, zpp, zpp, zpp, zpp.* Six, in all. When O'Hara put a loaded magazine in, that would mean six bullets.

O'Hara was fully satisfied.

P.C. Kemp went into the Divisional Station for his mid-shift break, and, as always, looked at the notice-board. A new notice, marked *URGENT*, was pinned up below one about a darts match with Hammersmith.

The notice read :

James Gregory O'HARA — American Citizen
(See Previous Notice)

A report must be made immediately of any American or Canadian or individual speaking with an American or Canadian accent living in this district. If any such person owns a 16-mm. ciné camera this should be reported immediately to the Superintendent's office and in emergency to Commander Gideon at New Scotland Yard.

Particular attention should be given to resi-

> *dents in hotels of all kinds, guest houses,*
> *boarding-houses, and apartment houses. The*
> *man believed to be O'Hara might be with a*
> *party, might be with a woman, or might live*
> *on his own.*

> *No risks should be taken with anyone sus-*
> *pected of being O'Hara.*

"See that, Dick?" another constable asked. "Got to check every hotel and boarding-house. Wonder what they want him for? Got to have eyes at the back of your head, these days?"

Michael Lumati left his studio on the following Sunday afternoon, took a Number 11 bus to Fulham Broadway, then sauntered towards North End Road, where the litter from the previous night's market had not yet been properly cleared. He turned into a public house, and went upstairs to a private lounge. He could hear a man whistling : *Some Enchanted Evening*. He tapped at the door, the whistling stopped, and Alec Sonnley called :

"That you, Lummy?"

"It's me, Sonny Boy."

"Come right in." Sonnley was standing by a window hung with dark green curtains. An aspidistra stood on a small table in the middle of the room, which was like one preserved as a mid-Victorian relic.

"What are you going to have?" he asked, and turned to a table on which were dozens of bottles of beer.

"I'll have a pale," said Lumati, and sat down in an old-fashioned saddleback armchair as Sonnley poured out.

"Got those samples?" Sonnley asked.

Lumati didn't answer.

"Now listen, Lummy, have you got them or haven't you? If you're still worrying about the busies, forget it — we've got those souvenir programmes to show we're in legitimate business together. But if you're thinking of asking for more than fifty-fifty, forget that, too. I'm taking

142

just as big a risk as you are. You know that as well as I do."

"Yes, I know," said Lumati.

"Don't tell me you don't trust me."

"I trust you," said Lumati, eyeing the little man very closely, "but I'm not sure I trust your pal, Klein."

"Listen, Lummy," said Sonnley, drawing nearer the artist and looking like an earnest sparrow, "I've worked with Klein for over ten years. They don't come any smarter, but I wouldn't trust him round the corner. Klein's not in this. He's looking after the usual business for me. He's been up in the North and the Midlands, making sure we don't have trouble with those boys. I'll spread your stuff round myself with the takings from my branches, and I'll pay a lot of my bills with them. I'll spread some out with bookies, too. Don't you worry. I'll get rid of most of it in a week. Now, where's the samples?"

Lumati took an envelope from his pocket, and handed it over. Sonnley slit it open, and pulled out the notes inside; there were five. He rustled one in his fingers, put the five down on a table and flipped them like a bank teller. Then he took them to a window, and, standing to one side, held one up to the light. The thread showed through clearly, so did the watermark; it was a remarkable job of printing. He swung round and clapped Lumati on the shoulder.

"That's the best job I've ever seen in my life, Lum! It's an absolute winner."

"It's the best job that's ever been done," said Lumati. His little beard waggled in his excitement. "And I've got fifteen thousand of them. It's a deal, then. You won't tell Klein—"

"Cross my heart."

"You pay me fifty per cent of the face value, on delivery."

"Lum, just to show how much I trust you, I've brought three thousand quid in real English dough along with me —it's in that little case over there. Don't get it mixed up with your own speciality, will you? I wouldn't like to get yours contaminated!" Sonnley went over and picked up a small leather case, opened it, and showed the small wads of one-pound notes, wrapped in fifties with gummed paper bands. "How about that, Lum? You get three thousand quid on account."

Lumati stared down at the money, his eyes glistening, his mouth dry, his lips parted.

When Sonnley left, soon afterwards, he was whistling as merrily as could be, his green Tyrolean hat stuck jauntily on one side of his head. He whistled all the way home, all the way up to Rosie, and all the time he was washing his hands before lunch. He was half-way through a steamed steak-and-kidney pudding of mouth-watering succulence when the telephone bell rang.

"I'll get it, Sonny," Rosie said, and puffed a few straying hairs away from her nose as she leaned on the table, got up, and waddled across to the telephone in a corner; she knew how Sonny Boy disliked being interrupted when he was eating.

"Hello, who's that?" she inquired disinterestedly, and then she said: "Oh, Mrs. Whittaker, hallo, dear, how are you? . . . Well, I *am* sorry . . . Well I never . . . Well, what a funny thing to happen. Has he tried olive oil? It's ever so soothing . . . Oh, I see . . . Well, he's busy now, dear—" She glanced across at Sonnley, who was scooping up a forkful of succulent brown meat and gravy-soaked suet crust. He waved his knife at her, and she went on: "He's just come in, dear, wait a minute." She covered the mouthpiece with her podgy hand as she called to Sonnley: "Dicky Whittaker's burnt his hands something cruel. He's had to go to a doctor."

"The damn fool, he's due to start work next week," Sonnley said disgustedly, and grabbed the telephone. "Sonnley speaking. What's all this about . . . ?"

He broke off, listening more intently, and when he spoke again his voice was subdued and the expression in his eyes was very different, and very thoughtful.

"All right, tell him not to worry, I'll stake him," he said curtly, and rang off. He stared at his wife, who sat down

144

placidly although she had just learned that one of the cleverest pickpockets in the business had burned his hands so badly that he would not be able to operate during the Visit.

Someone had smeared vitriol on the handle-bars of his motor-scooter.

When Klein came into his office, next morning, Sonnley sat reading some letters, without looking up. Klein stood by the desk for two minutes, then deliberately sat on a corner. Sonnley took no notice. Klein took out cigarettes, lit one, and dropped the spent match into an ash-tray close to Sonnley's right hand.

"Remember me?" he said.

"I've got to have some bad luck," Sonnley still read.

"You said it," said Klein, flatly. "I've got news for you."

Sonnley looked straight into his eyes for the first time, paused, and then asked :

"What news?"

Sonnley never admitted it to a soul, but Klein's answer took him completely by surprise, and almost broke up his poker face. The answer was one word, spoken with that guttural accent, taking on a kind of menace which Sonnley had not known for a long time.

"Cops," said Klein.

Sonnley needed a moment's respite, and he said :

"What's that?"

"Cops."

"What the hell do you mean, cops?"

"I mean busies, dicks, bloody flatfoots," said Klein. "They're watching my van. They followed me this morning. There's a couple outside now—one of them was at the station when I got back last night, one was outside here when I arrived. Think he was waiting to pass the time of day with me? What have you been doing?"

"I don't believe—" Sonnley began.

"You take a look," invited Klein.

Sonnley stood up, slowly, and went to the window. He had lost his perkiness and heartiness as he stood at one

145

side of the window, to avoid being seen. On the other side of the street, standing by a telephone kiosk and reading a newspaper, was a tall, heavily-built man, and Sonnley knew that Klein was right. There was another, taller, thinner man, strolling along the street.

"What have you been up to, to bring them as close as this?" demanded Klein.

"It's just routine," Sonnley said uneasily. "That's all it can be."

"Okay, then, it's just routine," said Klein. "But if I start collecting the stuff from the boys and girls and get copped, I'll be back on the Moor, and that's a routine I don't like. I've got some more news for you."

"Now, listen, Benny—"

"I want out," said Klein. "I want five thousand quid as a golden handshake, and then I'll just fade out of your life. I'm not taking any more chances, and it's time I got my bonus."

Sonnley returned to his desk, sat down, and looked into the other man's bright grey eyes. There was nothing there that he liked, nothing remotely reassuring. He had known that one day a break would come, but he hadn't expected blackmail, and he hadn't expected it to come so suddenly. He took out a check green and white handkerchief, and dabbed at his forehead. Klein didn't shift his gaze. He had one hand clenched on the desk, another with the palm upwards, the fingers crooked and beckoning.

"Give," he said.

Sonnley still didn't speak. Klein leaned across the desk so that Sonnley could feel the warmth of his breath, and repeated :

"Give."

Sonnley said thinly : "Not a penny."

"Say that again, and I'll break your neck."

"Then you'll go inside for the rest of your life."

Klein's eyes narrowed, as if he hadn't anticipated such tough resistance.

"Sonny Boy, don't get me wrong," he said. "I want out

and I want five thousand quid, and that's how it's going to be."

"Benny," said Sonnley, in a voice which shook a little, "you aren't going to get another penny from me unless you see the next ten days through. You can please yourself."

Klein was towering over him, lips drawn back. There was silence and stillness in the room for what seemed a very long time, and with every second it looked as if Klein would explode into action. Before he did, while the breath was hissing through his mouth, Sonnley said in a soft voice :

"Who smeared vitriol on Dicky Whittaker's motor-scooter?"

For a moment Klein's expression did not change; he still looked as if he would burst into violent action. Then he blinked. He closed his lips, moistened them, and said:

"What's that?" and drew back a pace, as if his rage had suddenly died away. "*What's* that?"

"You heard."

"Come again."

"Who smeared vitriol on the handle-bars of Dicky Whittaker's motor-scooter?"

"Someone did *that*?" Klein sighed.

"You've been back in London since last night, and no one told you?"

Klein said, still sighingly : "You're telling me, aren't you?" He moistened his lips again. "Because the cops were watching, I kept away from all the boys. I didn't hear anything. Sonny Boy, is this right?"

"It's right."

"Then Dicky can't work."

"He can't work."

Klein said : "Who did it, that's what I want to know? Who did it?"

"That's what I want to know too," said Sonnley. "If you want out and five thousand quid, you find out who did it."

"Who would hate Dicky as much as that?"

"Just find out, and let me know quick," said Sonnley, "because when I find out who did it, I'll break him. Understand?" He stared levelly, coldly, into Klein's eyes. "Whoever it was, I'll break him for good. Just remember that."

"I'll find him," Klein said. "I'll find the swine."

Sonnley watched as he turned away and went out, and saw no change in his expression. Sonnley jumped up from the desk, stepped swiftly to the door, pulled it open, and saw Klein half-way across the room beyond, still looking astounded; if he knew more than he pretended, he was covering it well. Did he know? Or was he as shocked as he made out?

Sonnley went back to his desk, sat down, then jumped up again and took three jerky steps to the window. The watcher by the kiosk hadn't moved, but the taller, thinner man was now farther along the street. Klein appeared on the pavement. The thin man turned and followed him. Sonnley watched them both go round the corner. The man by the telephone kiosk stayed put, which meant that Klein had been right, and that he, Sonnley, was being watched.

Sonnley's lips pursed, and he began to whistle, but it was a thin, grating sound, with no high spirits, no attempt to catch a tune. Now he had two problems, two big problems, and he had to decide which needed priority.

The question of priorities was Gideon's chief preoccupation, too, and it became more acute as the days passed. A week before the Visit, it seemed as if there was an impossible amount to do; masses of paperwork passed over his desk, and for days he hardly moved out of the office. That worsened his feelings of frustration and strengthened the urge to get out and about; but he could not, wisely. He was a little sore because he had advised Cox to go round to all the Divisions and check the arrangements and the men to be released for Central London work, and instead of jumping at it, Cox had looked down his nose as if it were a chore. But that side of the arrangements appeared to be working smoothly, and he did not allow it to worry him; he was getting used to Cox.

On the Monday before the Visit he spent less time than usual looking through reports and briefing his men, but a note from Abbott caught his eye. *"Beryl Belman will be here today—would you like to see her?"* Gideon looked across at Bell, and said:

"Tell Abby I'll go down and have a word with the Belman girl, will you?"

"Right."

"Anything more on Carraway?"

"Absolutely blank, Abby says—it's like coming up against a brick wall."

One of Gideon's telephones rang, and he lifted it while glancing at another report. It was Christy of N.E. Division.

"Yes, Hugh?"

"Funny thing happened you ought to know about," said Christy, without preamble. "Remember Dicky Whittaker?" On the instant Gideon pictured a tall, very thin, sorrowful-looking man, who had often been inside for picking pockets and snatching handbags; he was probably the cleverest man in London at either job.

"I remember him."

"He's burned the skin off his hands. Someone smeared his scooter handles wih vitriol, and put him out of business."

Gideon gave a snort, smothering a laugh,

"Well, who's complaining?"

"I'm just telling you," Christy said. "While I'm on, George—half a mo'." Christy wasn't a man to waste time, so Gideon scanned another report and started on a third before Christy came back. "One of my chaps got punched on the nose by a drunk, he's just come in . . . What was I going to say?"

"You tell me."

"Oh, yes—I had Ray Cox here last night. Kept me here until half past ten, the so-and-so."

"Did he?" Gideon asked, mildly.

"Seems to be right on the ball," said Christy. "He knows exactly what he wants and how to get it, if you ask me. Thought you'd like to know you're in good hands! 'Bye."

Christy rang off, and Gideon put his receiver down slowly, rubbed his nose, shrugged, and went on with his reports. But his spirits rose a little; that was the first cheering report he'd had about Cox.

His telephone bell rang again, and Abbott said:

"Beryl B's downstairs in the waiting-room, George. I don't think she can help us over Carraway, though—but she can put Little away."

Gideon was surprised by the girl's attractiveness, her feathery hair, and the likeness to her dead sister. She looked pale, her eyes were very bright, and she spoke in a subdued voice while looking him straight in the eyes. He felt quite sure that she was telling the truth when she said that she had wanted to see Carraway, but had never met him.

Gideon talked for ten minutes or so, and then stood up.

"I'm sure Mr. Abbott's told you how sorry we are about what happened, Miss Belman. If we can do anything to help you, or your parents, let Mr. Abbott know."

"He's been ever so kind, sir," said Beryl earnestly. "My father says he'll always respect the police much more than he used to, after this. Mr. Abbott's been ever so good to me, too, and I would like to thank him personally."

Abbott was almost preening himself, Gideon saw. He would make the grade now, so one uncertainty was past, and the morning's upward trend continued.

Gideon went out, feeling as if the weight was lifting. He was much more cheerful when he opened the door of his office, and was surprised to see Violet Timson at his desk. She moved away from it quickly, almost guiltily?

"I was looking for a report on the Little case, sir, for the Assistant Commissioner," she said. "Mr. Bell's out, too."

Her cheeks were flushed, and she sounded as if she expected a sharp rebuke. If he gave one, it would undo all the work done towards a better understanding, so he simply said :

"You'll find it on his desk."

"Oh, how silly of me. Thank you," she said hurriedly, and went across to the other desk and picked up the file. "Mr. Rogerson wants to talk to the Solicitor's Office about another remand." She went out briskly.

Gideon put his hand in his pocket, then smoothed the bowl of his pipe, and stared at the papers. He saw one thin file which wasn't quite squared with the others, pulled it out, and read : *Australian Party*. She had been checking to find out if there was any further news of Wall. Well, there wasn't. He smiled thoughtfully to himself, and put the report aside, wondering how serious the *affaire* was going to be.

He had been alone for ten minutes when there were brisk footsteps outside, and before the sharp, peremptory knock came at the door, he knew this was Cox.

He steeled himself.

"Come in."

Cox came in, briskly, glanced at Bell's empty desk, advanced to Gideon's, and said :

"Good morning, Commander. I think we've got everything we need, now. Plenty of reserves, the Divisions all organized for the first three days of next week, everything laid on." He was hearty, and brisker than usual, as if making a big effort to create a mood of *camaraderie*. "There are two things I'd like your advice on."

This was sensational.

"Pull up a chair—" Gideon began.

"I won't, if you don't mind. I'm going over to the City in five minutes, just called in on my way." Cox put papers on Gideon's desk. "Do you think it would be a good idea if we—you and I, I mean, personally—did a kind of tour of inspection together later in the week, or next week-end ? Keep everyone on their toes, and make sure that nothing slips up."

Gideon said : "Anything that would take me out of this

blurry office is right with me. We'll fix two separate half-days, shall we?"

"Whenever you say," said Cox. He was very newly shaven, his eyes were bright, his long thin neck and jutting ears made him look just a little comical. "The other thing is really something to be tackled at Divisional level, but in order to be at full strength next week a lot of leave is being taken this week. The Divisions are pretty short of men." This was elementary. "There's a missing neighbour case down in Streatham." Streatham was one of London's older, more sedate suburbs, in a quiet Division. "A woman's been missing for several days, and a neighbour's been worrying the sub-divisional station, because there's a heap of fresh soil in the garden. As a matter of fact, I would have recommended that the Division goes and digs that soil over, but if I'd asked Miller for anything else I think he would have snapped my head off."

"I know what you mean," said Gideon. At least one Divisional Superintendent disagreed with Hugh Christy on Cox's merits. "Uniform reported it, and Divisional C.I.D. is sitting on it. That right?"

"Yes."

"Give me the name and address," said Gideon. "I'll pick it up from a Divisional report—there's bound to be one—and ask Jeff Miller to have that plot dug over. He can get a warrant on the grounds that we're looking for stolen goods. Job like that shouldn't take long. If the earth's fresh and there's been no effort to cover it over, I wouldn't expect to find much there. What's the name?"

Cox answered almost blithely:

"The woman's a Grace Smith, Mrs. Grace Smith. Miller says that the husband's a sour piece of work, and thinks that this is just a neighbour's spitefulness. Just as well to be sure, though."

Cox spoke like a schoolboy who was very conscious of good behaviour.

"You couldn't be more right," Gideon said.

He called Miller, of the Division, and Miller—preoccupied with some other problem—promised to get the warrant at once. Gideon expected to have to remind him, but within three hours the report came in. *Soil at 41, Common Road dug over as requested. Result, negative.*

"All right as far as it goes," Gideon said to Bell. "But where did the soil come from? Put in a call, and ask Miller, will you?" He sorted through some papers, as he went on : "Did our Vi bring that Little file back?"

"She brought it in full of apologies," answered Bell. "If it wasn't for that Aussie I'd think she had quite a crush on you."

Undoubtedly Donnelly and Webron were anxious, but they had the comfort of knowing that every possible action was being taken in London to trace O'Hara, and by now they had some idea how thorough the check would be, from top men in the Divisions down to the youngest flatfoots on the beat. It would not have surprised them to know, for instance, that Police Constable Kemp was very thoughtful about the wanted American.

Kemp had come to know which of the hotel managers and manageresses of the smaller establishments were helpful. From time to time he had to go and check the registers of guests, and this was the excuse he made when he called at the Lambett Guest House on the following morning. He saw the name Hann in the book which Mrs. Lambett showed him. She was a pleasant, if somewhat reserved woman, who charged more than most and catered for a better type of guest.

"Now this Mr. Hann, he's an American, I see," Kemp remarked. "Here for the Summit, is he?"

"I understand that he is planning a long holiday in Europe, and England is his first stop," answered Mrs. Lambett.

"Nice chap?" asked Kemp.

"He is a very satisfactory guest."

"I know one thing, these Americans can afford a lot more on cameras than I ever could," said Kemp. "How many's he got? Two or three?" He made a joke of it.

"As far as I know, he has only one, a ciné camera," replied Mrs. Lambett.

Without pressing too hard, Kemp could not learn more from her, but he did find out that Hann was coming in for a midday meal. So he made it his business to watch the street, and saw Hann turn from the corner of the High Street, without knowing for sure who he was; but he did see a likeness, if a vague one, to the photograph. He also saw the camera, and thought it looked big enough for a sixteen millimetre.

At the station, Kemp checked on the details of O'Hara's description; height and weight were about right, but this man's hair was jet black, not pale brown turning grey. The possibility that it was dyed made him suspicious. He reported to the C.I.D. branch at the Division, but the sergeant who took the report said disparagingly:

"That's five we've had from here alone. The Yard must be flooded out."

"That's up to them," said Kemp. "I've done my bit."

17

KILLER-CAMERA

GIDEON stood in the doorway of the *Information Room*, watching, listening to men's quiet voices, the tap-tap-tap of the teleprint machines, the subdued buzzing of bells. Nowhere was the ceaseless activity of the Yard more evident than here. At the long desks with the conveyor belt running between them, carrying urgent messages so unhurriedly, uniformed men sat with casual-seeming intentness.

No one seemed to hurry, but the pace was always steady, and much faster than it seemed.

A man was saying :

"Two youths, age about nineteen, robbed a grocery shop in Whitechapel at 2.31 p.m. and got away with seventeen pounds one shilling. No description available."

Another was taking a different message :

"Two private cars were in collision at the north end of Lambeth Bridge at 2.32 p.m., both cars badly damaged, one driver dead, the other injured. Traffic has been reduced to single line . . ."

A third message came over the teleprinter as Gideon watched the tape ticking through.

"Attempted bank robbery at Lloyds Bank, Richmond, Surrey, at 2.30 p.m., two men and a girl involved. A bank clerk raised the alarm. The girl and one man have been held, the other man escaped with a bag containing about two thousand three hundred pounds in used treasury notes . . ."

The messages were distributed to the departments concerned without comment. Within a few minutes Bell would be checking with Division about the bank raid ; it looked as if that had failed, so luck was holding.

Another message came through on the machine :

"Message from C.D. Division." That was from Kensington and Cromwell Road area. "Police Constable R. E. Kemp reports an American who might fit the description of the man O'Hara. He says that this suspect's hair is jet black and looks as if it might have been recently dyed. The man is staying at the Lambett Guest House under the name of Hann."

The Chief Inspector in charge of *Information* came up and said :

"Another O'Hara false alarm."

"One of them's going to be the McCoy sooner or later," replied Gideon. "That gone up to Donnelly and Webron?"

"It's on its way."

"Thanks," said Gideon. "I can see I'm not needed down here."

In fact, all the Yard was fairly quiet because of the lull in major crime, and the day-to-day commonplaces could almost look after themselves. It was just the right afternoon for a jaunt, and it would do no harm to go out with Donnelly and Webron. They would then be able to report back to Washington that the Commander in person was concentrating on O'Hara. Smiling at his own humbug, Gideon went upstairs to the Americans' office, and found it empty. A sergeant, passing by, said :

"The two Yanks have just gone out, sir."

"Oh," said Gideon. He didn't like "Yanks" but one could overdo punctiliousness. He thought ruefully that the pair hadn't lost a moment ; that was probably a measure of their anxiety. He lifted a telephone, called Bell, and said :

"Joe, I'm going out for a stretch—over to take a look at that latest O'Hara."

"Enjoy yourself," said Bell.

Gideon went downstairs, to find a chauffeur at the foot of the steps ; Bell had uncanny ability in arranging that. Gideon told the driver where to go, and sat beside him, watching the traffic, studying the quick reactions, knowing that at one time this man had been a star driver of the Flying Squad ; he was now nearing sixty.

"In a hurry, sir ?" he asked.

"We needn't break our necks," Gideon said.

He was glad to be out, no matter what the excuse, and quite expected to find two disappointed Americans when he reached the Division.

Little more than half an hour after P.C. Kemp had made his report, Donnelly and Webron reached the corner of the street where the Lambett Hotel was, Webron at the wheel of a grey Austin Cambridge. They waited for twelve minutes, before a larger car turned into the street, and as it passed, Webron exclaimed in surprise :

"There's the great Gideon."

"I don't believe it," Donnelly scoffed.

"You'll believe it," Webron said. "Does he know anything more ?" He opened the door of the car and got out as Gideon's car stopped.

Gideon glanced up at the newly painted private building, with *Lambett Hotel* painted shiny black on big white columns, then glanced along and saw Webron. He waved, and strolled towards him, looking huge against the stocky American, whose dark hair was ruffled by a strong wind, and who looked up with a half grin.

"Special information ?" he inquired.

"No. I just thought that dyed hair worth looking at," explained Gideon. "Do you know if Hann's in ?"

"He's in," said Webron. "Your Divisional man has been watching, and he told us ; he's put two men at each corner."

"We don't want anything to happen to our guests," Gideon said drily. He watched his car moving along, and strolled after it, content to feel the pavement solid beneath his feet. It carried him back twenty-nine years, to that time when he had first pounded a beat, and there was a positive nostalgia about it.

He heard a soft toot on a car horn, and glanced round. A man was turning away from the Lambett Hotel. He was of medium height, with jet black hair, and had a camera slung over his shoulder. Hebron was only a few yards in front of him. Donnelly was getting out of the car into the road, and a small van, coming along fast, honked its horn wildly. Donnelly dodged back. Gideon swung round and began to stride towards the stranger, and as he did so, he saw Webron's expression change, and saw horror on Donnelly's face as he rounded the car. Although the suspect had his back turned to him, Gideon saw the swift movement of the camera strap and the position of his arms; the man was levelling the camera at Webron, so Webron might be face to face with death.

Gideon opened his mouth and yelled: *"Police!"* He saw the suspect start; he saw Donnelly leap forward, trip on the kerb, and fall headlong. The man with the camera jumped away from him, and Webron dived in turn. In the moment of furious confusion, Gideon was still twenty yards away. He saw the suspect rush towards the porch of the hotel; somehow, Webron flung himself sideways, to stop him. Then the man with the camera jumped towards the steps which led down to the hotel's sub-basement, and managed to slam the waist-high iron gate behind him. He was on one side of the gate, and Donnelly was helpless on the other. Webron was going forward with cold-blooded determination.

The "camera" was trained on them both.

"Get away," Hann said, gaspingly. "Get away from me. Let me go or I'll kill you."

"Stop the talk," Webron said. The edge on his voice told Gideon how tense he was; and how afraid. He took a step nearer. "You've had your day, O'Hara. Just drop that—"

"Get away from me or I'll shoot you both."

"Mr. O'Hara," Gideon called in a level voice. He was only a few yards away, approaching with long, deceptively leisurely strides. Donnelly, picking himself up, glanced at him as if in astonishment, and Webron moved forward again. "It's one thing to assassinate your President, if you believe he is betraying your country," Gideon

158

went on conversationally, "but it's another to commit cold-blooded murder. These men are just doing their job. You might injure them, or even kill them, but you can't get away. The hotel is surrounded, and I can have armed men here in a few minutes." He put a hand to his pocket, calmly, took out his wallet, and extracted a card. "I am Commander Gideon of the Criminal Investigation Department." He held the card forward and saw O'Hara staring at him, lips already beginning to work, strength and purpose failing.

The camera dropped before Gideon touched the man.

"Commander, I just want to tell you that was the coolest nerve I've ever seen in a man," declared Donnelly.

"Amen to that," Webron said.

Gideon sat back in his chair behind his desk, looked from one man to the other, and said:

"That was the biggest slice of luck I've had in years. I couldn't let it slip through my fingers. O'Hara isn't a killer as such. I didn't see how the appeal could fail." He meant exactly what he said. It seemed to him that the day had changed the whole outlook of the Visit; everything had started to go right, and he was positively light-hearted.

Later, when he talked to Kate about the newspaper account of this, he was to say honestly that it had not occurred to him that there was really any danger; and she was to believe him. Now he went on: "It's our biggest headache over, anyhow." He thought: *I'm a blurry fool. I ought to have told them they had all the guts in the world, too.* But that would be an anti-climax now. "O'Hara's downstairs, praying. We'll charge him with being in possession of a fire-arm without a licence, and that will keep him on remand in custody for eight days. By then we should have an extradition warrant ready. That what you two want?"

"Commander, that's exactly what we want," Webron replied. "Is there anything we can do for you?"

"Yes," said Gideon. "Go out to Kensington, and have a word with Constable Kemp."

"We'll be glad to," said Webron. "Is there any rule against taking him out to dinner?"

"Make it a good dinner," Gideon urged.

On that same evening, Matthew Smith turned into the gateway of his house, went round the side as he usually did, hesitated at the back door, and then went towards the workshop. He did not even glance towards the heap of soil which he had dug up from beneath the workshop, and did not yet know that it had been examined; his neighbours were not likely to tell him. He did not notice that the woman next door was watching him through a window.

He unlocked the workshop door, stepped inside, glanced at the spot where his dead wife lay, and quickly looked away. Thought of her vanished from his mind as he stared at the hiding-place where he kept the bomb. His heart began to pound, and blood throbbed through his ears. It was so very near; the great moment was almost in his grasp. He could not wait to take that bomb and hurl it at the hated creature in the gilded coach. He could not wait to hear the roar of the explosion, to see the horses rear up, to see a devil being blown to pieces. He did not give a thought to the people who would be in the stand behind him.

On the Saturday, the day London would be flooded with visitors, and the first day intended for a series of widespread raids by Sonnley's men. Sonnley had not whistled much in the past few days. He was worried, although there were some reasons for thinking that the worst of his worries might be over. The police were taking comparatively little notice of him, and he knew that they were stretched very thin. Probably the watching earlier in the week had been in an effort to scare him and Klein.

He did not know what to make of Klein.

After the news of the "accident" to Whittaker, Klein

seemed to have become obsessed with the idea of finding out who had smeared those handle-bars, but he had failed. No other burnt fingers had been reported, and as far as Sonnley's scouts in the big provincial cities knew, there was no movement towards London. Klein seemed to have paid them to stay out of the big smoke, as instructed, and that was just as Sonnley wanted it.

But how far could he trust Klein?

He told himself that Klein was reliable at least until he had been paid off, but would have to be watched very carefully afterwards. Meanwhile, Sonnley double-checked his own arrangements for the Visit.

He meant to have an alibi which no one could possibly break. He had to make sure that the money was collected and paid into the bank quickly, and that the stolen goods were moved quickly, too. He also wanted to distribute Lumati's money—he had collected it days ago, and it was stored in the cellar of one of his shops—but for a reason which he could not explain to himself, he held that back. He had collected it, and it was safely stached away. There was no hurry with the money, and the police might be on the look-out for forged notes.

At the back of Sonnley's mind, there was one way in which he could use the slush, but his immediate concern was to see that his own plans worked smoothly.

On the Saturday morning, he gave Rosie a peck of a kiss, and went outside. It was bright and sunny, and by the time he reached the garage at the back of the flats he was whistling cheerfully; good weather was just what his "artists" wanted. He slid into the driving-seat, switched on the ignition, and took the wheel. Immediately he felt something sticky and wet, that puzzled him for a moment. Then, only seconds before the acid began to burn, he realized what it was.

He snatched his hands away, and sat absolutely still, eyes glaring, hands crooked, the burning pain worse with every passing second. Soon he made choking noises in his throat, as if he were fighting for breath.

That day, the day which should have been Sonny Boy Sonnley's greatest harvest, his "artists" left home for the West End of London, each of them very careful with the handle-bars of bicycles, scooters and motor-cycles; none of them used cars, because of the need for quick getaways. All of them went among the crowds for the first of their jobs. The weather was so lovely that it made the people happy and careless, and pockets and handbags were easy game. In all, fourteen of the men made good first pickings, and hurried back to their machines.

Exactly the same thing happened in each case, in dozens of different places.

Each man gripped the handle-bars, and started off; after a few seconds, each man pulled into the kerb, snatched his hands from the bars and looked down. Each saw hands and fingers which were already red and blistering, and which were beginning to cause agony.

Man after man jumped off his machine, bystanders staring at them as they waved their hands about wildly.

The police were soon alerted.

Superintendent Lemaitre pulled up in his blue Humber outside Gideon's front door, early that afternoon, and Gideon saw him from the bedroom, where he was mending a spring blind. Kate was out shopping. Gideon was on call, and judging from Lemaitre's expression, this was an urgent one. He smiled to himself as Lemaitre disappeared along the path, and carried a mind-picture of the tall, thin, rather gawkish man, with spotted red-and-white bow-tie, grey overcheck suit which somehow contrived to be loud, and narrow-brimmed trilby set at a jaunty angle on the side of his head.

The bell rang twice before Gideon could get to the door.

"In a hurry, Lem?" he asked mildly.

"In a blurry hurry," Lemaitre cracked, and there was excitement but not anxiety in his eyes. "Gottabitta news for you." He came in, almost as familiar with the house as Gideon, and went on boisterously: "Remember old

Dicky Whittaker? Poor old Dicky with the blistered fingers?"

"Well?"

"We've had nine cases of blistered fingers reported this afternoon," Lemaitre announced, joyfully. "Every one of them a Klein and Sonny Boy man! How about that, George?" Without giving Gideon a chance to respond, Lemaitre careered on, taking a slip of paper from his pocket. "Every one of the baskets was caught with his pockets stuffed with loot, too. Every one's a dead cert for three years inside, after hospital treatment. Some of their hands—you should see! Raw isn't the word. But the thing is, George, I know what's on."

Gideon said cautiously : "Do you?"

"That's right, that's right, tell me I'm jumping to conclusions again. This time I'm bang on the ball." Lemaitre waved the slip of paper in front of Gideon's nose. "Now listen to me, George. Here is a list of the boys who've been burnt. They can't work, understand? One might have been an accident, but nine makes a campaign, and there may be more to come. So as soon as I heard there were several of them, I checked round with the provincial cities. You want to know something?"

"Try me."

"Jock Gorra's boys left Glasgow last night and this morning. Some by train, some by road. And remember, Klein was up there, with Gorra, and they behaved like dear old pals. You can take it from me, the Glasgow Blacks are coming to take over from Sonnley, and all we've got to do is pick 'em up as they arrive, and have 'em sent back to Glasgow. Now wait a minute, wait a minute!" pleaded Lemaitre, as Gideon tried to get a word in. "I've telephoned Glasgow. They've put out an official request for all of Gorra's gang to be sent back for questioning. It's only a matter of finding them. They won't be likely to come by road, not all the way, it's a hell of a drive. I think those who started out by road will catch a train further south, maybe in Carlisle, and we ought to be able to pick them up at Euston."

"Got the stations watched yet?" demanded Gideon.

"Attaboy," said Lemaitre, and his grin seemed to split his face in two. "I've done better—action, that's me. We got seven of the so-and-so's off the *Flying Scot*, and nine more at the Victoria Coach Station. Don't they hate London!"

Gideon joined in his laugh, and felt a deep satisfaction.

His hands bandaged and free from pain, Sonnley was sitting at the window of his apartment, staring down into the street. Now and again he muttered harshly:

"I'll get the swine. I'll get him."

Most people in London were happy, however, and among these was a certain Arthur Ritter, from Worcester, who was driving a car hired from Carraway without caring what it cost. At that time, he was alone.

So was Doris Green.

18

TICKETS FOR THE STAND

LITTLE Doris Green, pretty in her new flowered hat, was not happy; in fact she was scared.

She had been to London twice, each time with her mother, who was now dead; her father had been dead for many years. She stood forlorn and lonely on that Saturday evening. The soft light gentled the rather hard green of her tweed suit, a neat and fashionable little outfit. She looked nice. Somehow the cut of the jacket and the high neck of the yellowish blouse beneath it emphasized the roundness of her bosom and the smallness of her waist. She wore flesh-coloured stockings on legs which were rather too full at the calf, thus accentuating her small ankles and brown-clad feet.

Along the row of tall, grey, porticoed houses in Cromwell Road were the signs one after another : *No Vacancy. Full. Sorry, Full Up.* Two youths walked past her, turned, and walked past again. A coloured man stood on the other side of the wide road, looking at her. Massive red buses and little dark cars would cut him off from sight momentarily, and back he would come again. A sports car slowed down, and a man with a black wavy moustache called :

"Like a ride, baby?"

One of the youths, approaching for the third time, called : "How about a bit o' rock-on'-roll, doll?"

Doris was more than ever scared, and walked quickly along towards a traffic junction and another busy road. At the corner, a dozen people surged off the pavement and she was nearly bowled over. She recovered, went with the crowd, and was knocked from the far side. When she felt a tug at her left arm, she thought nothing of it until she reached the far pavement. Then she discovered that her handbag was gone.

She was so shocked that she stood absolutely rigid. People pushed past her, a man said "Sorry", another growled : "Want all the pavement?" She moved towards the side of a house, staring blankly at her left wrist, where the bag had been hanging.

In a strangled voice, she said : "No, oh, no."

Then tears filled her eyes; she had to fight against crying out. She had no idea who had stolen the bag, no idea what to do; she was beyond thought.

For in that bag was thirty pounds; every penny she had.

Arthur Ritter had been a widower for seven years. He was rather shorter than average, stocky, with iron grey hair, a young face, and clear brown eyes. He dressed well and walked well. He owned a small pottery near Worcester, was comfortably off, had no particular vices and few of what he would recognize as virtues. Now and again, because he was lonely, he visited a woman in a town near his home ; he always came away feeling a little ashamed.

That Saturday evening, he had driven from his hotel near Piccadilly to see an old friend in a guest house in the Cromwell Road. His car was parked a hundred yards away, and walking towards it after visiting his friend, he noticed the girl in the green suit and the little flowery hat on a mop of golden-coloured hair. He noticed the two youths and the man in the car, too, and felt annoyed with them and sorry for the girl. She looked so forlorn. He saw when she crossed the road, noticed the youth who bumped into her, and saw him quicken his pace and then turn a corner. A moment later, the girl stumbled, and two more men bumped into her. She went to the side of a big house with round, cream-coloured pillars and a high porch, and looked as if she could stand no more.

Everyone else ignored her.

Ritter went towards her, feeling awkward and shy, and yet genuinely sorry for her. He stood a yard or two away, close enough to see the tears glistening on her eyelashes.

He could keep quiet no longer.

"Excuse me," he said, with a frog in his throat. "Excuse me, but—can I help you?"

She stared at him without speaking, her lovely violet eyes still glistening.

"I don't want to butt in, but—I'll be glad to help if I can."

Hesitantly, tremulously, she told him what had happened.

It was a strange, touching little encounter, a father-and-daughter-like meeting. She mustn't worry, she mustn't cry. He would see the police for her. She would almost certainly get her money back. He would find out where the police station was. Where was she staying?

"*Nowhere!*" he exclaimed. "You mean your home isn't in London?"

"No."

"And you've nowhere to stay?"

Pathetically, she said: "And I haven't got any money, either."

The police at a nearby sub-station were affable but not really hopeful; and of course they asked for Doris's address. Almost without thinking, Ritter said:

"The Welchester Hotel."

"What room number, please?"

"Seven-o-seven." He gave his own, for there was no other to give.

"Look here, my dear," he said, when they were outside. "I'll lend you some money. I'll be happy to."

"It's ever so kind of you, but—"

"Look here, young lady," said Ritter, suddenly masterful, "you can't wander around London without any money and without anywhere to sleep. We'll go and find you a hotel for the night, anyhow. I'll drive, and you look out for a place on your side."

No Vacancy. Full. Full Up. No Rooms. Fully Booked, the signs read, and it was dark by the time they had given up.

"You *must* have somewhere to sleep," Ritter said, desperately. "Perhaps my hotel has a room."

He took her there. As they approached the Reception Desk through the crowded foyer, three applicants for rooms were turned away.

"You *can't* stay out all night," he said, in a funny kind of voice, for by then he was beginning to realize what might come of this. "I can't allow it. You—you must have my room."

"Oh, I can't possibly!"

Instinct or premonition told him that she could and she would, and in his heart he knew exactly what was going to happen. His conscience worried him a little because she was so young, but she wasn't a *child*.

"I'll tell you what," he said. "There's a settee up there."

She was shaken and scared and lonely, and he was old enough to be her father. She was not at all frightened of him.

His bedroom was more luxurious than any room she had ever been in. There was a bathroom, too, and the settee was plenty long enough for her. He wanted her to take the bed, but she refused, almost gaily. He sent for some sandwiches, and she hid in the bathroom when the waiter brought them. When she came out, they laughed conspiratorially.

Arthur locked and bolted the passage door. *Arthur* went into the bathroom while Doris slipped off her clothes and put on a pair of his pyjamas. *Arthur* came out, breathing a little fast and roughly. He went over to her, and bent over her, and leaned down and kissed her, softly—gently—passionately.

It was the first time that Doris had known a man. Ritter knew that, as he took her so gently yet so daringly, so guiltily, and yet with such ecstasy.

"Of course I'm not ashamed," Doris said, next morning. "Arthur, you mustn't be, either. I-I-I *loved* being with you."

168

They did not leave the room until nearly twelve o'clock, and they walked out together, as in a dream. Near the hotel an office was open, selling stand tickets for the Procession, the lowest price left being twelve guineas each. Ritter bought two; he would have bought them at double or treble the price.

Alec Sonnley went out by himself, to collect the tickets for the Procession stand. When he had them, he went to a telephone booth and, with great difficulty, inserted the coppers and dialled the number where he expected to find Klein. It rang on and on for a long time, while he scowled straight ahead at people passing in the street. Nothing would go right.

Then the ringing stopped, and Klein answered:

"Benny Klein speaking."

"Benny," Sonnley said, in a low-pitched voice; he managed to make himself sound anxious.

"Who's that?" demanded Klein, and then caught his breath. "Is that you, Sonny Boy?"

"Listen, Benny," said Sonnley, with soft urgency, "I know who fixed that acid now. It was that flicker from Glasgow, Jock Gorra. I can't do anything to Gorra yet, but the day will come. Listen, Benny—"he broke off.

"I'm listening," Klein said, as if he could not really believe that Sonnley was affable.

"I'm throwing my hand in," Sonnley declared. "I can't take any more of it, Benny. I'm past it. So I'm throwing my hand in, and I want to make sure the cops don't get anything on me over the grapevine. I want you to keep your mouth shut about me, Benny."

Klein said, swiftly: "What's it worth, Sonny Boy?"

That was the moment when Sonnley felt sure that Klein had taken the bait, and after a long pause he smiled for the first time since his fingers had been burned. Then he said anxiously:

"We agreed on five thou', didn't we?"

"*How* much, Sonny Boy?"

"Five thou'—"

"It's a deal for ten thousand," Klein said. "Ten thousand will make a lot of difference to me, but a rich man like you won't notice it." There was a sneer in his voice.

Sonnley muttered: "I'm not so rich, but—well, I don't want trouble, Benny. I'll make it ten. But my hands are all burned up, you'll have to collect it. You'll find it in the cellar at the Norvil Street shop. It's packed in television set cartons—I thought I'd need plenty of change. You've got some keys, haven't you?"

"I've got some keys," Benny said. "Okay, Sonny Boy, you can sleep easy."

When he stepped out of the telephone booth, Sonnley stood for a moment, wiping his forehead with the back of one bandaged hand. Then he turned towards his home. His lips puckered as he began to whistle.

On the Sunday morning, Mildred Cox got up first, glad that Ray was asleep. She had never known him so tired, never known work take so much out of him; in a way, he had been worse at home since she had persuaded him to try to get on with Gideon. She knew the truth, of course; he could never bear to play second fiddle, yet something about Gideon made him feel inferior.

He slept until ten o'clock; when he woke he was irritable and sharp-voiced, so that young Tom was subdued.

"I'm going to check progress along the route," he told Mildred. "I can't be sure when I'll be home."

He drove to Parliament Square, where the flags were up, and the flowers at the window-boxes of the government buildings were at their loveliest. Crowds were already thronging the streets. Cars were parked beyond the various barricades. Traffic was already too thick to allow it in Whitehall, Parliament Square, St. James's Park or the Mall. Cox recognized a lot of C.I.D. men mixing with the crowds, and wasn't surprised to see Parsons.

"About what you'd expect today," Parsons remarked when they met. "Half the pickpockets and bag snatchers in London. But the big boys aren't out—you heard what happened?"

"Eh? Oh, the acid."

"That's it," said Parsons, drily. "And the Glasgow boys have been sent off, with fleas in their ears. You all right?"

"Can't see anything I've missed," Cox said, rather tartly.

"Tell you one thing I forgot," said Parsons. "Gee-Gee asked me if your wife would like a stand ticket for Wednesday. He'll be glad to fix it."

After a fight between a cool rejection and Mildred's interest, Cox said : "She'd like one very much."

There was much activity on that Sunday in other parts of London, and in Paris, Bonn and New York.

The airport security measures were checked for the last time, and Gideon drove to London Airport to see a rehearsal. Airport police and officials were with him at the control tower.

He watched ground crews, airport maintenance men, rescue service squads, both fire and medical, going through their drill with satisfying precision and speed. From lift-boy to door attendant, news-stand assistant and restaurant worker, everyone had been screened. All scheduled aircraft were re-routed or re-timed, to keep the air, runways and services clear for the three Presidents and their retinues. Two helicopters were detailed to keep continual surveillance. Watch-tower crews were doubled. The pilots of the four aircraft concerned were briefed by radio-telephone down to the most minute detail. Security men and women, as well as police, were stationed at every possible danger-point. The roof-top Observation Point was closely checked, too, and officials stationed there. The day-by-day and hour-by-hour routine of the airport was set aside. Few officials minded, but passengers complained bitterly in all tongues from English to Finnish, from Urdu to Japanese.

Satisfied as far as he could be, Gideon joined Cox, as arranged. He sensed the man's tautness ; but at least he was civil and even overdid his thanks for the stand ticket.

They checked as the greater London Police Forces went

into action along the route from the airport to the embassies and hotels, drove the whole route, where men were stationed every hundred yards or so. They drove over the roads to be closed, too, so as to make sure the main route could not be affected on the big day itself.

"Don't think we've missed much," Gideon said, when they had finished. "How about a drink, Ray?"

After a startled pause, Cox said : "I could do with a pint. Thanks."

In and near the embassies, Security keyed itself to the biggest efforts ever.

Everywhere, the crowds gathered, quiet, thoughtful, interested, quickly and easily stirred to laughter, thickening during the day until by early afternoon London was nearly as full of people as it would be on the day itself.

Carraway's cars were everywhere, but London crowds had seldom been less troubled by expert pickpockets, bag snatchers and petty thieves.

Gideon, at the Yard, went across to look at the river; then heard footsteps outside breaking the Yard's Sabbath quiet. The door opened, and Ripple appeared.

"Hallo, George!"

"Hallo, Rip. Glad you're back."

"How are things?"

"All under control, I think," Gideon said.

"I counted twenty-seven of our chaps at the airport and on the way here," said Ripple. "I hope nothing crops up to cause a distraction."

"And don't I!" said Gideon.

Matthew Smith was waiting almost in anguish for Wednesday : all he could think about was throwing his bomb. Violet Timson was waiting very contentedly for Ricky Wall, who was back in London. By coincidence he had come on the same plane as Ripple. Doris Green was blissfully happy because already Arthur had talked of marriage. Carraway was doing a big business, feeling quite secure; and Eric Little's wife was trying to make her children understand the long wait for their father. Beryl Belman was pleasantly surprised that her mother was already perking up. Sonnley was waiting until the moment came to cut Klein's throat; and Klein was trying to grasp what had hit the Glasgow Blacks, for Jock Gorra was already back home, held for questioning about an old robbery with violence. Klein had virtually nothing to do, had no money and no goods to collect and sell—and he knew now that Sonnley would be out to get him if he once suspected the truth. Parsons was waiting for a chance to send the Italian procurer out of the country, with some of his beauties, but giving up hope—and the security officers from the four great countries could hardly wait to get the Visit over.

19

ARRIVALS

ON THAT crucial Monday, the skies were clear, there was a zephyr wind of six miles an hour, and near-perfect visibility. London went about its normal business, shouldering aside the inconvenience near the Procession route, where the hammering took on a more urgent note, and sightseers from out of town and overseas began to give even dingy streets a festive look.

One after another, the aircraft with their important passengers flew in, landed quite trouble-free, and emptied. Britain's Queen and her consort, the Prime Minister and the Foreign Secretary, were there to greet them. Sleek cars rolled along the highways leading to the city. Crowds were thin at first, with groups of children gathered in wide places, waving flags of four nations; cheering, eager, showing hope and faith in the world that these men were trying to fashion.

Nearer the heart of London, the crowds grew thicker and the cheering louder; but it soon faded as the cars stopped at embassies and hotels, their passengers stepped out, paused again for cameras and flashlights, then disappeared to relax for a while, and to gear themselves for the first of the great occasions.

The great occasion would be Wednesday's Procession.

On the Tuesday, late in the afternoon, Sir Reginald Scott-Marle stood up from the end of the large table in the Conference Room, and looked at the group assembled there: Rogerson, Gideon, Ripple, Cox, Mollet, Bayer, Webron and Donnelly, the British Head of Immigration, and Mullivany, the Yard's secretary. Mullivany had sat throughout the last hour, listening to the final plans and the up-to-the-minute reports without a word of complaint or disapproval.

"Everyone is satisfied, then," said Scott-Marle. "Apparently we all have reason to be. I shall be available in the morning until ten o'clock, an hour before the Procession leaves the Palace. If there is any kind of emergency or anxiety, call on me." His voice, his way of barely moving his lips when he spoke, added a curious emphasis. "Now shall we adjourn to my office for a drink?"

He turned round, and the door leading to his office was opened by a youthful-looking man; beyond, the bottles and glasses were on a table by the window. The sun was shining on the bottles, firing them with a hundred colours.

Ripple followed Gideon through the doorway.

"It will be over tomorrow, thank God."

"We'll just be clearing up the mess," said Gideon, and added under his breath : "I hope."

When Gideon got back to his office, after the cocktails, he sat on a corner of his desk and ran through reports that had come in. One was from Lemaitre :

"All the Glasgow boys have gone home, George. Bob's your Uncle!"

Gideon grinned.

Another report said that there was no indication as to where the soil heaped up in a suburban garden had come from. The Divisional Superintendent simply said : "Will check when opportunity arises," and Gideon decided that it was not worth too much trouble.

"We can check that when the rush is over," he said to Bell.

"Rush? What rush?" asked Bell.

Gideon laughed, thought warmly of Bell, and then lifted a telephone : "Get Mrs. Gideon for me," he said, and sat swinging his leg. There was an empty sense of anticlimax now that so much was over, and the persistent feeling of uneasiness had no specific cause. The trouble was that he had nothing active to do, and he needed action.

Bell had gone home early.

The call was a long time coming through, which probably meant that Kate was out.

"Mrs. Gideon, sir."

"Hallo, Kate," Gideon said. "Like to know something hard to believe?"

"You're not coming home tonight," said Kate philosophically.

"I'm free now. Care to come up, and have a stroll along the route? I'm told they're gathering pretty thick already."

Kate began : "I promised Priscilla I would—"

"She home?"

"They're all home."

"Bring 'em all up," said Gideon expensively. "I'll lay on a meal somewhere."

"No, don't do that, it'll be hopeless getting a meal out tonight," said Kate. She was obviously pleased. "You get something at the Yard, and we'll have a snack here and be in Whitehall at nine o'clock. Is that all right?"

"Couldn't be better," said Gideon.

At five past nine, he saw Kate, Priscilla, Penelope and young Malcolm, all hurrying because they were a few minutes late, all looking eager and fresh, Malcolm leading the way through the crowd, the girls behind him, Kate bringing up the rear, a head taller than any of them. A lot of men looked at the Gideon girls and as many took notice of Kate.

They met at the corner of Parliament Street and Parliament Square ; Kate and Gideon touched hands, and then they began to move among the crowds thronging the square, and walked back along Whitehall past the thousands of people who planned to sleep out all night.

It was warm, the weather forecast was good, more and more people were streaming along, and the front seats were already taken. Rubber cushions, little stools, airbeds, all of these gadgets and a hundred others were in use. The crowd was high-spirited and good-tempered. A crowd of young Australians had a spot nearly opposite Downing Street, and were shouting exchanges with a smaller crowd of French students, and some middle-aged Americans.

"I ain't done such a thing as this in my whole life," a woman said, with a Southern drawl. "But nobody's going to stop me tonight, Jim. I'm staying right here."

"You do just that, *Maaaaam*," an Australian mimicked.

The Gideons reached the narrow stretch of pavement in front of the stand where Kate would be next day. The pavement here was crowded, but only one row of all-nighters was allowed on the kerb. Gideon took no special notice of them.

Malcolm Gideon actually stepped over Matthew Smith's legs.

The programme sellers, the sellers of cardboard and cheap mirror periscopes, the souvenir pedlars, were out in their hundreds, and Gideon wondered how much of the stuff being offered had been stolen. There were reports of a strained relationship between Sonnley and Klein, but crooks had been known to use a quarrel as a smoke-screen, and if anything it made Gideon more suspicious. He saw pound notes and ten-shilling notes changing hands freely, for London crowds were always free with their money on nights like these.

He saw Donnelly and Webron, on the other side of Whitehall; they waved. There was no sign of Mollet or Bayer, but as he reached the Mall he saw Parsons, on his own, looking like an evangelist. Gideon felt Kate's hand touching his. Some Australian detectives were in the Mall, but Wall wasn't among them. The Mall was already jammed tight with people.

Near the Palace, Gideon saw Ripple, mingling with the crowd; they exchanged glances, but otherwise did not acknowledge each other.

20

GREAT DAY

LONDON stirred . . .

Along the route of the morning's procession, Londoners woke in their thousands after the long, uneasy night, cramped, stiff, hungry, unwashed, unshaven, bleary-eyed, dour at first, but quick to find good humour.

The trek to the toilets began. The trek of the hawkers and barrow boys, the programme sellers, the souvenir sellers, began. The cameras began to click, for the sun had risen early and the sky was a clear blue : the unbelievable perfect day. It was warm at six o'clock, warmer at seven, getting quite hot by nine o'clock; but long before then the crowds were thronging in from the suburbs. The extra buses were carrying massive loads; the unseen, unheard tubes were running through London's bowels, and disgorging passengers from the stations at Westminster Bridge, Piccadilly, Charing Cross and Trafalgar Square, at Victoria, Dover Street and St. James's. Scarlet buses dropped their passengers as near to the Procession route as they were allowed to go; and masses walked across the bridges, the young hop-skipping-and-jumping, many parents flagging already, the middle-aged and the elderly showing a curious earnestness.

This was a great occasion, one of London's great days, second only to a Coronation.

The restaurants open for special breakfasts were crowded, and long queues waited outside them. The coffee bars could not serve lukewarm coffee and stale buns fast enough.

The scene along the Mall was at once so familiar, and yet so strange, that visitors from overseas were baffled and bewildered by the packed throng, the masses of paper used overnight as sheets, the mess, the muddle, the good temper, the colour, the drabness, the bare arms, the men's shirt-sleeves.

And out of London's Divisions came the uniformed policemen, to relieve those who had been on duty all night.

In the Information Room, Gideon and Cox followed their movements as the Units reported.

They came from the perimeter of London and all the outer Divisions, in black marias, in buses and in coaches. Each policeman carried his shiny rolled cape because England's June could not be trusted. Each man was dressed in heavy dark blue, each helmeted, each was already hot, slow-walking, firm-footed, quite unperturbed by the occasion, knowing that his job was as much to keep the crowd in humour as to keep them in order; the contented crowd would offer little trouble.

The police walked in their dozens, in twenties, in thirties and forties, under the command of sergeants from the central Divisions. They took up their places along the route, in front of the crowds, standing quite close to one another. The ribaldry began to flow from the people behind towards the policemen, who stood at ease and joked among themselves, but did not tempt fate by answering back the civilians.

"Perfect job, your chaps," Gideon said, and Cox smiled mechanically.

Then came the first of the troops, from the Navy, the Army, the Air Force : battalions of them marching in military precision to the places *en route* which they must line ; heels clicking, arms swinging, more unbending then the police, obeying barrack-square voice orders, some looking a little apprehensively up at the sky. If it didn't cloud over before long, it was going to be stinking hot, and hours standing under this gruelling heat was no one's idea of a joke. They talked in asides, ignoring the banter of the crowd. Horns honked on the outskirts.

The Special Branch and C.I.D. men mingled with the crowd. All the windows on the buildings were watched.

In each of the buildings officials checked that no unauthorized person got in. Men from the Special Branch climbed up through skylights to the roofs, and some took up positions which they would hold all day. The television and newsreel cameras were at their various vantage points, click, click, clicking in practice runs.

Big Ben boomed out, impersonally, resonantly. The sun rose higher. The prospects of the hawkers grew less, but they were well satisfied, many already packing up and going home; but the newspaper sellers were out in force. The pigeons in Trafalgar Square had a forlorn and neglected air; their turn would come when the crowds started to move again. Now only a few children fed them corn, and few cameras clicked at them.

At Wellington Barracks the Guards foregathered : the Horse Guards, the Household Cavalry, the Life Guards. The big, black horses were saddled and bridled; collar chain, breastplates and sheepskin were checked; all that was metal gleamed and glittered. The men were marshalled, medals shimmering and plumes erect as a fox's brush, tunics tight across packed shoulders and deep chests, pouch belts looking as if they were powdered with unmelted snow, white breeches stiff as with starch or pipe-clay, spurs glistening behind the jackboots, forever a threat but never to be used on the flanks of the big black horses. The gauntlet gloves were pulled on firmly; each state sword was held fast by its white sling.

The orders rang out.

The Guards moved into position, as if horses and men were moved by the same reflexes and the same impulses, and they rode along the Birdcage Walk towards the Palace, where the State Coach and the Coaches for the Heads of States had been waiting—with Security Police from all four countries watching surreptitiously, looking for anything which was even slightly amiss.

Huge crowds, gathered on the steps and the fountain opposite the Palace, broke into cheers before they were due. People laughed and shouted and chattered and eased cramped muscles. Time ticked slowly by until the first roar went up as a row of police from the Mounted Branch led by their Inspector clattered out of the Palace gates and clip-clopped smartly up the Mall and along the whole route; to clear the way, to tell their colleagues on the sides and among the trees, at the roofs and at the windows, that all was well further along the route, and that the Procession would soon start in earnest. The police riders looked straight ahead, winning some cheers touched with irony, as many with admiration, bringing cracks from the crowd to the standing uniformed men—*"Didn't your mother teach you to ride a horse, Charley?"* or *"Mind he don't bite you, Bert,"* or *"When are we going to see the real thing?"* But it wouldn't be long, now, and the crowd knew it. There was a kind of tension among them all; faces were turned right or left, towards the direction from which the first of the Cavalry would come.

Suddenly there was a great roar of cheering as the golden coach appeared in the Palace yard, the clattering guards in front and behind it, a figure in gold-coloured satin sitting on one side, the Duke in his uniform as Admiral of the Fleet on the other.

Now the deep-throated cheers rose in waves along the Mall, and the periscopes went up. The tall and the tiny went on tiptoe, fathers lifted pleading children, and the cries of protest came. *"Expect me to see through your blooming head?"* Small feet kicked against stiff shoulders and chests, the lucky six-footers stood at the back, looking disdainfully over the masses of heads. The troops lining the route clicked to the salute as the royal carriage drew near, and then the other Heads of State, first the American, then the French, then the German . . .

The Special Branch and C.I.D. men were keyed up, even the most experienced of them tight-lipped and hard-eyed, watching, watching for any trifling tell-tale sign of danger. The men from the four countries were with their English colleagues now, watching, hopeful, admiring; still a little anxious, in case the one thing they could not prevent should come about. A shot *could* ring out; a fool *might* try to rush towards the carriages.

But nothing happened to alarm them. The Queen's Guard rode by in sun-bathed splendour, the gilt of the coaches and the beauty of the dresses, the radiance of the Queen, the calmness of her consort, the massive elegance of the President of France, the tall, slim figure of the President of the United States in a morning suit, the President of West Germany, liked a carved figure from the Black Forest, face unsmiling.

The Procession was at its height.

The coach in which the President of France and his lady rode turned out of Admiralty Arch towards the Houses of Parliament.

Gideon was now in his office with Cox, a more relaxed Cox, watching a television picture of the corner of Parliament Street and Parliament Square, so he had a bird's-eye view of all this pomp and panoply. His anxieties were drawn out of him by the beauty and the splendour, and by the thought of the hopes which mankind based on this one day.

Further along, in the House of Lords, that golden chamber, the members of both Houses were waiting. The police who protected Parliament were on duty at the gates, and what happened once the coaches were through was no direct concern of Gideon's. If there were to be trouble he believed it would be on the way in—any time, now; any moment. But there had been hundreds of processions before; he himself had taken part in dozens; and there had been no serious trouble at any, yet, no single act of madness.

He saw a picture of the stand where Kate was sitting, very glad that she was there. Malcolm was somewhere among the crowds; the two girls had stayed away. Then he frowned. The pavement in front of the stand was jammed tight with people, although he had ordered two lines only. He glanced at Cox, and saw Cox's face suddenly pale and drawn, saw his hands clench.

"I—" began Cox, and gulped. "I forgot to order that pavement clear. I—God!" He was sweating.

"It won't do any harm," Gideon reassured him quickly. "Bound to have something go a bit wrong. It's been near perfect. Forget it."

He saw a little man in front of the stand, the very front. Then he looked at Kate again.

Kate Gideon was watching with a feeling almost of enchantment, like most of the women in the stand. About her were the Americans, the French, the Germans, the Indians, the Africans—people from all countries and all continents, with huge cameras or with small cameras, now whirring, now clicking. Some people were silent, watching, holding their breath, eyes strained to get the nearest vision of the Queen. Glasses pressed tight against a thousand eyes, the magnified figures showing something of the radiance.

Kate looked her fill at the Queen, who seemed younger at each of these great occasions, and then watched the Household Cavalry clattering and clicking behind. She saw the white horses of the coach in which the President of the United States was sitting; after that would come the President of France. His carriage would be here in two or three minutes. The whole procession would not last for more than seven or eight, but every second was well worth while.

Rosie Sonnley was in the stand, sucking peppermints. Cox's wife was there, within waving distance of Kate. Doris Green sat with her hand in Arthur's, warm and snug. She knew how much older he was, but it did not seem to matter to her; this was like a golden dream. They sat behind two empty seats, with a wonderful view.

Detective-Inspector Ricky Wall, of the Sydney C.I.D., was sitting half-way down the stand, actually on the steps, to allow a little woman next to him to get a better view. Just below him was Donnelly. Webron was somewhere in the Mall. A place where Lemaitre was to have been on duty was vacant, but few noticed that. Wall felt the kind of emotional excitement which he had thought himself proof against; he saw Donnelly wave his hands, and thought he heard his cheers, as the President of the United States went by, completely self-assured, his lovely wife perhaps a little over-awed.

Donnelly, still cheering, saw a man sitting on the kerb open a small case and take out a vacuum flask. That seemed so odd at such a moment that Donnelly stared.

The man Donnelly noticed was at the front, and must have been there all night, but when the cheering was at its height, when the moment was supreme, he was taking out a vacuum flask! Wall watched him closely, too.

Donnelly saw that the man did not unscrew the top, but held the flask by his side. He would not have been able to see so clearly, but the police had kept the road itself clear, and there was a gap where a party of children stood. Why take out a flask at such a moment? And why take out a flask at any time and not pour out?

Then Donnelly remembered talking to Ripple about a bomb disguised as a vacuum flask, captured from Algerian extremists. Donnelly jumped up and ran down the steps, then saw Gideon's *aide*, Joe Bell, on the street corner near the man. To shout would be a waste of time.

Donnelly vaulted over the front of the stand, by the steps; a woman cried out, but her voice was drowned. The nearest soldier swung round to face the crowd. Donnelly landed on the pavement. Bell saw the movement out of the corner of his eyes, swung round, and recognized the American. Bell came pushing his way through the thick crowd, cursing the fact that the pavement here hadn't been kept clear.

"What is it?"

"Look at that guy!" Donnelly shouted close to his ear. "The man with the flask!"

The French coach was coming now, the clip-clop-clip of the horses' hooves sharp and clear, the coachmen holding the reins as if born to it. The President was bowing, his wife smiling and inclining her head. Cheers from the crowd of French students rose in wild waves, then they swung into the first bars of the *Marseillaise*. Bell turned to see the little man in crumpled clerical grey holding the flask in his hand. He raised his hand high, then drew his arm back, as would any man who was going to throw.

The people alongside him were too anxious to see the procession to take any notice, and the soldiers were watching Wall, Bell and Donnelly.

Bell roared: *"Stop that!"* and sprang forward. The little man must have heard him, for he half-turned, arm drawn right back, the flask tight in pale, thin fingers. Bell was only two yards from him, when the man swung round and hurled the flask into the air. As he did so, a guardsman saw the danger, stuck his rifle forward, and caught Matthew Smith on the forearm. Instead of going towards the President of France, the flask rose high into the air, then curved more quickly down towards the front of the stand, behind Smith.

Smith began to kick and struggle. Bell put a hammerlock on him, thrusting his arm up, and saw the flask dropping downwards. For an awful moment he thought that it would fall into the stand. He let the prisoner go, and flung himself towards the falling object. Another C.I.D. man came running, but was too far away to help.

The flask hit the front of the stand.

Bell saw the white flash, and it blinded him; heard the roar, and was deafened. On the instant, he felt as if his body had been ripped into pieces. Immediately behind him were two empty seats—and behind them a man and a young girl; Doris Green with her lover. A piece of metal smashed into her forehead, killing her instantly. Another gashed Arthur Ritter's left eye; he died before the police reached him.

Out on the road, horses reared up, startled heads turned; people began to scream.

Watching, with horrified fascination, Gideon could hardly think at first. Then he realized that the carriages were not damaged, the worst had not happened. It was terrible, dreadful, but—

"My God!" he breathed. "Kate."

He searched among the faces on the screen, transfixed with a deeper sense of horror, until suddenly he caught sight of her, talking to Ray Cox's wife.

For a few minutes that relief seemed to ease the shock of Bell.

21

DAY'S END

"The bomb hit the front of the stand, which took the brunt of the explosion, and Bell took the rest," said Donnelly to Gideon, when everything was over. "I think he thought if he could smother it with his body he would save a lot of lives. Two others were killed, and a dozen hurt, but none of the injured are too bad. The man who threw the bomb is over at Cannon Row, gibbering. He's the nearest thing to crazy I've ever seen. It seems as if the failure drove him round the bend."

Donnelly looked sick and pale. So did Wall, who was with them.

"If it hadn't been for sheer luck, I'd have been there," he said. "So would half a dozen of us. We'd have been goners, too."

Cox caught his breath, and Gideon glanced at him, nodded understanding of his great relief, and then asked : "Was anyone else in the stand hurt?"

"No, except a few cuts," Donnelly said.

Gideon was sitting at his desk, and looking across at Bell's desk, and the chair which would never be Bell's again. That was the hardest thing to realize. The death of Bell affected him more, at the moment, than the fact that there had been an attempted assassination.

Ripple was with Rogerson and Mollet, and the Commissioner was on his way back. The Heads of State were in the Gilded Chamber. Except for that one little patch of horror now cordoned off, everything in London was normal, although rumours of what had happened were spreading fast.

One of Gideon's telephones rang. At moments like these it had been Bell's habit to lift his extension, and make sure

that his boss wasn't harassed unnecessarily. *Joe, Joe, Joe.*
Gideon lifted the telephone and said :

"Gideon."

"Now the show's over, I can tell you something," a man said. It was Lemaitre. "I've picked up some of Sonnley's boys flashing phoney fivers about. We've made four arrests, and they all say that Benny Klein gave them the money. Shall I pick up Benny ?"

Gideon said : "Get him, but have someone else do it, Lem. I need you here."

Cox looked at him, and saw how drawn his face was ; and realized what a terrible blow Bell's death was to him. Yet this man had thought to glance reassuringly at him because of the ironic good consequences of that forgotten order. Cox felt suddenly very humble, but it was a long time before he realized just what the emotion was.

Soon Lemaitre came in, followed by Mollet and Ripple. Mollet just raised his hands, and went to the window. Lemaitre said :

"Queer thing, George."

"What is ?"

"The assassin's a chap named Smith—there was a report about his wife being missing. Remember ? Some digging done in the garden."

"I remember."

"The digging was under the floor of a workshop in the garden ; his wife was there."

Gideon said : "Good God." He closed his eyes for a moment, and then said : "You tried, Ray—God knows you tried that one."

Mollet turned round.

"This assassin—when will he be charged ?" he asked.

"This afternoon," replied Gideon. "We'll hold a special court. Why ?"

"I would like to be able to give Paris the latest information," said Mollet. "I will telephone." He went out, still badly shaken, and Ripple and Cox went with him ; Gideon saw Ripple glance at Bell's desk as he went out.

Lemaitre was on the telephone, giving instructions about Sonnley, and Gideon said to Donnelly and Wall:

"Going back to the route for the return procession?"

"I don't want any more of that," said Wall. "I had a bellyful."

"Go and see if Miss Timson's free, will you?" Gideon asked. "If she is, ask her to lay on a car for me at once, my own's not here. I want to go and see Mrs. Bell." He noticed the alacrity with which the Australian went out, but there was no brightness in his own eyes or lightness in his heart when he looked across at Lemaitre.

And Lemaitre, after a moment's hesitation, deliberately sat down in Bell's chair; the chair Lemaitre had occupied for several years before Bell had taken on this job—the job that had killed him.

"Lem," said Gideon, his throat dry, "how about Sonnley's shops?"

Donnelly said: "I'll be seeing you."

"Clean as a whistle," reported Lemaitre. "I've checked with four Divisions. Might have some stolen stuff, but there's nothing we can pin on to them for certain. They look as clean as—*hey*! Think Sonnley's fixed Klein? Blimey!" went on Lemaitre, and gave a choky kind of laugh. "We'll get the pair of them. Klein will squeal all right."

There was a tap at the door as he finished, and Abbott came in. It was difficult to define the change in Abbott, but it was there—as if the Carraway case had forged a kind of steel in him.

"If Carraway had any part in the murders of his partner and of Marjorie Belman, he'll get away with it this time," Abbott said. "I think we ought to go it alone, and charge Little with the girl's murder."

"Right," said Gideon. "I'll talk to the Public Prosecutor. Anything else, Lem?"

"Anything special you want me to do?"

"Pass all your current jobs on to someone else, and take over Joe's desk, will you?" Gideon said quietly. "We're going to need a lot of help today, this bloody thing won't stop—"

A telephone bell began to ring.

One or the other kept ringing, and it wasn't until nearly one o'clock that a call which Gideon was waiting for came through.

It was Christy, of N.E., brisk to a point of brusquesness, and hard-voiced.

"I've heard about Joe Bell, George."

Gideon said : "I suppose you have."

"I can't say—"

"Hugh," Gideon interrupted harshly, "have you got Klein?"

After a long pause, Christy said : "Yes. Picked him up with five thousand pounds in new pound notes. They're so good that our expert can't swear whether they're real or false, except by the tintometer—the ink's the wrong colour. No doubt about it, he says. Klein swears that Sonnley gave him the money, but Sonnley says he doesn't know a thing about it. He says he knows Klein just sold him out to Gorra, why should he pay him anything? I doubt if we'll get Sonnley this time."

"His day will come," Gideon said heavily.

He was heavy-hearted all the time he was in his office, and he was there until after nine o'clock.

Outside, London was still noisily awake, thronging the procession route, traipsing over the carpets of old newspapers littering the ground, the litter and the debris of the crowd.

The President's escape did little to soften the impact of Bell's death ; Ripple too took it badly to heart. Miss Timson worked very late that night, because there had been a hitch in the plans for the flight back to Australia of the touring detectives. How would the future work out for her? Did Australia really beckon?

Gideon checked the arrangements for the hearing against Little, looked over the report of the brief proceedings in which Matthew Smith had been charged with using an explosive to the public danger and remanded in custody. The court had been so crowded that even Mollet had had difficulty in getting in.

Gideon drove home about ten o'clock, and the front door opened as he pulled up outside. He recalled Joe Bell's wife, short, dumpy, fluffy, shocked to a stupor of silence. When Kate came towards him, hands outstretched, his eyes stung. He felt very tired—but at least the Visit was nearly over.

THE END

BOOK TWO

Gideon's River

CONTENTS

Chapter One

BIG SHIPS, LITTLE SHIPS

They came into the Port of London from every corner of the world, the big ships and the little ships, the tankers and the tugs, the liners and the banana boats, the modern ships and the old. They came by day and by night, hindered only by the tides, or by fog; or on those days when the men who worked the docks withdrew their labour in protest for some cause, probably real and vital to them, but often mysterious and frustrating to the rest of London.

For London and all Londoners depended on the Port of London for more than they realised; in fact the Thames was the lifeblood of the nation's capital. Muddy and grey near the open sea and at its wide, waiting estuary, in the upper reaches it was clear as a mountain stream. Far up, even as far as Hammersmith and Putney, Richmond and Teddington, the laden barges sailed their sluggish way with coal and wood and grain and oil and countless other vital goods which could be taken by water more cheaply than by rail or road. At Tilbury where the great stretch of docks began, no bridge spanned the river; but the Pool of London was made by the Tower and by London Bridge as well as by London's history.

But not only was the river the highway for the food which fed the nation, it could also be the highway for those who fed on crime. True, there was much more crime on the land on either side than on the river itself, but much of that crime started on the river, and

7

it was sometimes difficult to understand where responsibility began and ended for the investigation into crimes committed on land or on water, on docks or in warehouses, in pubs or in pleasure boats.

In fact, four police forces controlled the river, all working closely together.

On the broad expanse of the water itself the Thames Division of the Metropolitan Police was in control, its ceaseless patrol of small boats and swift launches keeping a constant vigil both day and night. One small stretch of water, from Tower Bridge to the Temple, was however controlled partly by the City of London Police; but the two forces acted as one in the defence of London's property and people.

The docks which led off the river, docks with such names as Royal Albert and Victoria, London and Saint Katharine, Surrey and Millwall, were walled and protected like mediaeval cities, with policemen at the gates to check and control the lawful flow of lorries and carts, dockers and lightermen, port authority and Customs officers. These docks were protected by a different force, the police of the Port of London Authority, who had a close and intricate knowledge of the wharves and warehouses, quays and berths, repair shops, storage sheds and transport.

These police worked in the closest co-operation with the other two forces having the same objectives, rules and grievances, the same sense of dedication too seldom understood by civilians who worked in or on the river, and beyond.

Finally, there were the Customs men, two groups, each dealing with quite different aspects of the business of London: the Landing Branch who dealt with cargo only, and the Water Guard who dealt with ships' stores, passengers and crew.

If in fact the Customs force could be regarded as two forces, then the Metropolitan Police should be also, for the Thames Division with their reefer jackets, white shirts and white collars and their caps, were quite distinct in appearance if not in purpose; so, in all, six different forces of police guarded different parts of London's river.

Occasionally, very occasionally, each of these became involved in the same crime and the same series of crimes.

Probably none of the others would ever have admitted it, happy though their relations were with one another, but when all six became involved the man in over-all command was likely to be the Commander of the Criminal Investigation Department of the Metropolitan Police—George Gideon. He would have been the last to claim control and yet, subconsciously, would no doubt have exerted it. And the other branches, knowing and accepting the need for co-ordination as well as co-operation, would almost certainly have accepted his authority without question.

On the night when a certain series of crimes began on the river, Gideon was at home, with his wife and one of their six children. He was 'on call'—he was nearly always on call. He was always instinctively aware that, in the London he so loved, during every minute of the day and night some crime was being planned or committed; and that any one of these crimes might bring a time of great testing for any one of London's police forces. He was not consciously preoccupied with that at this particular moment, however. An exceptionally pretty girl with an exceptionally nice figure was singing an exceptionally ugly tune on television. Kate, Gideon's wife, noticed the intentness with which Gideon watched, and smiled affectionately to herself.

Mary Rose was also an exceptionally pretty girl with an exceptionally nice figure. She should have been light-hearted and gay, as the singer appeared to be. Instead, she was terrified. She had been terrified ever since Tom and Dave had started to quarrel in the pub. Tom had sneaked her away, hoping that Dave wouldn't notice; but he had. They had cut across a building site, hearing the engine of Dave's car start up, knowing he was giving chase. Tom had dashed down the alley leading to the quay steps, but Dave might have seen them from the car, there was no way of being sure.

She stood at the bottom of the steps, hearing the river water slapping the stone walls and plopping against the sides of a small boat. Tom was standing in the boat, unsteadily, half-drunk. Across the water a few lights showed at warehouses and barges, some distance up-river a pub was gay with coloured lamps. Now and again a car or lorry passed along the road behind them, lights ghostly in the gloom, but none stopped. Perhaps one was Dave's; perhaps they were safe.

Mary Rose could just make out Tom's lean figure as he sat down. She heard sounds she could identify, of oars grating on the rowlocks. Another car came along the road, its engine very clear. She turned her head and stared up towards the top of the steps.

'Come on!' Tom whispered.

'I—I daren't!'

'Come on, don't waste time!'

'I—I can't, I'm too scared!' she gasped.

'You'll be more scared if they catch you.' he growled hoarsely. 'They're so drunk they'll do anything. We've got to get away.'

'Tom, I——'

'Are you coming or aren't you?' he demanded, his

roughness cloaking his own fear. 'If Dave catches you while he's drunk, he'll slash your face to pieces.'

'Oh, God,' she gasped. 'Don't say it!'

'Come *on*, then, get a move on.'

He was right, she knew. Dave would slash her, she would lose her beauty she would be scarred for life. He had slashed other girls. Taking a timid step forward on to the green slime on the step, she nearly fell.

The car slowed down.

'It's them!' cried Tom, in anguish. 'Are you coming, or aren't you?'

A car door slammed, and another. Footsteps sounded, sharp and urgent. Mary Rose leaned against the wall and groped with her right foot for the boat. Now Tom was leaning forward, hand outstretched to help her. She took it.

'*Jump!*' he urged.

She could not make herself jump, but she clambered over, crouching, scraping her legs and knees painfully, ruining her stockings. Footsteps clattered in the narrow cut leading to the steps, hard leather and metal heel-tips on the uneven cobbles. Tom sat back and pushed with one oar against the wall. The boat rocked, and Mary Rose gave a little groan. Tom slid the oar back into the rowlock and started to row. The clatter drew nearer, and drowned another sound on the river itself—the even beat of the engine of a motor-boat, some distance away.

The rowing boat was only ten yards from the steps when a torch shone out, bright beam dazzling. When Mary Rose twisted round she saw behind it only darkness, but the beam shifted and shone on the oily-looking surface of the river. Another torch beam cut the darkness like a knife.

A man called: 'There they are!'

'See them?'

'There's Mary Rose!'

The light shone on the back of her head then passed either side, losing itself in the mirror of water. Something fell heavily close to the boat; plonk. Tom rowed desperately, but did not seem to draw any nearer to safety. Mary Rose, feeling the boat rocking more and more, held tightly to the sides. One torch went out but the other focused on her, and something thudded into the side of the boat. 'They're throwing beer bottles,' Tom muttered.

Beer bottles . . .

They must have brought beer bottles to smash and jab into her face and Tom's face. All this, for a kiss and a hug—not knowing Dave had been in the pub. Oh, God!

'Why don't you get out into the river?' she gasped.

'We're too close.'

'I'm—I'm rowing as hard as I can.'

'We're closer than we were!' she muttered in sheer terror; and as if he had heard her a man on the bank said clearly:

'They'll never make it, Dave.'

'Never thought they would,' another man said. He raised his voice. 'Come and get it, you whore! Come and get it.'

'Tom—Tom, row *harder*!'

'They're in an eddy—' It was the first man speaking— 'going round in circles, see?' Both men began to roar with laughter.

It was true, they *were* going round in circles, Mary Rose realised in awful fear. That was why they were no further from the steps.

The man with Dave spoke clearly. 'I got an idea, Dave.'

'What's that?'

'Sink 'em,' the man said, simply.

'Sink 'em?' echoed Dave.

No, oh no, no!

'There's these old barrels, right here,' the man with Dave remarked. ''Roll 'em down the steps, that would rock the boat all right.'

'Not a bad idea,' Dave said, with drunken intentness. 'I'd rather carve them up, but they'll be better off dead.'

Oh, God, why had this happened to her?

'Come on!' the second man said. 'Let's get them rolling.'

The torch light changed direction, pitched on to the steps and showed the dark silhouettes of the men. Dave's long hair was like a wig—a golliwog's hair. Tom rowed more desperately than ever but was gasping for breath and could not get the boat away; he never would, now. Mary Rose sat in numbed despair, not even praying. She heard the men on the steps moving about, and suddenly something came crashing down on them and hurtled into the water. There was a great splash, and the boat keeled over very steeply.

Mary Rose screamed.

Again Dave's friend roared with laughter. 'One more will do it!' he bellowed. 'Heave, there, heave!'

Then without warning, a bright light shone out from the river and a glow of light appeared in the road behind the steps. An engine roared, making a strange echo on the river, and a patrol boat drew close to the steps and the helpless couple. Another clatter of footsteps sounded on the steps.

'It's the cops,' Tom gasped. 'It's the bloody cops.'

Observing lights and unaccustomed activity at Fiddler's Steps, the Thames Division patrol report read, we called assistance from the land and a car moved on

13

to the source of the trouble from land while we approached by water. Two arrests were made. David Carter and Samuel Cottingham were subsequently charged with attempting to cause grievous bodily harm to Mary Rose Shamley and Thomas Argyle-Morris by attempting to sink the boat they were in and throwing bottles at them. The charges were made at . . . It was a short report, giving no idea of the skill required by the patrol to approach the steps so cautiously, nor of the almost instinctive way in which the patrol had first noticed that something unusual was happening, and had called for help from land. Scissors operations like this between Thames Division, NE Division and the City of London were so common that no one thought it worth special comment.

When the first morning daylight patrol of the river between Greenwich and Blackfriars Bridge was about to start off, 'Old Man River' Singleton, who was in charge at Divisional H.Q., strolled down the ridged gangway towards the landing stage where three vessels were moored. The three-man crew was already aboard. One was a bearded sergeant, at the helm, the second an elderly constable and the third a youngster who had been in the Thames Division for little more than a year.

'Take a close look at Fiddler's Steps. Tidy, and examine that dinghy. If there are scratches where the bottles struck, we need to know.'

'Right sir.'

'When will that pair be charged?' the young man asked.

'Teach him his ABC,' Singleton said, caustically.

There was a general laugh; any policeman who forgot that the charge would follow in the morning as day followed night, really did need to go back to school.

The patrol boat moved off, slowly, into mid-stream and then up-river.

Behind it was the magnificence of Tower Bridge and the Pool beyond, seen through the grey stone frame of the two main pillars of the arch. The sun, rising above the roof tops of warehouses and the spidery tops of cranes, brightened the masts and the bridge of a Uruguayan ship of about seven thousand tons which was unloading grain.

'Ships are beginning to use the river a bit more than they did, not going into the docks so much,' remarked Sergeant Tidy. 'There was a Frenchie at Hay's yesterday and a Yank at London.'

He spoke casually as he scanned the ruffled surface of the river. Fiddler's Steps were only a few hundred yards down, not far below Wapping Old Stairs, and 'taking a close look' would be the first job; they could almost drift towards the spot on this ebb tide. A piece of driftwood clunked against the propeller, but none of the men took any notice when the boat shuddered. Some straw and a cigarette carton drifted past, the carton making a splash of crimson against the yellow straw. They saw this as they saw everything the still and silent barges moored in the roads, the men working on wharves and in warehouses, here and there a car close to the water's edge. Everything on the river and on the banks appeared to be normal, the sun was beginning to catch the water, giving it a beauty they did not fully understand. A tanker from Holland, of three or four thousand tons, passed them up-river; none of the crew gave it more than a cursory glance.

The patrol boat drew closer to Fiddler's Steps, where a floating barrel was bumping gently against the wall of the recess by the side of the steps; another, further away, was trapped in a kind of pontoon of driftwood which had collected in a corner, as a result of an eddy which was always here at high tide. The little row-boat, one of the few still used to reach barges which had become loose in the roads, was moored to a ring in the wall of the steps.

The youngest man, Addis, said: 'What's that?'

'What's what?' asked Sergeant Tidy.

'That.' Addis pointed towards the pontoon, and following his gaze, his companions saw a small brown packet caught in the driftwood. Tidy turned the boat, but they could not get near enough to pick it out by hand. Addis unhooked the hitching pole and prodded for the packet, caught it and drew it in cautiously. The elderly constable leaned over and picked it out of the water.

'That's a special waterproof container—look how it's sealed,' Addis remarked. The constable turned it over, and saw a faint ring on one side but made no comment.

'Wonder what's in it?' said Addis.

'Tell you what,' said Tidy, 'we'll take that straight back and let Old Man River open it and find out.' He throttled hard, turned the boat swiftly, and raced back towards the landing stage.

Chapter Two

SCOTLAND YARD

At Scotland Yard that morning, there was a curious sense of alertness, almost of tension, which developed without warning and lasted for a few minutes two or three times each day. It was never quite possible to explain it. Certainly George Gideon, Commander of the Criminal Investigation Department, did not want to create such an atmosphere when he arrived to start the day's work, but inevitably he did so. The only other man who had this effect was the Commissioner, Colonel Sir Reginald Scott-Marle, and this sometimes puzzled Gideon for he did not see himself in any way like the aloof, austere soldier who directed the affairs of the Metropolitan Police with military detachment from its men. In fact, most of the Force held Scott-Marle in awe, although some would never have admitted it. Without exception, they held Gideon in deep respect. Whether he liked it or not, and sometimes he disliked it very much indeed, he had become a kind of father figure at the Yard.

On that particular morning, a stranger might have understood why he earned such respect and gave the impression of almost paternal benevolence. Stepping out of his car, big, heavily-built, with thick shoulders and a big head thrust slightly forward, iron grey hair brushed back from his forehead like thick, crinkly wire, he gave an impression of power. As a man hurried forward to hold the door for him, however, the stern expression on his face altered, he smiled and said casually:

'Hello, Simms. How's that daughter of yours?'

Simms, as old as Gideon and still a sergeant, was craggy-faced and burly. His eyes lit up.

'Fine, sir, thank you.'

'Did she have those twins?'

'False alarm, sir, but a whopping big boy. Nearly ten pounds he was.'

'Don't know how they do it these days.' Gideon said, nodded and started up the high flight of stone steps towards the main hall. A uniformed man saluted.

'Good morning, sir.'

'Morning, 'morning, good morning, 'morning.

Footsteps rang out on the cement floor, voices all held a hollow ring in the bare passages.

'Morning. Good morning sir. 'Morning, 'Morning, 'Morning.

Gideon opened the door on the right, and a shaft of sunlight struck him in the face. He put his hand up to shade his eyes quickly, blinking, and went to his desk. It was empty and almost forbidding, the IN, OUT, PENDING, in fact all the trays shiny and polished. He was not yet used to Hobbs as his second-in-command, instead of Lemaitre, who had served him for so many years. Hobbs, with his sturdy old English name, was the public school and university man; Lemaitre, with a name which had come over with the Huguenots, was a cockney to his marrow. Gideon, who had recommended Hobbs for the post of Deputy Commander and was still sure he had been right, nevertheless felt a certain nostalgia. Until a few weeks ago the desk in the corner would have been littered, Lemaitre would have been sitting there with his colourful bow tie, his slightly beady but alert eyes, his lined and wrinkled face. And a pile of reports would have been on Gideon's desk with some notes on top, all in Lemaitre's copperplate hand.

Now it was almost too tidy.

The door opened, slowly.

'Good morning,' Hobbs said.

He carried a batch of reports under his arm, in a much tidier parcel than Lemaitre's had ever been. He was a compact, dark-haired man with regular features, dark grey eyes and a touch of severity about an expression culled more from Scott-Marle's background than Gideon's. But he was a dedicated policeman. Some older men at the Yard disliked him but none denied that he had met them on their own ground, in the

18

detection of crime, and beaten them. A year as Super-intendent of one of the East End's toughest divisions had proved his quality beyond all doubt.

Ever since they had met, there had been moments when Gideon felt slightly ill-at-ease with Hobbs, and those moments had become rather more frequent during the period since Hobbs' wife had died. In a strange way it was as if part of Hobbs had died with her, and Gideon was seldom wholly free from a sense of awkwardness; but it never showed.

' 'Morning, Alec,' he said. 'What have we got this morning?'

'Nothing of special interest,' Hobbs said. 'Only two new cases we need worry about.' He implied that the rest of London's crime could be dealt with that morning by the men out in the divisions. 'Van Hoorn is coming over from Amsterdam about the industrial diamond smuggling; he seems certain that the diamonds are coming into England.'

'Does he say why he's certain?'

'Only that they've caught one of the thieves, a man known to fly to and from London regularly.' Hobbs put a file on Gideon's desk, fairly full and fat. Gideon opened it and saw a typewritten note summarising what Hobbs had just said, and finishing: *Inspector Van Hoorn is due at London Airport on Flight 1701 KLM Airlines at eleven-fifteen this morning.*

'Who are you sending out to meet him?' asked Gideon.

'I thought you might like to go.'

'No, thanks!'

'Then Micklewright.'

Gideon conjured up a mental image of a tall, spare, sandy-haired Detective Superintendent who was one of the Yard's experts on precious stones and whose knowledge of diamonds was a by-word.

'He's not very good with foreigners,' he remarked. 'Either they put his back up or he rubs them the wrong way, I'm never quite sure which.'

Hobbs made no comment.

'All right, he can go.' Gideon agreed. 'I'll have a word with him first, though.'

'I'll send for him,' promised Hobbs. 'The other case is out at Richmond. A thirteen-year old girl has disappeared.'

Gideon's heart dropped; if there was one kind of crime he hated above all it was an offence against a young girl.

'Since when?'

'She should have been home at half-past seven last night, and at nine o'clock the father reported her missing. She'd been home to tea and gone back to school to play tennis. She didn't stay long with the girls she played with, but went off on her own.'

'Anything known?' asked Gideon.

'There have been some complaints about young girls being molested in Richmond Park, but nothing very serious,' Hobbs answered.

'Did you talk to Hellier?'

'Yes. He's asked the adjoining divisions for help, and would like assistance from us.'

'Does he want the river dragged?'

'He appears to think it might be too soon for that,' Hobbs said, making it clear that he had asked the Divisional Superintendent about dragging. 'I've had a word with the Thames Division at Barnes, to alert them.'

'Good,' Gideon said. 'They can have all the help they want.' He took more reports from Hobbs and spread them over his desk, making it look much more familiar, then glanced up. 'Did you ask how Hellier is going about it?'

'He's using a hundred men in groups of twenty-five. One group's at the river, one checking the neighbours, one checking the school and the girls the child was playing with, one in the park. They're examining all newly-dug soil and any turf which seems to have been disturbed recently.'

'All right, all right,' Gideon interrupted. 'I shouldn't have asked.' He turned back to the files. 'What about the Hendon bank robbery?'

'No news.'

'The Fulham smash and grab?'

'The injured jeweller isn't as badly hurt as it was first suggested. We've found fingerprints on a patch of smooth cement on the brick, but they're not in *Records.*'

'Hm.' Gideon thumbed through the remaining reports; on those where there was nothing new Hobbs had clipped a duplicated *Nothing to report* on the top document. 'Send Micklewright in, will you?'

'At once,' said Hobbs.

He went out of the door from which he had come, and as it closed behind him Gideon heard a murmur of voices. Almost at once there was a tap, and on Gideon's 'come in' a tall, sandy-haired, freckle-faced man entered, all arms and legs and hands and feet; Gideon never saw Micklewright without thinking of a music hall comedian. He realised that Hobbs had anticipated whom he would send to the airport and also that he, Gideon, would want a word with him.

'Sit down, Mick,' Gideon said, and in a fluster of movement Micklewright obeyed, sitting on the edge of a straight-backed chair and crossing his legs; his right knee seemed to make a football in his trousers. 'How's Susan?'

'She's fine sir, just fine.' Micklewright's voice was pitched somewhat high.

'Good. Do you know Inspector Van Hoorn?'

'I couldn't say I know him,' answered Micklewright, 'but I know the man by sight and to talk to.'

'He speaks good English, doesn't he?'

'Aye, when he's a mind to.'

'Mick,' Gideon said, 'we had three letters of complaint from Oslo after you'd been over there on the Vigler jewel job, and they're not as touchy as the Dutch.'

'They didna know a thing about jewels, mind.'

'Van Hoorn probably knows more than you about diamonds.'

Micklewright stopped fidgeting and, as a result, seemed to be uncannily still.

'That I take leave to doubt,' he said, precisely.

Gideon grinned. 'Prove how much you know then, and don't rub him up the wrong way. And Mick——'

'Yes, sir?'

'I don't want any more complaints. Lay off the Scotch.'

'I'll behave,' Micklewright said with a rather sad smile. 'Don't worry, sir, don't worry at all.'

But in his way, Gidon did worry, for Micklewright had only recently started to drink much. Irascible at the best of times, never able to suffer fools gladly, some new influence was making him very edgy these days. Domestic affairs? wondered Gideon. He had an attractive wife but she was surely too old to be——

Gideon's train of thought was cut short when one of his telephones rang; the one from the Yard's exchange. The door closed on Micklewright as he lifted the receiver.

'Gideon.'

'Mr. Worby, sir, of Thames.'

'Put him through ... Hello, Warbler,' Gideon used an old nickname without thinking—'haven't heard from you since the Centenary Dinner. How are you?' There followed rather more small talk than usual with Gideon, for this was an old friend, but at last he said: 'What can I do for you?'

Chief Superintendent Worby of Thames Division had a half-jocular manner of talking, as if even when he was serious he wanted to kid whoever was at the other end of the line.

'Ever heard of industrial diamonds, George?'

Gideon's expression hardened but his voice was quite controlled.

'What about them?'

'A little bird tells me Amsterdam is worried about some going astray.'

'I don't know any Dutch bird,' Gideon said, still flat-voiced.

Worby chuckled.

'Tell you what's happened, George. We've a lot of trouble with your land boys, always doing their job for them, and last night we helped them to pick up a local would-be gangster who was terrifying the life out of his girl friend and her new boy friend. The pair took refuge in a boat. The would-be gangster pitched a couple of barrels on to them, hoping to sink the boat. He didn't, lucky for him, or he'd be on a murder charge. But my boys keep their eyes peeled, George, and they went to the scene of the crime this morning. Lodged on a pile of drift-wood they found a water-proof packet. Guess what was in it.'

'Was it big enough for a packet of diamonds?' asked Gideon, and pressed a bell under his desk.

'It was. About two thousand quid's worth, I'd say.'

Hobbs came in.

'Send it up to Waterloo Pier right away,' Gideon said into the telephone. 'We'll have a man waiting to pick it up. Hold on . . . Alec, get Micklewright back, don't

23

let him leave the building. Tell him a packet of industrial diamonds was found in the river this morning and they'll be at the Thames Division station at Waterloo Pier in about half-an-hour's time. He can examine it on his way to see Van Hoorn.'

Hobbs said: 'Yes, at once,' and went out.

'Still there, Warbler?' asked Gideon.

'I've laid that on,' Worby told him. 'The packet will be there in twenty minutes or so. Nice timing, was it, George?'

'Very nice timing,' Gideon approved. 'Thanks. Where do you think the packet came from—one of the barrels?'

'Could have, but it would only be a guess. I've got the barrels in for inspection.'

'Good,' said Gideon, 'I'll call you later.'

That was the very moment when Wanda Pierce, whose daughter had been missing for nearly eighteen hours now, was saying in a weary voice:

'Only three days before her birthday. Oh, what an awful time for anything like this to happen. What an awful time.'

Her husband took her hand gently, very gently.

'She'll come back,' he made himself say. 'She'll come back in time for her birthday. You needn't worry.'

'Of course I worry!' the woman cried, snatching her hand free. 'How do you know she'll come back? How do you know she hasn't been killed? Go on—tell me! How do you *know*?'

24

Chapter Three

ANGUISH

David Pierce felt his wife's fingers biting into his fore-arm, saw the glassy brightness of her eyes—usually a beautiful blue, like Geraldine's. Oh, God, like Geraldine's. She had not slept all night but he had dozed once or twice during that awful waiting, after the police had almost carried him home at the end of the first day's search.

Everything—everything hurt so much.

The dread in her eyes; the tautness at her lips; the pallor of her cheeks; the weight in his chest, as if it were forcing his heart down to his bowels. The sheer physical anguish of it all was almost unbearable; how could fear be so physical, send such pain through his body, his arms, his legs, make him feel sick with nausea? The shrillness of Wanda's voice hurt, too.

'... How do you know she hasn't been killed? Go on—Tell me! How do you *know*?'

He did not know.

He feared what Wanda feared, that their beloved Dina, their only child, had been lured away by some maniac, who——

But he must pretend for Wanda's sake.

'*Tell me!*' Wanda screamed.

'I just feel it in my bones,' said David Pierce, flatly. 'I just don't believe anything has happened to her.'

'Of course it has, she's *dead*. Some devil attacked her and—oh dear God, what's happened to my Dina? What's *happened* to her?' Tears filled the woman's eyes although she had cried so much it seemed there could be no tears left. 'Those little beasts who call

25

themselves her friends shouldn't have let her go off alone. That's the truth—she would have been all right with them. It's *their* fault.' The tears were dried up in sudden fury. 'I'm going to see those mothers, I'm going to tell them it's *their* fault, if they'd brought their children up properly——'

'Wanda, please——'

'I'm going, I tell you! How would they like it if this had happened to their child? Don't try to stop me! I'm going.' She thrust him aside with more strength than he had expected, or known in her before, and sent him staggering. He was so helpless, and she—she looked so like Dina. The same dark hair cut just above the neck, the same slender hips, the same free, swinging movement.

A policeman appeared from the kitchen, where he had been for some time. Big and solid, he blocked the doorway. A cup of tea steamed in his hand.

'Thought you might like a cuppa,' he said affably. 'Don't mind me finding my way about your kitchen, I hope.' He drew the cup back quickly as Wanda Pierce struck at him, and tea slopped into the saucer. 'Take sugar, do you?'

'*Get out of my way!*' screamed Wanda.

'Oh. Sorry, ma'am.' The policeman, round-faced and still affable, drew to one side in the narrow passage, and Wanda pushed past him, rushing towards the front door. She snatched at the handle, as the policeman dropped the saucer. It broke with a noise like a shot, and Wanda swung round, in shocked alarm. The policeman stood there stupidly, cup in hand.

'You clumsy fool!' Wanda cried. 'Look what you've done.' She stood at the closed door, hands clenched and raised. David moved uncertainly towards her, not knowing what to do, hardly recognising his wife of fifteen years. Suddenly, she collapsed against him, sobbing, and in her anguish there was a momentary easement of his own. He led her back to the dining-room and as she passed the policeman, the man winked. He had dropped the saucer deliberately to distract Wanda.

A ring at the front door was almost a relief—and then, suddenly, a cause of tension: this could be *news*. Wanda's body went rigid.

'I'll go,' offered the policeman. A moment later, his voice changed. 'Good morning, doctor!'

Doctor? They had sent for no doctor.

There was a murmur of voices before short, dapper, young-looking Dr. Wade came in, brisk and forth-right.

'Good morning, Mrs. Pierce,' he said as Wanda freed herself and stared at him. He nodded to David. 'I think it's time——'

Wanda cried: 'Is there any news of my daughter?'

'Everything possible is being done to find her,' Dr. Wade said in a matter-of-fact tone. 'She probably ran away in a fit of temper. You know, Mrs. Pierce, you aren't going to be able to help if you don't have some rest.'

'*Rest!* How on earth *can* I rest, when I don't know where Dina is? When I don't know——'

'Mrs. Pierce,' Dr. Wade interrupted sharply, 'when Geraldine gets back she will need your help. If you're in hysterics, you'll only make her feel worse. Now I'm going to give you an injection. You won't feel it, and it won't make you sleep too long. Just hold out your left arm.'

'I—I don't want an injection!'

Dr. Wade looked into David Pierce's eyes and took a small box out of his pocket. David gripped his wife's hand and pushed her left sleeve back above the elbow, and as Wanda stiffened in stubborn resistance, he held her tightly. Wade rubbed a spot on her arm with a piece of cotton wool, pinched the flesh, and put the needle in, all very swiftly.

'I don't want an injection!' repeated Wanda, but she didn't pull herself free.

'You need some tea or coffee with a lot of sugar,' Wade said, briskly. 'And I'll see Geraldine the moment she's found. That's a promise.'

'Promise!' Wanda echoed, stupidly. 'Promise!'

'Hold her!' Dr. Wade said sharply.

David Pierce felt her dead weight fall against his body. Almost at once he saw Mrs. Edmond, a neighbour from across the street, and another woman whose name he did not know just behind her.

'We'll take her upstairs,' said Mrs. Edmond, also matter-of-factly.

'Like me to carry her?' asked the policeman. Without waiting for a reply, he lifted the unconscious woman, and carried her from the room with no apparent effort, followed by the two visitors.

David Pierce watched them disappear up the narrow staircase then turned back to the dining-room and stood by the closed french windows, which opened on to a small garden with a patch of grass bright and trim, some roses, and a bed of multi-coloured antirrhinums, as fine as any he had ever grown. His expression was one of bleak despair. There were movements above his head as the neighbours busied themselves: and Wanda had never had much to do with neighbours, but how lost they would be without them, now.

'You could do with some rest, too,' Dr. Wade told him.

'I'm all right,' muttered Pierce. 'If Wanda's all right, I am.' He broke off, 'I'd better telephone the office, as soon as I can. My—my boss won't like me being late.'

'He won't mind at a time like this, surely.'

'He's—he's a funny chap. I must telephone.' Pierce closed his eyes. 'Doctor—*is* there any news?'

'Not yet, I'm afraid,' Wade said, gently.

'What—what do the police really think?'

'They're doing everything they can to trace her, you can be sure of that.' Wade tried to be reassuring, just as David Pierce had tried to be with Wanda, and his words sounded just as empty. 'Have you a telephone?'

'No. There's one in the High Street, though.'

'Mrs. Edmonds has one,' said Dr. Wade. 'I'm sure she would like you to call from there.'

'Really, Pierce, you know how busy we are,' said Edward Lee, Pierce's employer. 'Yes, of course it's worrying but you don't know that anything's happened to her yet . . . Come in as soon as you can, we must get the Seaborne analysis finished this week . . . I shall expect you to work late, of course . . .'

That was the time when David Carter and Samuel Cottingham were standing in the dock at Greenwich Police Court and Chief Inspector Singleton was giving evidence of arrest.

The magistrate was a very big, very deliberate man.

'And have the accused anything to say?' he asked.

'Not guilty,' Dave Carter said quickly. He was surprisingly small, very wiry-looking and had a suspicion of a hare-lip. 'It was just a lark, sir, that's all.'

'That's right,' said Cottingham, whose hair was as long as a girl's and whose nose was almost as pointed as Cyrano de Bergerac's. 'Not guilty, me lord.'

'What do the police ask for?'

'A remand in custody while inquiries are being

made, sir,' Singleton said.

'Custody?' queried the magistrate.

A youthful, shiny-faced man stood up at the back of the court.

'I'll put up surety, in any reasonable amount, sir,' he announced.

'For both the accused?'

'Yes, sir, if it's not too high.'

In the well of the court, Mary Rose and Tom Argyle-Morris sat close together, almost as frightened as they had been the previous night.

'What do you say about bail?' the magistrate asked Singleton.

'We oppose it, sir, having reason to believe that the two witnesses might be menaced by the accused.' Singleton spoke without any expression or apparent feeling.

'Why that's crazy!' cried Dave Carter. 'It was only a lark, I tell you!'

The magistrate looked at him levelly. 'A very unfortunate lark, I must say. I shall remand you both in custody for eight days.'

Carter caught his breath. Cottingham rubbed his nose. The shiny-faced man muttered, audibly: 'That's persecution, that is.' Quite clearly, Carter said: 'Flicking bastard,' but the magistrate and his clerk pretended not to hear.

Both Mary Rose and Tom looked noticeably relieved as they left the court. Singleton left just after them, satisfied, but preoccupied about the packet of industrial diamonds found in the water at Fiddler's Steps.

Detective Superintendent Micklewright waited as the KLM twin-engined jet taxied towards the entrance to the Customs shed at Heath Row. The

30

Customs men knew him well; it was surprising how often he came here over smuggling and theft investigation. He saw two nice-looking women, a girl and several business men come out, followed by Van Hoorn. The Dutchman had the widest pair of shoulders Micklewright had ever seen on a man; he was only about five feet seven and that made his breadth of shoulder even more noticeable. He carried a small shiny black attaché case.

'Looks like a bloody hangman,' Micklewright muttered under his breath, then beamed and went forward, splay-footed, big hand outstretched, feeling as if Gideon's hand were on his shoulder. 'Good morning, Inspector, very glad to see you again . . . We needn't bother with Customs, we trust all policemen!' He led the way through a side door and out to the front of the terminal building, where his car and driver were waiting.

'You are very kind,' Van Hoorn said stiffly.

'Pleasure, Inspector, pleasure.' Micklewright started to slam the door, saw Van Hoorn's thick fingers on the frame and snatched his hand away. The driver was there to close the door, anyhow. He walked round the back of the car and got in the other side, kicking against Van Hoorn's foot as he sat down. 'Sorry. Have a good flight?'

'It was uneventful,' stated Van Hoorn. His voice was slightly guttural, and yet high-pitched at the same time. 'I studied all the documents, and depositions of the man we caught. I hope you will agree there is much evidence that the stolen jewels do come to England.'

'Wouldn't be at all surprised,' said Micklewright, opening his own battered pigskin brief-case. 'We had a bit of luck last night. Quite fortuitous,' he added slyly, but Van Hoorn gave no sign that the word puzzled him. Micklewright took out the waterproof packet, now unsealed, and held it towards the Dutchman. 'Is this one of the Dutch consignments?'

Van Hoorn's slatey grey eyes shone suddenly with excitement; the expression put life into his face, and he seized the package.

Something outside the car caught Micklewright's eye—an airport policeman, waving. Just beyond this man was a woman and on that instant Micklewright thought it was his wife. His heart seemed to expand, then slowly, very slowly, to shrink. It wasn't Clara; it couldn't be Clara. The woman just happened to have Clara's attractive kind of grey hair with a slightly blue tint, and a black and white check suit, like Clara's; and she had an absurdly small waist—Clara's waist.

She passed.

Micklewright rubbed his sweaty hands together, and stared in the other direction oblivious of the rustling of the polythene bag which Van Hoorn was easing out of its outer waterproof container, and of the curious whistling sound which Van Hoorn made as he took a fold of linen from the bag. He opened this and peered down at the scintillating diamond chips which were fastened to the linen's wash-leather lining by strips of transparent plastic.

'Yes,' he breathed. 'This is one of the missing consignments. The inside packing is exactly the same. You will see.' He opened his case and took out a folded pad exactly like the one found in the Thames. 'There can be no mistake. This is good, very good.' He almost dropped the 'y' in 'very', almost added a 't' after good. 'Where did you find it?'

Micklewright was staring out of the window, Chin thrust forward, eyes narrowed, lips set tightly, his hands spread over his knees like an octopus with its tentacles tightening round a victim. Van Hoorn raised his eyebrows and fell silent. They crawled out of the parking area and were soon on the underpass and out on the main highway. Van Hoorn continued to inspect the diamonds on the two pads, as if trying to see any dissimilarities.

Micklewright turned his head, as if with an effort. 'Er—sorry,' he said. 'You said something.' The weight lifted and he went on in a stronger voice. 'Oh, yes, the industrial sparklers. Is it one of your consignments?'

'I am quite sure that it is,' replied Van Hoorn, patiently. 'This is a big step forward. May I ask you where it was found?'

'A big slice of luck,' Micklewright said, and explained in detail. 'It may have been in one of those barrels but more likely it was dropped or thrown overboard from a ship. No use guessing. We'll cover all the possibilities as soon as we can.' By the time he finished, they were moving fast along the Great West Road. 'I've told the Thames Division to lay on some lunch for us, and we can have a look round from there. And I've told the Port of London Authority chaps to expect us this afternoon sometime. Tell you one thing, though. If the crooks are bringing the stuff in by the river—or taking it out by the river if it comes to that—what price the man you caught who flies between here and Amsterdam so often?'

'It is one of the problems we have to discuss,' Van Hoorn said stiffly. The sympathy he had felt for the Scotland Yard man because of his obvious troubles, dried up. Micklewright had a reputation in Amsterdam, Brussels, Paris—in fact in most of the European capitals—for being far too insular, a difficult man to work with and one who was always trying to score off continental detectives. Now he was virtually telling him, Van Hoorn, that the Dutch police had made a mistake over the suspect who had been arrested in Holland. Van Hoorn geared himself for a difficult time.

Chapter Four

GIDEON WALKS

No one knew about the cave in the old quarry except the man who had discovered it several years before and who had made his home there. To reach it, he had to climb down one shallow side of the quarry and cross ten yards or more of water; this water was several feet deep, except in the middle where an earth fall had made a kind of bridge; even after heavy rain the water there never rose higher than his ankles, and he always wore boots which came halfway up his calves. He had furnished his home gradually, piece by piece, from furniture found on rubbish dumps. In a recess there was an old oilstove, a frying pan, a kettle and a saucepan, and he always kept a bucket of rainwater there. Near the stretch of water opposite the cave was an old shed, once used for tools, but now empty and derelict. Rainwater dripped off the corrugated iron roof into an old drum, from which he refilled his bucket. Very few people ever came near, and when they did, they could not see the cave, which was hidden by a jutting piece of sandstone. Behind this, and across the mouth of the cave he had built a ramshackle wooden wall, with a tiny window and a door which he could bolt from the inside. This gave him a sense of protection and security.

Jonathan Jones—for such was the man's name—

was gearing himself for a difficult time; as Van Hoorn had done. He sat in a rocking chair, lurching gently to and fro, to and fro. On the one narrow bed, in a corner and beneath the hole which served as a window, lay a girl, asleep.

She was a pretty child, with full lips and a snub nose. She had dark, bobbed hair and, even as she lay, her figure appeared more a woman's than a girl's. She had a tiny waist, drawn in tightly, a dark red skirt and a grubby white blouse. She appeared to be sleeping quite naturally.

Now and again Jones shook his head.

Suddenly, he leaned forward and stretched out his right hand, touching the child's ankle; his touch was still light as he ran his hand up and down the calf of her leg. She wore no stockings, and her skin was enticingly soft. He rocked and stroked, rocked and stroked. The chair made a slight creaking noise, the only sound.

His difficulty was to decide what to do with her.

She was nice; very nice.

He hadn't frightened her; not really.

But when she woke she would remember and when she remembered she would want to scream, and if she got away it would not be long before the police arrived.

It was a very, very difficult time. He had to decide what to do, soon. He did not know how long she would sleep, but it would not be for more than two or three hours. That wasn't very much time in which to make such a decision. He did not want to kill her but on the other hand he did not want to be caught by the police. If he were caught he would be sent to prison, and goodness knew what would happen to him there.

It would really be better if the girl did not wake; it would solve so many of his problems.

To and fro, he went: to and fro.

Up and down went his hand over the satiny skin: up and down.

Gideon heard a man laughing.

It was a pleasant laugh, perhaps little more than a chuckle, as if the other were deeply amused, and hearing it, Gideon's pre-occupations faded. He was in St. James's Park, watching the lake, the wild ducks so nearly tame, the masses of flowers, the people sauntering over grass and along the paths. A thicket of bushes hid him from the man, but a few yards further along he saw what was happening. A child of four or five was trying to stand on his head. Up he would go, legs waving wildly, scarlet in the face, supporting himself with his hands; then over he would tumble, only to be up again on the instant game for another try. He wore very short blue shorts and a singlet. The man, wearing a short-sleeved shirt of pale blue, looked spruce and scrubbed. Neither child nor man said a word. The child tried twice again, so intent and so earnest that Gideon also began to smile.

Then as the child thumped down with the inevitable tumble, the man said: 'That's enough, kiddo.' As the boy started again he moved forward, grabbed and swung the lad over his head. Now it was the boy's turn to chuckle. Gideon started to move on; he hadn't been noticed yet, and there was something curiously private and personal about the little scene.

Swinging the child to the ground, however, the man turned and came almost face to face with him. On that instant his expression changed, he lowered his arms quickly but in full control.

Gideon had a shock: for the last time he had seen this man, he had been in the dock in the Old Bailey; it must be seven or eight years ago.

'Hallo, Mr. Miller,' he said. 'Haven't seen you for a long time.'

Miller stared, his face and body tensed; then, very slowly, he relaxed.

'No, we haven't met, have we?'

'Your son?' inquired Gideon.

'You could say so,' Miller replied. There was a curious twist to his lips which puzzled Gideon for a moment; then the penny dropped and he was appalled by his own gaucheness. Miller had served six years at least, and the child could be no more than four or five.

Once again Miller gave that pleasant chuckle.

'Let's say, adopted son,' he said. 'I'll settle for that.'

'Lively youngster,' Gideon observed. 'How long have you been back in London?'

'Six months or so.'

'Everything all right?'

'I've my own little haulage business, thanks to my wife,' said Miller. 'Yes, everything's fine, now.' His eyes filled with laughter and it came to Gideon that he was a happy man. 'How are tricks in your line of business?'

'Too many for my liking,' Gideon said.

'Daddy——' the child began, its patience wilting.

'Okay, kiddo, we'll go and look at the ducks. Good day, Mr. Gideon.' He took the child's hand.

Gideon nodded and passed on, his thoughts carrying him back over the years. Miller had been a cashier for one of the big Joint Stock banks, and had helped thieves to break into a suburban branch where he had once worked. Now he had a haulage business, 'thanks to my wife'. What exactly had that meant?

Gideon, already later than he had intended, stepped out more briskly.

He was due for a conference at Savile Row Police

Station with two divisional men and an insurance broker. There had been a lot of fur robberies in recent months, mostly in Mayfair, and the police had been too long a time without making an arrest. The conference could easily have taken place at the Yard but then three men would have had to travel, and Gideon wasn't under any particular pressure that afternoon, moreover the walk through the park, then past Clarence House, up to St. James's Palace, across Piccadilly and along Bond Street to Savile Row, had attracted him. This was part of his old 'manor', his square mile; seeing it now filled him with nostalgia—in a way, the encounter with Miller had done the same thing.

He turned into Savile Row Police Station five minutes late, at twenty past three. Almost immediately a sergeant accosted him.

'Excuse me, Commander.'

'Yes?'

'You're asked to contact your office at once, sir.'

'Right, thanks,' Gideon said. 'Where's the nearest phone?'

'As a matter of fact, sir, I saw you pass the window, the Yard's on the line now.'

'Thanks.' Gideon glanced keenly at the sergeant, an eager-faced man in his thirties obviously out to make a good impression. Well, he had.

The telephone was in the charge room, and as Gideon lifted the receiver he heard Hobbs' voice. *'Is Mr. Gideon there?'*

'Yes,' Gideon said. 'What's on?'

'Hellier wants to use frogmen to drag the river for the Pierce girl,' Hobbs told him, almost too abruptly. 'Her school satchel was found washed up on the bank near Teddington weir.'

Gideon pondered, his spirits suddenly cast down.

Hobbs would have given authority had he felt it justified; the very fact that he raised the query meant that he was doubtful. And he was right to be doubtful. Once frogmen were used the case would become a major newspaper sensation, and that would tear the hearts out of the parents and could put ideas into the heads of men already teetering on the brink of that half-world of lust and lunacy which made them long sexually for a little girl. If one traced the incidents of this kind of crime, one found that they came in cycles. There might be months without a single one, then a sensational case, and half-a-dozen would follow.

Gideon pulled himself up short; there was no certainty, yet, that a crime had been committed.

'No,' he said. 'Only if Hellier's virtually certain he'll find the body in the river.'

'I'll see to it,' said Hobbs.

Gideon rang off, the sergeant with his eye on the main chance was entering notes in the duty ledger. As Gideon nodded to him and went out, a neatly-dressed, nicely made-up young woman came in, nervousness and anxiety clear on her face.

'Good afternoon, Madam.'

'I'm sorry to trouble you but I *think* someone's broken into my house . . .'

So it went on, day in, day out, crime following crime in a shapeless pattern, playing on human fears and emotions, harassing and harrowing. It had given Gideon his livelihood, he was dedicated to its service; but *why* did it happen with such remorseless, unending regularity?

The two divisional men and the insurance broker were waiting in a smoke-filled office overlooking the street, and a fur salon with a single sable on display was immediately across the road. The broker was Jewish, bright-eyed and alert, with a soft, attractive voice;

the two senior policemen obviously had a great respect for him. They were big men of the same type, difficult to distinguish one from the other.

'Very glad to meet you, Commander ... As I've told these gentlemen, nine out of eleven fur robberies in the West End area in the past three months have been from stores whose insurance goes through my hands. If it happens much more I shan't get any business, everyone will think I'm responsible.'

'Are you?' asked Gideon, with heavy humour.

'No, I am not, and it is no joking matter,' said the insurance broker. 'But as many of the robberies take place when new stocks have just been delivered and in some cases are still in transit, I think it possible that a member of my staff might be involved. What I should like to do, sir, is to have one of your detectives on my staff for a while.'

'A woman?' Gideon asked.

'Oh, a woman, of course.'

'Be much less noticeable,' The Divisional Superintendent remarked. 'But it has to be someone knowledgeable about furs, and we haven't anyone here.'

'I'll see what we can produce at the Yard,' Gideon promised. 'And we'll watch all the shops and the warehouses as new stocks go in and out. What's worrying you in particular, Mr. Morris?'

The broker leaned forward in his chair. 'As a matter of fact, Commander, a very large collection of Russian sable and Russian and Canadian mink is due tomorrow. It's for a special mannequin parade to be held next Monday and Tuesday on the river between Chelsea and Tower Bridge. It's going to be a very big show, Commander.'

'I hadn't heard of it,' Gideon said, suddenly interested.

'It's been widely advertised by word of mouth in

the trade and in society,' said the broker, 'but no one will know where it's to be held until the last minute. The furs will be transferred to the boat from Chelsea pier, I'm told.' Morris was obviously taking this very seriously indeed. 'I am responsible only for the insurance of the furs, but there will also be displays of jewellery, and of course the guests will be very wealthy people. I'm very troubled about it, Commander.'

'Have we been officially notified?' Gideon demanded.

'Not to my knowledge, sir, but I am not the organiser.'

'Who is?'

'Sir Jeremy Pilkington. He's hiring the *River Belle*, I believe, and several other boats besides. The proceeds will be for charity, Sir Jeremy is a very prominent gentleman in organising such affairs. One of the features of this one is the mystery—on the other hand, I feel so strongly that these furs should be *fully* protected that I felt I should tell you—in strict confidence, of course.'

'Yes,' Gideon said. 'We appreciate it. Monday and Tuesday, you say?'

'Yes, in five days' time.'

'We'll keep an eye on things,' Gideon promised, 'and I'll see whom we can find to join your staff for a longer term purpose.'

'I'm very grateful, Commander.'

Gideon left the office just after four o'clock, this time stepping into a car which the Divisional men had laid on. Traffic was so thick that it took him almost as long to reach the Yard as if he had walked. He was very much more thoughtful, quite able to understand why Morris had preferred not to come to the Yard and realising that the implications of the insurance man's story could be very widespread. He turned into his own office and opened the door to Hobbs's.

Hobbs wasn't there.

Gideon went to his own desk and picked up the telephone.

'Get me Mr. Prescott, of AB Division,' he ordered. 'And when I'm finished get Mr. Worby of Thames.' He put down the receiver, then lifted another telephone which was direct to *Information*. A man answered: '*Info*'.

'This is Commander Gideon,' Gideon said heavily. 'Is there any news from Richmond about the missing girl?'

'No, sir, nothing fresh. Mr. Hobbs was just inquiring about it.'

'Is he still with you?'

'Left a minute ago, sir.'

Gideon grunted and rang off as the other telephone rang.

'Mr. Prescott, sir.'

'Good afternoon, Commander.' Prescott was bright, brisk, breezy, a man in his middle fifties who never seemed to grow older.

'Hallo, Lance. Have you had any request for special parking near Chelsea Bridge next week?'

'No? Should I have?'

'I wouldn't be surprised. Has Lex, do you know?'

Lex was the Superintendent in charge of ST Division, which controlled the riverbank on the Surrey side.

'Nothing big, anyhow—I had lunch with him today, and he would have said if there had been.'

'Thanks.' Gideon rang off, pressed the bell for Hobbs, and stood up, going to the window and staring at the shimmering surface of the river. With the huge Shell buildings on the other side, as well as the Festival Hall, the South Bank really had a massive and impressive skyline.

Hobbs came in, almost at once.

'You heard what Sir Jeremy Pilkington's up to?' asked Gideon abruptly.

Hobbs, unexpectedly, gave a quick smile.

'Not lately!'

'Do you know him?'

'Yes. Not well, but I know him.'

'According to some news I picked up——' Gideon broke off, leaned towards the telephone and lifted it, adding: 'Listen to this ... Hallo, Warbler ... Anything from Micklewright and Van Hoorn? ... Well, it can wait... Have you heard of a special river parade due to take place next week? Sir Jeremy Pilkington's said to have hired the *River Belle* and is having a flotilla or something between Chelsea and Tower Bridge? ... Yes, I'll hold on.' Gideon kept the receiver at his ear and spoke to Hobbs. 'I got this from Morris, the insurance chap, he's worried about it. Hello? ... Yes, Warbler ... yes ... let me make sure I have it straight. You've been told that the *River Belle* has been chartered for a special party and that there will be some small boats with her but you haven't been told what it's about. Right... Do the Port of London Authority know any more? ... Find out, will you? ... I'm checking but I think you may have to make special arrangements for those evenings. I'll let you know. Thanks.'

He rang off, hardly aware that he had said so much in few words, and completely unaware of the fact that Hobbs was looking at him with a kind of amused admiration.

'We could be making a fuss about nothing,' he remarked to Hobbs, 'but I don't want to be caught napping. Can you find out unofficially what Pilkington has in mind?'

'Yes,' Hobbs said promptly.

'Good. Things still quiet generally?'

'Fairly quiet,' Hobbs answered. 'It must be summer sloth!' He was beginning to show much more of his human side. 'A nice time for a river trip,' he added drily.

'Now what are you getting at?' Gideon asked.

'You mentioned a week or so ago that you haven't been on the river for a year or more, and suddenly there's a crop of river investigations. It might be a good idea if you had a day on the river tomorrow.' Hobbs was obviously serious.

Slowly, thoughtfully, Gideon remarked: 'Not a bad idea at all. I might do it, if the weather's right.' It passed through his mind that it was a long time since anyone at the Yard had suggested anything *he* should do, it was usually the other way round. Was it really possible that Hobbs was going to share his burden, the very real burden, of the Commander's job?'

It was a funny thought, which made Gideon feel a little rueful, even a little old. But it did not stop him from hoping that it would be a nice day tomorrow.

Chapter Five

NICE DAY

Gideon woke soon after seven o'clock the next morning, to bright sunlight. Kate, his wife, lying next to him, was also beginning to stir; suddenly her eyes opened and stayed open with that half puzzled, half

44

comprehending expression which often comes on the moment of waking. Her eyes, even though her back was to the windows, were very clear, bright blue.

'Good morning, love.'

'Hello, George,' Kate said. 'What's the weather like?'

'Sunny.'

'The television said it would be,' Kate said. She stretched, luxuriously, with a hint of sensuousness, and Gideon was acutely aware of her. Their bodies were close. 'Didn't you say you might go on the river today?'

'Yes.'

'I'm going over to see Pru,' Kate said. 'She might like a day by the river, too.'

'I'll keep an eye open for you.'

'I don't know that I like the idea of the police looking out for me.' Kate gave a little smile which screwed her mouth up in a way which had attracted him for nearly thirty years. Quite suddenly, he kissed her; and for a few moments his arms were very tight around her. It *was* early. Gideon glanced at the window again —then heard a chink of cups at the door, breaking the spell.

'Anyone awake?' It was Malcolm, their youngest son, who was not usually up so early.

Gideon eased himself away from Kate and over on to his back.

'Come in, Malcolm.'

The door turned, the youth entered with the tray balanced precariously on one hand; he was beaming, obviously very pleased with himself. At sixteen, he showed some signs of being as big as his father, but his features were narrower and more like Kate's.

'Just to show you that I *can* wake by myself,' Malcolm said.

'Mal, be *careful*.'

'Pooh, I won't drop it.'

'Where are you going today?' demanded Gideon. 'Not having a day by the river, too, are you?'

'No, worse luck. Victoria and Albert Museum. *Art*,' added Malcolm with a grimace; he was the least artistic of all their children. 'As a matter of fact I've got a game of tennis before school, I'll get my own brekker, Mum.'

'Knew there was some reason for you waking up,' Gideon remarked. His mood was so good that he had almost forgotten that he had been interrupted.

An hour later, bacon and eggs, coffee and toast inside him, he started off to the Yard, choosing to drive along by the Embankment. Traffic was already heavy, and diesel fumes from a petroleum carrier nearly choked him. Through the fumes he could see white smoke billowing majestically from the four chimneys of the Battersea Power Station. The sun, coming across the river but already fairly high, misted the graceful span of the Albert and the more prosaic stretch of Battersea Bridge. There was faint mist over the pleasure gardens, too.

As he passed the lorry he drove faster until, at the new, square Millbank ministry building, he slowed down, affected as always by this view of London, the Houses of Parliament, the Abbey, the wide grandeur of Whitehall beyond Parliament Square. The same man who had taken his car yesterday sprang forward.

'Nice morning, sir. Just right for a day on the river.'

Gideon looked at him sharply but forbore to ask whether the remark was a coincidence, or whether rumour had spread. If Hobbs had told Worby of Thames Division then it might well have leaked out and the whole of the Yard would know it now. It was still very much a village in these days of radio and swift communication. As he turned towards his office, Micklewright appeared.

' 'Morning, Commander.'

' 'Morning. How are things?'

'Going very well, very well indeed,' Micklwright reported. 'Van Hoorn thinks we have a police force after all.' He followed Gideon into his office. 'There isn't much doubt that that package came from a ship fairly recently, although it *could* have been in one of the barrels Carter and his friend pushed down Fiddler's Steps. In which case someone could have been planning to collect it from the barrel. Only certain thing is that it was meant to stay in the water—the water-proofing was perfect. Someone hides packets like it in the water, a colleague on land picks them up. Or *vice versa*.'

Gideon said: 'Yes. It certainly looks like it. Any specific ideas?'

'I've asked the Warbler to let us have a crew to show us all the places where small packets could be hidden easily.'

'H'mm,' Gideon said. 'Going on the river today?'

'Yes. Picked the right day for it, haven't I?'

Gideon frowned. 'I'm not sure you should go, Mick,' he said slowly. Pressing the bell for Hobbs, he watched Micklewright's face, realising that it made no difference at all to the man whether he had his day out or not. Hobbs came in. 'Alec, the Superintendent was planning to go on the river with Van Hoorn today. Van Hoorn's known to Customs, to the P.L.A. people, and to anyone who uses the docks regularly; if they see him on the river they'll know we've special reason to search there and may guess that we've found the packet of diamonds. I think the search should be left to the Thames Division.'

'So do I,' said Hobbs.

Micklewright glanced from one to the other. 'While Van Hoorn and I try the airport and the diamond merchants, as if we haven't a clue?' he suggested.

'That's what I think,' said Gideon.

'You're absolutely right,' said Micklewright. 'Why don't I think the way you do? I'll tell you one thing. This job could be very big.'

'How big?'

'Van Hoorn estimates that the diamonds stolen in the past year are worth considerably more than a hundred thousand pounds.'

'Does he indeed,' said Gideon. 'How long is he staying?'

'As long as it seems worthwhile.'

'Have him come here and see me tomorrow,' Gideon said, adding without pause: 'Might as well make it lunch—you come too, Mick.'

'Be delighted!'

'Any other clues at all?'

'Not yet,' Micklewright said. 'It's early days, though.'

When he had gone out, Gideon pondered for a few minutes. Micklewright's manner was brittle and bright, but even at this hour there was the smell of whisky on his breath. Preoccupation about this was driven from Gideon's mind as two telephones rang at once. Hobbs picked up one, Gideon the other.

'Deputy Commander speaking.'

'This is Gideon.'

'Commander,' Hellier of Richmond said in an uncompromising way, 'there's still no trace of Geraldine Pierce, and I really think it's time we searched the river. I don't want to be stubborn, but we shouldn't leave it too long.'

'Get the Thames Division to start dragging,' Gideon agreed. 'I'll see you some time late this morning and if we have to call the frogmen out, we will then.'

'Right!' Hellier was obviously satisfied. 'Look forward to seeing you, sir. I'll tell you one thing we *did* find while we were looking for the kid.'

'What?'

'Body of a day-old child, strangled and buried in the park,' Hellier said. 'Some poor young bitch got herself in trouble.'

There was no need for any special instruction about the murdered baby. Infanticide by half-demented mothers was not infrequent and, shocking though it was, sympathy for the mother was almost inevitable. Gideon rang off, again momentarily depressed. He told Hobbs what he had done, and in a few seconds was free from depression and looking forward to going on the river.

'Will you have the Superintendent's launch, or a patrol boat?' Hobbs asked.

'A patrol boat on its beat,' Gideon decided. 'Have 'em pick me up at Westminster Pier in half-an-hour.'

'There's one waiting there for you,' said Hobbs.

So the fact that he was going out on the Thames *was* known, and Hobbs and Worby had guessed he would prefer a patrol boat. Gideon made no comment, went through the other cases pending, and then found a coloured postcard from Algiers at the bottom of the pile. He picked it up, thinking: Scott-Marle's on holiday there. It was from Scott-Marle, and almost an unprecedented gesture from the Commissioner. Gideon felt a moment of pleasure, put the card down, and remarked:

'He'll be away for another two weeks.'

'Yes,' said Hobbs.

'Did you see Pilkington?'

'No, he's in Paris,' Hobbs answered. 'But I saw his

wife. He *is* arranging a kind of gala mannequin parade on the river, between five o'clock and eight o'clock next Monday or Tuesday evening. He plans to have floats with top fashion models showing all kinds of clothes, jewellery and furs. It will be quite a sensation.'

'So I imagine,' Gideon grunted. 'What's all the secrecy about? They usually like to get as much publicity as they can for this kind of stunt.'

'They're planning a big campaign in the week-end papers and on television,' answered Hobbs. 'The proceeds are for a World Food Campaign. All the invitations have gone out, and the guests told to look for the time and venue in the newspapers. The press have been invited in strength, of course. No one knows exactly how it will be done, and the secrecy is intended to heighten the effect. It should be very effective, George. Pilkington is the brains behind it, and he's obviously put a lot of effort into the preparations. Some of the best designers, furriers and jewel-merchants will exhibit.'

'If it hadn't been for Morris the first we'd have heard of it would have been Sunday,' grumbled Gideon. 'As it is, we'll have to put all the Divisions with waterfronts on special alert, and warn the City chaps and port of London and the Thames Division. They'll have a major job on their hands. I'll tell Worby when I see him; you see to the rest.'

'I will. What is your feeling about letting our precautions be known?'

Gideon pursed his lips.

'Pity to spoil their surprise—if that's how they want to do it, it's up to them. We needn't talk about it. Just put out a special alert to the Divisions affected. Better cancel all leave except the usual holidays, and arrange for overtime where it might be necessary.'

'I'll have a report ready by morning,' Hobbs promised. 'There is one particular thing, George.'

'Yes?'

'I told Esmeralda—Lady Pilkington—that we took a dim view of the fact that we hadn't been warned, and that the least they could do was to see we have a few complimentary tickets. I thought perhaps you'd like to take Kate, and if Priscilla will accept an elderly escort, I'd be happy to take her.'

Gideon warmed to him in a way he never had before.

'Kate will love it, and if Priscilla hasn't a passionate boy friend at the moment, she will, too.' He glanced at his watch. 'I'd better be off.'

It was only a step to the pier at Westminster Bridge. The patrol boat was waiting with Old Man River Singleton and P.C. Addis standing by, and Sergeant Tidy at the helm. It was the crew which had saved Tom Argyle and his girl, and found the packet of diamonds, although Gideon did not know this; nor did he know that they had all volunteered for this special spell of duty. Stepping over the polished side, he moved to the centre of the boat. It was pleasantly warm in a hazy sun. Two pleasure boats and several river trip launches were hove-to, one of them already loading passengers. A man with a croaking voice kept calling out:

'*Tower Bridge—Pool-a-London—Bloody Tower—London Bridge, all for three bob. Tower Bridge—Pool-a-London—Bloody Tower—London Bridge, all for three bob.*' There was no variation in his tone or expression.

The youngest man in the police crew cast off.

Gideon settled down at the seat in the stern. Old Man River Singleton balanced himself evenly, looking at Gideon. The engine began to growl. They went slowly towards midstream before heading down river. For the first few minutes Gideon forgot practically everything—the coming water parade, the diamond thefts, the missing Pierce child, all the crime that was taking place in London, all those conditions which 'invited' crime, everything but the sensuous pleasure of feeling the sun on his face and the gentle sway of the boat.

Geraldine Pierce also felt the sun on her face. And it fell on the head of the man who now had his back to her. She could not move, for she was tied to the bed; she could not shout, for she was gagged. She lay in a kind of stupor, conscious and terrified and yet numbed.

It was the first time in her life she had felt fear.

It was not fear of a repetition of what had happened soon after the man had brought her here, not fear of being ravished—it was fear of being killed. She did not know what was in his mind, but she was no fool. She read newspapers, and she knew that this man, with his gentle, almost soothing touch and his soft and rather pleasant voice, was frightened of the police.

He had given her milk and bread and butter, some ham and some cheese.

He had cut the cheese with a knife.

He kept the knife close at hand, kept touching it, and turning to look at her.

If only he would take the gag off, she could plead with him.

Wanda Pierce looked at the tall, square block of a man, Superintendent Hellier of the Divisional force which served Richmond division. He towered over her. She did not think of it consciously, but there was something hard and ruthless about him; about his rather small eyes which seldom blinked, the stubby brown eyelashes, even the brickish colour of his skin. His cheek bones were prominent, his jaw very square, even the way his hair grew on his forehead gave a square, symmetrical effect; not at all rounded. He had a harsh penetrating voice.

'So there's no news,' Wanda said, emptily.

'No, none. I'm sorry.' That was almost perfunctory. 'I have given instructions for dragging the river, Mrs. Pierce. If we find anything we will inform you.'

Wanda's heart seemed to become a ball of lead.

'Commander Gideon, the head of the Criminal Investigation Department, is coming to visit the scene in person,' Hellier went on. 'That gives you some idea of the importance we are attaching to this sad affair.'

Sad—*Sad*? Dear God, it was agonising!

'Thank you,' Wanda said stiffly.

The neighbour with her, plump and fluffy Mrs. Edmonds, said almost in despair:

'I'm sure she'll be all right, Wanda dear, I'm *sure* she will be.'

Hellier thought bleakly: She hasn't got a chance. We'll find the body in the river. He did not say this, but something in his manner conveyed that impression. He turned and went out, and as the front door closed he heard the neighbour exclaim:

'What a brute of a man! He shouldn't be in the police.'

The friendly policeman who had shown so much sympathy and understanding, was at the door. He must have heard the comment but made no sign.

Chapter Six

HARD SHELL

Dick Hellier got into his car outside the Pierces'
home. His movements were always brisk but deliberate, almost as if he controlled the reflexes of his body
as he controlled—or tried to control—the reactions of
his mind. He sat back in the car and said to the
driver:

'River.'

'Yes, sir.'

As the car moved off, two reporters drew near and a
photographer leant down and took a photograph
through the car window. Hellier was acutely aware of
the fact that they hadn't approached him closely until
he had settled into the car. They had just watched,
blank-faced, almost sullen. They disliked and resented
him, of course; in a way, they feared him. He knew
that, just as he knew that the way he had talked to
Mrs. Pierce had seemed harsh and unfeeling to her
and her neighbour.

'*What a brute of a man! He shouldn't be in the
police.*'

And Constable Luckley had heard, of course; Luckley probably agreed.

Hellier, son of a Swedish sailor and an English
mother who had been killed in the late stages of the
bombing of London in 1944, did not understand why
he felt as he did at this moment; almost savagely resentful. He had not meant to sound cold and indifferent, he had formed his words carefully so as to create a
different impression, but he had failed. He always
failed in his relationship with people, he thought bit-

terly. There was some quality missing in him.

When he had first heard of this case he had felt furiously angry, and determined at all costs to find both man and girl. Deep down inside him, only half-admitted, there was a special reason.

He knew the child, as he knew the mother; by sight.

Each had a quality which was rare, a quality he knew about vicariously but which he had not experienced personally for nearly twenty years. They had a sexual attractiveness, the kind of attractiveness which made them natural seductresses. He did not think the mother was aware of this quality in herself, and that might mean that she was unaware of it in her daughter. Hellier found it very hard to describe. It was far above anything which made youths turn their heads and whistle. It was not simply the fact that men would notice their slender legs and their slim hips. It was not their faces, attractive and alike though they were, nor their figures. It was something in the way they stood, walked, glanced about them; a kind of regality, an assurance of their own ascendancy.

Nonsense?

Hellier, groping for words as he sat still and outwardly morose in the back of the car, didn't think so.

The girl hadn't quarrelled with her three school friends. Why then, had she left them early? Why had she taken the long way home, by the river? Because thought Hellier, she had known that along the river she would find youths and young men loitering and would revel in the effect she had on them. He suspected that the other girls had let her go alone because they knew that she would attract all the attention.

They, and their mothers, had virtually told him as much when he had questioned them.

And so Geraldine had gone off on her own.

And someone——

Some brute of a man!

Hellier drew in a sharp, hissing breath.

For a reason he could not understand, the thought and the momentary hurt drew him out of this mood of introspection and he became what he appeared to be to most people who knew him; a calculating machine, weighing up facts and drawing conclusions. He had one invaluable asset as a detective—a memory for names and faces, as well as for details of everyone he knew. He was a kind of walking records office where this Division was concerned.

An instance of his gift came at that moment, when a black Jaguar swept round a corner leading from the river. At the wheel was an austere, very handsome woman; Hellier, although he did not know her, recognised her immediately as a Mrs. Tollifer, from Rivers Meet. She and her husband lived in some style in a house with grounds which ran down to the river. Tollifer, a stockbroker, was reputed to be several times a millionaire, a big, genial, fleshy man. His wife appeared as cold as he, Hellier, was thought to be. For the first time Hellier wondered whether she was as frigid as she looked on the surface.

On the next corner, a milk dray was parked, safely tucked in but seemingly deserted; milk, cream, eggs and orange drink bathed in the afternoon sun. The milkman was Constantin Duros, a remarkable name for a milkman; he was a Greek, with a roving eye and a caressing voice and an indisputable attraction for his housewife customers. It was not unusual for this dray to be parked for half an hour or more, while Constantin Duros was nowhere to be seen.

'Don't know how he does it,' Hellier's chief assistant had a habit of saying. 'Three times a day sometimes and he must be over fifty!'

Coming along the street on his bicycle was 'Daddy' Paterson, the postman, also in his fifties, with iron grey hair, iron grey eyes, a stalwart of the local council, a man who never wasted a word, was involved with nearly every do-gooding organisation in the district, and who had never looked at any woman since his wife had died seven years previously.

Hellier could place and catalogue an incredible number of people in his manor, their weaknesses, their idiosyncrasies, their likes and dislikes, even their potential for good or bad. This served him in remarkable stead in his job, which was in some ways the best organised division in the Metropolitan area, with a much higher ratio of solved cases than in most. This part of Richmond, of course, did not lend itself to much professional crime, but there was some: and pocket-picking, shop-lifting and car stealing was as rife here as in most Greater London areas.

He reached the pier at Barnes, where Gideon would come ashore, ten minutes before Gideon's patrol boat arrived. Several reporters had wind of who was coming, and stood close by. So did the Thames Division men, with whom Hellier worked closely. They got along well enough, for Hellier's efficiency was respected by everyone and personalities counted for very little. He stood talking to the Chief Inspector in charge of Barnes as the boat came chugging round the wide bend in the river.

Someone said: 'There's Gideon—standing up.'

The big man seemed to dominate not only the boat but the smooth expanse of river. In the other direction three patrol boats were dragging, systematically, and crowds lined the banks to watch. Several pleasure boats were moored close inshore, crowded with passengers watching this search for the body of a child.

'Lot of ghouls,' stated Old Man River Singleton, roundly. 'I'd send the blighters packing if I had my way.'

Gideon, standing while the other man now sat, nodded and said tritely: 'Takes all sorts.'

Gideon watched as the patrol boats gently moved, all going up river, all with the drags out. Unless it were weighted down, a body would float and be caught. Usually, he knew, it was possible to recognise that it *was* a body, but sometimes it floated too far beneath the surface for there to be any indication. There was a matter-of-fact air about all the men involved, those on the banks as well as those in the boats.

This one drew alongside with hardly a jolt. Gideon climbed out, the Thames man, Chief Inspector Bill Bell, shook hands.

'Glad to see you here, Commander.'

'Haven't seen you for years,' Gideon remarked, and was slightly vexed with himself; everything he said today seemed trite. It wasn't exactly an inspection, but even the river men, with their reefer jackets and curious air of informality, were on their best behaviour. 'Any sign of the child?'

'No, sir.' Bell looked like a sailor, even to the faraway expression in his eyes.

Gideon saw Hellier, who was standing on one side, nodded, but didn't go towards him at first. Bill Bell, a little self-conscious, glanced up river, and his expresson changed.

'They've got something!' he exclaimed.

Every man on the pier and in the boats, every newspaper man, everyone in sight, spun round and stared at the middle one of the three boats which were dragging. One man was standing up with the hitching pole ready: something heavy was caught in the drag.

The man with the hitching pole leaned forward and pulled gently. A camera clicked. Gideon took a swift look round and noticed Hellier's set profile, the thrust-forward chin, the obvious tension in his body.

Someone on the bank cried:

'They've got her!'

A woman turned away from a little group and scurried off, mounted a bicycle and raced along the path. Everyone in the pleasure boats craned their necks, a dozen cameras pointed at the swirl of water around the drag. Another police boat drew nearer. A man close to the rail of one pleasure boat suddenly retched and was sick. Gideon, forcing himself to study the policemen near him, read compassion and sadness in Singleton, a tight-lipped distaste in Sergeant Tidy, matter-of-factness in most of the others. Young Addis, the youngest member of the crew of his boat, said *sotto voce*:

'I'll never learn to like it.'

Hellier stood like a rock; a man *made* of rock. Heartless? Gideon did not know him well, and liked little of what he did know, his main interest being in the fact that Hellier was one of the best detectives in the Force.

Someone cried shrilly: 'It's only a dog!'

One of the men on the nearer boat nodded his head and relaxed. In a few moments the body of a big dog appeared clearly above the water. Orders were shouted, and one man called: 'Bring it in.' Someone gave a high-pitched laugh; a siren blasted, a bicycle bell tinkled.

'Anyone would think it was something to celebrate,' grunted Singleton. 'Haven't found the kid yet, then.'

Gideon said to Hellier: 'Do you still want those frogmen?'

Hellier turned, and seemed startled, as if he had been shaken out of a coma.

'Er—yes. Yes, sir. If you please.'

Gideon turned to Singleton. 'Will you fix the frog-man team, Superintendent? Get them here as soon as possible.'

'Right, sir.'

'I'll have a look round here and come to your office when I'm through,' Gideon said to Hellier.

'Very good, sir.' The answer was almost mechanical. Hellier half-turned, and then added. 'Thank you, sir. About the frogman team.'

'Fixed,' Gideon said.

Singleton came off a telephone.

'They'll be on the way in five minutes,' he declared.

While Gideon was looking over the Barnes sub-station of the Thames Division and Hellier was going through all the reports which had come in that day from the parks, the river banks, the neighbours and the school friends of the missing child, Geraldine her-self was lying on her back and looking into the eyes of the man who sat rocking to and fro. The knife was no longer near him. He had given her some more milk and some biscuits. The scarf with which he had gag-ged her was in his hands, stretched taut. She managed to smile—a smile which seemed almost trouble-free.

'Please don't gag me again,' she said. 'I won't shout, I promise.'

He gave her his slow, rather vacant smile.

He was thinking: 'I couldn't use the knife, I couldn't stand the blood.' Almost immediately he thought: 'If I put this round her neck she couldn't talk and there wouldn't be any blood.'

She wondered what was really passing through his mind, as she said again:

'*Please* don't gag me. I *promise* I won't shout.'

But she would, of course, she would. He had no doubt. He would have to kill her and throw her body into the river, after dark. That was how he had disposed of her satchel, and it hadn't been traced to him. Her body wouldn't be, either.

At that precise moment the woman who had cycled away from the scene when the drag had caught something without knowing that it was a dog, turned into the street where the Pierces lived. She pulled up outside their house, rang the bell, and as Mrs. Edmonds opened the door, she gasped:

'They've found the body! I saw them with my own eyes! They've found her!'

Wanda Pierce, in the kitchen of her neighbour's house, heard every word.

Chapter Seven

CONSPIRACY

Hellier, obviously determined not to overdo the deference, did not come out of his office to greet Gideon but simply stood up from his desk. It was a larger office than most, with a big pedestal desk looking disproportionately large because it was empty but for four trays, two with a few papers in them, and two telephones. Behind Hellier was a map of his district, on the right-hand wall a map of the Metropolitan Police Area, on the left a map of the Thames Division along its whole length.

Everything here was so clean it looked new; even

the maps.

'Please sit down, Commander.' Hellier's manner as well as his movements were stiff.

Gideon sat down. There was still nothing he liked about the man's manner, but he had learned from the Thames Divisional sub-station how completely Hellier was known to be on top of this job, and he was thoughtful about the signs of tension in the man which he had seen at the riverside.

'What makes you so sure the girl's in the river?' he asked.

'I'm not absolutely sure, sir. I would think it's a ten-to-one on chance.'

'Any particular reasons?' asked Gideon.

'Her satchel was found in the mud on the bank. She was seen going towards the river. She was known to walk along the towpath, often alone, as it was only a slight detour on the way between her home and school. I've just had confirmation that her footprints have been found on a muddy patch, up to a place called the love nest.' Hellier was too earnest to say this lightly. 'That's a patch of shrubs frequently visited by courting couples.'

'Any sign of her having been *in* the love nest?'

'No sir. But it's on a rise in the ground and it's bone hard there. We wouldn't see prints.'

'Combed it?'

'Inside out. Would you care to see what I have done, sir?'

'Yes.'

Hellier rose from his seat and crossed to the Divisional map. Beneath it was a narrow shelf from which he picked up narrow strips of metal in many colours. He placed one after another on to the map and each stayed put; obviously they were magnetised.

'I've four groups working, as you know, sir. The

blue strips represent men covering the river area in conjunction with Thames Division.' He placed the blue strips into position. 'Red is for my men who have interrogated the neighbours . . . green is for the men who have been and are searching all the parks, including Richmond Park . . . yellow is for the men who are working on the schools. If you will watch closely, sir . . . The areas shaded in pencil have already been covered once . . . The dead infant was found here.' He put a black cross above a green strip. 'The girl was last seen here . . .' As he went on Gideon was more and more impressed by his complete grasp and his computer-like mind. 'I have personally questioned seven men whom I believe to be capable of waylaying and raping the girl.'

'How did you get on to them?' asked Gideon.

'Three have records of interfering with minors, two are suspect—they're known to hang about near the river and in the parks when the girls' schools are playing there, two were seen by all four girls when they were playing tennis. One is the local tuck-barrow man, I've had him watched for some time. He does a lot of hand-holding and head-patting several parents have complained. I don't know of anyone else who can be considered an obvious suspect. I've a fairly complete list of men living alone—there are several in caravans near the river and on waste land, and a great many living alone in one room. One can find this out by studying the electoral register, sir—when there's only one person of the same name at any address, I have them checked. Comes in useful when co-operating with the Welfare Officer. All these are being visited in turn, sir, and I should have the last one questioned by nightfall. I've a hundred men on this operation, thanks to help from the Yard.'

Gideon thought: All this, although he's convinced

the girl's in the river. He searched for a way of saying he was impressed without being patronising when he heard a shout from outside, footsteps, a stentorian bellow of:

'Come back!'

More footsteps thundered, from stairs to landing, as Hellier moved swiftly towards the door. As he reached it, it burst open and he had to dodge aside to avoid its full weight. A wild-eyed man rushed in, grabbed Hellier by the lapels and began to shake him furiously.

'Where is she? Why didn't you tell *me* first? Why, you swine——'

Hellier could have crushed this man of lean build and medium height, but he backed away under the onslaught, while the man went on shouting and a plainclothes man, and another in uniform hovered unhappily in the doorway.

Suddenly, Hellier said sharply:

'We haven't found your daughter, Pierce. Stop this nonsense.' The violence seemed to be cut off, and Hellier shrugged himself free. 'Who told you we had?' he asked.

'Someone——' Pierce half choked on the words—''someone said you'd pulled her out of the river.'

'Then they were mistaken.'

Pierce backed away. Hellier waved briskly to the men in the doorway and they closed the door without a word. Gideon moved quickly, thinking that Pierce might collapse; the colour drained from his face and he swayed, his eyes feverishly bright.

'But—she said she was there. She said she *saw* her.'

'We found something but not your daughter,' Hellier said. 'If there had been any other discovery I would have been told by radio telephone.' He moved stiffly to his desk, opened a cupboard and took out a bottle of whisky and a glass. He poured out a finger and gave it to Pierce, who stared at it vaguely, then suddenly raised it to his lips and tossed it down.

'For you sir?' Hellier asked Gideon.

'No, thanks.'

Pierce muttered: 'I thought my wife would kill herself. I really did. I—I rushed from the office when—when I heard Mrs. Edmonds telephoned me, she said —she said the other woman had *seen* Geraldine's body. Why did she lie?' His voice rose. '*Why did she lie?*'

Gideon laid a reassuring hand on his shoulder. 'It was a mistake, Mr. Pierce. Something was caught in the grab, and a lot of people thought it was your daughter. I'm very glad it wasn't.'

'Isn't there—isn't there *any* news?' Pierce was suddenly terribly pathetic.

'No,' Hellier said. 'None at all.'

'Not yet,' Gideon tried to soften the blow. 'I'm from Scotland Yard, Mr. Pierce, and in a life-time of experience I have never known a search for a missing person handled so swiftly or so thoroughly. The river is being searched as a precaution; every other possibility is being explored, including the possibility that your daughter has been abducted.' After a brief pause to allow Pierce to speak if he chose to, Gideon went on: 'All the Metropolitan Police and all the police of neighbouring counties are co-operating. I assure you truly that *everything* is being done.'

Pierce muttered: 'Oh, Oh, I see. Thank—thank you.' He closed his eyes and pressed the tips of his fingers against his forehead. 'Could you—could you say that to my wife? She doesn't——'

Hellier said awkwardly: 'Commander Gideon has to go back to Scotland Yard.'

Gideon said quickly: 'I can go via Mr. Pierce's house, if you think it will help.'

65

'Oh, if only you will!' Pierce looked pathetically grateful. 'My wife seems—seems to think that no one cares. Could you——' he hesitated, gulped, and went on hurriedly: 'Could you drop me at my office? I really ought—ought to get back.'

Startled, Gideon said: 'Must you go back to the office at a time like this?'

'It's—it's stocktaking time,' said Pierce, miserably, 'and Mr. Lee has cut up rough already. I'm the chief clerk, you see.'

Gideon began: 'Does he know——' and then he broke off. Obviously Pierce's employer must know, and there was no point in exacerbating the situation.

Hellier rang down for a car, and ten minutes later Gideon dropped Pierce off at a small block of offices near the Green, and was then driven round to Mrs. Pierce. It was a strange case for him to become involved in, but when he saw the woman he was glad that he had taken the trouble. She still had neighbours with her, and was nearly prostrate when he arrived; but the knowledge that it had been a false alarm, that her daughter might still be alive, put a thin flicker of fresh hope back into her.

Gideon was driven back through the summer beauty of Richmond Park, the trees heavy with leaf, here and there the scent of new mown grass. Soon he was back on the river, being taken slowly past the meadows, seeing the sweeping arches of the bridge, feeling an acute sense of nostalgia as he was reminded of the days of his youth when he had courted Kate along these very banks.

It was so peaceful and quiet ... as if fear and violence belonged to a different world.

Fear and violence made up the world of Thomas Argyle-Morris.

When Carter and Cottingham had been remanded in custody he had felt at least that he had a breathing space. Now, he did not.

He was followed everywhere he went.

He knew the men; he knew their viciousness; he knew there was no cruelty of which they were not capable. He did not really know why they were after him, unless it was that they were friends of Carter.

Carter was bad enough; there was no doubt that Carter would gladly have drowned him and Mary Rose. He was vicious in his jealousy; when a girl was 'his' she was his absolutely until he had finished with her. To this day, Argyle-Morris could not understand what had persuaded him to kiss Mary Rose; but that was over and done with. Dave Carter was the leader of the Cockles, and the Cockles were a small-time gang in the protection racket.

The men who were following Argyle-Morris belonged to a bigger and more powerful gang—a deadly gang. He knew of their existence, knew that Dave Carter sometimes worked for them, but he could not understand why they were so interested in Dave's love life.

Even in his fear, Argyle-Morris knew that this did not make sense.

But Screw Smith made sense.

Screw was a nickname which had grown up with Smith since, at the age of nine, he had seen a thumb-screw in a museum and had started to practise with a clamp on smaller or weaker children. By the time he was eleven, he had won his nickname.

Now, Smith could make anyone talk, simply by showing them the thumbscrew he had himself manufactured out of odd pieces of metal.

Why was he after him, Tom Argyle-Morris? *He* didn't know anything.

67

Argyle-Morris was sweating.

He was a shipping clerk who lived in one of the new blocks of council flats near Wapping High Street, with his mother and three sisters. He had a room of his own and he paid his mother three pounds a week for food and board, whether in a job or out—he preferred temporary posts, and made as much money as he needed by judicious smuggling and the selling of contraband. He spent very little time with the family. Now, in dread, he turned a corner and looked up at the flats. Each had a small balcony. Washing was blowing from some of them, while two women were talking on another. Above his own window, hanging geraniums trailed their vivid scarlet against the yellow brick wall.

He glanced round.

Screw Smith was fifty yards away, a little, carroty-haired man with very thin features and a pointed nose; a man whose cruelty showed in the twist of thin lips and the glitter in small, green eyes. Behind him was big, heavy Captain Kenway of the Salvation Army, the man in charge of the Army Canteen and refuge, who made a habit of going to see men whom the hostel had once housed; he was a one-man Auxiliary Probationer Service. He strode past Smith and glanced down.

Smith pretended not to notice him.

Argyle-Morris crossed the road, hearing Captain Kenway's footsteps close behind him, feeling a kind of security in the shadow of the big man, who drew level on the far pavement.

'Hallo, Tom,' he said. 'Everything all right with you?'

'Sure. Sure, everything's fine.' Argyle-Morris wiped the sweat off his forehead.

'Is your father back yet?'

'No, he won't be back much before October.'

'That will be five months at sea—that's a long trip.'

'He likes long trips.'

'I know, I know,' said Kenway. He was flabby and pale-faced and his lips as well as his hands were a little moist, but the expression in his eyes was very shrewd. 'What's worrying you, Tom?'

'Nothing's worrying me!'

'If Dave Carter's boys are after you——'

'They're not after me, no one's after me!' If Smith saw him talking to the Army man it would get round that he was asking the Army for help, and they would skin him for that. He quickened his pace and almost ran into the big building. A lift was standing open. He pressed the fourth-floor button as a girl from a flat beneath his came running. The lift door nearly trapped her. Belatedly, Argyle-Morris held it back.

'Okay?'

She looked at him thoughtfully as the lift stopped at the third floor. He wiped the sweat off his forehead again and gulped as it went up to his floor. The door opened. The front door of his flat, nearly opposite, was closed. He opened it with a key and slipped inside.

He heard a quick movement—and Mary Rose appeared by the living-room door.

'You've got to save me,' she gasped. 'You've got to!'

'What—what the hell do you mean?' he muttered. 'What's up?'

'They're after me.' She could hardly get the words out.

'Don't be crazy, they're in clink.'

'Not—not *them*, I don't mean *them*.'

'Then who the hell *do* you mean?'

'Screw's lot!' she gasped. 'Screw Smith's!'

Argyle-Morris clenched his teeth to try to stop them

from chattering.

'You've got to tell them I don't know anything!' she went on fearfully. 'You've got to make them believe you.'

Feeling physically sick, he said. 'You're crazy! No one's after you.'

'You're lying to me. Screw's after you too, I *saw* him. He's down in the street now. You've got to tell him that I don't know anything.' She grabbed his arm and half-dragged him into the living-room which was dominated by a huge television set in one corner. 'Look down there!' she cried. 'Is he there or isn't he?'

Tom Argyle-Morris peered down from the window. Screw Smith was crossing the road and looking up, as if he knew they were staring down. Mary Rose clutched Tom's arm tightly, and was gasping for breath, while he could hardly breathe, he was so frightened.

Smith reached the near pavement and then disappeared, beneath them.

'He's coming here,' Mary Rose gasped. 'I've got to get away—I've got to!'

A man from the doorway said very softly:

'Not until we want you to, doll.'

Chapter Eight

THE WAREHOUSE

Mary Rose and Tom swung round.

A stranger to both of them moved forward, tossing a key into the air and letting it fall; it struck the floor sharply, brassily.

70

'I won't need that again,' he said.

Mary Rose's fingers bit so deeply into Tom's arm that they seemed to burn. Her body was tight against his, too, as if she wanted to sink into him and so hide herself from this man with the sneering voice.

Tom muttered: 'Where—where'd you get that key?'

'From your kid sister,' the man answered. 'I took it out of her handbag in the Supermarket—she's out shopping with her ma.' The sneer was even more pronounced.

'Don't, don't let him hurt me,' Mary Rose pleaded. 'Don't let him hurt me.'

'No one's going to hurt you,' the man said, 'unless it's Screw Smith.'

She gave an agonised squeal.

'No, no, no, *no*!'

'Nice fingers and thumbs you've got, doll. Remember that.' He glanced round and went on: 'Okay, Screw, they're ready for you, all nice and ripe.'

Screw Smith came into the room.

At close quarters he was vicious and cruel-looking; it was hard to believe that anyone could like him. He needed a shave and he needed a haircut, and when he raised his hands they showed up grimy, with blackened, broken fingernails.

'You talked to them?' he asked.

'I just told them the facts of life.'

Tom moistened his lips and muttered: 'I don't know what you want, I don't know anything.'

'I don't either. I swear I don't!' cried Mary Rose.

'Tom, you're coming along with us,' Smith said. 'We want a little talk.'

'But I don't——'

'Shut up,' Smith ordered. 'You're coming.'

'I'll call the cops! I'm not coming with you—I'll

71

As he spoke, both men moved with bewildering speed, the stranger gripping Mary Rose's arm and wrenching it free, Smith kicking Tom savagely in the groin. Tom doubled over, clutching his stomach, and staggered about the little room. The stranger pulled Mary Rose to the table, dumped her into a chair, and forced her to lean back. Screw moved to her side and took her right arm, bare to the elbow. He stretched it across the table, hand palm downwards, and with his free hand took out the little instrument for which he was so notorious.

Mary Rose began to sob.

'I didn't know what I was doing, Screw, I swear I didn't. I got scared when he started kissing me, I thought you'd think it was my fault. But it wasn't, I swear it wasn't.'

Slowly, Tom Argyle-Morris straightened up, his face grey with pain and terror. Yet there was shock in his expression, as if he could hardly believe the girl would say such things—would try to blame him, alone.

Smith said: 'Okay, Tom. You come with us quietly, or the girl gets a squeeze from this. She likes being squeezed. If she wasn't a lying bitch you wouldn't be in this situation—*would you?*'

'Oh, God. No, no, no,' moaned Mary Rose. 'It wasn't my fault, *it wasn't my fault.*'

'Here's one squeeze she doesn't seem to want,' Smith said. He spoke in a flat, emotionless voice, as he took her soft, white thumb between his thumb and forefinger; and the other man held her arm firmly on the table. She had nice hands, well-kept, and with beautifully shaped nails. 'Coming with us Tom, old man? If you do, okay, Mary Rose can go and get herself cuddled by some other poor mutt.'

'Tom,' moaned Mary Rose. 'Don't let them hurt me. You know it was your fault, you know it was.'

Tom Argyle-Morris stared at her, gulped, then looked at Smith and muttered: 'How do I know you won't hurt her if I come?'

'We won't need to, because you're going to tell us all we want to know.'

Tom moistened his lips again. He didn't really blame Mary Rose but he felt she had let him down. He still felt the physical nausea from the kick, and it was worsened by a nausea of fear of what they would do to him. But if he didn't go with them then they would get to work on her, and he couldn't stand by and see them hurt a woman.

He said thinly: 'I don't know a thing, but—but I'll come.'

The stranger loosened his grip on Mary Rose's arm. Smith released her hand. She sat there, pale-faced, her eyes rounded into saucers, her fear despoiling her prettiness.

'Don't hurt him,' she said weakly. 'He didn't mean any harm.'

'Okay,' Smith said. 'Let's go.'

As they got into a black Ford Anglia parked outside the block of flats, Captain Kenway noticed them, noticed Argyle-Morris's pallor, and wondered uneasily what was going on. A quarter of an hour later he passed the flats again and this time saw Mary Rose come out, freshly made-up, her walk jaunty, her hips swaying provocatively. Captain Kenway stopped her.

'Mary Rose, is everything all right with Tom?'

She looked pertly into his flabby face.

' 'Course it is, why shouldn't it be?' she answered. 'Excuse *me*, I haven't got time to stand here talking to *you*.'

Tom Argyle-Morris sat in the back of the Ford Anglia, with Screw Smith; the other man drove along Wapping High Street, past the huge high warehouses with their drab-painted doors, past the Headquarters of the Thames Division Police, tyres grumbling over the cobbles. Soon they were going faster in a more open area; here more people were about, nice-looking girls, some wheeling prams, older women, a few old men with nothing to do, truck drivers, groups of men from the docks, capped and mufflered. Huge lorries lumbered past and towered over them, exhaust fumes, acrid, stifling, seeping into the car.

'Where are we going?' muttered Tom at last.

'You'll find out.'

Ten minutes later they turned into the No. 2 Gate of the West India Docks. A Port of London Authority policeman stopped them, and Tom bit his lips and looked away.

'We're crew from the *Sugar Queen*,' the stranger said.

'Got anything with you?'

'Nothing we didn't take out.'

The policeman stared ruminatively, then waved a hand towards Tom.

'What's the matter with him?'

'He drank too much bad liquor, and he's paying for it,' the driver said.

The policeman let them pass.

They drove along Poplar Docks, over the bumpy railway lines, past Blackwall Basin. Now and again through gaps in the big sheds they saw sugar freighters and banana boats, now and again they glimpsed the huge new buildings of the Granary and the Flour Company's mills. There was a lot of traffic, and no one took any notice of them. Cranes were being worked, and there was a constant clatter of noise from pneumatic drills used in the erection of new warehouses and new sheds. They slowed down near a small, green ship and Tom read the name: *Sugar Queen*.

Were they really going to take him on board?

The ship was being unloaded, two gangs were busy by the big open hatches, and the smell of fruit was strong, almost heady. Nearby were two big sheds, one with a hole gaping in the roof, another half-demolished by bulldozers and excavating machines. The noise was ear-shattering. The stranger swung the car into a side road between the two derelict buildings, then pulled in behind the one with the hole in the roof. On this side it seemed to be in fair condition.

'Out,' Smith ordered.

Tom climbed out cautiously, still feeling shaky and slightly nauseated. Smith climbed after him, then caught hold of his arm and pushed him across the broken ground where weeds grew tall and grass was the only softness, into a doorway.

The driver revved his engine and drove off.

'Don't run,' Smith ordered.

He kept his hand firmly on Tom's arm and led him across the big shed; which stank with rotting fruit which had been tossed there when sacks or crates were accidentally broken. It was nearly dark. Over in one corner was a huge pile of disused hogsheads, once used for bulk sugar, now replaced by metal containers. A gap had been cleared in this pile and Smith gave Tom a shove towards it.

'Keep going,' he ordered.

There was hardly any light; only gloom and the stench and the noise. *Noise.* Tom kept shivering. *Noise.* Wherever Screw Smith worked there had to be noise to drown the sound of screaming.

Tom was sweating.

Then he stepped into an office, hidden by the hogsheads, clean and tidy, the walls lined with hardboard which kept some of the noise out. There was less stench in here, too, what there was being partially masked by the aroma of cigar smoke. High in an outer wall a closed window let in some of the light from outside. Lower down on the same wall were two strip lights, beneath which sat another man whom Tom Argyle-Morris had never seen before.

'We got him,' Screw Smith announced with proud satisfaction.

The other man, big and massive, took a cigar out of his mouth, and spoke with a hard, guttural voice.

'Now all you've got to do is make him talk.'

Tom gasped: 'I don't know anything, I swear I don't!'

The big man said flatly: 'You stole a packet of industrial diamonds which was floating on the river near Fiddler's Steps, the night you and your girl ran away from Dave Carter. I want to know what you did with it.'

Tom almost screamed: 'It's a lie! I didn't know there was anything there! I don't know anything about any diamonds. You've got to believe me!'

The driver of the Anglia came in, walked straight to Tom, put a lock on his arm, then held the arm out towards Screw Smith.

In the exercise yard at Brixton Jail, Dave Carter said to Cottingham:

'They've just about started on Tom-Tom, now.'

'You fixed him all right,' congratulated Cottingham. 'If they think he pinched those sparklers———'

'*Think?* They know, I made sure of that,' Carter said, grinning. 'Better they think *he* did, than me. If they hadn't gone down Fiddler's Steps I wouldn't even have known there was a racket going on.'

'But you do now,' Cottingham said. 'I'll bet you turn the screw on when you get out of here.'

'Don't make any mistake, I will,' Carter asserted.

A warder drew near, disapprovingly, and they stopped talking.

Sydney Roswell was the Chief Superintendent of the North-East Division of the Metropolitan Police, the Division which covered the land area coinciding with that section of the Thames patrolled by the crews based on Headquarters in Wapping High Street. He was an elderly man, with a deep and exhaustive knowledge of his district, of the people in it, of the crimes which were carried on within its boundaries. He was also a deeply religious man who, when off duty, served a Methodist Church and the clubs associated with it, and also worked with other Christian groups in this rough and often brutal part of London.

The telephone on his desk rang, about the time that Tom Argyle-Morris was pushed into the secret 'office' at Millwall Docks.

'Hello?'

'Captain Kenway of the Salvation Army is on the line, sir.'

'I'll speak to him,' said Roswell at once. 'Hallo, Percy, I promised to ring you about the inter-denominational meeting, but——'

'I'm not calling about that,' said Kenway. 'I'm worried about a youth named Argyle-Morris, Thomas Argyle-Morris. Do you know him?'

Roswell sat up, startled.

'Yes. What about him?'

'I met him this afternoon and he was obviously badly worried. Frightened, I would say. And he was with Screw Smith. I'm sure you know who I mean, don't you?'

'I certainly do know whom you mean,' agreed Roswell grimly. 'Tell me just what happened, will you, Percy?'

As he spoke, Roswell opened a folder on his desk, marked: *Diamond Smuggling—C. Supt. Micklewright*, and as the Salvation Army man recited what he knew, Roswell took notes in his own brand of shorthand.

Gideon had been back in his office for only ten minutes when his telephone rang. He felt pleasantly tired and relaxed, reassured by the thoroughness with which Hellier was working. It had been a smooth and wholly uneventful voyage back, with the sun behind his left shoulder most of the way and shining with striking effect on all the riverside buildings, old and new. He had stepped off by Westminster Bridge, as Big Ben struck five, and walked across to the Yard.

Now, picking up the receiver, he heard the operator say: 'Sorry to keep you sir. Mr. Roswell of North-East is calling.'

'I'll talk to him,' Gideon said. He was almost glad to have something to take his mind off the memory of Pierce and his wife and the grief which they shared. 'Hallo, Syd, what's on?'

'I would have talked to Micklewright but I can't get hold of him,' Roswell said apologetically. 'Remember Argyle-Morris, the youth who——'

'I remember,' Gideon interrupted.

'Screw Smith seems to be having a session with him,' announced Roswell.

Gideon said sharply: 'Is he b'God! Do you know where?'

'Afraid not,' said Roswell, as Gideon lifted the other telephone and dialled *Information*. 'He was driven off in a black Ford Anglia . . .' He told Gideon all that he knew.

78

Soon, Gideon was saying to *Information*:

'Put out a call for Screw Smith and Thomas Argyle-Morris. I want to know where they are and where they've been. Send it to Thames Headquarters and the Port of London Police, ask Customs and the City Police to keep an eye open, too. And tell Mr. Mickle-wright I want a word with him.' He rang off, made a few notes for Hobbs, then stood up and stared out at the river which was so much part of his life.

He could picture the beauty near Richmond.

He could picture the squalor in parts of the East End.

He could picture the curious way the water had risen, like a molten mound, over the corpse of a dog thought momentarily to be a child.

In a way, it was his river—all the romance, all the commerce and all the crime that its tides carried, were part of him. It held many secrets, secrets which it would seldom yield up to him as it did to such a man as Singleton. Old Man River Singleton. Gideon smiled a little grimly. Singleton would be badly missed when he retired, but other men were slowly acquiring his knowledge of the river, men who already had a love for it. That was something Gideon had almost forgotten: The Thames Division men loved the river and were dedicated to keeping it as clear from crime as they possibly could.

This diamond smuggling might stretch them to the limit of their resources.

There was no way of telling himself why he suspected that, but suspect it he did. He hoped they would soon find Thomas Argyle-Morris. And the Pierce child. He wondered where Hobbs was, and when he would be back. And then, by some trick of memory, he remembered promising to let the insurance broker, Morris have a detective on his staff, and he made a note.

Chapter Nine

FLOATING CASINO

'Alec, darling,' Esmeralda Pilkington said. 'I've a nasty feeling that you are going to be a policeman again. It isn't that I don't like policemen, but I can never get used to the fact that you're one. Jeremy hasn't done anything *very* criminal, has he?'

She was an attractive woman, in her middle thirties, with ash-blonde hair and a fair but slightly sun-bronzed face which made her eyes seem a very bright grey. Alec Hobbs had known her when she was in pig-tails and a gym tunic and he had been at Eton with her brother and Pilkington. She still had the figure of a girl, slim, thin-hipped, with shapely arms and legs. On this warm summer afternoon she looked fresh and elegant.

'He hasn't done anything criminal yet,' said Hobbs, 'he's just been his usual slap-happy self. Did you speak to him?'

'Yes, poor dear. He had to stay in Paris for another night. Some difficulty, I understand, with the Paris models. He told me to give you every facility, Alec, and I've told Hugh St. John that *he* must, too.'

'That's something,' Hobbs said. 'Where is St. John?'

'He's somewhere in London, I haven't any idea where, but he'll be back this evening. Why don't you come to dinner? You can talk it over then.'

Hobbs was tempted.

There would be no harm in it, either; there was nothing in police regulations to say that he could not dine with an old friend and discuss business at the same time. But he came at last to the conclusion that with Esmeralda and Jeremy it would not be wise.

'I should love to,' he said, almost too casually, 'but I shall be working late.'

Esmeralda stretched out and touched his hand.

'Still grieving, Alec?' When he didn't answer, she went on in a soft voice: 'You shouldn't, you know. Helen would want you to be happy.'

Had Gideon, had anyone else, said that or anything like it, Hobbs would have stiffened with an aloofness not far removed from resentment. In a way, Esmeralda was very like a sister, and whatever motive she might have had in asking him to dinner, he knew she was now thinking, in genuine concern, only of him.

He smiled, quite freely.

'Yes, I grieve much of the time,' he said. 'But it isn't an obsession any longer, and it isn't why I work late so often. Believe it or not, the Yard is seriously under-staffed.'

'I thought that only applied to policemen in uniform.'

'They're worse off than we are, certainly,' Hobbs agreed, 'but there's a great deal of work waiting to be done, all the time. What I would like to do,' he added before she could interrupt, 'is go over the boat.'

'*Now?*'

'Preferably now, yes.'

'But Hugh isn't here——' she began, and then laughed and stood up; she moved with a deliberate slowness but was very graceful. 'I suppose there's no reason why I shouldn't take you. That's if you don't mind me coming along.'

'Esmeralda, dear,' Hobbs said, 'don't fish.'

He got to his feet, and Esmeralda, slipping her arm through his, led him towards the garage.

Ten minutes later she was at the wheel of a grey

Bentley, driving with nonchalant ease through the traffic in Park Lane, round the whirlpool of cars at Hyde Park Corner, then along Grosvenor Place towards Chelsea and the river. Hobbs glanced at her from time to time but she was never looking at him, was always on the alert for other cars, and obviously revelling in being at the wheel. Soon she was in Chelsea Bridge Road; she paused at the traffic lights, which turned from red to green almost at once, then turned on to the Embankment. It was very wide where she stopped, and comparatively quiet. She pulled in not far from the bridge, and they got out and walked towards the steps which led down to the landing stages and pier.

This was a new one, installed for pleasure cruises only, and moored alongside were two large river steamers, one the *River Belle*, the other christened the *Belle Casino*. Only a few men were about on the *Belle Casino*, but a small army was working on the *River Belle*. A young man with long hair and very tight trousers came hurrying to the gangway and helped Esmeralda on board.

'I'd no idea you were coming tonight, darling.'

'Superintendent Hobbs persuaded me to bring him,' Esmeralda said. 'Superintendent, Timothy Gentian is in charge of all the arrangements for the actual show.'

Hobbs had heard of but never met Gentian, who looked in his early twenties but must, thought Hobbs, be in his middle thirties at least. He had a high reputation as a dress designer, an equally high one as a choreographer. His eyes were clear, his skin fresh, there was something youthful and frank and zestful about him.

'How do you do, Superintendent.' Gentian turned back to Esmeralda. 'We had a Chief Inspector from the Thames Division here this afternoon to see what we were up to—he went off with Hugh, to the Port of London Authority. I had no idea that one had to make plans in advance for a little trip up the river.' He was only half-jesting. 'Do come and see . . .'

Hobbs had seen the *River Belle* on a Saturday night, packed to the rails with roistering merry-makers, decks, salons, restaurants so crowded it was difficult to get through. He was astonished at the change. Gentian had draped the interior with velvet in pale greys and blues. Along the main deck were raised platforms, some of them already completed. Electricians and engineers were erecting floodlighting, a row of three lights were suddenly switched on, bright in spite of the sunlight. Hammering and banging was ceaseless—and so was Gentian's commentary.

'We're using the main *salon* for the girls and the two smaller bars for the male models, all the changing will be down there. The spotlight on the funnel—d'you see?—will be focused on the main staircase, and the models will parade right round the ship . . . The seating is being made ashore, it shouldn't take long to erect . . . The buffet will be on one of the attendant boats which will be secured on the right hand side—do hope you're not a sailor, Superintendent!—and there will be a flotilla of smaller ships with the press, models of furs and gowns which can't all be stored on board. Newspapermen and furs will be ferried to and fro as it were. It has been a very complex arrangement to make.'

'I can imagine,' Hobbs said drily. 'What else is planned for your guests?'

'Don't you think enough is being done?' asked Gentian. 'They will see the finest collection of furs and gowns ever displayed, a magnificent display of jewellery, many of the world's most beautiful women.

83

There will be a buffet with food of quite exquisite delicacy, and the best of wines. *Can* they ask for more?'

Hobbs smiled. 'Some will.'

'Alec, what *is* on your mind?' demanded Esmeralda Pilkington.

'Gambling,' Hobbs said.

'Oh, the casino.' Gentian spread his hands delicately. 'That is available on the other boat for those with money to lose.'

'Isn't it an official part of the show?' asked Hobbs.

'Show?' Gentian echoed deprecatingly. 'No, Superintendent, it is *not* part of the presentation. An arrangement has been made I believe for our guests to become temporary members of the *Belle Casino* and to get aboard, but that is no part of my business.'

'It's Hugh's though,' Esmeralda pointed out.

They went ashore, Gentian handing Esmeralda over the side, and inclining his head slightly as Hobbs said goodnight. Hobbs walked with Esmeralda to the Bentley.

'Where can I drop you, Alec?' she asked.

'Parliament Square will be a great help,' Hobbs said as they settled in. 'Esmeralda—ask Hugh to come and see me tomorrow, will you?'

'But surely you *will* come and dine——'

'No,' Hobbs said decisively. 'Thank you, but I really must work.'

'Alec,' Esmeralda said as she slowed down outside Westminster Abbey, 'you're worried about something to do with the show. What is it?'

'The presentation,' Hobbs reminded her, with a faint smile. 'I don't want Jeremy to get himself into trouble, and from now on this has to be official police business. Just a formality,' he added, and patted the back of her hand. 'Thanks for the lift.'

He saw that she glanced round as she drove off, but

made no sign that he noticed, and walked briskly to the Yard, wondering whether Gideon had gone home. Big Ben struck the quarter; that would be a quarter past six, thought Hobbs, he might just catch him before he left.

Gideon was clearing up his desk when Hobbs tapped and entered from the passage door.

'Now what's on your mind?' Gideon demanded, on the instant.

'Is it as obvious as that?' Hobbs asked wryly. 'I've just come from the *River Belle*.'

'What did you find on board?' Gideon was taking a bottle of whisky and some glasses out of a cupboard in his desk.

'I found enough to worry me,' Hobbs said. 'There will be a quarter of a million pounds' worth of furs, at least as much jewellery, and a fortune on the casino boat. And all of that adds up to an almost irresistible temptation to thieves with ambition and ingenuity. Don't you think so?'

Gideon poured two drinks, and pondered as they drank. Finally, he said: 'A damned sight too great. We must have that parade or whatever they call it guarded as if they were showing the crown jewels. We'll have to talk to Worby—' he hesitated. 'Tell you what, Alec. We'll have Worby, Prescott and Singleton here for a conference, and it might be a good idea to have someone from the City Police and the P.L.A. There's a lot to discuss. Officially we can call it for these high jinks, and then tackle all the other things at the same time. Ten o'clock, say, in the morning.'

'I'll arrange it,' promised Hobbs, and finished his whisky.

'Another spot?' asked Gideon.

'No thanks—but I needed that one,' Hobbs said.

Soon afterwards, Gideon was on his way home. Kate would be waiting for him and directly he began to think about her he realised that her first question would be about the Pierce child. He flicked on his radio and asked *Information* if there was any news from Richmond.

'Not a word,' *Information* told him.

'Let me know at home if any comes in,' Gideon ordered.

It was very dark in the quarry cave.

Geraldine lay still, very drowsy but aware that she was still alive. Now and again the man moved, but he offered no threat now; he was asleep. Gradually, full wakefulness came to the girl, and with it memory and fear—and hope.

She kept thinking about her captor.

She kept thinking about the way he fondled her, how he loved touching her skin.

She kept thinking about all that had happened since she had met him and allowed him to bring her here. She had known it was wrong, known it was risky.

She could almost hear her mother, too, warning her against men; there were times when she thought that her mother actually *hated* them.

'They only want one thing, and don't you forget it. Do you hear me, Geraldine? They only want one thing, and when they've had it then they've finished with you. You're a big girl now, I've seen how attractive you are to men. Listen to me, darling ...'

Now Geraldine was listening, over the months that had passed.

She was wide awake, and thinking, and remembering that strange look in the man's eyes, a kind of glazed expression, when he had held her scarf in his hands. She had been almost sure what was passing through his mind. He had gagged her again, not too tightly, and tied her to the bed before rocking to and fro, to and fro, until at last the rocking chair had stopped creaking.

He stirred.

Soon she realised that he was awake, too; she could just make out the shine of his eyes. The chair creaked again and she knew that he was getting up. He came across to her and she felt his hand groping about her, about her shoulders, then about her face. He fumbled with the scarf behind her head, loosened it, then drew it away. Without a word, he moved to one side; a match flared, dazzling her. When she opened her eyes wide again she saw a candle, flickering slightly. The light grew stronger, but when he came to her again his body hid the actual flame. Gently he began to massage her cheeks and chin and mouth. Soon, he loosened the rope round her waist, helped her to sit up, and held a cup to her lips.

It contained milk, cold and greasy and none too fresh, but it eased the dryness in her mouth, her parched throat, and she drank eagerly.

When she had finished she drew her head back. 'You're nice,' she told him. To her, the words sounded hoarse and over loud. Be natural, be natural, she told herself.

'What did you say, child?' he asked.

'I said you were nice,' Geraldine repeated. 'Very nice.'

He looked at her eagerly. 'Do you really think so?'

'Of course I do. I think you're very nice, and—I love you touching me.'

'You—you *do*?' His voice grew shrill.

'Yes,' she whispered. 'I really do.'

She felt his hands upon the satin smoothness of her legs.

She heard him draw in his breath, as if he had difficulty in breathing. He pressed harder. She wondered what he was thinking, believed that while he was doing this at least he would not kill her.

He was thinking with a kind of exalted desperation: She likes me . . . If she likes me she won't shout . . . If she likes me. Perhaps it's a trick. Perhaps she's lying to me. If she's lying to me I'll choke the life out of her, I'll choke her to death.

She whispered again: 'You're very nice.'

She was not yet fourteen.

Chapter Ten

CONFERENCE

Gideon opened the door of his office at half-past eight next morning, and found Hobbs sitting at his desk, telephone in hand. He waved to Hobbs to stay where he was and glanced through a file of reports on a corner of the desk.

Hobbs said into the telephone: 'Then you'll have to put it off. Be here at ten—Commander Gideon's office.' He rang off and stood up. Whereas Lemaitre would have grumbled about whoever was raising difficulties and named them, Hobbs made no reference to what had just occurred, saying only: 'That's everyone.'

'Nice and early,' Gideon said drily. He felt in a brisk, assertive mood this morning, without knowing why. The day was dull outside and the atmosphere sticky and unpleasant. 'Anything new about the

Pierce girl?'

'No.'

'The baby killing?'

'Hellier is questioning a girl now—he seems pretty sure she's the right one.'

'Micklewright?'

'Nothing new—except that he seems to be getting on all right with Van Hoorn.'

'We'll see them at lunch,' Gideon said.

'I wondered if it would be a good idea to have Micklewright in on the conference,' Hobbs said.

Gideon frowned. 'Why?'

'He's been concentrating on the river, and he may have something useful to contribute,' answered Hobbs.

Gideon's frown deepened.

'I suppose so. And you're right in principle, any-how—I should have thought about it. We want to talk to the City and the P.L.A. people about both the parade and the smuggling, and ought to have the Customs here, too.' He was annoyed with himself because he hadn't thought of these things before. 'Kill two birds with one stone,' he added, feeling once again that he was speaking tritely.

'I asked the P.L.A. to check if Customs could have men available if we should need them,' Hobbs told him.

Gideon's frown faded into a wry, amused grin.

'That's good—we will have 'em all.' He looked round the office. 'Can't get 'em all in here, though. Better use the small conference room. Have coffee laid on for eleven-fifteen.'

'I'll do that,' Hobbs promised.

'Is there anything new?' asked Gideon.

'Nothing which need worry us this morning,' Hobbs assured him. 'There was a small bank raid at

Lewisham yesterday afternoon and a post office was broken into during the night at Chelsea.'

'Any news of that chap with the high-falutin' name? Argyle-Morris?'

'No.'

'I'll talk to Roswell,' Gideon said. 'You carry on.'

Hobbs nodded, picked up some of the papers, and went out. Gideon leaned back in his chair, drumming his fingers on his desk. He suspected that there was something on Hobbs's mind which he didn't yet want to talk about. Oh well, he'd just have to wait until Hobbs decided to mention it. Stretching for the telephone, he put in a call to Roswell.

It came through almost at once.

'No, nothing's turned up,' Roswell said. 'Not even Argyle-Morris.'

'What does that mean exactly?' Gideon asked.

'He didn't come home last night.'

'What about the girl?'

'She's home and as bold as brass,' replied Roswell. 'You'd think they'd learn, wouldn't you?'

'Learn what?'

'She nearly gets drowned because she plays fast and loose with Dave Carter, and now that the new boy friend's away for a night she's up most of it with another one. We kept an eye on her after Argyle-Morris left with Screw Smith.'

'Who's her third boy friend?' asked Gideon, thoughtfully.

'Not one of Carter's gang, as far as we can find out,' Roswell said.

'Might be a good idea to check very closely on him,' said Gideon.

'If you think so, George.'

Gideon only just bit back a rough: 'I do think so.' Roswell was old in the service and a little inclined to take things easily. He was equally inclined to feel that only he really knew how to handle his Division; and in one way he was right. Gideon rang off and pushed thought of the Divisional man from his mind—and almost at once the telephone rang.

'Mr. Hellier of Richmond for you, sir.'

Gideon's heart began to beat faster.

'Put him through . . .' there was a short pause. 'Good morning, Hellier.'

'Good morning, sir.' Hellier's voice betrayed no emotion at all. 'We haven't found the body in the river, for what that's worth. The frogmen finished half an hour ago.'

'So the child may still be alive.' Gideon's voice was gruff.

'Could be, sir.' There was a fractional pause before Hellier went on: 'I've just talked to the young mother who killed her infant child.'

'She admitted it, did she?'

'Yes, sir. She's seventeen. Parents haven't helped at all. I'm charging her this morning and asking for remand in custody. The Welfare people can see what they can do, then.'

'Right.' Gideon wondered whether this was all Hellier had called him about.

'One other thing, sir,' Hellier went on. 'There's a possibility that Geraldine Pierce is on the other side of the river.' He meant, 'not in my division', and that told Gideon a great deal. Obviously he was not sure that the police on the other side would search in the way he thought necessary. 'So far we've taken it for granted that she's on this side, sir.'

Gideon could have said: 'I haven't taken anything for granted.' In fact he said: 'I'll have a word with them.'

'Thank you, sir.'

'What was that about Pierce losing his job?' asked Gideon.

'His employer is an old skinflint,' answered Hellier, 'but I don't think he'll be fired, he's too useful. His boss may make life hell for him, but he won't cut off his nose to spite his face.'

Gideon grunted and rang off.

'Pierce, you're nearly an hour late again this morning,' Edward Lee said to his chief clerk. 'You know how important this stock-taking is. I have no objection to you leaving early if you've finished, but you must be here on time.'

Pierce thought: You humbug, you know you expect me to work overtime every night. He said: 'It's a very worrying time, sir.'

'I appreciate that. Nevertheless . . .'

As he listened, Pierce gritted his teeth and clenched his hands; and when at last he was alone at his desk in a tiny office, all he could see was first his wife's face, then Geraldine's, dancing before his eyes.

He turned to the stock cards.

In a way it was better to have something to do.

Gideon was five minutes late getting to the small conference room, delayed by a telephone call from Oslo about some forged öre notes being circulated in the United Kingdom. It was probably just as well, for Worby was only just arriving, and he prided himself on his punctuality.

The room was almost filled by an oval table of light-polished walnut, with ten chairs around it. In front of each man was a note pad and pencil, between each two an ash-tray. The window was small and high, overlooking the main courtyard. It was open, and the noise of cars starting up, of men talking, of men laughing, drifted into the room. Each chair had wooden arms and the largest was one of three which were vacant. Gideon took it.

Hobbs was on his right; Worby, dark, well-preserved, a little too heavy at the jowl, was on his left. Micklewright sat next to Worby, big knuckly hands clasped on the table in front of him. Next to him was Chief Superintendent Prescott of AB Division; next to him in turn, Roswell of NE. These two men might have been father and son, Roswell looking older than his fifty-nine years, balding, grey, with creases in his forehead and jowl, and unexpectedly merry blue eyes, while Prescott, of similar build, bore the same creased face, the same hint of enjoying life to the full. Next to Prescott was Superintendent Yates of the City of London Police, big, blond, military-looking, with a high complexion, improbably curly hair, and china blue eyes. He seldom said anything at conferences, only after them.

Gideon knew all of these men well.

He also knew Superintendent Hennessy of the Port of London Authority Police, for before joining the Port of London Authority Force Hennessy had been in the Metropolitan Force, resigning at sergeant's rank because he could not get what he so badly wanted—transfer to the Thames Division. Hennessy was a spare time yachtsman who loved the water. He was short compared with the other men, stocky, with very broad shoulders, nearly black hair and well-marked eyebrows, a rather beetling forehead and a broad snub nose.

On either side of the Port of London Authority man were Customs officers—one of whom Gideon recognised as Nielsen, a senior officer in the Water Guard branch which dealt with crews, passengers and ships' stores. Nielsen was a fine-looking, fair-haired and fair-complexioned man, of mixed English and Swedish parentage. The other, obviously from the Landing Branch of the Customs service, had charge of cargoes both going out of and coming into the Port of London. He was the youngest-looking man present.

Hobbs turned to Gideon. 'I think you know everyone except Mr. Cortini of the Customs Landing Branch, Commander.'

'How are you, Mr. Cortini?'

'Commander.'

'Good of you all to come at such short notice,' Gideon said, and saw Prescott shoot a smug glance at Hobbs; so probably he had been the one to make difficulties. 'The major problem is this mannequin parade that's been sprung on us. As it's going as far as Greenwich it goes through all our divisions and spheres of influence.'

'Sprung on us is right,' said Worby. 'We'll only just have time to make arrangements.'

'What arrangements need take all that time?' Prescott asked.

'Don't need telling you're a landlubber,' Worby retorted. 'We've got to make sure the river's clear—no big vessels moving in and out, or they'll swamp the little boats. We've got to check the tide, make sure it's not likely to be high, and patrol the river for the idiots who'll hire boats and get as close as they can to all that mink. And once the pleasure boats get wind of the river parade they'll put on special trips or divert their regular trips up and down the river. Every water man with a small boat and a wife will be there—and most of their families, too.'

Worby wiped the sweat off his forehead as he finished and even Prescott looked slightly abashed.

Gideon asked mildly: 'Anything you can't cope with, out of all that?'

'Not if everything goes to plan,' said Worby. 'But one boat capsizing, or one model falling overboard, could make a lot of difference.'

'Overtime laid on?'

'Yes—oh, we'll manage, Commander. I've got all the specials on duty, too.'

'Haven't lost much time,' Gideon approved. 'What about the bridges?'

'Bound to be crowded,' remarked Roswell.

'Crammed,' agreed Banks.

'A general rider for double duty for all traffic police has gone out,' Hobbs reported. 'I've followed the general plans for the *Evening News* pageant. The same streets will be non-parking areas after two o'clock in the afternoon, and I've warned London Transport to be ready for extra demands for buses and trains.'

'Do you really think it will be *that* big?' demanded Roswell, sceptically.

'I think it might.'

'Could be a damp squib,' Prescott objected.

'Then we'll be able to send everyone home early,' Gideon said soothingly. 'Better that than be caught half-prepared.'

'Can't understand why they haven't given us more warning,' Worby complained. 'Pilkington isn't a fool —didn't he have something to do with the Fire of London pageant?'

'He co-ordinated the plans for the business houses floats,' said Hobbs stiffly.

'Thought there was something, Geor—Commander,' Worby frowned. 'Pilkington *must* have known what a sensation this would cause. Given a fine night we'll have a million people by the river. Londoners love to see any kind of pageant, and mannequins on parade will draw them like bees round a honey-pot.'

Gideon thought: Yes. And it is puzzling. Aloud, he asked: 'Does this affect you, Mr. Cortini?'

'We've been told there will be two ships from Calais with a bonded cargo of furs,' Cortini said. 'The jewellery from the Continent is coming in by air.'

Gideon wrote *Airport P* on his note pad.

'This is rather an exceptional case, Commander,' the Customs man went on. 'As the furs won't be unloaded on land but simply transferred to the *River Belle*, they won't strictly be liable for duty, but the moment any of them are sold they could become liable. And they may be sold on board the ship and brought ashore by the buyers—they sometimes prefer to do this rather than have them delivered.'

Gideon frowned. 'That's a point.'

'Didn't think of that,' said Hennessy.

'Even the P.L.A. forgets things sometimes,' said Cortini drily.

'What are you going to do?' Gideon asked.

'The organising committee has put up a bond. The purchasers will be charged the usual import and purchase tax rates, and we'll get a copy of the bill to keep the record straight when the organisers clear the bond.'

'There's a good chance that someone will cheat, surely,' Hobbs remarked.

Cortini smiled drily. 'I'll have men mixing with the guests. So will Nielsen.'

'I have ten men detailed,' Nielsen boasted. 'It isn't that I think anyone will deliberately cheat, but just in case they fall to temptation.'

There was a general chuckle.

'How *did* we get on to this?' asked Banks. 'Until Hobbs phoned me, I hadn't an inkling.'

'The insurance broker involved was worried,'

Gideon answered.

'Can't say I blame him,' said Roswell, his scepticism dispersed. 'The more I think about this the crazier I think it was to hush it up for so long. There's a limit to stunt advertising. If we're not careful we'll have a great River Robbery on our hands. There could be upwards of a million involved in this show.'

'We're here to make sure that nothing goes wrong,' Gideon said, mildly.

'No need to worry about them getting away with a River Robbery as they did with the Great Train job,' Worby said reassuringly. 'You land chaps forget that you can't move around on the river like you can on land. Big ship or little boat, it has to be secured, has to be unmoored, has to get under way slowly. You can't hurry when you start anything on water. That's why we have little real crime on the river. Why, there wasn't more than a hundred thousand pounds' worth stolen last year!'

'As far as you know,' said Roswell slyly.

'We know how much is lost from stuff coming into the port,' said Hennessy, 'but a hell of a lot is almost certainly lost on ships going out. Don't discover the loss until it's at the port of destination, that's the trouble.'

Two or three others made a comment and Gideon did not interrupt, for he was brooding over what Roswell had said. There *was* an obvious risk. And if any group of criminals knew of the parade in time, they might well plan a raid—and if they did, then they would make as sure as possible that they could get away with it.

Could they?

He felt uneasy, without quite knowing why, but at least he was satisfied that all normal precautions had now been taken. He must give Micklewright his head soon. The man was obviously unable to restrain his impatience.

He was about to change the subject to the industrial diamonds case when the telephone rang.

'I gave instructions that we shouldn't be disturbed,' Hobbs said, lifting the receiver. 'Who . . .' He broke off almost at once, and handed the instrument to Worby. 'It's your man Singleton, he says you told him to call you if he had any news of Argyle-Morris.'

'So I did,' Worby said. 'Excuse me, Commander . . . Yes, Jack, what is it?' There was a pause before he went on in an ominous voice: 'Oh, *has* he.'

Chapter Eleven

RIVER'S VICTIM

All that Tom Argyle-Morris could think of was pain.

There was pain in his thumb, awful pain in his thumb; and in his face, his eyes, his mouth, his stomach, his chest. Everywhere.

He was so full of pain that he could hardly remember how it had begun, who was causing it. He was hardly aware when they were asking questions or shining blinding lights into his eyes.

He was on fire with pain.

No one had spoken for some time, he was aware of that; no one had shone the light, no one had touched him. Yet they seemed still to be there, menacing shapes and sounds hovering or whispering close by. He knew that he was quivering, that he could not keep still, that there was warmth on his hands and fingers, on his toes.

But no one seemed to be touching him now.

He felt himself lifted, suddenly, and tried to scream, but hardly a sound came from his lips. He was lifted. Oh God, what next, what next? He was carried. A man stumbled and brought fresh waves of agony. He felt coolness—he was out of doors. He felt himself pushed into the back of a car. Was it an ambulance? The doors closed behind him with a bang.

The car moved.

Every bump was agonising, every swerve at a corner, every railway line. They were taking him out of the docks.

To hospital—please God, to hospital.

Soon they drove over a smooth road and now only the vibration of the engine hurt. At last he opened his eyes—and found that it was dark. He could see street lamps and lighted windows, that was all. He closed his eyes again. Suddenly the car stopped, and he heard the men coming towards the back, rubber soles making little noise. The doors were opened. He tried to raise his head, but a hand closed over his face and rammed him down with a thump which sent new waves of agony through his naked body. They pulled him out savagely, one holding him by his ankles, another by his wrists.

He opened his eyes and saw light shining on the water.

Terror struck him dumb as they swung him to and fro three or four times and then let him go.

He had his mouth wide open in a vain attempt to scream when he struck the water. He tried to struggle, but he could not stop himself from going down.

It was Superintendent Jack Singleton, out with his crew next morning, who saw the tell-tale mound of water which always rose above a floating body. It was

Sergeant Tidy who used the hitcher and the drag to pull the body in. It was Singleton who took one look at the bruised and battered face, another at the pulped thumb, and who felt sick.

The senior officers gathered about the table at the Yard were silent, Worby listening, the others—including Gideon—looking at him with tense interest. Finally Worby said:

'Yes, pull her in ... and pick up that man she was with last night ... and pick up all of Carter's gang for questioning ... Every one of the sons of bitches, yes.'

He rang off, then turned to Gideon. 'Thomas Argyle-Morris was pulled out of the Thames half-an-hour ago. He'd been tortured—savaged—and tossed in. Singleton thinks he was thrown in near Fiddler's Steps—there's a current which carries flotsam from there to the place where the body was found.'

The Customs men, who knew nothing of the significance of this, looked their curiosity. Micklewright cracked his knuckles, and said:

'Well, Carter didn't do *that*.'

'It's not a Carter gang job,' said Worby, with absolute assurance. 'He'd beat a man up but he wouldn't torture him. We want Screw Smith and we want to know who Screw's been working for.'

Hobbs said: 'I'll go down to *Information*.'

'Yes,' said Gideon. He stopped himself from telling Hobbs what to do and waited until the door closed on the Deputy Commander. Then he looked at Micklewright.

'Will you tell us just what's happening about these industrial diamonds, Mick? And where this murder comes into it.'

Micklewright straightened up, momentarily taken

by surprise, then launched into the story with a lucidity that could not have been greater had he prepared a report for this very moment. Something of his awkwardness seemed to fall away from him, he became a police officer of obvious acumen. He told of the Dutch concern over the extent of the losses, of Van Hoorn's visit, of the evidence that the packet found by the Thames Division patrol was one of those stolen from Amsterdam. Then, taking the actual waterproof container from his brief-case, he went on:

'Amsterdam says that four or five lots, worth between two and three thousand pounds each, are stolen every month. And a lot of uncut diamonds are stolen, too. That makes it very big business. If Argyle-Morris was killed because he was involved and might have talked, then we know the organisation is big enough for the criminals to take murder in their stride.'

Into the silence which followed, Roswell asked in a small voice: 'Big enough to think up a Great River Robbery?'

Van Hoorn's guttural voice had a penetrating quality which could be heard all over the dining-room. Gideon, seldom self-conscious, was very aware of the attention the Dutchman was attracting during the hour he spent with him and Micklewright. And he could see the signs of rebellion on Micklewright's face as Van Hoorn kept saying:

'It was as I said in the beginning, Commander, there is a big criminal organisation which buys stolen industrial diamonds here in England. Where else they go I do not know. It is easy for anyone to steal, yes, but as I said in the beginning, who would steal if they did not know there was a buyer?'

Micklewright said: 'The Inspector thinks there is a

widespread sales organisation in this country, Commander.'

'What makes you think this, Mr. Van Hoorn?'

'I go to Oslo, Stockholm, Copenhagen, Brussels, Paris—all the cities of Europe. I am told by the diamond merchants that sales are lower everywhere—ten per cent, fifteen per cent. But the industrial users, what do they say? They say they *use* more. Commander, industrial diamonds, as you well know, are used in precision engineering and——'

Micklewright made a grimace, his lips appearing to form unspoken words, the last two of which seemed to be: '. . . suck eggs.'

'. . . So we have more diamonds used, less diamonds sold,' Van Hoorn remarked. 'And we have many diamonds stolen. It seems to be a matter of certainty, Commander—these stolen diamonds are placed on to the market by illegal sellers, at low prices.'

'Can you prove that?' asked Gideon.

'Not yet, sir. It is a difficult matter to prove. Industrial users who buy unofficially do not wish the source of their supplies to be known.'

Micklewright leaned forward in his chair. 'All right, then you think there is a big organisation which sells the diamonds. But why insist that its headquarters are in England? Why not *Holland*? Or if it comes to that, America? They're the world's super salesmen. And they have access to the South American diamond supplies. Why pick on us?'

Van Hoorn spoke almost angrily. 'But I have told you. We have arrested one known thief, he comes to England often by air. And you yourselves find the diamonds in the river. It is easy to send them from Holland to England and easy for England to absorb them, she is so much a bigger country than Holland. Commander, I say to you—I believe in England there is the heart of a big diamond smuggling and stealing ring—very big indeed. I ask that you request Superintendent Micklewright not to shrug his shoulders at this.'

'If it exists, we'll uncover it,' Gideon said soothingly. 'How long will you stay in London?'

'I have to return tonight for conferences, but the day after tomorrow I come back.'

'Can you wait for five days before coming back?' asked Gideon.

'Five *days*?' The Dutchman looked startled. 'May I ask why, Commander?'

'We shall be having one of the biggest searches of the river in the next five days,' Gideon told him, 'and an opportunity to examine the possibilities very closely.' He turned to Micklewright. 'Did you tell the Inspector about Argyle-Morris?'

Micklewright looked uneasy. 'No.' His hands, large, ungainly, moved clumsily, knocking against the handle of his knife; dripping with thick gravy, it fell on to his trousers. 'Oh, what the hell,' he muttered.

'I will, of course, wait five days,' Van Hoorn said. 'And Commander, permit me to say how kind you are to spare this luncheon for me. I am deeply honoured.'

'Pleasure,' Gideon made himself say, and was glad it was over.

'Mick,' Gideon said, in his office after the luncheon. 'What's worrying you?'

'That damned Dutchman,' Micklewright muttered.

'I thought you were getting along with him nicely.'

'That was before he manufactured a big anti-Dutch plot by some master minds among English criminals. It's just as easy to smuggle stuff into Germany and France from Holland.'

'But he's found no evidence of that whereas he has

found evidence that some are coming here,' said Gideon. 'You're not giving him a fair crack of the whip, Mick. He could be right. In any case we've got to make sure whether he is or not.' Slowly, he went on: 'When did you last have a holiday?'

'In the spring. But I'm not over-tired, if that's what you mean.' Micklewright bridled.

'Then what *is* the trouble?'

'Forget it, George.' Micklewright spoke harshly. 'I'm getting old and I don't like Continentals. That's about the size of it.'

Even more deliberately Gideon went on: 'Would you like to be relieved of the job?'

Micklewright went very still; and for a long time the office was silent. Then he pushed his chair back, and said stiffly:

'That's up to you, Commander.'

'If I relieve you of the job, what will Clara say?' Gideon demanded.

'*Clara? She* won't care.' Micklewright sounded bitter, but the next moment he recovered himself 'Nothing to do with Clara, anyway,' he added hurriedly. 'Is that all, Commander?'

So it's trouble at home, thought Gideon. He saw the misery on the other's face, and for a few moments could think of nothing to say. Certainly it wouldn't help to pursue the Clara issue now, this would only drive Micklewright further back into his shell. 'Well, Van Hoorn's off your back for a few days,' he said at last. 'Keep at it yourself, and if you need help, let me know. It's beginning to look as if Argyle-Morris was killed by some pretty nasty customers, and it could be tied in with those diamonds. We don't know that he wasn't trying to escape with them, do we?'

'He swears—he *swore* when we talked to him, that he'd never seen the packet. Don't think I'd overlook a simple possibility like that, do you? I'll ask Worby to find me a desk down at Wapping for the next few days. That all right?'

'Yes,' said Gideon.

Micklewright stood up, moved towards the door, hesitated, then said awkwardly:

'Thanks, George.'

He went out.

'Warbler,' Gideon said to Chief Superintendent Worby, 'Micklewright's going to work from your manor for a few days. Keep an eye on him, will you?'

'Still on the bottle, is he?' Worby asked.

'Something's eating him,' said Gideon slowly. 'And I'd like to know what.' He rang off and sat back in his chair, wondering whether he should have gone so far. Worby and Micklewright were old friends and Worby would know that he, Gideon, was genuinely concerned for the other man, but it wasn't good to have one senior officer watching another.

The truth was that if Micklewright went on as he was going he could no longer be trusted with major assignments. It did not matter how sorry one was for a man, the police had to get results—and results only came from detectives who could give their very best to the job.

Making a conscious effort, he put Micklewright out of his mind, turning his thoughts towards Sir Jeremy Pilkington's parade. A show of jewellery and an international ring of diamond thieves. It had to be coincidence. Gideon kept turning it over in his mind, then went over what had been said and planned at the morning conference; at least they'd had *some* warning.

Supposing a ring of jewel thieves *did* use the river for hiding and delivering precious stones . . . and supposing the same ring decided to try to stage a robbery at the parade ... couldn't the hiding places and the disposal plans for the industrial diamonds be used for the more valuable jewellery?

Fanciful? he wondered.

He'd known stranger things happen.

It was nearly seven o'clock when he left his office and drove back to his home in Fulham. As he opened the front door, he heard Kate coming along the passage; so she had seen him and, he guessed, was excited about something.

Almost at once, she said: 'George, you didn't tell me about the River Parade.'

'What do you know about it?' Gideon asked in surprise.

'Four invitations were delivered by hand only twenty minutes ago,' Kate told him, '*and* a brochure! It looks as if it's going to be magnificent.'

It was good to see her so pleased, and Gideon made a mental note to tell Hobbs about her pleasure. It was less good to see her expression, at the dining-table, as her thoughts obviously veered to something unpleasant.

'George,' she said. 'Do you think there's any hope for that Pierce child?'

Chapter Twelve

TO KILL OR NOT TO KILL

'What's your name?' asked Geraldine Pierce timidly.

The man said roughly: 'Never mind my name!' He rolled off the bed and stood glaring down at her, his face demoniac in the candlelight. 'What do you want to know my name for? Go on, tell me!' He thrust his hands on to her shoulders and shook her violently, banging her head up and down on the hard pillow. His voice rose. '*What do you want to know my name for?*'

In her terror the child gasped: 'Don't shout! People will hear you. Don't shout!'

The warning stopped him; people did come down to the quarry, especially children. He drew back, releasing her, and his rasping breath seemed to go in and out in time with her shallow, frightened breathing. It was very quiet. The candle flickered in a faint breeze from the door. After a while he leaned over her again but this time he did not touch her.

'Go on, tell me, why do you want to know my name?'

'I—I want to call you something, that's all.'

'You don't have to call me anything.'

'I—I just wanted to.'

'Why did you want to?'

She was still taking in those quick, shallow breaths as she stared up into his face.

'I—I *like* you,' she said. And after a pause, she added: '*You* know *my* name.'

'Yes, I do. *Geraldine*. But that doesn't mean you have to know mine. You can like me without knowing my name.' He nodded, as if to emphasise the fact that his argument was unassailable.

Geraldine hesitated before beginning:

'I know, but——'

'But what?'

'It doesn't matter,' she said wearily.

'It matters to me!'

'I'm sorry,' she said. 'I just wanted to know. I thought it would be friendlier.'

'You're not lying to me, are you?'

'Of course I'm not! Why on earth should I?'

'You could want to know my name so as to tell somebody.'

'Who—who is there to tell?' she asked helplessly.

He frowned, then lowered himself to the rocking chair and drew it closer to the bed. She watched him uneasily. He was like one of the younger kids at school, it didn't matter what she said he would find an objection, no matter how silly. He *did* behave like a child; like her father did, sometimes, when her mother had vexed him. This time he did not answer but placed his hand gently on her leg, just above the knee. He *was* gentle when he was stroking her, whenever their bodies were close; touching. Except when he was angry about some imagined slight or genuine fear, he was very gentle.

'You can call me Dick,' he said.

'Oh, that's lovely!' She was about to ask if that meant that his name was Richard, but thought better of it. 'Dick—that's a *very* nice name.'

'Do you really like it?'

'Yes, I do. It's *lovely*.'

'I'm glad you like it,' he moved his hand gently upwards. 'Do you like that?'

She felt the pressure of his hand. She felt the stirring of strange excitement which she had already felt with him—and sometimes when she had thought about 'men', when on her own.

'Do you?'

She whispered: 'Yes. Yes, Dick, I do.'

'Do you—mind—what I do?'

'No,' she said. 'No. I—I love it.'

And in a way, she did.

And in another way, she knew that she must humour him. Because when they were close together she was not tied and helpless.

And—once—he had nearly dropped asleep.

If he was asleep and she was free she could creep off the bed and get out of this awful place.

Afterwards . . .

Afterwards, exhausted, he lay by her side, breathing very heavily. Soon Geraldine began to think that he *was* asleep. He was on the outside of the bed but she could slide downwards and climb off the foot. That was the only way. She began to ease herself downwards and he did not stir. She felt her legs go over the foot of the bed. Scarcely breathing, she managed to touch the floor. Then she was on her knees at the foot of the bed. The candle-light shone on the back of his head and his bare shoulders. Slowly, cautiously, she stood up, and turned towards the door. She did not know that this door had been built, in the first place, to keep out draughts; that outside it was concealed by rocks and sand, with only just room to squeeze through.

She reached the door, glancing fearfully back at the huddled figure on the bed. She saw her own shadow, dark and gigantic against the cave wall; almost frightening her. Then, feeling for the handle, she turned it, slowly, gently, and pulled.

The door did not move. She pulled again, but still it did not move. Looking up, she saw that it was bolted. Standing on tiptoe she began to slide the bolt back, but this wasn't easy. Holding her breath she went on, exerting more and more pressure—until suddenly it shot back, and metal struck metal with a noise like a bullet shot.

She heard Dick move.

She snatched at the handle but the door still did not open. Terror rose up in her as she heard the bed creak. He sprang from it and swore at her just above his breath, vicious, filthy words. She swung round before he reached her, to try to fend him off, and felt his fingers touch her neck and then slide off.

'No!' she gasped. 'No!'

He seized her by the neck and she felt his thumbs pressing into her windpipe and she knew that she was near to death. She slumped against him, pleading with her body, making no attempt to struggle, sensing that it would be useless to try.

As she leaned her weight against him, he had to bend his arms at a more difficult angle and there was less strength in his grip. Now she could breathe more freely. She sobbed as if her heart was broken, put her arms round him and pressed against him, looking up into his face, her lips parted in an invitation which was unthinking and wholly natural.

Gradually his anger began to die away.

Gradually, his grip on her neck slackened.

'Don't ever do that again,' he said. 'Don't ever do that again.'

She felt the change in him as his hands fell gently to her shoulders and he began to caress her. The tumult in her heart quietened and soon she began to doze.

She was going to tell the police, Jonathan Jones thought.

She would have told them all about me.

She's very lovely, but she won't be any use to me if they take me away.

So long as I can keep her here, he thought, everything will be all right.

The following morning Hellier stood in his big office, studying the progress of the magnetised markers and the reports which had come in from all the groups of officers. There was no sign at all of the missing child.

If she's dead and buried it isn't in my manor, he thought. We'd have found her if it was. I wonder if Gideon talked to the others? He went to his desk and sat down heavily. 'She isn't in a boat or a boat shed,' he said aloud. 'She isn't in a caravan. She isn't in an allotment shed. She isn't in a disused garage. She isn't in an empty house or flat.' As he spoke he laid aside folder after folder with reports of investigations into all these places. 'She isn't with any man who is known to be living alone. She isn't in a hotel or boarding house. So if she's in this division she's in a house where other people live. She isn't hiding for a joke, and she's no need to run away, so she must have been abducted. We've checked all the families with sons who are weak in the head, and whom we know need watching. So it must be someone we don't know—and most of the ones we don't know are families who've moved into the district in the last six months, say.'

His face cleared as he lifted a telephone.

'Yes, sir?' His second-in-command answered promptly.

'I want someone to go round to the Town Clerk's office, see the Rating Officer and get a comprehensive list of all families known to have moved into the district in the past twelve months. Send others round to all estate agents to get lists of furnished houses or flats rented in the same period.'

'Right, sir.'

'Get it done quick,' ordered Hellier.

He felt better when he rang off; at least he had started another line of inquiry, one it would have been easy to overlook.

Wanda Pierce was at the kitchen sink, preparing vegetables for lunch. David made a point of coming home to lunch, these days, although Mr. Lee didn't like it. In a way, it helped her. She knew what she was doing but did it mechanically. There was no relief from the mental agony she felt, no relief from the perpetual cross-examination of herself. She had *known* Geraldine was too easily flattered by men. She had *known* that she was extremely attractive and physically very well-developed for her age: she could pass for sixteen or seventeen anywhere.

'I tried to tell her. I tried all I knew,' Wanda said drearily.

The words seemed to echo back at her from the empty garden.

She was alone. Mrs. Edmonds would look in during the afternoon sometime, but she had her own family to look after. And none of the other neighbours came in often.

It was half-past eleven, and David would soon be back. Poor, useless, helpless David. If only he had some spirit! He should have left Lee years ago. *She* had always wanted to emigrate, to Australia preferably, but he had never had the necessary drive.

What would they do now?

At heart, she knew that only Geraldine had kept them together; left to herself she would have walked out on her husband years before.

Mr. Lee opened the door of David Pierce's office and found Pierce staring blankly out of the tiny window. He did not even look round as the door opened. Lee took the one stride needed to reach the desk.

'Pierce!' he barked.

Pierce started and looked round, wildly.

'What on earth are you doing? You take enough time off, these days, you should at least be giving your job your full attention when you *are* here.'

Pierce didn't speak.

'Are the July stock-sheets ready yet?'

Pierce spoke slowly. 'No. Not quite. They will be by middle afternoon.'

'That won't be time enough,' rapped Lee. 'I want them in my office by two o'clock at the latest. Don't make any excuses.'

He went out, closing the door with a snap.

Pierce turned to the loose-leaf ledger in front of him, with its interminable lists of stationery stocks, all entered in his own small, neat handwriting. He had been doing this ever since he had left school, when he had taken over from an elderly clerk very soon after he had obtained the job.

The figures swam in front of him.

He looked at the big, round-faced clock on the opposite wall, and saw that it was nearly twelve o'clock. To get these lists ready by two would mean staying here throughout his lunch hour, and that would mean sending a message to tell Wanda that he wasn't coming home. He could imagine her expression when Mrs. Edmonds told her. He knew that she almost despised him, and instead of the disaster drawing them closer together it seemed to be tearing them further apart. She couldn't help him and he couldn't help her. But he knew that she hated to be alone, and pehaps he *did* help a little by going home to lunch.

He stared at the clock.

He heard Wanda's voice in his imagination.

'You ought to be out looking for her!'

It was true; he ought to be.

Very slowly he stood up, put a marker in the ledger, put on his jacket, and went through the small general office, where two girls were typing and another at the little switchboard was making entries in the day-book.

The girls paused in their typing as Pierce walked towards the outer door. He reached it, and turned round.

'Tell Mr. Lee that I will come back *after* my daughter is found.'

He did not wait for an answer but went out, down the narrow stairs, out into the side street which led into the High Street and so to the river. He did not cross the bridge but walked to the police station. It was a quarter-past twelve when he asked for Hellier.

'What can I do for you, Mr. Pierce?' Hellier asked.

'You can give me something to do which may help me to find my daughter,' Pierce said.

'Mr. Pierce, we are doing everything we possibly can. Amateur help will not——' Hellier began, and then he broke off, realising that once again he had said the wrong and cruel thing. He simply could not help being clumsy with words.

'But there must be something I can do. There *must* be,' Pierce sounded desperate.

'But what about your work?' Hellier asked, shifting his ground weakly.

Stonily, Pierce answered: 'I have left my job until Geraldine is found.'

Awkwardly, Hellier dissembled. 'Give me time to consider this, Mr. Pierce, and I will find the best way to use your services. Will you telephone me this afternoon?'

'I'm not on the telephone,' Pierce replied. 'Will you please send an officer to me with the message?' He turned and went out of the office, leaving Hellier staring after him.

Chapter Thirteen

PROMISE

Sir Jeremy Pilkington, tall and handsome, came down the gangway from the BEA aircraft at London Airport with two beautiful young women in front of him and two equally beautiful young women behind. They were slender and exquisitely dressed, and as elegant as anyone presented by Dior and Jean Patou should be. At the entrance to the Customs hall a battery of at least a dozen cameras was turned towards them, several from television and the news reels. Trained to perfection, the young women posed without appearing to, were vivacious and attractively natural.

With the photographers were a dozen newspaper men.

'Just a moment, Sir Jeremy.'

'Will you stand in the middle? Thank you, sir.'

'If the blonde will change places with the tall brunette . . . Thank you.'

'Just one more, sir, please.'

'Will you tell us exactly where the parade is to be, Sir Jeremy?'

'Is it to be on the river?'

'Teddington?'

'Westminster?'

Sir Jeremy, obviously in his element, slipped his arm delicately round the brunette's waist.

'You'll know all about it in the morning,' he promised. 'I can tell you now that it will be the most magnificent show of furs, gowns, jewels and beautiful women ever staged in London. The spectacle not only of the year but of the decade.' He spied his wife, on the fringe of the newspaper men and strode towards her, arms outstretched. 'Hello, m'dear.' He kissed her lightly on either cheek. 'Lovely to see you, you ought to be *in* the show, not simply organising it.'

'Will you do that again, sir?'

'Could you move a little closer, madam—*and* you madam. *And* you.' The speaker motioned first to Lady Pilkington, then to the models.

Pilkington laughed. 'That's enough now, gentlemen—more tomorrow.' He inclined his head towards his wife. 'Hugh here?'

'Yes, just coming.'

'He can look after the models,' said Pilkington. 'Aren't they charming?'

'Most charming.'

They both laughed.

A few minutes later Esmeralda was driving her husband out of the airport, while Hugh St. John, manager of the parade and renowned in London fashion circles, shepherded the models, allowed them to pose for a few more photographs, and then climbed after them into a big Chrysler.

Next to his wife, Pilkington was saying:

'What *is* all this about Alec Hobbs and his merry men, darling?'

'He's very put out because you didn't tell the police about the parade.'

'But it would have spoiled the whole show if they'd started making preparations!'

'I told him that, but he didn't seem to think it important. Jeremy.'

'Yes, m'dear?'

'I think *he* thinks there could be a robbery.'

'Oh nonsense! Tosh! Rubbish!' Suddenly Pilkington seemed almost angry. 'Alec *can't* believe such balderdash. Didn't say anything to suggest it, did he?'

'Only that he was afraid of it.'

'How did he hear about the parade?'

'Morris, the insurance man, told him.'

'I'll have to talk to Morris, said Pilkington. 'Secrecy is secrecy. *You're* not worried, are you?'

Esmeralda half-frowned. 'I would hate anything to go wrong, darling.'

'My God, so would I!' Pilkington sat back for a few seconds, then touched her hand—resting lightly on the wheel—as if he had forgotten that she was driving in the thick traffic of the Great West Road. 'Perhaps it's as well Alec knows. The police won't let anything go wrong. As they know all about it, we needn't worry. Angel, you look absolutely *splendid*. Whenever I leave you for a few days I always wonder how I could have been such a fool.'

Esmeralda laughed, but was obviously pleased.

Gideon, at the end of that day, was in one of his more dissatisfied moods. He felt as if he had been tied by hidden bonds to the desk, and this always irked him. Only now and again, as Commander, could he take any active share in an investigation; for the main part he could only guide the detectives in the field, from his office.

At the moment, except for the Pierce child, the coming parade, and the industrial diamonds problem, there were no major crimes going through. Summer was often a quiet period, which was just as well; school holidays meant holidays for policemen with their families as well as for criminals with theirs. But this was a quiet period in other ways, too. For years there had been the uncertainty about Lemaitre and his, Gideon's deputy; and there had been a strong move to promote him, Gideon, to the post of Assistant Commissioner. All of these things had helped to create pressures and tensions, and Gideon heaved a great sigh of relief when they had passed. Yet the truth was that he missed them.

Now that he had been on the river there was no excuse to go out into the Divisions, and this made him feel restless. He had given all the thought he could to the Pierce case; in fact there was nothing he could do which Hellier couldn't do at least as well.

A tap at the door made Gideon look up from his desk, and as he did so the door opened, and Hobbs came in, closing it carefully behind him. In some contradictory way Hobbs's calm and unquestioned efficiency both took a load off Gideon's shoulders and, at the same time, added to his restlessness.

'What's on, Alec?'

'Nothing new of any significance.' Hobbs said that as if it were routine. 'I've just heard that Pilkington is back from Paris, and has promised the press a statement by tomorrow morning.'

'That's what we expected, isn't it?'

'Yes——' Hobbs paused, and then added: 'George.'

'Yes?'

'Prescott and Roswell worried me.'

' "Big River Robbery", you mean?'

'Yes.'

'Got under my skin, too,' Gideon admitted. 'It obviously sprang to everybody's mind.' He did not add that it had also drawn attention from the waterproof bag story; no one had been particularly interested in that, although each had examined the bag.

'*Is* there a way it could be staged?'

'Meaning, is Worby over-confident?' Gideon pursed his lips. 'Worby's always inclined to be, of course. In this case—I don't know. He's quite right in his assertion that it's difficult to start anything quickly on the water.'

'Yes.' Hobbs frowned. 'Yes, I suppose so. Or under it.'

'But not above it,' said Gideon slowly.

Hobbs stared.

'Above?'

Gideon frowned. 'I don't know what protection those jewels will have, but if they *were* all in one place, if someone aboard *did* steal them and get them on to the deck, say, and if——' he hesitated, feeling that the possibility which had entered his head was too ridiculous to utter, then went on—'and if a helicopter was hovering, ostensibly to take photographs, but with someone on board ready to signal when it was worth swooping down and using a grab——'

Hobbs gave a low-pitched whistle.

'Great River Robbery, Method One!'

'I know it sounds absurd.' Gideon sounded almost apologetic.

'But it *could* happen,' said Hobbs excitedly. 'One swoop, and a crate could be plucked off the deck, and dropped beside a waiting car or van almost anywhere in London, within a few minutes of the robbery.'

Gideon began to rub his chin.

'It *isn't* absurd,' Hobbs argued. 'And I wouldn't like to take any chances,' he added.

'Nor would I,' growled Gideon. 'We've two clear days before the damned thing starts.'

'Nearly three,' Hobbs corrected. 'It starts at six-thirty, to miss the worst of the rush-hour. From what I saw of the *River Belle* they'll be working right through the night to get the *décor* finished. Care to look over it yourself?'

'No, I'll leave that part to you. But I'll drive home along the Embankment and see what they're doing on the pier.'

In fact, there was very little to see, except an army

of workmen on the pier and on the river boats, as well as several tradesmen's vans parked nearby. A Superintendent of the Division was talking to a uniformed Inspector, obviously about parking and re-routing traffic. Gideon didn't stop, but raised a hand to them. Just beyond the pier the *Belle Casino* was gay with bunting, but practically no one was aboard; gaming seldom started in earnest until after dark.

When he turned into the gate of his home in Harrington Street, Gideon heard the first theme of a Beethoven Concerto, being played in his front room. So Penelope was home and practising. Bless the girl, she spent every moment she could at the piano. He let himself in as the majestic notes rolled out, and for some absurd reason almost tiptoed past the half-open door. There was no one in the kitchen or the living-room, and he wondered if Kate were out. There was no note. Suddenly the piano playing stopped and Penelope came hurrying.

'Is that you, Daddy? Oh, *there* you are!'

Penelope was twenty-two, and the least attractive of the Gideon daughters, but she had a merry expression in her brown eyes, a snub nose, and nice lips. She was the most vivacious of the family. Giving Gideon a hug, she went on: 'Mummy's gone over to Pru's and is going to stay the night . . . There's a casserole in the oven . . . Neil's out until midnight, and Priscilla will be late too.'

'So that leaves you and me,' Gideon said.

'Leaves you,' said Penelope, briskly. 'I've a rehearsal, and a date afterwards, I just waited to say hello-goodbye.'

'Hello, goodbye,' Gideon said ruefully.

He ate the contents of the casserole, and a large slice of apple tart, then went into the living-room and switched on the television. Almost at once there was the sound of shooting, sure herald of a Western. He picked up the evening newspaper and half-watched the screen while skimming the headlines, read a small paragraph about the Pierces, another about the infanticide, an inside page story of the finding of Tom Argyle-Morris's body. The Yard wasn't getting anywhere with any of the main inquiries, he thought despondently, that must be why he was feeling so depressed.

He put the paper down and, despite the figures cavorting across the screen, began to doze. It was pleasant and comfortable. Then, suddenly, the telephone bell disturbed him. He was so near sleep that he wondered, at first, what it was; then how long it had been ringing. If it was the Yard it would go on and on, if it was a family call it would probably stop ringing before he reached it.

It didn't stop, and he lifted the receiver.

'Gideon.'

'George, you were quite right to ask me to keep a weather-eye for Micklewright.' It was Worby speaking. 'One of his sisters-in-law has just phoned me. She says he's drunk as a lord and swearing that he's going to kill his wife. Did you know she'd gone off with another man?'

Gideon sat in the back of a car which had been sent from the Yard and was being driven along the Embankment. Now that it was dark, the *Belle Casino* was ablaze with light, and across the river, Battersea Park Pleasure Gardens, lively survivor of the 1951 Exhibition, was gay and gaudy with lights of a dozen colours, reflecting with rare beauty on the dark water. Gideon was aware of these things, but thinking only of Micklewright and his wife.

Why hadn't he made Micklewright talk? The man

must have been at breaking point for days, if not for weeks. With a little more effort he could have been persuaded to tell the whole story.

Self-reproach was a waste of time, though.

Micklewright was believed to be somewhere between his own home in Stepney, and the flat where his wife was known to be living, in Greenwich, and Worby had alerted the Division which covered Greenwich.

'According to his sister-in-law, he's twice been forcibly restrained from attacking his wife,' Worby had reported.

'Is the wife's place being protected?'

'He won't get through, George, don't worry.'

'I hope not,' Gideon had said, grimly.

Now, as the car sped along through London's night, all the other factors went in and out of his mind. There was Micklewright's personal problem, which explained so much. There was the fact that tension and too much whisky were stopping him from doing his job well. There was the fact that he had upset Van Hoorn. There was the fact that he would have to be taken off the inquiry, and it was always a bad thing to put a new man in charge halfway through a case. There was another, in some ways the most important, factor of all: if Micklewright did reach his wife and attack her it would be a major sensation, and would do great harm to the public image of the police. That image was better now than it had been for some time, but it needed comparatively little to blur it. There might be no fairness in a situation by which one policeman's personal tragedy could affect the reputation of the entire Force, but it could and, if this got out, it would.

'Have the press learned about this, yet?' he had asked Worby.

'Not as far as I know, George.'

The best way to Greenwich by night was across London Bridge and then along the Old Kent Road through New Cross and Deptford. The Tower Bridge was vivid in floodlights. Gideon had only to turn his head to see the floodlit walls of the Tower itself. The road, which seemed deserted, was poorly lit. Every moment he expected a message by radio, but none came. At last the car drew up alongside another police car at the end of a tree-lined avenue. Two men came forward: first, Joe Mullivan, Superintendent in charge of QR Division, then the last man Gideon had expected, Old Man River Singleton.

Joe Mullivan, big and massive, one of the few men in the Force who was bigger than Gideon, opened the door.

'Any sign of him?' Gideon demanded at once.

'Not near here, sir.'

'Anywhere?' growled Gideon.

'We've had a report that an acquaintance of his saw him in a pub in Deptford half an hour ago.'

Gideon frowned. 'Does his wife know what's happening?'

'No,' Mullivan said.

'She ought to be warned,' put in Singleton gruffly. 'That's my opinion, sir.'

He glared almost defiantly at Gideon.

'What are you doing here?' demanded Gideon.

'They're both old friends of mine, sir. I could see this marriage was heading for the rocks years ago. I want to go and see Clara but the Superintendent refused to allow me to go up to her place until you arrived. I'd like your permission, sir.'

Chapter Fourteen

THE MURDEROUS POLICEMAN

In the shadows cast by the street lamps were several detectives, their faces pale shapes, their bodies dark. Beyond Gideon was the driver, in front of him Mullivan and Singleton—and Singleton was obviously fighting to retain his composure. Here was a case where the human, emotional side of a policeman was getting on top of his official side. A couple came round a corner, walking briskly as they turned into the street, slowing down when they saw the cars and the men. All of these things flickered through Gideon's mind. There was more than enough to worry about without Singleton, but the wrong attitude towards him now could do a lot of harm in several ways. Even in the few seconds while he deliberated, Gideon saw a hardening of defiance in Singleton's craggy face, in full expectancy of a refusal.

'It's a long time since I've seen Clara Micklewright,' Gideon said. 'I think I'll come along with you.'

The defiance, the half-formed resentment, vanished into thin air.

'That's going to *make* her take it seriously!' Singleton was almost jubilant.

'I hope so. Superintendent——' Gideon turned to Mullivan—'What's the position?'

'The house is watched back and front, sir, and we've men in the gardens of neighbouring houses, even got two men on the roof opposite.'

'With long-beam lamps?'

'Yes, sir.'

'Good.' Gideon turned and walked along the street

of tall, terraced houses with Singleton, who suddenly seemed tongue-tied.

'Anything about the Pierce girl, sir?' he asked at last.

'Not yet.'

'Hell of a thing to happen.'

'Yes,' Gideon said. 'And this is a hell of a thing to happen to Micklewright. You say you've been expecting it?'

'For years,' answered Singleton. 'It was one of those misfit marriages from the beginning. God knows what Clara ever saw in Mick. Easy to understand what he sees in her, though.'

'Much younger than he is, isn't she?'

'Fifteen years. She was *too* young, I suppose. Hero-worshipped him, in a way—remember when he won that life-saving medal?'

'Yes,' said Gideon, turning his mind back to the time when Micklewright had plunged off Chelsea Bridge to rescue two children who had fallen from a pleasure boat.

'They met about that time. Er—I'm not talking out of place, sir, am I?'

'Not a bit.'

As Gideon spoke, they reached a gate where a man stood on guard and another was close by. Bushes grew in the small garden beyond, and whitened steps led up to a dark front door. There was a light over the door and a light at a high window. On one side of the porch were several bell pushes, each with a card underneath; Singleton pressed the top button as he went on:

'Everything was all right for a few years. They had one child, a girl—but she died at the age of six. She'd held them together. Mick buried himself in his work but Clara hadn't anything to bury herself in, so she got a job as a model, and—well, she's enough to make most men lose their heads.'

Gideon asked, rather grimly: 'She lived it up, did she?'

'Yes, sir—but she didn't let Mick down. Not for years, anyhow. She kept their home clean as a new pin, and she's one of the best cooks I know. He didn't seem to mind the rest.'

'Did he know what was going on?'

'Oh, he *knew* all right.'

'Then what's this trouble about?'

Singleton pressed the bell-push again, and said:

'She asked him for a divorce, and that changed things. A year ago, that was. She met this chap she's living with, Jonathan Wild, and fell in love. They wanted to marry, but Mick wouldn't go along with divorce. He said he'd shut his eyes to an affair and wouldn't make any trouble provided she stayed in his house, as his wife. Didn't make any demands on her—what the hell is happening?' He rang the bell again. 'They usually press the button upstairs and the door opens.'

'Sure they're in?'

'There's a light on at their window.'

'Do you come here often?'

'Once most weeks,' answered Singleton. 'As a matter of fact I knew Jonathan before——'

'Who's there?' a man asked from the other side of the door.

Singleton raised his voice.

'It's Jake and a friend.'

'Hang on a moment.' There was a sound of a chain being taken out of its channel, then a creak as the door opened. The light from the hall was behind the man who opened the door, but a street light shone on to his lean, hatchet-like face. Gideon had an impression of an overpoweringly handsome man with shining dark eyes. 'Hello, Jake,' he said. 'Who's your friend?'

'Commander Gideon,' Singleton answered.

Wild's eyes widened almost ludicrously.

'This *is* an honour. Do come in.' He stood aside for the others to enter, then closed the door. 'I suppose you've come because Mick is on the rampage again,' he added. He said 'Mick' with a kind of friendly familiarity which surprised Gideon.

'How did you know?' Singleton asked quickly.

'Jessie telephoned,' answered Wild.

'Clara's sister,' Singleton interpolated.

'And I thought I'd better not release the street door from upstairs,' Wild went on. He kept his voice low as he led the way up a flight of narrow stairs, which curved round at a landing. The ceilings were high, the walls dark, the landing lights dim. 'How much does the Commander know?'

'You can speak quite freely,' Gideon said.

'Then I will. He did get in once, three weeks ago, and really scared Clara. Until then she didn't take his threats seriously, but she does now. Everything's all right until he hits the bottle. Then it can be hell. I—*My God*, what's that?'

Across his words from high above their heads came a high-pitched scream.

'Don't! a woman cried, 'No, no no!'

'He's up there!' cried Wild, and he sprang forward as if there were springs in the heels of his boots.

The woman screamed again, in wild terror.

'Micklewright!' roared Gideon in a tremendous voice. 'Stop that!'

Then Wild tripped on the stairs.

As he tripped and fell, he banged his head heavily on the wall, grunted, and sprawled down. Gideon was just behind him, the woman was screaming; a door on the next landing opened and a man appeared, calling out ineffectually. Gideon dodged as Wild slipped down another stair, then sprang over him, holding tight to the banister.

Upstairs, a door slammed.

Gideon took the stairs two at a time, swung round another landing, then, in the dim light, saw a door at the next one, shut and dark. Reaching the door, he tried the handle and thrust hard, but found it would not budge. Drawing back three feet, he hurled himself against it, his great weight making it creak and groan. He drew back again. The screaming had stopped. He had an awful fear that he was too late, and summoned still greater strength for his second attempt.

With a deafening crash the door swung open.

In front of him, back towards him, Micklewright had his hands round his wife's neck. She was pressed against the wall, her head held tight against it, her eyes huge and staring, her mouth open, her teeth bared.

Gideon swept his right arm round and struck Micklewright a tremendous buffet on the side of the head. Micklewright swayed and his grip on his wife's throat slackened. Gideon hit him again. This time his hands fell and he staggered, struck a chair, and crashed to the floor. His wife, hands at her throat, was beginning to slide down the wall. Even in that strange and tense situation, Gideon noticed the beautiful shape of her hands, and the soft pink of the lacquer on her nails. He thrust an arm round her waist and drew her away from the wall, as Singleton said:

'I'll look after her, sir.'

Seeing a couch on one side of the room, Gideon carried the woman over to it, laid her down gently, and drew back. She was breathing harshly, painfully. Singleton, pushing in front of him, knelt beside the couch and began to loosen the waistband of her skirt.

Wild came in, limping.

Micklewright began to claw himself to his feet.

Wild glanced at him without expression, then hurried towards the couch.

Singleton looked up at him. 'Turn the bed down, get hot water bottles, then hot coffee,' he ordered.

'Right.' Wild turned away, glanced at Micklewright again, then went out of the room. He said something under his breath; it sounded like 'thanks.' He disappeared. Gideon took Micklewright by the arm and held him steady. His eyes were bleary and bloodshot, his nose was red and shiny, but his cheeks were the colour of pastry and his lips looked faintly blue. He kept moistening them and touching the side of his face as if wondering why it stung so much. His gaze did not focus properly, and he began to sway to and fro. Gideon felt a mingled disgust and compassion.

And he began to face up to the things that would have to be done.

First—get Micklewright to a police station; next, sober him up—no, next have a police surgeon and an independent doctor examine him, *then* sober him up. Get a psychiatrist to examine him, tonight. Charge him with attempted murder——

Must he?

He could charge him with common assault.

No, Gideon thought, that would be impossible. Too many people had heard of his threats, dozens had probably heard him tonight. The neighbour on the landing below had heard everything and may have seen much. There could be no whitewashing. God damn it! Gideon suddenly roared within himself, there shouldn't *be* any thought of whitewashing! What was the matter with him? The charge would have to be attempted murder. And as soon as Micklewright was at the station someone would tell the press and tomorrow the court would be crammed full to overflowing.

As for the evening paper headlines——

Again, but with less vehemence, he thought: Oh, hell, what's the matter with me? He *did* it. In another two minutes his wife would have been dead. He had a brainstorm while he was drunk.

In fact, it wasn't going to be as simple as that; but at least from the police point of view it was nothing like as bad as a charge of corruption.

Singleton stepped to his side.

'She's all right now,' he said.

'Thank God.'

'And thank you, sir. If you hadn't got that door down when you did——'

'Where was Micklewright hiding?' Gideon asked.

'As far as I can find out, sir, he forced a downstairs window, came through the ground floor flat while the family was watching television, and let himself into the hall. Seems to have been hiding in a landing cupboard for a long time—before the alarm was raised, I would think. The cupboard stinks of whisky and there's an empty bottle on the floor. God knows what he meant to do, but he was crafty enough to stay in hiding.'

'Awaiting his chance, I suppose,' Gideon said.

'George ... George ...' Micklewright began to mumble 'George ... Gee ... *Gee-Gee*! Commander.' He drew himself up to an unsteady attention ' 'Evening, sir.'

There were other men here now, including Mullivan. Micklewright looked at them all as if puzzled,

130

turned back to Gideon, and said thickly: 'Commander Gideon, sir!'

Gideon turned to Mullivan. 'Take him, will you. Get our doctor and another G.P. and ask them to call a psychiatrist. Don't charge him until I come—I'll be with you soon.'

'Right, sir,' said Mullivan. 'Are *you* all right?'

'Yes. Why shouldn't I be?'

'Er——' Mullivan grunted, turned to Micklewright and gripped him lightly just above the elbow. 'Come on, Mick,' he said, his voice surprisingly gentle.

Gideon moved across to a chair and sat down, a little annoyed with himself because he felt so very weary. Almost as soon as he relaxed, Jonathan Wild came towards him, limping, carrying a bottle of whisky in one hand and a glass and a soda syphon on a tray. He was smiling twistedly, but Gideon's impression of a remarkably handsome man was stronger than ever.

'Will you have a drink?'

'Thanks.'

Wild poured out a generous tot.

'Soda?'

'Fill it up, please.'

The soda water gurgled and fizzed.

'Thanks.' Gideon lifted the glass.

'Commander, I can't hope to tell you how—how grateful I am.'

'You don't need to try.'

'But I *shall* try,' said Wild. 'And another thing, I would like you to know that I——' he hesitated— 'that I really do love her.'

Gideon thought: Yes, I can see that he does. Aloud, he said: 'I'm very glad she's all right.'

'And I want you to know that I hope it will be possible not to charge Mick.'

'Mick' again.

Gideon frowned. 'Assault is assault.'

'He's a sick man, Commander. Some will say I helped to make him sick. All I want you to know is that if there is any way I can help him now, I will.'

'Mr. Wild,' Gideon said, 'we aren't going to be vindictive. You can be sure of that.'

Wild's lips seemed to curl.

'But the law is the law and because he's an upholder of it will have to be punished with the utmost vigour. Yes, I see. Don't you sometimes hate the law, Commander?'

After a few moments reflection Gideon drank again and then replied: 'If you want to invoke the aid of the law for Superintendent Micklewright, the best way is to get a lawyer who really knows what he's doing. If the lawyer is briefed before he's called to the police station, it will help.' He finished his drink and went on: 'I needed that!'

'Another, Commander?'

'No, thanks.'

There was a long pause, then Wild gave a jerky little nod, and said: 'I'll do just what you recommend.'

Chapter Fifteen

THE THREE MEN

At about the time that Gideon was drinking his whisky and soda on the south side of the river, three men were sitting round a table in an apartment on the north side, less than a quarter of a mile from Scotland Yard. One of these was the big man with the guttural voice who had been in the disused shed at the Royal Docks. He wore a dinner jacket which was rather too small for him, and a big-winged bow tie; the unlit cigar jutting from his lips looked like an extension of his face. Opposite him in a high-backed armchair was a very much smaller man with a curiously baby-like face, smooth and peach-pink, and fair, silky hair. He was also wearing a dinner jacket.

The third man was Hugh St. John, Sir Jeremy Pilkington's chief *aide*.

St. John wore the grey suit with green flecks that he had worn at the airport that afternoon. He was good-looking in an un-English way, with thick dark hair rising high from his forehead, a sallow complexion, full lips and a long, down-curved nose. There was something very finicky about his movements and his attitudes; sitting there he gave an impression of impatience, of disdain for his two companions.

'I want to know exactly what happened in Paris,' the big man said.

'I don't know what happened in Paris,' St. John replied.

'You are paid to get the information.'

'Holmann, I am sure St. John is being wise not to claim to know everything,' interpolated the man with the baby face.

'That's right,' said St. John. 'I get paid for telling you what I know. Not what you would like to know. I'm not sure that I get paid enough.' There was a supercilious expression on his face as he glanced from the big man to the small man. 'What do you think, Morro?'

The baby-faced man said: 'You will be well paid when we have the jewels.'

'And if you don't get the jewels?'

133

'None of us will be well paid,' murmured Morro.

'What are you talking about—we are going to get them,' said Holmann. His English was good but rather precise and with a momentary hesitation before certain words. 'That is, if you do your job.'

St. John leaned back in his chair. 'The jewels will be on the *River Belle*. The value will be approximately half-a-million pounds. They will be insured for seven hundred and fifty thousand pounds, at Lloyd's. In all there will be seventy-two different pieces—twelve models will wear six pieces each. The models will be given the jewellery only two or three minutes before they appear before the guests. Cheap costume jewellery will be used at rehearsals, including the dress rehearsal an hour before the real event occurs. Each piece, with a numbered tag, will be taken out of the portable fire-proof safe and given straight to Gentian, who will pin it on to the model and will take it off when she has finished. An insurance representative, two Securial officers, and I, will be present all the time. I will take the jewels out of the safe and hand them to Gentian, and he will give them back to me to put back into the safe.'

He paused, to sip from a big brandy glass.

Morro murmured: 'It is very thorough.'

'It must be thorough,' Holman said. 'This is good, I agree.'

St. John gave a wry, thin-lipped smile.

'I am glad you think so. There will be spotlights shining on each model in the bar where she is given the jewels. The safe will be under a spot-light all the time. The jewels will be in the full view of at least six people every moment, and for most of the time in full view of hundreds—including some very important policemen.'

'What is that?' exclaimed Morro.

134

'Of Scotland Yard?' asked Holmann.

'Pilkington has invited Commander Gideon and his wife, Deputy Commander Hobbs and a friend, and two officials from the Thames Division,' St. John informed them. 'There will be Customs officers as well as Thames Division officers on board all the time.'

'Naturally,' Holmann was quite unflustered.

'The portable safe will be locked by the Securial officers and kept on board overnight, with a four man armed guard on duty,' continued St. John. 'Police, Customs and Securial officers will escort it from the bank to the *River Belle* and back late on the Tuesday evening. The Customs will check item by item on Tuesday evening at the bank and it will then be collected by the different jewel merchants who are lending it for display on Wednesday morning.'

Morro was looking earnestly at Holmann.

'It is very thorough, isn't it? Our only opportunity to get the jewels will be as they are brought to the river, or as they are taken from it.'

'There will be at least twenty Securial men at the landing stage and on the Embankment, and probably twice as many police,' St. John answered, and when neither of the others spoke he went on: 'Now do you see why I doubt if we'll get the jewels, Holmann?'

'You are paid to provide information,' Holmann said, drawing at the unlit cigar. 'Not to consider whether we shall get them. Or *how* we shall get them.'

'I don't think you can,' St. John retorted. 'That's why I wonder whether a thousand pounds is enough for the risk I'm taking. If you make an attempt, and fail——'

'I do not fail,' said Holmann, harshly. 'Have you a plan of the ship?'

'I'm no draughtsman, but I've some rough drawings.'

'Did I not understand that Gentian had drawings of the interior of the ship so that he could perfect the *décor*?'

'He has only one copy.'

'There are such things as cameras.'

'Oh, no,' said St. John. 'I'm not going to take that much of a risk. I'll pass on what I learn in the way of business but I won't do anything which will point to me if I were seen or caught.'

'St. John——' Morro began, nervously.

'It is a reasonable attitude,' said Holmann, unexpectedly. 'We do not want him caught any more than he does himself. Show me these rough drawings, please.'

St. John lifted his flat, black brief-case from the side of his chair, unzipped it, and took out a folder. He opened this and handed it over the table to Holmann, then looked at the brandy decanter.

'Please,' Morro said. He pushed the decanter closer to St. John, who first selected a cigar, clipped the end, cut it, and then helped himself to more brandy. Holmann was scrutinising the drawings which were in dark pencil and had a number of annotations and indications of dimensions. He looked from one page to another—there were four in all—and finally back at St. John. He was smiling faintly; the curve to his lips made him look vaguely like a tiger.

'These are good,' he announced.

St. John bowed sardonically. 'They're the best I could do.'

'How did you do them?'

'They were done for Securial, and I kept a copy.'

'Good,' repeated Holmann. 'These sizes, are they accurate? Especially the width of the doors . . .'

He asked questions, searchingly, most of which St. John was able to answer. Holmann seemed even more satisfied when he had finished. He placed a pudgy hand on St. John's shoulder, then took out a fat wallet and selected a number of ten pound notes. He placed these in front of St. John.

'I hope you will feel better rewarded with this extra money,' he said.

Without counting the notes, St. John picked them up and nodded.

'Thank you.'

'And you are not likely to be called on for any other service until after the river parade,' Holmann added.

St. John stood up, looking intently into his eyes. They were slightly yellowish, with an outer fringe of green round the pupil, the lids sallow, with tiny folds of flesh about them. St. John did not voice any questions but plenty were in his expression.

'I will come to the lift with you,' said Morro.

Again, St. John nodded.

A few minutes later he stepped into a black Jaguar $3\frac{1}{2}$ litre parked in the forecourt of the block of modern flats. A doorman stood and watched him, indifferently. There was a hint of rain in the air but not enough to call for windscreen wipers. St. John drove towards the Embankment, with Victoria Station behind him. It was very dark until he drew near the *River Belle* and the *Belle Casino* over each of which was a glow of light. He parked fairly near the pier and looked across at the lights of the pleasure gardens, then walked past two policemen, towards the gangway leading to the pier. Three couples, the women beautifully dressed, came up from the casino. Two doormen were at the pier, another man stood on the gangway leading to the *River Belle*. Lights shone all over the old boat, two floodlights on the bows were slowly being swivelled round, and there was a sound of hammering.

St. John went into the main salon.

Gentian and two girls, all wearing pale mauve pants and primrose yellow shirts, were draping the windows with gold-coloured fabrics. Gentian had a mouthful of pins and was mumbling:

'How about the height, dear . . . Not *on* the floor, but not more than half-an-inch above it . . . Is that right?' He put in a number of pins, then looked across, saw St. John and widened his eyes in surprise. He took the pins out of his mouth carefully.

'What are we doing wrong now? If anything?'

St. John raised his eyebrows. 'I didn't come to see what you were doing wrong, I wanted to find out if anything was going right.'

The girls exchanged meaning glances. Gentian made no comment.

'What chance is there of being ready on time?' asked St. John.

'If we don't get any more interruptions we shall be ahead of time,' retorted Gentian.

'*And* if we work all night,' said one of the girls.

St. John ignored her. 'Has Sir Jeremy been here this evening?' he asked Gentian.

'No.'

St. John nodded, and went out. As he disappeared and while he was within earshot, one of the girls said feelingly:

'How I *hate* that man.'

'He probably doesn't like you very much,' Gentian remarked. 'Now, the other window, dear . . .'

St. John strolled on to the deck, looked about him, seeing the beauty of the lights reflected from the Embankment and the bridges on the dark water, then crossed to the landing stage and walked towards the *Belle Casino*. The men on duty stood aside. He went in and sauntered about the crowded room. The two big roulette tables were besieged by well-dressed men and women, the blackjack nearly as crowded. Two red-headed girls and several long-haired youths were at the craps table, the girls giggling, one of them shooting the dice. In a far corner two tables of poker seemed to be part of a different world.

The cashier was near the craps table, and the office was behind it.

St. John went to the door of the office and tapped. It was opened after a few seconds by a hard-faced, middle-aged woman who stood to one side. An elderly, grey-haired man was at a pedestal desk, with a safe behind him.

'Well?' he said.

St. John laid the money which Holmann had paid him on the desk. The man took it, counted it, and handed him five notes back. Then he opened a drawer and took out an I.O.U. for four hundred and fifty pounds, signed by St. John. He handed this across.

St. John picked a book of matches from a big glass ash-tray and set light to a corner of the paper and watched it burn. In everything he did there was an air of calculated insult.

'St. John,' the man said, 'don't ask me for money again.'

'I won't ask you for anything again,' St. John said. He nodded and went out. The two red-heads were on their way to the powder room, and both glanced at him. He went to the roulette table, waited for ten minutes, then bought fifty pounds' worth of counters and placed them on Number 7, straight. The croupier pushed other counters about, no one spoke, smoke was very thick. The croupier called:

'*Rein ne va plus*,' and paused momentarily before he spun the wheel. The soft whirring of the running ball sounded clearly against the background noises from the rest of the room, then slowed down to a hushed murmur.

The ball almost settled in twenty-nine, and then went over seven into twenty-eight.

St. John turned away. Two or three of the officials watched him thoughtfully. He spoke to no one but, outside, paused to take another look at the still surface of the river before moving up to his car.

Another car, a red Mini Minor, started up just ahead of him and turned out into the Jaguar's wake. At the wheel was a young man, by his side a girl with a lot of blonde hair which fell almost to her shoulders.

At the Greenwich Police Station, Gideon was saying to Mullivan: 'It will have to be attempted murder.'

'Yes, I know.'

'Wait for an hour,' Gideon advised. 'You may find he'll be legally represented by then. How is he?'

'Honestly, sir, I don't know whether he's still blind drunk or fooling. He doesn't seem to make any sense at all. Our doctor thinks he's drunk, the other man thinks it may be a nervous collapse.'

For the first time, Gideon seemed to brighten.

'If they prove that, it could help,' he said. 'Hell of a job, whatever happens. Is Singleton here?'

'No, but he left a note for you,' Mullivan replied, and handed Gideon a sealed envelope. Gideon did not open it until he was in the back of the car being driven home to Fulham. Then he read:

Just want to say thank you very much, sir.

His spirits lifted a little, and on the way home he was able to relax enough to reflect, a little sententiously, on the fact that just as two hours ago he had had no idea of what was in Micklewright's mind, so at this moment he had no idea of what was being planned anywhere in London.

Was there a plot to raid the River Parade, for instance? *Was* there a big organisation behind the industrial diamond losses? *Was* Geraldine Pierce alive, and if so, what ordeal had she suffered? What was going on in the minds of her parents? What other men, driven to drink and despair by the loss of their wives, might go berserk tonight? How many practised criminals were out on their furtive work, how many people were committing a crime for the first time in their lives?

There was no end to the questions.

And there was no end to the secrets in this vast, sleeping city through which the wide river flowed so silently and mysteriously, burdened with ships and their cargoes moving to and from so many parts of the world.

Chapter Sixteen

RING MARK

Police Constable Charles Addis of the Thames Division had spent the first ten years of his working life, from fifteen to twenty-five, at sea as a merchant sailor. He had obtained his master's certificate, then had met the girl he had wanted to marry and no longer desired to leave London for months at a time. So he had joined the Metropolitan Police force, going immediately to the Thames Division and soon becoming a member of the crew of a patrol with Chief Inspector Singleton in charge, and Police Sergeant Tidy, ten years his senior, as second-in-command.

Addis lay long awake that night, his wife Elsie sleeping soundly beside him.

Everything was fine between him and Elsie—even though she didn't like it when he was on night duty and had a secret longing for him to leave the Force. But this he didn't know. Their first child was on the way, which delighted him and rather frightened Elsie. That night, however, he wasn't thinking about Elsie or the child, he was thinking about that packet of industrial diamonds.

He had hooked it out of the water; had been the second man to touch it. He had a proprietorial attitude towards it—this was *his* case. He knew everything which had been done, had taken Micklewright and the Dutchman with the wide shoulders on a beat from Greenwich to Hammersmith and had heard them talking freely. Van Hoorn was sure there was a big organisation at work, and that the packet he, Addis, had found had been one of many. Micklewright had doubted this but had been prepared to look.

Short of searching every ship which came in from the Western European ports, there was nothing else to be done. Van Hoorn had said to Micklewright only the previous day:

'It is possible, surely, to have the Customs search every ship.'

'Give us proof or even a good reason, and they will,' Micklewright had said.

So Addis, taking a chance, had talked to an officer of the Water Guard, a man whom he knew slightly.

'Search every ship?' the Customs man had echoed. 'You'll be lucky! It's a filthy job, takes a hell of a time—you ever crawled along the propeller shaft and got yourself covered with stinking grease, mate? And we wouldn't do it unless there was a hell of a good reason. Do you know what you're asking? With those freighters we might get fifty in a day! Fifty! Have a heart!'

And he was right.

'Besides,' the Customs man had added, 'they could be in a waterproof container, made to float, and tossed overboard in the Estuary, miles before Tilbury even, and picked up by a small boat. If you suggest this lark, chum, you'll be the best hated man in the Water Guard.'

He had laughed and slapped Addis on the shoulders.

Addis could almost feel the force of the blow as he lay there.

To make such a search even for one day *would* be impossible, unless there was a very powerful motive. It would require thousands of men from the Force, Customs, City and Port of London police. If a couple of coppers were bumped off, now——

'Don't be a bloody fool!' he muttered, half serious, half laughing at himself.

It would need that kind of sensation. All the same, there must be a way of cracking this problem.

He began to think of the packet, picturing it in his mind's eye. There had been that round mark on one side, the kind of mark that was caused by rubber feet standing on a plain surface. He had a typewriter which made the same kind of mark on paper, even on a table. Could that have any significance? The packet was at Scotland Yard, trust them to hog everything there was in the way of evidence. But there were some photographs of it at the Wapping station.

It was nearly dawn—five o'clock, he guessed. He turned over and looked at the bedside clock; it was ten to five. He could lie awake no longer; he'd had it. He got out of bed cautiously, and, thank goodness, Elsie didn't stir. It wouldn't surprise her if he were gone when she woke, he was due off soon after seven, anyhow—always waking himself rather than putting on the alarm early enough to wake Elsie. He dressed very quietly, went downstairs and made himself some tea, then set off for the Wapping High Street Station.

His wife heard the front door close.

She stretched right across the bed, pulled his pillow under her, and dozed off again, slightly resentful.

Why did he always have to wake her up?

Perhaps if they had twin beds it would be better.

The night duty men were still at the Wapping High Street Station when Addis arrived. The man on duty in the Chief Inspector's room made the inevitable crack: 'Your wife kick you out, Charlie?' He went out, through the boat shed where one of the small patrol boats and the Superintendent's launch were being serviced. Round the propeller shaft to the patrol boat was a coil of thick steel.

'Got to take the prop shaft off to put *that* right,' a mechanic complained.

'My heart bleeds for you,' Addis remarked, and went out towards the pier. Here the river was wide and smooth. On the far side were the warehouses and wharves; not far off were the big piles of timber in the Surrey Docks. Two lighters, each towing four barges, were following each other up river. Not far off, a ship's siren blasted—either as the ship arrived or when it was about to leave. A Customs cutter went past, busily. Over on the far side, in the roads, were at least a dozen barges: on one of them was a man. Addis turned away from the water, which put new life into him, and looked into the Inspector's room again.

'Anyone seen the man on the barges at Elbow Roads?'

'Fred went over and had a look. He's a Rodent

Officer, they've got some rats over there,' the duty man replied. 'They used to call 'em rat catchers.'

'That's when they caught rats!'

Addis went into the C.I.D. room, where the photographs were pinned on the wall next to a notice about a Police Federation meeting. He stood studying them intently. There were six—one from each side of the packet, one from each edge, which all looked the same. The faint ring showed up more clearly in the photograph, because of the way the flash had been positioned. Addis began to frown. He had seen something like this before. It was like the ring impression made by a suction cap. Mines were stuck on to the hulls of ships with small round suction caps.

His heart began to beat very fast, and he could hardly wait for Old Man River to come in.

Gideon was up next morning before Penelope or Malcolm, grumbled to himself while he made some tea, decided to breakfast at the Yard, and was there before eight o'clock. The night duty men were just going, all with that rather worn look that nightworkers always had, the day duty men were coming in, with some of the office staff. It was a bright morning, much more crisp than yesterday. He rang for a messenger, and an old, retired constable now on the civil staff came in.

'Bacon and eggs for a hungry man, Jim!'

'Yes, Mr. Gideon. Coffee as usual?'

'Everything as usual,' Gideon said, reflecting that it must be three months since he had last had breakfast at the Yard. He went into Hobbs's office, but no new reports had reached Hobbs yet, not even about Micklewright. It was strange but he, Gideon, wanted to shut out the recollection of what had happened last night, and even resisted a temptation to telephone Mullivan.

The messenger brought in an enormous breakfast. 'Thought you could manage three eggs, Mr. Gideon.'

'How right you were!' Gideon knew that he was being over-hearty, but knew also that this was the best way to treat this particular messenger. He watched the man spread a white cloth over a small table and lay knives and forks and everything needed for breakfast. Then the messenger said:

'Is it true about Mr. Micklewright, sir?'

Gideon looked at him levelly.

'What have you heard, Jim?'

'That he's been charged with the attempted murder of his wife, sir.'

'I'm afraid it is true,' Gideon admitted, quietly.

'I couldn't be more sorry,' the messenger said. 'A very kind gentleman, Mr. Micklewright.'

'So it's all over the Yard,' Gideon remarked.

'Proper buzzing with it, sir.'

Gideon nodded, sat down and gradually began to concentrate on his breakfast. The messenger brought in three morning papers: there was nothing about Micklewright, but the *Globe* carried a front page picture of four attractive looking girls and Sir Jeremy Pilkington, Pilkington looking gay and very handsome. The caption read: *Sir J. Pilkington and Parisienne models in London for a Big River Mannequin Parade. See p. 7.* The other papers also carried the story. Tucked away in a corner was an account of the unsuccessful search by frogmen near Richmond. Gideon finished eating—and almost at once the telephone bell rang. He leaned across to take the call.

'Mr. Worby, sir, of Thames Division.'

Worby, to commiserate.

'Put him through.'

Worby's voice was pitched on a high note, without a

hint of commiseration, and he announced without preamble:

'George, one of my chaps has had a brainwave.'

'Good,' said Gideon. 'What kind?'

'He thinks that packet of industrial diamonds might have been stuck to the hull of a ship, and come off by accident.'

Gideon said slowly: 'Yes. Yes, it *is* a possibility, he's quite right.' He thought: What's the matter with us, why didn't someone think of this before?

'What I want to do is get the frogmen team busy,' went on Worby. 'They can cover a lot of the river if they start early—no searching needed, just a quick glance round the ships. We can say we're after a body, perhaps that Pierce child.'

'Go ahead,' Gideon agreed without hesitation.

'Right!'

'Which of your chaps was it?' Gideon wanted to know.

'You may remember him—the young one who was with you when you had your river trip.'

'Addis, wasn't it?'

'Charlie Addis, that's the chap. Once he's on a job, he doesn't let go.'

'He should make a good policeman,' said Gideon. 'Right.'

'I'll get cracking,' said Worby. ' 'Bye—oh, *George*!'

'What is it?'

'Er—I—er—couldn't be sorrier about Micklewright.'

'Nor could I,' Gideon said drily.

'Have a problem with Van Hoorn now, won't you?' Worby asked.

'He's gone back to Holland for a few days, so that can keep,' Gideon told him. 'What about the River Parade?'

'Everything's set,' said Worby. 'Including the newspapers. Have they gone to town on this!'

'You'd expect them to go to town,' Gideon remarked.

He rang off, and almost at once heard a movement in the next room. Was Hobbs in at last? He pondered young Addis's idea, recalled the eager, youthful face, then got up and went towards the door. It opened as he reached it, and he came face to face with Hobbs, who dropped back.

' 'Morning, Alec.'

'Good morning,' Hobbs said. He came inside as Gideon, in turn, backed away, his face finely drawn, obvious signs of anxiety in his eyes. 'I haven't been down to *Information* or collected any reports yet,' he said. 'I've only just heard about Micklewright.'

Gideon nodded, studying this man who came from such a different background and was dissimilar in so many ways, yet felt as deeply and as keenly for the reputation of the Force as any man who had been born and bred to it. He nodded again.

'Coffee?'

'No, thanks.'

'Alec,' Gideon said, 'if I'm not careful the Micklewright case is going to become an obsession. It mustn't.'

Hobbs gave a tight-lipped smile.

'Every newspaper, every television newsroom, the Home Secretary and our own Commissioner won't let us forget it. I had two newspapers on to me at my flat before I left.'

'I daresay,' Gideon weighed his words. 'I don't mind how I feel or you feel or anyone else feels. This is a human problem. We've done our job, we've got to hand the papers over to the Legal Department to brief the Public Prosecutor. Except for preparing the details, it's out of our hands. I've got no comment to make and I want word to go out to every station— send a teletype message to all Divisions and sub-divisional stations, telling them to make none, and to warn all the men on their strength to say absolutely nothing.'

'I should have realised you'd already decided what to do,' Hobbs said.

'The real problem is to find someone quickly to replace Micklewright,' went on Gideon. 'Any ideas?'

Hobbs pondered.

'Do we want a man with a good knowledge of precious stones or someone with knowledge of smuggling up the river?'

'A river man,' Gideon answered promptly. 'Someone who knows the river and the different Forces concerned with policing it—he must know them well.'

'I think I agree,' Hobbs said. 'There's only one man I can think of who answers to all that.'

'Who?'

'Singleton of Thames Division,' Hobbs said.

Gideon had been concentrating on possible successors to Micklewright among men at the Yard, and had not given a thought to anyone at the Division. He was surprised and, after the first few seconds, pleased that Hobbs should think of a man close to retiring age who might easily be allowed to wear out slowly. Singleton—Hobbs probably didn't know—he was a friend of Micklewright. Gideon recalled all that had happened last night, remembered the challenge, the defiance, the gratitude.

'Alec, talk to Worby and put it to him this way. That you think Singleton would be the right man but until he, Worby, agrees, you don't want to put it up officially to me. You could even ask Worby to sound me out on it.'

Hobbs's eyes crinkled at the corners as, for the first time that morning, he began to smile.

'I'll do just that.'

'Make it your first job. Worby's in, he's already told me . . .' Gideon briefed Hobbs about what had happened, and Hobbs went back to his own room to talk to the Thames Division chief. Almost before he sat at his desk Gideon's telephone rang again.

'Yes.'

'Mr. Hellier, sir, of EF Division,' the operator said, and on that instance switched Gideon's thoughts from diamonds and Micklewright to the missing Pierce child, of whom nothing had been heard for three days.

'Yes?' Gideon said.

'We know where the Pierce girl is,' announced Hellier, without a word of preamble.

Chapter Seventeen

GERALDINE

Geraldine Pierce was still in the cave.

She was wide awake, but 'Dick' was asleep.

She was dizzy with hunger for they had not eaten during the previous day. She had a dull headache and a sense of nausea.

She was secured by the strap and could not get at the buckle; she could move only a few inches. She felt cold, despite the touch of the man's body against her; her toes were freezing. She had a sense of hopelessness, brought on by hunger, pain and utter helplessness. She *knew* what would happen if he caught her trying to get away again, she could still imagine the tightness of his hands round her throat.

There was nothing, now, that she could do.

Last night, late, as he had lain with her, she had pleaded and promised. If he would let her go she would tell no one, she would pretend she'd got lost or been on her own—even run away. As she had pleaded she had seen the dull light in his eyes and had doubted whether he really heard what she said.

Afterwards, in that state of exhaustion she had become used to, she had said:

'You will let me go tomorrow, Dick, won't you?'

And he had said: 'I'll never let you go. You're *mine*.'

She had not uttered a word after that but had fallen asleep after a long time; and now she was awake, with the memory of his words and of his expression as he had uttered them. He had bared his teeth and spoken from deep in his throat.

'I'll never let you go. You're *mine*.'

Now she began to think, drearily: 'I can't get away. He means it, so I'll never get away.'

Tears had flooded her eyes but she had repressed the impulse to cry for fear of waking him. After a while she began to toy with the idea of hitting him; if she could only be sure that he wouldn't wake she could wriggle and wriggle and get at the bucket beneath the bed.

How could she knock him out?

She stared at his weak face, the two days' old stubble, the slack mouth and eyelids smeared with white 'sleep.' There was nothing heavy or hard within hand's reach, so all she could use were her hands.

Hands.

His were very strong and he could kill her just by tightening them round her neck. Were *hers* strong enough? She moved them cautiously, to study them.

151

They were quite long, dirty because she hadn't washed for several days, and her nails——

'Geraldine! How often have I told you to file your nails!'

Oh, Mummy, Mummy, Mummy!

She let her hands drop to the bed. They certainly weren't strong enough, and in any case she couldn't turn over and get them round his neck so as to grip tightly. It was hopeless, utterly hopeless, unless he were to go out and leave her. He had said something about going shopping today.

Even that was useless, though; he would tie her up so tightly she wouldn't have a chance. She hadn't any chance at all.

Unless——

She held her breath as an idea came into her mind. She saw his teeth and the top of his slack tongue as his head lolled forward awkwardly from the pillow. The *pillow*. She had seen a television picture only the other day—that age ago when she had run in and out of her home whenever she had wished. In the film, a woman had placed a pillow over a sleeping man's face and then pressed and pressed until his convulsive struggles had ceased.

The *pillow*.

She shifted round with infinite care so that she was facing him. She stretched her left arm over him and pulled the pillow a little further away from his head. He did not wake. She drew it free and his head fell just a little further forward. She could hardly breathe as she raised the pillow in one hand. Her mind was working very swiftly, and she could hear one of her school mistresses saying:

'*Think*, Geraldine, think before you *act*.'

Think——

If she shifted her right arm high enough from the

bed to touch part of the pillow beneath it, she could then hold it fast by lying on it. And she could stretch out her right arm and hold it tight on the other side. How long would it be before he stopped struggling? How long could *she* hold the pillow in position? Was she absolutely sure there was no other way?

She thought, no, no, there isn't.

She took a tighter hold on the pillow and eased her body up, drew the pillow across Dick's chest inch by inch, watching him tensely, frightened every moment that he would wake. If his eyes began to flicker that would be a sure sign.

She got the pillow beneath her body.

Her breathing was harsh and shallow and she was afraid that would disturb him. Now she had to decide whether to drop it on his face suddenly and put all her weight on to it, or whether to draw it gradually over his chin and then his face.

Gradually.

Gradually, gradually.

It was on a level with his chin, she steeled herself to make the final movement, when a dog barked close by.

On the instant, Dick woke.

He woke out of a sleep troubled by strange dreams of weird creatures and weird faces and staring eyes and beautiful bodies, to a loud yapping. He felt the pillow beneath his chin and knew immediately what Geraldine was trying to do. He flung himself backwards off the bed, snatched up the pillow and brought it down on to her head and face. He left it there and spun round towards the boarded-up window. The dog barked again and a boy called:

'Sprat, come here! Sprat.'

The dog yapped again, less furiously. The boy

called more gently:

'Leave it, Sprat, leave it.'

At that moment, Jones made his great mistake; pushing back the bolt, he opened the door and peered out to find that some of the protecting sandstone had fallen. Across the stretch of water, only three or four yards away, the boy stood looking at him.

And as they stared at each other, Geraldine screamed:

'*Help me! Help me! Help me!*'

Jones jumped away from the door, saw Geraldine leaning on one elbow, her face suffused, her eyes screwed up, her mouth wide open; a series of high-pitched screams followed one another in quick succession. He sprang towards her and gripped the sheet, screwed up a corner and rammed it into her mouth so that her screams faded into a hoarse gurgling sound. Flinging the pillow over her face, he ran back to the door. He could hear no sound now, but saw the boy, fifty yards up the shallow side of the quarry, the dog at his heels. They were scrambling up, dirt and stones falling after them. Jones knew exactly where the path was, reached it and started after the boy, who saw him and made a wild effort to go faster. He drew level, only ten feet or so away from the boy, who would have had no chance but for the dog.

The dog leapt at Jones. Jones kicked out, missed, and kicked again. The dog stumbled, steadied, and leapt at the man's hand. Its teeth buried themselves into the fleshy part of the ball of the thumb. Jones screamed in pain, lost his footing, and fell down several feet. The dog raced away; and a few seconds later both dog and boy reached the top of the quarry and disappeared. Jones came to rest nearer the foot of the path than the top, blood streaming from his hand, face scratched, knee suddenly painful where he had

banged it on a stone. He picked himself up and staggered towards the mouth of the cave.

He went in.

He saw Geraldine, lying very still, the pillow on
one side but the corner of the sheet still in her mouth.

He thought: she will tell the police what I have
done.

He thought: I didn't hurt the boy, he doesn't matter. She mustn't tell anyone what I've done.

They'll put me away for ever if she tells them, he
thought.

Her eyes were closed, and she did not seem to be
breathing. He pulled the sheet slowly away from her
mouth and dropped it. He picked up the pillow, held
it in both hands, then lowered it slowly on to her face.

The boy was seen by a motorist, who stopped to see
what was the matter.

The motorist drove furiously to the nearest house
and telephoned the police.

The police were at the edge of the quarry in seven
minutes and inside the cave in ten.

'We've found her, sir,' Hellier said on the telephone to Gideon. 'She's dead. Only been dead a few
minutes, too.'

'Have you tried——' Gideon began, helplessly.

'Tried the kiss—tried everything,' Hellier said.

Gideon asked heavily: 'Do the parents know?'

'I'm going to see them now,' answered Hellier.

When he rang off he put the receiver down and sat
at his desk for several minutes, with no comfort but
his thoughts, and they were little enough. The girl
had been in his manor. It was a well-hidden place but
it should have been found. Whichever uniformed
man covered the area would be in trouble for this, so

would the detectives who had searched the quarry. In fact Hellier could not blame himself, but nevertheless he did. Not bitterly, but with a dull, aching sense of failed responsibility.

Now he had to go and tell the Pierces.

God knew how they would react.

And only yesterday Pierce had thrown up his job and joined in the hunt for his child. Poor devil. Poor, poor devil.

He sent for a car and was driven to the Pierces' home. No one had yet alerted the press, thank God, no one was outside the Pierces' house. It was after nine o'clock. Two school-children ran from a front door, hair and satchels flying, and a woman called from the open door:

'Mind you're careful in the High Street.'

A bright-eyed, red-haired girl cried: 'Okay, Mummy.'

A smaller boy called: ' 'Course we will.'

They raced past the police car without a glance at Hellier, but a woman opposite, brushing down a doorstep, stood up and stared across, then waved vigorously at someone out of Hellier's sight. He stepped out of the car and opened the iron gate of the Pierces' house, walked with long strides up to the front door, hesitated for a moment, then rat-tatted; the door seemed to shake. He waited, his face set, but there was no answer. He knocked again and pressed a bell-push at the side of the door. Then he glanced round. Faces were close to several windows and three women were now on the spot where the one had been. A car passed, the driver looking towards him.

The Pierces surely weren't out.

He knocked again and at last footsteps sounded on the stairs. A man's. Hellier drew himself up, massive, an almost forbidding figure. Pierce, with a red dressing-gown pulled but not tied about the waist, thin hair awry, face unshaved, peered at him.

Slowly, Pierce's expression changed. The tiredness drained away. The lines seemed to fade. A strange, defensive expression crept into his eyes, and Hellier knew that his mission had already been accomplished. Pierce realised why he had come. They stood absolutely still, and said nothing. Then Mrs. Pierce called from upstairs.

'Who is it?'

Pierce moistened his lips but didn't speak.

Hellier called 'It's me, Mrs. Pierce, Superintendent Hellier. I'm afraid I've—I've bad news for you.'

Again there was silence; utter silence. Pierce moistened his lips again and moved back a step. Hellier did not know what to say or do. Pierce backed further away, and turned round; Hellier had an odd feeling that the man had forgotten he was present.

Wanda Pierce appeared at the head of the stairs.

'So she *is* dead.' There was the flatness of resignation in her voice, a kind of fatalism, none of the hysteria which Hellier had expected.

'Stay there, Wanda,' Pierce said in a level voice. 'I'll come up to you.' She ignored him and came down a step. 'I said, stay there,' he ordered.

'Superintendent, have you seen my daughter?' Wanda demanded.

'Yes,' Hellier said.

'Is she—disfigured in any way?' asked Pierce.

'No,' Hellier wanted to add: 'Thank God,' but he could not even put a warm or sympathetic inflection into his voice, he felt so taut.

'Where is she?'

'The——' he hesitated, boggled, over 'mortuary' and said, 'At the police station.'

'In the mortuary?'

'Yes.'

'My wife and I will want to see her. Please send a car for us in an hour's time,' Pierce said.

He turned towards the foot of the stairs and then went up, slowly, to his wife. She hadn't moved again; she was all eyes in a pale, pale face. Hellier felt that they were oblivious of him, that he was utterly unimportant. He saw Mrs. Pierce's face pucker as her husband reached her, saw Pierce put an arm round her, had a strange sense that this weak little man had found a strength that he, Hellier, had not suspected him capable of possessing.

Mrs. Pierce began to cry.

Her husband led her out of sight, and a door closed. The sound of crying was shut off. Hellier closed his eyes and turned round slowly, as the woman from next door, Mrs. Edmonds, came hurrying into the hallway.

For the first time, Hellier spoke in a relaxed and gentle voice.

'She's dead,' he said. 'But I think they'll be all right. I shouldn't go in yet, if I were you.'

He did not hear Mrs. Edmonds say in surprise to her neighbour: 'He's got a heart after all.'

Chapter Eighteen

'NEW' JOB

'Inspector! Mr. Worby wants you!'

Singleton looked up from the patrol boat into which he was stepping as a younger man came hurrying down the pier, kicked against one of the ridges and nearly fell.

'Pick 'em up, pick 'em up,' growled Old Man River. 'We don't want to have to fish *you* out.' He strode up to the repair shop, past the stores, saw the store-keeper and young Addis sparring, pretended not to notice, and climbed the stone stairs to Worby's office. He tapped.

'Come in, come in.' Worby was close to the door, just beneath the crossed cutlasses on the wall, souvenirs of the days when the River Police were armed with pistols, blunderbusses, knives and cutlasses. ' 'Morning, Jim,' he went on, putting a book of regulations on a shelf. 'What have you been up to?'

'What am I supposed to have done?' Singleton struggled not to go on but lost the struggle. 'Didn't upset the Commander last night, did I?'

Worby's half-grin faded.

'About Micklewright, you mean? Sad business that. Bloody sad. No. No, whatever you did certainly didn't upset him. Deputy Commander Hobbs put you up for a special mission and the Commander approved. So that leaves it up to me.' The grin returned to the rather fleshy, almost sensuous face.

'Head messenger in chief?' asked Singleton, suspiciously.

'Replacement for Superintendent Micklewright on this industrial diamonds job, which means the Argyle-Morris murder, into the bargain,' Worby said flatly.

At first Singleton did not take this in. Worby's words 'Replacement for Superintendent Micklewright . . .' seemed to rebound off his mind. Then he thought: 'The Warbler's ragging me.'

'Come again.'

'The Commander wants you to take over where Micklewright left off. He wants a man who knows the river, knows all the law enforcement groups who have a finger in river business, and who doesn't hate Dutchmen.' Worby paused, as if he knew that the older man would need a few seconds to absorb what he was being told. 'You'd have an office at the Yard, and the chaps who were working with Micklewright would be under you. And you'd keep your office here with all the usual facilities, and any two men you think would help most.'

Singleton stared as if still not fully comprehending; and then he had a quick mind picture of his wife's face, and suddenly he beamed.

'I can't wait to tell Maggie,' he said, in a near-falsetto voice. 'I can't wait.' Then he sobered, the weight of the responsibility of this assignment already making itself felt on his shoulders. 'Thank you very much, sir.' Worby liked to be appreciated.

'Don't thank me, Jim.' The grin played about Worby's lips again. 'If you think I can't run the station without you, you'll soon find out! Okay, then?'

'You bet it's okay!' Singleton's chest seemed to swell. 'I'd like Tidy and Addis, please.'

'They're yours.'

'And Addis was telling me about this suction cap idea. You know what we want right away, don't you?'

'What?'

'The frogmen team.' Already Singleton's excitement and exhilaration began to lose itself in the actual task; the planning. The policeman took over from the man almost at once. 'They can operate in three pairs, leaving one in reserve. We can say they're looking for a body, people will believe that. All they have to do is swim round the barges and the lighters, anything tied alongside, and check if anything's stuck on. Right?'

Worby looked at him very straightly and without

the vestige of a smile, and said:

'You're in charge, Jim.'

Very slowly, Chief Inspector Singleton nodded. As slowly he said: 'So I am.'

Gideon felt as if he had been at the office all day, although it was only half-past eleven on that same morning.

The Micklewright affair had cut the Yard in two—one half saying in effect: 'Poor devil, shows coppers are human, too,' the other half saying: 'He's let the Force down.' In their way both were right. With the Commissioner away and the Assistant Commissioner of the Criminal Investigation Department at a conference in South America, the brunt of it all fell on Gideon.

By ten o'clock, an Under Secretary at the Home Office had telephoned.

'The Home Secretary would like full details, Commander.'

The Home Secretary would have to be satisfied with a brief précis of events.

By half-past ten, the senior public relations officer and the P.R.O. of the Home Office had been in his office.

'We want to make sure, Commander, that all our reports tally and that only the official statement is released to the press. Presumably you would like to approve the official statement.'

'Yes,' Gideon said. 'Preferably in one sentence: the charge without comment.'

'Commander, there will be a great deal of public interest . . .'

'Let's not make a meal out of it,' Gideon said. 'There may be a lot of ghouls about, but we don't have to feed them.'

'What about the work Micklewright was doing?'

'Chief Inspector Singleton has taken over,' Gideon said tersely.

After they had gone, the senior Press Officer of the Yard telephoned.

'I know you've problems, Commander, but so have we. Our telephones are ringing incessantly; we've been asked if a senior official will appear on a television programme tonight, and also on the radio. There will *have* to be a press conference during the day. And——' the P.O., an elderly man by Yard standards, changed his tone—'you're the best man for the job, George. Give 'em a show, let them bring the cameras in. You can handle them better than anyone here. If we refuse——' he paused, then went on into a silence which obviously worried him—'they'll put their own interpretation on it.'

'Oh, all right, but it's to be a general conference, not specifically on Micklewright,' Gideon conceded. 'What time?'

'Is two o'clock all right?'

'Yes, Where?'

'The Lecture Hall,' the Press Officer had answered.

Even when he had agreed to this, there was no rest from the case; it affected everyone he talked to, all the superintendents he briefed. But being Saturday, there was less briefing than usual, and no major crimes had been committed in the last twenty-four hours, so at least he could now concentrate on the two tasks which preoccupied him—the industrial diamonds investigation and the River Parade.

He spent some time pondering both, and just before twelve o'clock, rang for Hobbs.

'Going to Lord's this afternoon?' he asked, as the door opened and Hobbs appeared.

'No,' Hobbs answered. 'I've asked Worby to take

me up and down the river.'

'Sit down.' Gideon leaned back in his chair. 'Seen any fresh angle yet?'

'No,' said Hobbs, 'I still think the helicopter idea is the most likely way they'd raid the boat, but the more I think of it the less probable it seems. I've been through the whole file—had Prescott here most of the morning. He's absolutely satisfied that the protection from the Embankment is foolproof. Securial are co-operating, so is Pilkington.'

'Probably pass off without any trouble at all,' mused Gideon. 'Has Prescott noticed anything at all unusual?'

'No,' answered Hobbs. 'He's briefed all his men on all the shifts: if there's anything even slightly suspicious or unusual, they're to report. I'll check with Worby from the river—are *you* going to Lord's?'

'After this press conference, I thought I'd look in on Prescott.'

Hobbs gave an unexpectedly free smile.

'Don't know that it will get you anywhere,' he told Gideon. '*He's* going to Lord's!' Prescott was probably the most enthusiastic cricket fan on the Force. 'Shall I warn him you may look in?' he added.

'Don't think I would,' said Gideon slowly. 'Anyhow,' he went on, 'I may be so bad tempered after this press conference that I won't go near the place. That reminds me.' He reached for the telephone, but almost at the same moment it rang. He lifted the receiver. 'Yes? . . . Yes, put him through. *Worby*,' he added in an aside to Hobbs. 'Hello, Warbler . . . Yes . . . Good . . . Tell him to come and see me at three o'clock . . . Yes, I'll be here.'

He rang off.

'Singleton's got the frogmen out already, the Warbler says he's mustard keen.' He smiled, rather dourly.

'He'd like to report to one of us this afternoon.'

'Someone must have told him about the briefing sessions.' Hobbs said, and almost before his last word faded, the telephone rang again. But the two men were used to the almost non-stop sequence of events, and it seldom ruffled them.

'Your wife is on the line, sir . . .'

'Hello, Kate, what time were you thinking of coming back? . . . That's good, I'll be late . . . We'll go out somewhere tonight, and let the kids look after themselves . . . 'Bout six, then. Goodbye, dear.'

Hobbs was already at the door.

The Chief Press Officer was a tall, droll-faced man, with rubbery lips and a pointed chin, a thin neck and a prominent Adam's apple which he tried to hide by wearing a high collar a little too large for him. He came into Gideon's office just before two o'clock. Gideon had had a sandwich and beer lunch, and was at the window.

'All ready, sir?' said the C.P.O.

'How long do you think they'll want?' asked Gideon.

'Thirty or forty minutes, sir. Both television channels have sent a camera team. Er—I've briefed a couple of the Agencies and they'll lead in with easy ones.'

As he went along to the Lecture Hall, where special briefings were often held, Gideon pulled down his jacket and ran his hand over his wiry hair. Two uniformed men were outside the hall and opened the door. A babble of talk sounded and the room was full of smoke. Someone called out: 'The Commander,' and there was an immediate hush. Most of the men got to their feet; so did the only two women present. Gideon went to the front of the room where a table with a notepad, glasses and a carafe of water stood beside various microphones, marked B.B.C., B.B.C.1, B.B.C.2, A.T.V., Granada and several others. A small man tapped one of these and there was a curious kind of sound from the back of the room; so this was the public address microphone, thought Gideon. Two television cameramen and several other photographers were in the front row.

The C.P.O. cleared his throat. 'Gentlemen—*ladies* and gentlemen, I beg your pardon—Commander Gideon has been able to allocate you thirty minutes. The shorter your questions, the more he can answer.'

'Commander,' a man asked promptly, 'do you think that over half a million pounds' worth of precious stones should be shown on so vulnerable a place as the river?'

Gideon pursed his lips.

'Ask the Thames Division that and they'll tell you that the Thames is the least vulnerable place in London. They lose very little from the docks and wharves. As for the question—it's up to the people who own the jewels.'

'Do you disapprove or approve, Commander?'

'I would complain if they took unnecessary risks, but they don't appear to be taking any.'

'Were you allowed enough time to prepare?' asked another man.

'It isn't time we need, it's more staff,' Gideon countered. 'We can't police London as well as we'd like to, because we are fifteen or twenty per cent below strength.'

'Damned good point,' murmured the C.P.O. Pencils sped over note books of all shapes and sizes.

'Are you satisfied with the security precautions for the River Parade, sir?' A man called from the back of the hall.

'Yes.'

One of the women asked in a quiet voice:

'Do you think that special displays of this kind *should* be allowed to draw off police protection from other parts of London?'

'No. And it isn't doing so.'

'Surely it *must*, Commander.' She looked a little mouse of a woman, but she was persistent.

'All it does do is to cause a lot of policemen's wives to grumble because their husbands have to work over-time,' Gideon answered, and won a little laughter.

'Do they get paid for overtime, Commander?' asked the other woman.

'They either get paid or they get time off when things are slack.'

'Are things *ever* slack?' That was an American voice from the side of the hall.

There was a general, louder laugh.

'Sometimes even our bad men behave themselves,' Gideon remarked, and the laughter was redoubled. Gideon suddenly realised that he was enjoying himself, but he checked his tendency to encourage light-heartedness.

Into the tail-end of the laughter, a man with a Scottish accent asked: 'Were you satisfied with the way the search for Geraldine Pierce was carried out, Commander?'

The mood of the conference changed almost visibly. Smiles were wiped off every face, men sat up more erectly. Gideon, aware of the danger of relaxing as he had relaxed, gave himself a moment or two to think what best to say.

'I was satisfied with the way it was carried out, yes. Obviously I wasn't satisfied with the results.'

'Shouldn't the hiding-place have been found earlier?'

'It's easy to be wise after the event.' Gideon pointed to a map on the wall behind him, on which each division was shown in a pastel shade of contrasting colour, the river winding in dark blue through the centre. 'Constable,' he called one of the uniformed policemen, 'come and outline the area which was searched, will you?'

As he spoke, he thought: 'My God, I hope he *knows* the area.' But his fears faded as the policeman approached the map without a moment's hesitation and eased the tension by drawing out a truncheon to use as a pointer. 'That stretch of river is seven miles long,' Gideon said. 'Along much of it there is scrub and bush. There are hundreds of small boats, boat sheds, boat-houses, caravans and abandoned motorcars, and in the summer several official and some private camping sites. Every single place had to be searched . . . Point to Richmond Park, Constable— thank you. That is a Royal Park, open to the public by day, closed by night to motor traffic. Its area is . . . Now Ham Common, Constable.'

Gideon described the different sections of the area quietly and precisely, and at last he finished.

'The search took three days. To comb the area thoroughly needed twice or three times as many men working for at least a week. It was organised down to the last detail, and I don't know of anything else that could have been done.'

There was a long silence; and then, quite spontaneously, a little outburst of applause. Again Gideon felt a sense of satisfaction; and again, there was an immediate and sobering change of subject.

'Commander, do you think the arrest and charging of a senior official of the police will do harm to the public image of the police?'

Slowly, Gideon answered: 'I don't know whether it

will. I know that it shouldn't.'

'Do you know Superintendent Micklewright well, Commander?'

'Yes. Very well.'

'Are you aware that there are rumours that he was drinking too much?'

'Yes. I am aware that there are all kinds of rumours —including one that he took a sedative and had a drink afterwards.'

'Commander,' said a small man with a curiously lop-sided face, 'do you think that a man in Superintendent Micklewright's distraught and distressed state of mind should have been assigned to an investigation of international importance? Wasn't he *bound* to upset the Dutch police?'

That question, with the sting in its tail, was almost deadly in its impact, and Gideon felt every eye turn towards him, knew that everyone was hanging on to his words.

Chapter Nineteen

A REPORT IN THE AFTERNOON

Gideon's first thought was, I shouldn't have laid myself open to this. His second, I must be very careful indeed. His third, I mustn't hesitate too long. It did not occur to him to take the easy way out, the way which would no doubt be approved by the Home Secretary and his superiors at the Yard, and to say simply: 'No comment.'

He looked squarely at the sea of faces confronting him. 'Failure can be frustrating and upsetting,' he said slowly. 'The loss of industrial diamonds has been a harassment to the Western European police for some time. Only recently was there reason to suspect that some of the diamonds might be sent to England. We work closely with all the European police forces, sometimes in direct contact, sometimes through Interpol. In every case of joint investigation we assign the man whom we think most familiar with the kind of crime being investigated.

'Superintendent Micklewright is a world authority,' he added. 'He has been asked to advise on similar cases in South Africa, South America and the United States. He made—and helped to make—sufficient progress with the case for us to follow a different line of investigation—along the whole course of the river. At no time did he give any indication that he was not competent to carry out his duties. On the contrary, he carried them out well. Chief Inspector Singleton is now in charge of that particular line of inquiry and of the investigation.' He paused, looked round, saw the man with the lop-sided face start to speak, and went on in a tone of absolute finality: 'I have nothing more to say on that subject, gentlemen.'

Two would-be questioners sat down, without protest.

Gideon was asked a few more questions which he answered briefly, posed for half a dozen photographs, and then went out surrounded by a group of newspaper men. The constable who had used his truncheon as a pointer was at the door.

'Thanks, Constable,' Gideon said.

'Pleasure, sir.'

Gideon walked on, turned a corner and went back to his office with a chorus of 'Thanks,' 'Goodbyes,' and 'See yous,' following him. The Chief Press Officer was at his elbow.

'Don't want to sound pompous, Commander, but

that was a bloody good show.'

Gideon stared out of the window and went over the river, bright in the afternoon sun.

'I hope so,' he said. 'We'll see what they make of it tomorrow.'

'You won them over completely, sir.'

Gideon turned to look at him.

'That's the trouble,' he said, soberly. 'They shouldn't have to *be* won over. They ought to be on our side all the time.'

'There isn't one who won't make the point about us being under-established,' the other man prophesied. 'Er—is there anything I can get you?'

'No,' Gideon said. 'Chief Inspector Singleton is due at three o'clock. Try to make sure he's not button-holed by the press, will you?'

'They wouldn't get any change out of Old Man River,' the C.P.O. said confidently.

It was ten minutes to three before Gideon was on his own. No new reports were on his desk, and none on Hobbs's, but at half a minute to three there were foot-steps in the passage, followed by an over-loud knock at the door. This would be Singleton.

'Come in!' Gideon called.

Singleton looked a different man from the grim and defiant one whom Gideon had seen last night. Then he had had to brace himself to make an effort: now he had an almost buoyant confidence, and looked years younger.

'Sit down, Chief Inspector,' Gideon said. 'And while I think of it, your man Addis had a bright idea, didn't he?'

'*Very* bright, sir.' Singleton beamed. 'The frogmen found three more packets, too.'

With great deliberation he opened his black brief-case and took out three waterproof packets which had been found. These he placed, very precisely, on Gideon's desk. glancing up at Gideon each time he withdrew his hand.

Gideon stared at the packets, fascinated; it was so improbable that he could hardly believe his eyes. All thought of the press conference, the awkward questions, sudden depression, vanished. He met Singleton's gaze, and for a few seconds, noticed nothing. Then he saw the hint of triumph in them, and realised how elated the Thames Division man must be.

He drew a deep breath.

'It's a long time since I've been excited,' he remarked.

Singleton gave an explosive little laugh.

'Me, too!'

'Addis didn't plant 'em there, I suppose,' Gideon said.

'You could ask him, sir. He's in the room which Mr. Hobbs put at our disposal.'

'I'll take your word for it,' said Gideon. 'Where were they found?'

'One on a barge opposite the Millwall Docks,—the old section, sir. One on a lighter moored up river with eight barges in tow. And one on a Dutch coaster which came in with some chocolate and cocoa.'

Gideon picked up one of the packets, weighted it in his hand, then tossed it back to Singleton.

'Better make sure it *does* contain diamonds.'

Singleton nodded, and with very great care, slit one edge of the waterproof covering. Inside was a polythene bag. Singleton slit this with the same finicky care and took out a fold of linen. As before, the linen was lined with wash-leather, from which, kept in place by a strip of transparent plastic, innumerable diamond chips scintillated in all directions like tiny grains of sand.

All three packets contained the same weight of diamonds; each packet was worth about two thousand pounds on the commercial market. There was now no longer any doubt that Van Hoorn was right in believing that a substantial quantity of the stolen Dutch diamonds were being brought to London.

'Any ideas?' Gideon asked Singleton, after a long pause.

'May I report to date, sir?'

That was evasive, but no doubt Singleton had his reasons.

'Yes,' said Gideon.

'There wasn't any doubt that Screw Smith and a man not yet known to us took Argyle-Morris away from his flat. Captain Kenway was right about that. One of the P.L.A. gate policemen saw them go into the No. 2 Gate of the West India Docks and says he saw them leave about two hours later. He's not positive the same men were in it but he was sure the same car went out—a black Ford Anglia. And Screw Smith owns a Ford Anglia.'

Gideon nodded.

'Argyle-Morris's body was found at a place we call Dead Man's Rest—sometimes bodies come up there when the river's a bit lower than usual. There's a current that swings them out of midstream on to a point off the Isle of Dogs. Every time we've taken a corpse out of there we've discovered that the victim fell in somewhere between Wapping and Limehouse. That's a simple fact, sir.'

'Yes. Go on.'

'A Vauxhall Victor was seen along by Wapping High Street at half-past eleven the night before the body was found. It stopped for about three minutes. It was seen by a night watchman at a tea warehouse in the High Street—less than half a mile from our station, sir. We can't trace the Vauxhall Victor, but we're after it. And we *do* know that Screw Smith has been seen in a V.V. two or three times lately with a man unknown to the Divisional Police.'

Gideon said:

'Superintendent Roswell is giving you plenty of help, then.'

'As he did Mr. Micklewright, sir.'

'Good.'

'We could pick up Smith,' Singleton hazarded, 'and we might get something out of him, but I've just finished reading Mr. Micklewright's report, as far as he'd written it.'

Gideon waited.

'It's obvious that he was coming round to the Dutch view that this diamond racket is pretty big,' Singleton went on, 'and now we've found this little lot——' he motioned to the three packets—'it looks more likely than ever. It stands to reason that these packets come up from the estuary by night, a frogman goes over and fastens them on to the hulls with a magnet, actually, not a suction cup, and *another* frogman goes out later to pick them up. One of these packets has enough slime on it to show that it's been on the same spot for days, if not weeks. There's no telling how often packets are brought over, or how many there are in all, but apparently it's been going on for a long time, *and*——' Singleton hesitated, as if for the first time he began to wonder whether he was taking Gideon along with him—'it's very big business, sir.'

Gideon nodded, and echoed: 'Very.'

'And Smith isn't big business, any more than Dave Carter was. We could pick him up, we might even prove a case against him, but in doing so we risk losing bigger game.'

Gideon nodded again. 'So?' he asked, with raised brows.

'I'd leave him, sir, and I'd put these packets back—empty—and watch the vessels we took 'em from,' advised Singleton. 'That might lead us to the big fish.' He grinned suddenly, partly from tension, partly because of his native sense of humour. 'Wouldn't like Van Hoorn to know what we'd done, though.'

'No,' said Gideon thoughtfully.

'Think it would work, sir?' Singleton looked anxious.

'I think it might. When would you put the packets back?'

'Tonight, sir,' answered Singleton. 'I've got the frogmen standing by in case that's what you decide.'

Gideon hid a smile, and hesitated for a few moments before replying. He was attracted by the idea, and it certainly might work. He would have told Singleton to go ahead straight away, but for the murder of Argyle-Morris and the fact that Screw Smith might get away with that if the trail were allowed to go cold. The decision had to be made on a basis of what would give the best chance of catching Argyle-Morris's murderer.

'What about the girl—named Mary Rose, isn't she?'

'As a matter of fact——' Singleton sounded almost glib—'Addis reports that she's been going around in a Vauxhall Victor lately.'

'With a driver not yet known to us, I take it,' Gideon said drily.

'That's right, sir.'

'What about the man who started all this? Carter.'

'He's up for a second hearing on Wednesday—we should have a good idea of whether he plays any part in the smuggling by then,' Singleton answered. 'Roswell—Mr. Roswell—isn't sure he can make the attempted murder charge stick, as the girl's evidence won't be too reliable now.' Singleton was obviously making a considerable effort not to plead for his way, but the effort was putting a great strain on him.

Gideon said abruptly: 'All right, we'll give it a go. But keep tails on Screw Smith and ferret out everything you can about him as if you were going to charge him with murder.'

'I won't lose him, sir,' Singleton said confidently. 'He's a very nasty piece of work.'

Half an hour later as Gideon was driving along the Embankment, undecided whether or not to call in at the Divisional Headquarters, he remembered Addis, at the Yard; he should have looked in to see him. Pity. It was a remarkable development, and the more he pondered it the more likely it seemed that the river was being used for crime organised on a big scale. Anyone who planned this industrial diamond job and could both afford and be willing to leave a cache of diamonds hidden for several months, must surely be a master criminal.

There *was* a carefully planned series of crimes on the river with regard to the industrial diamonds.

There might also be a skilfully planned 'once only' raid on the River Parade diamonds. Any man bold and daring enough to organise the one might well be bold and daring enough to organise the other.

He shrugged the thought aside as fanciful, but it made him decide to go into the Divisional Headquarters. The Chief Inspector in charge was a youthful, blond man also named Smith, obviously anxious to make a good impression, and as obviously determined not to let his superior down.

'Mr Prescott's taken a few hours off, sir, but he'll look in later. Meanwhile one thing has cropped up. May be nothing in it, of course, but Mr. Prescott wanted to know everything that was unusual.'

'So do I,' said Gideon.

'It's a report from P.C. Toller, who signed on half an hour ago,' Smith reported. 'He's on duty at the pier head, we always have at least one man on duty at the *Belle Casino*. Last night he saw Mr. St. John—Sir Jeremy Pilkington's second-in-command, sir—go from the *River Belle* to the *Belle Casino*, and stay only for about ten minutes.'

'Is that unusual?' Gideon asked.

'Usually St. John stays longer. The peculiar thing about last night, though, was that a man followed St. John to the pier head in a Mini Minor. There was a girl in the car with him, and P.C. Toller says he recognised the girl.'

'Oh,' said Gideon. 'Who was she?'

'A Mary Rose Shamley, the girl friend of that poor devil pulled out of the river a couple of days ago,' Smith answered.

'I want to see Toller at once,' Gideon decided on the instant. 'If he isn't on the station, get him. And I want to talk to Mr. Singleton, at the Yard. After that to Mr. Hobbs, who's with a Thames Division patrol somewhere between here and Greenwich. Hurry!'

Chapter Twenty

GIDEON'S SPEED

'Singleton.'

'Yes, sir.'

'I want an Identi-kit picture of the unidentified man who's driven that Vauxhall Victor with the Mary Rose girl.'

'Yes, sir.'

'And I want you or Addis or anyone who's seen the girl out here at Division with the picture—*soon*.'

'It will be Addis, sir.'

'Ring me back when it's all in hand.'

'Yes, sir.'

Gideon rang off—and the telephone rang again.

'Mr. Hobbs, sir.'

'Alec, this is *very* urgent. St. John's had some heavy gambling debts and paid four hundred and fifty pounds off last night on the *Belle Casino*. I've talked to the manager. He paid off a thousand ten days ago. And he was followed by a man who may be an associate of Screw Smith. Got that?'

Hobbs said: 'Clearly.'

'I want you to see Pilkington, tell him—in fact have a confrontation with Pilkington, see if he can get anything out of St. John.'

'He could, too.'

'Where are you now?'

'Near Waterloo Pier.'

'I've told Pilkington we're sending someone to see him, he'll be there at half-past five,' said Gideon.

'So will I.'

'I'll be here or at home. Gideon rang off, then paused for the first time since he had heard about St. John being followed. Chief Inspector Smith, a little apprehensive and greatly impressed, saw the quality he had heard about in Gideon but never seen—this tremendous power of concentration. Gideon was also aware of it. From time to time an event acted on him like a powerful stimulant; he could think, reason, make decisions and move three times as fast as usual.

Now he was thinking . . .

Frogmen, underwater specialists, who was there in London? He spoke sharply.

'Smith!'

'Sir.'

'Get Colonel Abbotson of the Royal Marines. He's stationed at Greenwich. Find out where he lives, where he is now, get him for me.'

'By telephone, sir?'

'Yes.'

Smith turned and almost ran out of the office. Gideon pushed back his chair and breathed more freely. He could safely relax, for there was nothing more he could do himself at the moment. He felt very dry-mouthed and suddenly longed for a cup of tea. 'Anyone outside?' he called.

A man answered: 'Sergeant Mee, sir,' and a stout, middle-aged policeman appeared.

'Tell someone to send me some tea, in a pot, hot and strong.'

'Right away, sir.'

Gideon put his hand to his pocket and smoothed the bowl of a big pipe. He had not smoked it for years, all he ever smoked these days were cigars, but at times of stress he found himself doing this; there was something companionable about the briar. If Lemaitre were here he could think aloud. 'Lem,' he would say, 'I've seen a possibility that scares the living daylights out of me.' Lemaitre would ask him what and he would hedge. Funny, how one got used to the companionship of certain men, and how one missed it. Would Hobbs ever be that sort of companion? It wasn't likely. They came from different backgrounds, looked at things from different angles.

He was half-way through his second cup of tea when Singleton called:

'We've done better than an Identi-kit picture, sir.'

'What have you got?'

'A photograph—very good likeness, too. I'm having

copies run off. We can have twenty or thirty at once.'

Thank God for a man of quick intelligence!

'Send some over,' Gideon ordered, 'and get plenty done. Have those waterproof packets been replaced yet?'

'No, sir.'

'Get 'em back—fast.' Gideon was about to ring off when he had a moment of compunction—it was unfair to let Singleton work in a fog. 'It's possible those packets were stuck where they were as a precaution. There could be a daily inspection to check whether we've found them. If that's the case they'll know we have.'

'Good God!' exclaimed Singleton. 'I hadn't thought of that.'

'And today I don't want anyone scared off,' Gideon said. 'There could be a connection between your job and the River Parade—and keep that right under your hat, even from your assistants.'

Singleton said faintly: 'They wouldn't believe me, sir.'

Gideon almost laughed.

It was a quarter to six when Addis brought the photographs. By Gideon's standards he was young, but he was standing up to success and excitement very well, watched his words and his manner carefully, and was as neat as the reefer jacket of the Thames Division could allow. His white collar and tie almost glistened.

P.C. Toller, who had noticed St. John and put in the report, identified the man and the girl instantly.

'I'm *quite* sure they were in the Mini, sir, and just as sure the driver was the same man who drove the Vauxhall. The lighting's especially good just there—the Superintendent had it improved in case anyone tried to raid the Casino.'

Good for Prescott; very good for Toller. Toller

went out and Gideon turned to Addis, who was pinning a photograph of the unidentified driver of the Vauxhall Victor, side by side with Argyle-Morris's girl, on to a notice board.

'Who took the photograph, Addis?'

'I did, sir.'

'For any special reason?'

'Er—in a way, sir,' Addis said, a little hesitantly.

'Go on.'

'I don't think we—the Force—use photography enough, sir. I've always thought that we could have a small camera—concealed miniature would do, sir—as part of our equipment. It would facilitate identification and often be invaluable in court, sir.' Obviously Addis wondered whether he had been overbold, and was very formal.

'Worth thinking about,' Gideon conceded. 'Have you talked about this to Superintendent Worby?'

'Er—no, sir. He's above my——' Addis broke off and gave a broad, embarrassed grin. 'I've mentioned it to Mr. Singleton, though.'

'Have Mr. Singleton mention it to Superintendent Worby,' Gideon said drily. As he spoke the telephone bell rang and he nodded dismissal to Addis and picked up the instrument. 'Yes?'

'There's a message from Mr. Hobbs, sir.'

'What is it?'

'He says that both men are available and he's going in to see them right away.'

'Thanks,' grunted Gideon, and as he rang off, he knew that he had never wanted to be anywhere more than he wanted to be with Hobbs right now.

St. John found nothing surprising in the summons to Pilkington's flat overlooking Kensington Gardens; in fact he had rather expected it and had kept himself in readiness. He lived alone, and left his flat at half-past five. He did not notice that as he took the wheel of his Jaguar a Mini Minor turned out of a row of parked cars, following him so skilfully that the driver of the car saw him go into the building where Pilkington lived.

Nor did he, or his shadows, realise that the police had both cars under constant surveillance, and their progress was being reported to *Information*.

Pilkington was alone.

'Hello, Hugh,' he said, as he sprawled on a big couch, a little over-dressed, a little too flamboyant. 'One or two things I want to talk about, dear boy.' St. John's lips almost curled, he was so sickened by this man's foppishness; he and Gentian would make a good pair, he thought. Yet the 'one or two' things all proved pertinent, and no one could doubt Pilkington's intelligence.

Ten minutes after he had arrived, Hobbs came in. That was the first jolt to St. John's complacence, but he quickly reminded himself that these men were old friends. The second jolt to his complacence came with a change in Pilkington's voice; a hardening.

'Hugh, I've been hearing things about you I don't like,' he said.

'You should hear what I hear about you,' St. John retorted, masking a rising consternation.

'You've never heard that I've taken bribes to sell anyone out,' Pilkington replied.

St. John was so shocked that he could only stand and gape; then he turned and glared at Hobbs. He was breathing very hard.

'I've never taken a bribe in my life! If your bloody flat-foots——'

'That's a bit insolent, Hugh.'

'Insolent be damned. If the police——'

181

'The police would like to know where you obtained the four hundred and fifty pounds with which you paid off your gambling debts last night,' Hobbs said quietly, 'and where you obtained the thousand pounds you paid off a week ago.' He held out a photograph of the girl and of the driver of both the Mini Minor and the Vauxhall Victor. 'How well do you know these people, Mr. St. John?'

St. John stared, then said tartly:

'I've never seen them before.'

'The man followed you here this afternoon and is parked in Kensington Road at this moment,' Hobbs stated.

St. John caught his breath.

'He can't be!'

'Don't be a bloody fool, old boy,' Pilkington advised in a mild voice. 'He's there. Saw him myself when I looked out of the window. What's on? We want to know.'

'Nothing's on, I tell you!'

'Mr. St. John,' Hobbs said, 'you still have time to undo any harm you've done.'

'I haven't committed any crime,' St. John said harshly.

Pilkington stood up, and very slowly moved towards him.

'Hugh,' he said, 'if I have to I'll squeeze the truth out of you.' He had strong-looking hands. 'But Hobbs is right, you've time to make amends. And you may not have committed any crime—*yet*. But if there's any trouble on the *River Belle* and you're party to it——'

Hobbs interrupted him. 'This man——' he tapped the photograph— 'is wanted for questioning in connection with a particularly brutal murder.'

St. John paled. 'I don't know anything about a murder,' he rasped.

'What have you been up to, Hugh?' insisted Pilkington. He placed his hands on the top of St. John's arms. 'Let's have it, old chap.'

St. John began to sweat.

'I think it will save time if you come with me to Scotland Yard,' Hobbs said in sudden impatience. 'I'll keep you informed, Jeremy.'

'No,' St. John said, catching his breath. 'There's no need for that, I—I——' he drew himself up—'I've been selling information, but I don't know who to, or what they're planning to do.' He wiped the sweat off his forehead. 'At first I thought someone wanted to sabotage the Parade, but . . .'

He began to talk so freely that it seemed he was almost glad to get the burden off his mind.

'Go back to your flat, stay in all the evening, telephone Sir Jeremy if you are approached at all—just ask some questions about the Parade,' Hobbs ordered. 'Take no notice if you're followed. If you do telephone, we shall be told at once and we will get in touch with you. Is that clear?'

St. John nodded, mutely.

From the door he looked back unbelievingly at the man for whom he had had such little respect.

It was a quarter to seven when the telephone in Smith's office rang and the operator said: 'Colonel Abbotson, sir.'

'Put him through—and then telephone my wife and tell her I'll be later than I expected and may not get home until midnight,' Gideon said.

'Yes, sir. Colonel Abbotson on the line now, sir.'

Gideon tightened his grip on the receiver. 'Colonel Abbotson?'

'Yes, Commander.'

'I'm sorry to worry you, but I think you're the one man most likely to help in a problem we have on our hands,' Gideon told him. 'Where are you at the moment?'

'I've just come back from an afternoon of golf.'

'Can we dine together?' asked Gideon.

'Delighted.' Abbotson did not even pause. 'Shall we say eight o'clock? And if you'll come here it will help—the R.M. Club?'

'Thank you, I'd like that,' Gideon said.

As he rang off, reflecting on the pleasure it was to deal with men who wasted no time, Hobbs came in. Gideon did not need telling that Hobbs was fully satisfied with the way things had gone. He nodded slightly, and his lips curved in a faint, tight-lipped smile.

'We've got St. John, anyhow,' he said. 'He was taking bribes. We can't place the two men he dealt with, but he's given us a good description of each. Apparently they met in an apartment which is let furnished to a man named Brown—but this was obviously a blind.'

'No photographs?' Gideon asked, and then went on hurriedly: 'Does he know what's planned?'

'Only that they're after the diamonds and wanted details and dimensions of the *River Belle*.'

Gideon rubbed his chin.

'I wonder why.' He paused for a moment, then asked: 'Anything more to do tonight, Alec?'

'Not unless you can think of something.'

'I can,' Gideon said. 'You can square my conscience. Take Kate out to dinner. I'm going to . . .' He explained a little, watching Hobbs, seeing what he thought was a glint of pleasure in his eyes.

'I'll be happy to,' Hobbs said, and a smile curved his lips again. 'Can I know why you're dining with a

Colonel of the Royal Marines?'

'Yes,' said Gideon. 'Three or four years ago a Naval launch went down near London Bridge and there were some dangerous explosives on board as well as some secret apparatus. Abbotson was in charge of the salvage job, and it was quite a job.'

'It was a midget submarine, wasn't it? asked Hobbs, and on the instant his expression changed. 'Good God!' he exclaimed. 'Attack from *beneath* the water! Is that what's in your mind?'

'Yes,' said Gideon slowly. 'That's exactly what's in my mind.'

Chapter Twenty-one

THE RIVER PARADE

Colonel Abbotson looked about forty, was fresh-faced and keen-eyed, with close-cropped fair hair and a close-clipped fair moustache. He had a well-scrubbed look about him. He was standing in the hall of the small club, exclusive, Gideon knew, to holders of decorations for valour in both war and peace. It was an old Georgian house not far from Berkeley Square and might still have been a private home. The carved staircase was luxuriously carpeted, oil portraits of men with distinguished and often slightly mysterious war records were on the walls. There was ample room in the panelled dining-room, and Abbotson had selected a table in an alcove which was exactly right for a *tête-à-tête*.

'I imagined you would want to keep this quiet,' he said.

'Couldn't be more right,' said Gideon, 'and I couldn't be more grateful for your help.'

'Haven't got it yet,' Abbotson said with a smile. He paused as a waiter appeared at his shoulder. 'I can recommend the smoked salmon—the roast duck's pretty good here, too, if you care for duck—Good, I'll have the same. And a Montrachet, I think, or do you prefer something more robust?'

Soon, they were free to talk.

Gideon outlined the situation as it was, and then asked earnestly:

'What I want to know is, could small one- or two-man submarines come up the Thames from the estuary, or from a wharf or warehouse, plant these packets, or take 'em away, without being detected?'

Abbotson answered promptly. 'Unless we were looking for them, they probably wouldn't be detected. Expecting a modern Van Tromp, are you?'

'And are there small vessels which a man—a frog-man—can get in and out of, under water, without being seen?'

'Yes. Frogmen in certain branches are trained to it,' said Abbotson. He paused again as the waiter returned with two plates of smoked salmon and a third plate of finely cut brown bread and butter.

'I've been recalling all I can about this River Parade,' he continued as the waiter disappeared. 'There will be four or five hundred people on board, won't there?'

'Yes. And a safe full of diamonds and other jewels,' Gideon told him. 'What I'm wondering is whether one of these submarines could come close enough to fasten a limpet mine on the bottom of the *River Belle*, hover in safety until the mine went off, then move in during the pandemonium which would follow, get the safe, and take it away. Once it was in the water the weight of the safe wouldn't be quite so important, would it?' When Abbotson didn't answer at once, he went on a little self-consciously. 'I know it sounds melodramatic, but——'

'It sounds damned feasible,' Abbotson said firmly. 'If the crooks were indifferent to drowning a few dozen or so of the people in the ship it would be perfectly practicable. The people on the bridges and banks would be helpless, of course. In fact we *did* something like it on an exercise off the Isle of Wight a few months ago.'

'Did it work?'

'Like a charm.'

Gideon began to feel very much better, and he picked up his knife and fork and began to eat. He was aware of the delicate flavour of the salmon yet ate without concentrating on what he was doing. Abbotson helped himself to a piece of bread and butter.

'And you want us to watch the river on Monday evening. Is that right?'

'Yes,' said Gideon, simply.

'You'll have to pull some strings, and it's the weekend,' Abbotson said. 'I'd guess your safest way would be to get the Home Secretary to talk to the Minister of Defence. I could get everything ready for an exercise in the estuary,' he went on. 'We've a team at Shoeburyness, no need to worry on that score. We just want the word "go".'

'It is a difficult time,' said the Permanent Under Secretary at the Home Office, 'but if you think it essential, Commander——'

'I do,' said Gideon, uncompromisingly.

'Very well, Mr. Gideon, I will talk to my colleagues,' promised the Home Secretary.

'Thank you very much, sir.'

'If we've the men and equipment available, I don't see why not,' said the Minister of Defence. 'I imagine it will be a waste of time but it will give the Royal Marines an opportunity to exercise this particular team of under-water experts. I will see whether I can find the Commander-General.'

It was half-past four on the Sunday afternoon when the telephone woke Gideon out of a nap he had been quite sure he would never have. The sound of piano music came softly from the front room, as did Kate's humming. She often went there with the girls, and persuaded Penelope to play her favourite tunes.

Gideon got up and went to the telephone.

Colonel Abbotson said jubilantly: 'It's on, Commander!'

Gideon forgot the fact that he was drowsy, forgot everything but the almost sickening excitement at what might happen. He could not tell Kate. He could not tell anybody. He could only warn the Thames Division and the land divisions to stand by, and most of them expected an attack, if one came at all, from the Embankment, from one of the other ships, or from the air.

Only Hobbs knew.

Singleton was at Waterloo Pier, in touch by radio-telephone with Abbotson, believing that this precaution was against the possibility of a major robbery and an attempted getaway by water. He did not think it very likely but he was in no mood to be critical of Gideon. Addis and Tidy were in a patrol boat with another coxswain, also in contact by radio-telephone.

All that Monday the final arrangements were made on the *River Belle*. Gentian and his girls were in a last minute panic to get the final drapes up in time. The boat was being decorated with flowers, quite exquisite in their beauty. The electricians were putting the finishing touches to the lighting. The models were rehearsing in one of the big stores. The police and the Securial guards were having a rehearsal to make sure that all the precautions for the jewels were foolproof.

Kate, Gideon and Penelope were dressing for the great occasion, Penny with an excitement due at least partly to the fact that her escort was to be Deputy Commander Hobbs, Kate with a little disquiet, for she was sure that something was on her husband's mind. She was equally sure that he would tell her the moment he could.

. The team under Colonel Abbotson was already at action stations.

By two o'clock in the afternoon the first of the sight-seers took up their positions of vantage on the Embankment, on the bridge, every place, in fact, from which they could see the river. The police cleared the streets of any vehicles parked in the main thoroughfare leading to the Embankment. Buses and trains were as crowded coming into London as they normally were, at this hour, going out.

The models went on board at four-thirty.

. The jewels went on board at five-thirty.

Hobbs and Gideon approached the Chelsea Pier through the mass of eager Londoners, and Gideon felt a deep disquiet. If a bomb did go off, then the explosion might injure hundreds of spectators, both here and on the pleasure boats, which were already crammed with people. The one reassurance he had was that every conceivable contingency had been anticipated; if there *were* a disaster, the police, ambulances, fire-services, civil defence crews, were there to move in instantly. Police launches were on either side of the river, with reinforcements waiting at every pier. The whole establishment of the special constables of the Thames Division was on duty.

The hawkers called their wares, the children played and blew tin trumpets and let off caps from toy pistols. The newspaper sellers were out in strength.

And the sun shone.

Sir Jeremy Pilkington, and his wife, who looked dazzlingly beautiful, went on board at ten minutes to six, and Gideon and Kate watched them. Penelope and Hobbs were already on board with the other guests, the plain clothes policemen, the Customs men, and the Securial guards.

At five minutes past six, doors beneath the water-line of two barges moored in the roads near Surrey Docks opened; the sound detecting devices of the Royal Marine team picked this up, and immediately started in pursuit of two two-man submarines which were being launched from the barges. Some of Abbotson's team were frogmen, others were in one-man submarines. All of these headed up river. In a few minutes two more, smaller submarines started off from the bowels of a lighter which had been out of service for some months off the Millwall Docks.

On the *River Belle* the parade began.

In the *salon* which was so heavily guarded, the diamonds were handed out to model after model.

The four midget submarines drew closer to the *River Belle* as more of Abbotson's team moved from hiding-places in the Battersea Pleasure Gardens and on the wharves on Chelsea Embankment.

On deck, there was gaiety and applause and wonder.

Down below, Abbotson's men closed in on the raiders, who had no idea that they were suspected until more frogmen came from the *River Casino* and from the banks, giving the raiders no chance at all.

When they were caught, three of them were found to be in possession of limpet mines, each one enough to blow a hole in the *River Belle* and send it to the bottom.

At half-past seven the flotilla began to move down river, and the food and drink, from caviare and champagne to French bread and hot coffee, was served.

'It's *far* better than I expected,' Penelope Gideon said, enraptured.

'That's good,' agreed Gideon, trying to hide his preoccupation. As he spoke a plain clothes man came up and gave him a sealed letter. He opened it with great deliberation, his heart in his mouth. It read:

'*You were right. Operation completed. Four arrests made.*' Gideon turned to Hobbs and said gruffly: 'That was it, Alec. No need to worry. I'll be back.'

He went to the bridge of the old steamer and talked to Singleton and Worby, to Roswell and to Prescott. Every available man was concentrated on the launching sites for the submarines, Screw Smith and Mary Rose were picked up, but the still unidentified stranger remained at large.

He was still at large the next morning.

The frogmen and some of their accomplices ashore were caught in the mammoth raid. The newspapers splashed the story all over their front pages. *The Big River Robbery That Never Was* became the sensation of the year.

'But we still haven't got the ringleaders,' said Gideon to Singleton, two days later. 'We can't even be sure that the industrial diamond ring is run by the same people. You've a long haul ahead of you, Chief Inspector.'

'I'm used to long hauls, sir.'

'Yes. Have you seen Clara Micklewright and her friend Wild lately?'

'Not since the day before last,' said Singleton. 'You knew Wild was paying for the best legal aid, didn't you?'

'I hoped he was,' Gideon said.

In two days' time, Micklewright would come up for a second hearing.

In a few weeks' time, Carter and Cottingham would be on trial at the Old Bailey. Gideon could not see ahead to the time when he would learn that Screw Smith and his gang were employed by a man named Holmann—one of the two men described by St. John —and that they had feared Argyle-Morris had stolen the packet and had discovered their method of smuggling. Once certain he had not, they had simply made sure he could never give evidence against Screw Smith.

He could not know, either, that St. John had been watched so that Screw could be warned in time if he was interrogated by the police; and that when they learned he had been, Holmann and Morro had left the country, directing operations from Holland. These things Gideon would learn later.

But there were things Gideon did know.

Tomorrow, Van Hoorn would be back in London.

Tomorrow, a woman detective officer would start work in the office of Samuel Morris, insurance broker, and would watch Morris's staff.

Tomorrow, Hellier had told him, the Pierces were to go to Australia House and start on the long trail to a new life, with a greater chance of happiness than had seemed possible before.

And tomorrow, so Gideon had promised Kate, he would take a day off, if it were fine, and spend it with her on the banks of the river.

Gideon's Wrath

CONTENTS

Acknowledgments

The author is extremely grateful to all those who advised him on the facts of this book, particularly the Friends of St. Paul's Cathedral, the vergers there and elsewhere. the clergy and others at Westminster Abbey, Westminster Cathedral and the London Synagogue.

CHAPTER 1

THE WORSHIPPER

THE great nave was hushed and still. A pale light tinted a dozen colours as it filtered through the ancient stained glass of the window, touching the stone wall and the threadbare standard of a long-vanished regiment once carried by a man of valour long since dead. The light, subtle as the harmony of an old tapestry, changed in depth where it fell upon the polished brass of a plate which covered the last resting-place of a politician who had done all that any politician could to make himself right with God. Beyond this, the light faded into a pale glow, and vanished at the entrance to a chapel dedicated to a saint seldom remembered.

This chapel was bare and bleak and empty save for a few dozen hard and shiny wooden chairs, a dark oak bench running round the walls like that in a court of law, two or three paintings, each of the same saintly figure of half-forgotten history. The altar was covered with a cloth of handmade lace, and on it stood four candlesticks and a silver crucifix.

In front of the altar, at the rail, knelt a man.

There was so little light here that only those who came close could have noticed him. He knelt, in an awkward pose, on a tapestry hassock made by a half-blind woman who still lived to ply her needle and retained an uncanny sense of colour. One knee dented the middle of the hassock, the other edged to the cold stone floor. The man's hands were clasped on the rail, not in an attitude of prayer but tightly, as if in physical pain or mental anguish.

His breathing was laboured, almost sibilant. He had been in that position for a long time, as if unaware of the discomfort, his eyes sometimes closed and sometimes wide open. Now and again his lips moved.

'Oh God,' he would whisper, and after a long pause: 'Oh, Christ.'

After a longer pause, he would say:

'What can I do? What the hell can I do?'

Suddenly, after a longer pause, his breathing became stertorous and he began to choke and groan, until words burst out of him, loud and clear.

'I've killed her!'

The sounds died away, as if the anguish had suffocated him, until another whisper came: a name.

'Margaret . . . Oh, Margaret.'

And then, hardly audible, 'Oh, Christ, I've killed her.'

His hands, still tightly clasped, slid off the polished altar rail and dropped to his knees. Save for his breathing he was silent, his eyes tightly closed as if to shut out even the darkness. Outside in the nave the pale colours still glowed, and the hush was complete and profound—until a footstep disturbed it rudely.

The man at the altar rail jerked his head up and turned, staring at the tapestry colours on the stone.

Another footfall sounded, and he moistened his lips in fear.

A third footfall came and suddenly the filtering light was blotted out by darkness. The figure of a man showed black. The supplicant who had killed a woman now stared, teeth gritted. A second later the light returned as the solitary man passed on, his footsteps hardly audible.

A verger?

A steward?

A priest?

Another worshipper?

Another sinner?

The man by the altar began to move, with great caution, helping himself by pulling against the rail. His knees, one warm, one cold, were stiff, his movements slow and clumsy. He listened intently for the slightest sound, heard none except the agitated beating of his own heart. The spell of anguish and remorse was broken, fear replacing them— dread that he might be seen or recognised, which was nonsensical; dread that retribution would soon catch up, which was real.

He crept to the door of the chapel, careful to avoid those beautiful colours; staring towards the choir and the high altar beyond. He heard nothing and for a while saw nothing, until suddenly a yellowish glow appeared, startling in the darkness, wavering as if held in an unsteady hand. Soon, it settled on something which glistened, silent and golden. After a moment or two, shadows appeared; the glistening object moved, but not the light. Mesmerised by what was going on in front of him, the man by the chapel became aware of other things which glistened or glowed, all farther away from the radius of the pale light.

Another object disappeared; a rustling was followed by a faint clink of sound, a pause, a shadowy movement, another clink. Only after this had happened several times did the man who had killed realise what was happening; it was as if a voice within him cried: *'He's stealing the altar plate!'*

The fact, to him, was so monstrous that the enormity of his own crime was momentarily forgotten. Here, under his very eyes, was sacrilege. His mouth opened; a cry rose within him, but in the split second before it was uttered his danger swept over him again, paralysing the muscles of his throat, casting its own spell of silence. Gripped by an instinct that valued his personal safety above everything else on earth, he did nothing. The light moved, and so keen was his sense of perception and so much better his vision that he could make out the hands and fingers, even the shape of the thief's head and shoulders as the area of his depredations widened.

The man who had taken life turned his back on the man who was robbing the cathedral. He crept towards the door which was left open by the crypt so that those in spiritual need could come by night for solace or for help. Only when he reached the narrow wooden door, carved by a monk five centuries before, did he turn round. A strange and awe-inspiring sight met his gaze. There was more light. It came from the moon, risen higher in the heavens. This moonlight shone on the stained glass of a dozen windows and cast a pattern of lovely colours on the floor, the walls, the great pillars, the brass, the memorial wording cut deep into the walls. It was as if a rainbow had been broken and the pieces scattered. The thief by the altar, quite oblivious, was shifting his torch so that he could see still farther afield.

The murderer by the door pushed it, and the hinges creaked faintly. He caught his breath, but the other did not pause. Cautiously he pushed open the outer, much heavier door, and stepped into London's night.

It was cold. He shivered. He turned towards the main steps and the main doors, the shivering worsening like ague. His teeth chattered. His hands felt icy. In the distance a car engine sounded and soon a car hummed by, its headlights dipped and dim against the light from tall street lamps. The red light disappeared, like a banished demon, and the man by the cathedral steps saw it go, as he looked towards the emptiness of Ludden Hill and Ludden Circus.

Across the road the light of a telephone kiosk shone, hard and warning. He crossed to it, fingering the coins in his pocket, hesitated, then pulled open the narrow door. More light sprang up so that he could see the notices, how to dial, how to put money in the slots, how to call the police.

Dial 999. Of course.

He lifted the receiver, hand steadier now, and put the tip of his forefinger in the hole. 9—*brrrk*. 9—*brrrk*. 9—*brrrk!*

Almost on the instant, a man said briskly:

'Scotland Yard.'

'I want—I want to report a burglary,' the man said in a hoarse agitated voice.

'Thank you, sir. If you will give your name——'

'At St. Ludd's!' the man cried. 'There's a thief in St. Ludd's!'

He thrust the receiver down with frenzied vigour, all his bottled-up fear breaking loose as the man with that disembodied voice asked him for his name. He was near panic because for a dreadful instant he had nearly answered, so deeply ingrained was habit. He had nearly said: 'This is Eric Greenwood.' It did not then occur to him how unlikely it was that they would associate him with Margaret's lifeless body, her swollen throat. He swung round, pushing the door open, stepping out. A policeman stood only twenty yards in front of him advancing slowly from the faint white stone of the buildings of a great new group of buildings.

For a split second, the murderer stood rigid. The policeman, without quickening his pace, drew nearer. The murderer, nervous tension near to screaming point, turned suddenly on his heel and went back the way he had come, the voice inside him warning:

'Don't hurry. Don't panic.' All the time, his heart beat time to the refrain, racing so wildly that the self-injunctions ran into one another. *'Don't hurry—don't panic—don't run. Don't hurry don't panic don't run. Don't run don't run. Runrunrunrunrun.'* Because he knew the district well, he turned right, towards the Mansion House, passing the new buildings there; only when he was on the other side of the road did he look round.

The policeman had not followed him.

He turned again, and heard a car approaching at great speed, from Ludden Circus towards St. Ludd's. He also heard a squeal as of tyres, and glanced over his shoulder to see a car pulling up in front of St. Ludd's. The police, he thought, the police he had summoned, they would catch the thief who had dared to commit sacrilege, but not the man who had disobeyed the Commandment: *Thou shalt not kill.* As he made his way, something of the earlier anguish and fear and remorse returned, but the anguish was not so acute, not so obsessive. He could think, as well as feel. He could recall the picture of Margaret's face, so round and pretty and so gay, and the sudden change in it to distress, as she had said:

'I can't go on, Eric my darling! I can't go on.'

It had been like a great iron ball, smashing into his head.

'You must understand,' she had pleaded. 'I can't go on deceiving Geoffrey like this. I can't look him in the face. It was bad enough when he was away, but now he's home again it's impossible.'

He had thought in a spasm of wild fury: 'She wants to leave me. She wants *him*!'

'You're tired of me! That's the truth, you're tired of me!'

'No. It isn't that. It's just that I can't go on cheating him

—and I *can't* leave the children. Eric, you know I can't. Eric. *Eric!*' Suddenly, as his hands had closed about her throat, her voice had risen to a scream. '*Eric!*'

Now, she lay dead.

Now, he had prayed.

Now, he had to save himself from the consequences of his wickedness.

Although London slept and the great churches were as empty as the great blocks of offices, the museums, the stores and schools, the halls and stately homes, one place had earned the reputation of an ever watchful eye. That was Scotland Yard, the headquarters of the Metropolitan Police. In fact, however, only one section of the building was wide awake: that which housed the Information Room and the offices of the Criminal Investigation Department. From here, the centre of the web of London's police, the Divisions and the sub-divisional police stations were controlled. Each constable on duty in uniform or in plainclothes, each sergeant and officer of higher rank, was directed from one of these police stations, which themselves were directed from Scotland Yard.

A police constable named Glenn, on duty that night at St. Ludd's, was in fact from the City of London Police, another force; but the three men who appeared in the powerful car just after he had seen the man come from the telephone kiosk, were from the Yard. The two forces worked very closely together, sometimes almost as if they were one. The first car had only just stopped when another, from the City, pulled up on the other side of St. Ludd's, close to the Crypt Gate. At once, the men began to station themselves by the exits, and Glenn joined a man who stood by the statue of Queen Anne.

'What's up?'

'Had a tip off.'

'What about?'

'Burglar in there.' 'There' was indicated by a jerk of the thumb.

'Blimey!'

'If it's not a hoax,' the other remarked. 'You seen anyone?'

'Saw a chap come out of the kiosk. He was in a hell of a hurry.'

'Probably the one who tipped us off,' the Yard man remarked. 'Get a good look at him?'

'Not bad.'

'Might come in useful.'

Still another car arrived and two big men got out, going up the steps immediately and conferring with a man already by the main entrance to the cathedral. The whispering of voices sounded clear on the still air, and the shapes of the men were sharply defined in the soft light of the moon. Out of the gloom at one side of the cathedral a man in a dressing-gown appeared, tousled, bright-eyed. He was a verger disturbed by a call from the police. The whispering continued.

'What doors are open?'

'Only one, on the south side. Near the High Altar.'

'Quite sure of that?'

'Well, it's the only door which *should* be open.'

'We'll put a man at each of the others and try the one on the south side,' decided Detective Inspector Goodways of the City Police. 'No need for you yet, sir. We'll use torches, be easier to surprise this chap. If you'd care to put some clothes on——'

'But I can't believe——'

'Have to make sure, sir,' Goodways insisted.

'Yes, of course,' the verger said. 'Very well, I'll get dressed and send for the Canon.' He turned away again, obviously reluctant to admit that there might be a thief, as obviously determined not to be obstructive. As he disappeared, a whispered order was sent out, and soon four men converged on the door through which the murderer had escaped. Detective Inspector Goodways and Detective Sergeant Hodgson from the Metropolitan Force went in, making very little sound for such big and heavy men. But as they stepped into the cathedral itself, the door clanged sharply.

A yellow light, some distance off, seemed to glow brightly; then it went out.

'He's heard us,' Goodways whispered. 'Go ahead.'

On that instant, first he and then Hodgson switched on powerful torches as Hodgson called in a deep, carrying voice which echoed with strange resonance:

'Don't move! We know you're there.'

One torch beam shone on a pale statue, the other on the figure of a man carrying a big suitcase. At first, he did not move; it was as if he realised that he had no choice but to give himself up. As the two detectives moved towards him, however, and two more of lesser rank followed them in, the thief uttered an obscenity in a shrill, scared voice.

'—— you!'

He turned and began to run towards the great doors of St. Ludd's. The hurried, unco-ordinated sound fell as desecration in that house of prayer.

CHAPTER 2

GIDEON

No one with the name of Gideon could be oblivious of the fact that to many people the biblical connotation sprang immediately to mind. There were even those who said that, given a flowing beard, a voluminous gown and a thick and heavy staff, the Gideon who was a Commander at Scotland Yard would make a passable Old Testament figure. Hearing this, Gideon would laugh and make light of it, but it never failed to touch him with uneasiness. He was of an age, in the early fifties, and of a religious nonconformist upbringing, which could give a puritanical slant to most matters to do with religion, and he hoped he was neither as puritanical nor as forbidding as most Old Testament figures seemed to him.

It was characteristic of the man, physically so massive and powerful, mentally absolutely sure of himself in his job, that he should be sufficiently introspective to wonder whether any aspect of his character influenced the way he did that

14

job, and by so doing prevented a full understanding with his colleagues at the Yard. He wasn't worried about this, but occasionally he pondered it.

On the morning after the attempted theft of the altar plate from the cathedral, and the murder of Mrs. Margaret Entwhistle, nothing was farther from Gideon's mind. He had a family preoccupation as well as an administrative one, and it was the first of these that spilled over into the second. He couldn't help this, but did not like it; he wanted to concentrate on a matter of high policy in the Criminal Investigation Department, but was unable to get the face of his youngest daughter out of his mind's eye.

Poor, sad Penny; she had just failed her Royal College examination in music, an examination which was to have set her on the road to a career as a professional pianist. The letter had arrived just before Gideon left home, and so he had been delayed, which was exasperating in itself. But the sight of Penelope's glowing blue eyes, so like her mother's, the radiance of her face as she had opened the letter, had driven every other thought away. Both Gideon and Kate, his wife, had been less sure than their daughter of the result.

She had read . . .

Her face had dropped, until her expression had become one almost of despair. She hadn't trusted herself to look up at her parents, just stared down.

'No luck, Penny?' Gideon had asked, gruffly.

'No.'

'Oh, what a shame!' Kate had cried. 'They can't have——'

'I must have been really bad. And it was easy. I only had to play a selection from Liszt's *Hungarian Rhapsodies*.' Penelope broke off.

'Better luck next time,' Gideon had said, bleakly aware of the inadequacy of his words.

'There won't be a next time,' Penelope had said, drearily. 'I've failed, and that's that. Malcolm always said I was ham-handed on the piano, and this has proved it. I'll just have to give up. It doesn't matter really.'

Suddenly, like a frightened bird, she had darted away

15

from the front room of the Harrington Street house, run up the stairs, and into her room. Creaking springs told that she had flung herself on her bed. Husband and wife had looked at each other unhappily, and then Kate had forced herself to speak.

'She'll be all right, George.'

'Yes, I suppose so.'

'She always was too sure of herself. This might do her good.'

'I'd like five minutes with those examiners,' Gideon had growled, and then suddenly laughed at himself. 'I must go! Call me at the office if you think I can help.'

'I'll look after her, dear.'

And Kate would; no one better.

Gideon reflected on this as he parked his car near the main entrance of the old Commissioner's Office building, soon to be demolished, or at least vacated by the police, for stark new premises farther along the river. He must get the girl out of his mind. The funny thing was that when one's own child was hurt, one was so deeply, unreasonably, affected, even when that child was almost an adult. Penelope was twenty-one—a young woman, not an infant to fuss over and protect.

The courtyard was crowded with big men, standing by or moving to and from cars, two of which were being dusted. The police sergeant on duty said, 'Good morning,' and Gideon nodded. The morning was bright and the sky a vivid blue, but for him the dull red brick of the buildings cast a gloom. He walked up the tall flight of steps, noting that the hands of the clock in the hall touched nine-thirty, later than he had intended. Four Jamaicans, spruce and well-dressed, their dark faces showing an almost polished brightness, were sitting round the big table, talking earnestly; they were West Indian delegates here for a police conference. A constable said:

'Good morning, sir.'

' 'Morning.'

Gideon's office was up one floor, overlooking the Embankment and the Thames, just now shimmering with sunlight and gay with pleasure boats. Gideon hardly gave the view a glance as he sat at his desk of polished mahogany, seeing a pile of reports and documents in front of his chair. On the top was a note in heavy black lettering: 10 *a.m. Commissioner's Office.*

So he wasn't to have much breathing space before plunging into the administrative problem.

He pulled his chair up and paused to reflect, putting one hand on the report pile. There were at least a dozen different cases here, each requiring his immediate attention. Half would need studying closely, and he would probably have to talk to the Superintendent-in-Charge of at least six investigations. Allow half-an-hour for each of these cases, and that would see the morning out. Allow an hour with the Commissioner, and he wouldn't get round to the last case until mid-afternoon. He glanced up, forgetting that he now had a room of his own; and that his assistant had been moved next door. He pressed the bell-push as he lifted a telephone. The door leading from his assistant's room opened instantly, the operator answering at the same time.

'Get me the Commissioner's office.' Gideon raised a hand to the tall, lanky man who came in, bony-faced, bright-eyed, thinning black hair smoothed down with too much hair-cream, red-and-white-spotted bow-tie a little too flamboyant. This was Chief-Superintendent Lemaitre. 'Sit,' said Gideon, and a moment later: 'Colonel Scott-Marle, please ... Gideon.' Lemaitre sat down and Gideon asked: 'Who's waiting to see me?'

'Rollo, Simmons and Golightly,' answered Chief-Superintendent Lemaitre. 'As you were late I dealt with the others.'

Gideon nodded.

'Yes, Gideon?' said Colonel Sir Reginald Scott-Marle in his rather aloof voice; over the telephone most people found him hard to approach.

'Is ten o'clock the only possible time, sir?' Gideon asked.

'Isn't it convenient for you?'

'I can make it convenient, but there are one or two urgent jobs I'd rather attend to first.'

'Then make it eleven,' Scott-Marle said. 'And let me know what the Dean says.'

He rang off before there was time to answer. Gideon frowned as he replaced the receiver. Lemaitre was looking at him, eyebrows raised, lips parted in a set smile. What had the Commissioner meant by 'Let me know what the Dean says'? He did not ask Lemaitre if he knew; one way to preserve an oracle-like reputation was to find out the difficult answers for oneself.

'What's Golightly want?' he inquired.

'He's been over to M1 Division, a woman was strangled there last night,' said Lemaitre. 'Looks as if the husband did it.'

Gideon made no comment except a mental one; that remark, prejudging an issue about which he could not possibly have enough evidence, was characteristic of Lemaitre. It also made it easier for Gideon to form a decision when he saw Scott-Marle. He wondered if Lemaitre realised what the morning's conference was about; the Yard was a spawning ground for rumour, and none spawned so prodigally as those about appointments in the Force.

'I'll see Golightly first,' decided Gideon. 'Get him for me.'

'Right.' Lemaitre went smartly to the door. 'We can't keep the Commissioner waiting too long, can we?'

Was there a slightly malicious, or hurt, expression in his voice and in his eyes?

Gideon half-wondered as he picked up the first file, marked: *Murder: Margaret Entwhistle. C. Supt. Golightly,* the second marked: *Murder—Photo-Nudes: C. Supt. Rollo,* the third marked: *Fraud: C. Supt. Simmons.* The file beneath this was one he hadn't seen before, marked: *Attempted theft: St. Ludd's Cathedral.* He needed no more telling what Scott-Marle had meant about the Dean; obviously the Commissioner had assumed he would need time to start on this particular investigation. Yet another swift thought, more a reaction, passed through Gideon's mind: this kind of crime was sacrilege, over which the public conscience was likely to be very sensitive. The case would need careful handling.

The door opened, and Golightly came in.

It had often seemed to Gideon that names either fitted perfectly, or were complete misfits. Golightly's fitted like a glove. He was a comparatively small man by the standard of physique in the C.I.D.; neat, bland, gentle, soft-voiced; one seldom heard him approaching, so quiet were his movements. He was in the late forties, fair-haired, with innocent-looking grey eyes which always seemed to have a hint of surprise in them.

''Morning, Percy.'

''Morning, Commander.'

Gideon was looking through the thin file.

'Sit down.'

'Thanks.'

A married woman, attractive according to the photograph, had been found in her bed, strangled. Her husband, darkly handsome judging from a snapshot of him, said he had come in at three o'clock in the morning and found her dead in bed. Their three children, aged eleven, six and three, had been sound asleep—two girls in one room, the boy, an eleven-year-old—on his own. The husband, Geoffrey Entwhistle, had telephoned the police. The Divisional murder squad had gone over at once—arriving at three-thirty-one precisely.

'No one lost much time,' Gideon remarked. 'When did you get there?'

'Just after seven.'

'Couldn't you sleep?'

Golightly smiled dutifully.

'I'm still an early riser, and I called Information in case I could do anything on the way here. So I looked in at Entwhistle's place.'

Gideon's eyes were smiling.

'Just to pass the time of morning.'

'You know how the Divisions like someone to hold their hand,' rejoined Golightly. 'I haven't a big job on at the moment, you know.'

That was true. Moreover, this was his kind of job: the family crime, an investigation which affected people suffering from too much emotion. Such a condition was very relevant in Percy Golightly's opinion; he was hypersensitive to the undertones prevalent in crimes of passion and in a way he enjoyed burrowing into the causes of such crimes, perhaps because each taught him a little more about human beings, and so helped him in his job.

'Think this one's right for you?' asked Gideon.

'It could be.'

'Lem thinks the husband's worth keeping an eye on.'

'So do I,' said Golightly. 'And the lover-boy.'

'What?' ejaculated Lemaitre, from the door.

'So there's another man involved,' Gideon remarked.

'Not much doubt about it from what the neighbours say,' Golightly told him.

'There's the motive, then!' exclaimed Lemaitre.

'The lover's or the husband's?' asked Golightly, with his mildly perplexed and faintly knowing smile. 'M1 is deep in that bank robbery, Commander, that Division's got enough on its plate. This job isn't really right for them, anyway. They can give me all the help I'll need, but Fisherton would be glad to leave it to me.'

'I daresay,' said Gideon drily. Fisherton, the Superintendent at M1 Division, was nearing retirement, and since having a serious operation two years before had lost much of his vigour. He never missed a chance of passing the buck on any job. Golightly, cunning as he was, had anticipated the likely result of his call—probably Fisherton had telephoned Golightly at home. Gideon had to decide quickly whether to let him and Fisherton have their way, or make the Division take the responsibility. The real question was whether Golightly would do the better job; there was no point in being stubborn or cussed.

Gideon reached his decision.

'You take over,' he said. 'Get any help necessary from the Division; if you need any from here I want to know in advance.'

Golightly smiled much more freely.

'Thanks a lot,' he said, and stood up.

Lemaitre watched him go, leaned back in his chair, exploded: 'Lover-boy!' and jumped up. 'I'll go get Rollo,' he said.

Rollo was one of the Yard's glamour boys, the most worldly and probably the most licentious member of the C.I.D. His reputation as a bachelor made even hardened policemen whistle, shocking some and making others envious, but he had a professional etiquette as rigid as any doctor's. His *affaires de cœur*, as he referred to them, were strictly out of business hours; he was as cold-blooded with a beautiful woman witness as with a plain one. His peccadilloes affected his work in one way, however; he *did* know women, particularly the sophisticated ones and those who were promiscuous by nature. The Photo-Nude Murders probably concerned such women. Unlike the case which had preoccupied the Yard for years, that of the murder of prostitutes whose nude bodies were found in many parts of London, these were of young girls who were easily persuaded to be photographed in the nude. Three were known to have died in their one-room flatlets in Central London soon after being photographed—the same overdosage of barbiturates had caused death, and each had a print of a photograph by her side. The first two had been taken for suicide by overdoses of sleeping tablets; a third, in such identical circumstances, made murder seem a possibility. Chief-Superintendent Hugh Rollo now had the task of finding the truth. He was a youthful-looking forty-five, pleasant-faced rather than handsome, with a deep, melodious voice.

'What's new?' Gideon asked him.

'I've found a professional photographer we knew nothing about who has a collection of nude photographs that would rock the Folies Bergère,' answered Rollo. 'He works part-time in the Photographic Department of a big chemist shop and has access to every poison in the pharmaceutical book. He's got a nice little picture gallery in a cellar at his home— still lives with his parents, though. I'd like to check if he's got any pictures of the three girls who died. It would be an interesting common denominator.'

This was one way of asking for a search warrant, but there was probably more in the request than that.

'What else?' Gideon demanded.

Rollo laughed. 'Call this a confessional. One of his models used to be an acquaintance of mine. I don't know what you feel about my mixing past pleasures with business.'

Gideon grinned.

'Don't mix 'em too intimately,' he said. 'Does this chap know he's under suspicion?'

'I doubt it.'

'Don't forget how badly we want the killer,' Gideon said, and waved his hand in dismissal.

As Rollo stood up, two telephones on Gideon's desk rang. Gideon answered the exchange telephone, Lemaitre the internal one.

'Gideon.'

'Commander's Office.'

'Commander, the very Rev. Dean of St. Ludd's is on the line.'

'Hold him for one moment.' Gideon picked up the other telephone. 'Gideon.'

'This is the Back Room, Commander. I've got a bunch of press reporters here screaming for a statement on the attempted theft at St. Ludd's.'

'Tell 'em they can't have one for at least an hour,' Gideon ordered. He rang off, placed one hand over the mouthpiece of the other instrument, and looked across at Lemaitre, who was holding his telephone and obviously waiting to get a word in. 'What is it, Lem?'

'Simmons says he's on to something. Can he see you later, and not hang about for you now?'

'Yes.'

'Okay, Simmy,' Lemaitre said into his mouthpiece.

'Put the Dean through now, please,' Gideon said.

He noticed, without taking it in consciously, that Big Ben was striking ten; it was a good thing he had postponed the discussion with Scott-Marle.

CHAPTER 3

DELICATE MISSION

'Good morning, Mr. Howcroft,' Gideon said.

'Good morning, Mr. Gideon,' said the Very Reverend Dean. 'You have some idea why I am worrying you, no doubt.'

'No worry at all, sir.'

'That's most reassuring,' the Dean murmured; his voice was slow, and slightly husky. 'May I come and see you this morning?'

'How soon can you be here?'

'In five minutes or so, if that would suit you. I am at Westminster Abbey at this moment.'

Gideon did not understand why he was so surprised, but surprised he was and it took him a moment or two to say:

'I'll be free until five minutes to eleven, sir, when I have to leave for a conference.'

'Most co-operative of you. I know how busy you must be. Shall I come to any particular entrance?'

'The Commissioner's entrance—the man on duty in the yard will direct you, and I'll have someone waiting in the hall to bring you straight up.'

'Thank you again,' Dean Howcroft said.

Gideon rang off, rubbed his chin, saw Lemaitre staring at him with more than customary intensity and smothered a sigh. There were mornings which were simple routine, when one could just get on with the job, but too many were like this. Penelope, the administration problem, the fresh murder, the cathedral crime. He looked back at his assistant, friend and *confidant* of many years, feeling almost as if he were about to betray him. It was a nonsensical thought, but he could not rid himself of it. The best thing now was to face the matter squarely.

'Well, Lem,' he said. 'Know what the meeting with Scott-Marle is about?'

'I can guess,' Lemaitre answered, evading Gideon's eyes.

23

'And you'd be right. The decision about the new Deputy Commander can't be put off much longer.'

'And it's not going to be me.'

'No, it isn't,' Gideon agreed. He hated himself, yet went on defensively: 'We've talked this out a dozen times, and you've always agreed you don't want the job.'

'That's right, *I'm* the liar,' Lemaitre muttered.

He wanted the post desperately, of course, despite the fact that reason told him he was not right for it. He knew that well enough. Now and again, after an abysmal failure to handle a major investigation successfully, he would quip bluffly that he wasn't cut out for responsibility, that he was the natural assistant, born to subservience. Yet here was a dream of a lifetime, fading; after this morning, all hope, all illusion and all self-deception would be gone. The bony face seemed to become thinner, almost haggard, and the full lips worked.

'Lem,' Gideon said gently, 'I don't think the job is right for you.'

'Too true you don't. Why not let me have it straight? You don't think I'm right for the job of Deputy Commander, in line for promotion to Commander. Let's have it, George, the blunt truth.'

Gideon, deeply concerned, studied his friend, and then said quietly:

'I think Alec Hobbs is right for it.'

'Dear Old School Tie.'

Out of nowhere Gideon felt a flash of annoyance not far removed from anger, and it must have shown in his expression, for suddenly Lemaitre jumped up, clapped his bony hands together, forced a broad grin and said boisterously:

'Old bloody School Tie be damned! You and I went to the same type of school, George, London Elementary in the days before they knew what the eleven-plus was! Hobbs is the man for the job. I know it, and the fact that I'm *not* the man for it isn't your fault or Hobbs's. There's just one thing. Don't ask me to kow-tow to the slob.' Suddenly, he looked forlorn and anxious; he broke off again.

Gideon said: 'You kow-tow to anyone? That'll be the day!'

Lemaitre drew a deep breath, and stood very still. Then his whole body relaxed, and Gideon knew the crisis had passed. He thought (without consciously thinking), 'Thank God.' He gave a little smile, stood up, and with a gesture rare in him, placed a hand on Lemaitre's shoulder.

'Do you know Dean Howcroft?' he inquired.

'I'd know his face in a church, if that's what you mean.'

'He's probably in the front hall, now. Go and bring him up, will you?'

Lemaitre's eyes lost their strained unhappiness.

'Come to hallow the ground of the old place, has he? Must say he's taken his time. Okay, George.' He strode to the door, hesitated, turned round and said in a voice in which amusement overlay a suddenly revealed truth: 'Now there *is* a man I might kow-tow to!' He went out, and, before the door closed, began to whistle.

Gideon felt a marked lessening of tension.

He had two or three minutes in which to clear his mind of Lemaitre and the administration problem, and to prepare for the Dean. Standing in front of the desk, he skimmed through the file, which simply reported the facts: An unknown man had telephoned at one-twenty-one, saying that a thief was stealing the plate from the High Altar at St. Ludd's Cathedral. The caller had seemed breathless and agitated. The Flying Squad had been alerted, and cars from the City Police as well as from the Yard had converged on the cathedral. Entry had been made from the south door, near the Lady Chapel, by a detective sergeant from West Central Division, and by Detective Inspector Goodways, of the City of London police; Gideon knew both men by sight. The thief, caught red-handed, had attempted to escape and been cornered by a City policeman at the north-west door. He was an old lag with a record as long as his arm. Gideon glanced down the list of his offences, but saw none involving a church.

There was a sharp tap at the door.

'Come in!' he called.

'Here we are, sir,' said Lemaitre, as if he hadn't a care in the world. 'The Commander's expecting you.' The door opened wide. 'Commander Gideon, the Very Reverend Dean of St. Ludd's.'

Gideon held out his hand.

Dean Howcroft, a man in his early sixties, would have stood out in any gathering simply because of his snowy-white hair; quite beautiful hair which had a natural wave and was brushed straight back from his forehead, like a lion's mane. He was not, in other respects, particularly good-looking, for beneath an exceptionally broad forehead his nose was snub and his chin rather vague; nevertheless, his appearance was that of a fine-looking man. He had a reputation for pungency in his comments on social behaviour, a pungency which fell short of labelling him one of the lunatic fringe which lapped the Church.

He was shorter than Gideon, and perhaps a little too well-fed, for both his collar and his clerical grey jacket fitted over-closely. There was an unexpected briskness about his manner, however, and warmth in his smile.

'So we meet again, Mr. Gideon.'

'The last time was at the wedding of the Home Secretary's daughter,' Gideon remarked, pleased that the other had remembered him. 'Do sit down.'

'Thank you. This is an unhappy business, I'm afraid.'

Gideon said cautiously: 'Any crimes attached to a church could be considered so.'

'Yes, indeed. I understand you caught the man.'

'We did.'

'Such very quick work,' approved the Dean.

'Thank you.' Gideon was wondering what all this was leading up to. At the back of his mind there was Scott-Marle's reference to the Dean; someone had told the Commissioner in advance.

'Do you know the man?'

'He's a habitual criminal.'

'Are you sure?' The Dean's voice sharpened and he looked taken aback.

'We certainly are.' Gideon tapped the file. 'Four times in

26

jail, the last time he was sentenced he asked for seventeen other cases to be taken into account. He could hardly be more professional. He's always stolen silver or jewellery. I don't know him personally, but I shall soon have a report from someone who does. Have you any special interest in this man?'

'No,' said the Dean. He frowned, and a myriad wrinkles appeared at his eyes and forehead. 'Only in what he did last night. I am interested in certain other offences which may affect you, Commander. I have just been to the Abbey, as you know, where I discussed with the Dean a problem common to many of the big churches, perhaps more common than we like to admit. It is somewhat ironic that I've come to you as a consequence of a very different kind of offence, very different indeed.'

Why not say 'crime'? wondered Gideon.

'Why have you come, sir?'

'On a somewhat delicate mission from our point of view, perhaps a very ordinary one to you. I asked Sir Reginald Scott-Marle whom I should see, and he unhesitatingly said that I should see you.'

'Oh.' That was one little mystery cleared. 'What's the delicate problem, sir?'

'Commander,' said the Dean, leaning forward and looking very earnest, 'the Church—all churches—have many problems, perhaps the greatest being that of our relationship with the people. Forgive a blunt question, please. Are *you* a Christian?'

Gideon, momentarily taken aback, recovered and smiled at the directness of the approach.

'Nominally, yes, I suppose.'

'Ah,' said Dean Howcroft, repeating with a certain ironic inflection: 'Nominally. One of the great host of nominal Christians.' He hesitated, his slate grey eyes searching, and the wrinkles puckered his forehead again. 'And yet from my knowledge of you and your reputation, I would not have thought you would be nominal about anything.'

'Can *I* be blunt, sir?'

'Please.'

'I'm a policeman. I deal with criminals from all classes and all religions—Christians from all sects, Jews, Mohammedans, Buddhists, Hindus—I repeat, sir, *all* religions. Under the law, all men are equal whether they have any religion or none. As a policeman, I am committed to neutrality. That means nominal, surely.'

After a long pause, Howcroft said:

'And as a man?'

'I'm a policeman first, and you have come to see me as a policeman.'

'No,' said Howcroft, quite sharply. 'That is evading the question.' When Gideon stared at him expressionlessly, he went on: 'I'm sorry, Commander, truly sorry—and of course I, too, am being evasive in my own way. It is perhaps a simpler case than I am making it out to be. The Church cannot be quite so ruthless in its attitudes as other organisations. We cannot come to the police with the same alacrity as could, say, a business house or a hotel. We have a wider, more embracing duty to all people, even when they break the law.'

He paused, allowing a chance for interruption; Gideon let it go.

'And we have to worry about our public image, too. If we are severe with offenders, we are likely to be judged as being too harsh; if we try to help by understanding, we are judged as being too lenient. Either way, our image is smeared; and yet we need a clear, true image, Commander. Don't you agree?'

Gideon said: 'I hope you do, sir.'

'What do you mean by that?'

Gideon gave a grim little smile.

'A true image isn't necessarily a good one, is it? In the moral sense.'

After a moment's pause, the Dean smiled more freely than he had since entering the room.

'No indeed,' he conceded. 'But I will settle for an accurate one. I like to think you would find it good enough. I shouldn't have asked you if you were a Christian, you know; it was the wrong word. People are apt to jib at it.' He went on quickly: 'But I mustn't waste your time. Commander, in the past few months there have been a great number of trifling—I say trifling in the material sense—acts of vandalism in many churches. St. Paul's, the Abbey, Westminster Cathedral, St. Martin-in-the-Fields—all of these have suffered. So have many parish churches, both Church of England and, I believe, those of the Roman Catholic faith. Those of us who have to minister to the material needs of the Church are increasingly disturbed by these acts. No single case is sufficient to justify calling you in, but the sum total of damage and loss is becoming quite considerable. We have tried and failed to discover the culprits. We know we must now consult the Yard. I have been tempted to do so several times. Last night's sacrilege made it possible for me to see you, officially. I have talked with my very good friends the Deans of the Abbey and of St. Paul's. They agree that it would be wise to be wholly frank with you. Do you think you can help us to find out who is doing this—in fact, to find out whether it is organised or whether all the incidents are unconnected—and at the same time help us to avoid notoriety and disfavour with our—ah—nominal supporters?'

CHAPTER 4

RIGHT MAN?

GIDEON studied the alert, eager face, sensing the depth of the Dean's feeling, his anxiety to solve the problem and yet by so doing to cause no adverse criticism; to do good, without any risk of harm. That phrase entered Gideon's mind, and it seemed to him that it epitomised the attitude and the thinking of this rather prolix man. As he sat, considering, Howcroft could not keep quiet.

'I have made myself clear, haven't I? You do understand, don't you?'

'You've made yourself very clear, and I think I know exactly what you want,' Gideon said. Suddenly he smiled broadly, appreciating the other's acumen. 'And you've timed it perfectly! We can now take a closer interest in St. Ludd's and the other big churches, without arousing anyone's suspicions.'

'Precisely! And will you?'

'Suits us best, too,' Gideon pointed out. 'We also have to worry about our image, and if we get the reputation of spending too much time going after sneak-thieves in the churches instead of concentrating on the big criminals in business and society——'

He broke off, for the Dean was chuckling.

'Sir Reginald was right indeed,' he said. 'I'm most grateful. It goes without saying that I will do everything I can to help, and I can promise you the same from my ecclesiastic colleagues and friends. In our rather fumbling and amateur way we have already attempted——'

Gideon, an eye on the clock, interrupted.

'First things first, sir. We need the right man to look after this, someone with sufficient general knowledge of church background, regalia and customs . . .' He was thinking aloud and at the same time considering senior officers who might be familiar with the set-up and have the right temperament for dealing with churchmen. 'Give me a little while to think about it. We want someone who is sympathetic, but whose emotions won't run away with him.'

'Another nominal Christian, to be sure,' the Dean said, his eyes twinkling.

Gideon chuckled, and had a rare feeling—that here was a man whom he could grow to like very much, one who had both humour and humility.

'Up to you to convert him from nominal to practising,' he said, and stood up. 'If you'll let me have your telephone number and an address where I can always get you, I'll be in touch very soon.'

The Very Reverend Dean of St. Ludd's took a fat envelope from a mysteriously hidden pocket, and handed it across the desk.

'You will find everything you need in there, Commander, including the results of our own tentative investigations—futile, I assure you, hence our belated realisation that professional help was needed.' His handshake was firm, the twinkle remained. 'I will find my own way out——'

'Mr. Lemaitre will show you the way,' Gideon said, and opened Lemaitre's door. 'Superintendent, you've met Dean Howcroft, haven't you?'

Lemaitre's big hand shot out, engulfing the Dean's.

'Very glad to know you, sir. Not often an ex-choir-boy has the chance to shake hands with the Dean. It was Dean Ruston in my day, sir. Lived to be about a hundred!'

'He did indeed', said Howcroft, marvelling. 'And you are an old choir-boy at St. Ludd's? How very unexpected. You must come along and hear the choir again one day, we have two very beautiful voices—*very* beautiful indeed.'

He went out with Lemaitre. Gideon stared at the closing passage door, remembering. Lemaitre had often mentioned the days when he had been a choir-boy. Such a childhood's experience lay in many a tough man's recollection of it, covered by cynical comment or crude joke. Lemaitre, ex-St. Ludd's, was certainly no more than a nominal Christian, but his wife—his second wife—was a regular churchgoer. Well, well.

Gideon laughed suddenly: he was thinking in much the same way as the Dean talked.

It was five to eleven—time he went along to see Scott-Marle.

At five to eleven Eric Greenwood stood up from his desk in a tiny office which overlooked the Thames and a corner of Billingsgate Market, and stepped into the even smaller office, where his secretary sat at a typewriter which never seemed silent. Stubby fingers poised over the keys, she looked up. She was fifty-three, plump, coarse-skinned, grey-haired—and quite incredibly efficient. She had been secretary to the previous manager of this department, and by now was considered to be part of the furniture of Cox and Shielding, Importers and Exporters from the Orient. Behind her broad, innocently shining forehead there was more knowledge of out-of-the-way suppliers of exotic commodities than in any other brain in London.

'Yes, Mr. Greenwood?'

'I'm going across to see Shalimar's. Hold any calls, Bessie.'

'Yes, Mr. Greenwood.'

Before the flimsy door closed she was hammering away at the typewriter again, yet when her letters were finished they would be type-perfect. Greenwood stepped into a very narrow passage, with doors at regular intervals, each marked with the name of the department. There were: *Spices, Carpets, Woollens, Metalwork, Jewellery, Carvings* and several others. In a small way, Cox and Shielding's did a remarkable diversity of business. Greenwood was the General Buyer for the whole business and, with Bessie Smith, was almost indispensable. He pushed open a door at the far end of the passage. This led to the landing of the four-storey building, with its floor and steps of stone; there was no lift, and his heels rang out sharply. He stepped into a narrow lane, still cobbled, still with its iron hitching-posts, and walked briskly between tall, ugly office buildings to Upper Thames Street, then along another lane to the Monument, where a few tourists stood looking up at the ancient watch-tower built to ensure that London would not burn again. Here cars and vans were parked. An acquaintance from a shipping company nodded, but did not stop. Greenwood, walking with long strides through the crush of traffic, the lumbering buses, the mass of pedestrians, reached the approach to London Bridge.

Shalimar's, an oriental carpet and curio importing firm, lay on the other side.

The sun shone warmly, the river surface shimmered, the dozen ships in the pool of London were all being worked, booms and cranes and derricks clanged, some holds were being emptied, some being filled. In the distance, against the clear blue sky, Tower Bridge looked like an illustration out of a history book.

Greenwood stood in the middle of London Bridge, staring down. Ships and buildings, and the bridge itself, were reflected in the water, but all he could see was Margaret's face, all he could hear was Margaret's voice screaming: 'Eric!' His hands were tightly clenched, his lips set and thin, his eyes screwed up. Everywhere he could see and hear her, a never-fading reminder of the fact that she was dead.

They had met here; on this bridge; feeding gulls.

He could remember that meeting, over two years ago.

She had been alone on a warm summer's day, lovely, sweet and desirable. He would never understand what had happened to him; how utterly he had surrendered to her attractiveness. Nor would he understand the absolute nature of her surrender to him. It was almost as if on the instant of meeting they had known that their stars had ordained their union.

Her husband had been away in the tropics, on a three-year contract with an engineering firm; wives were not allowed on the project. Their three children had a young woman to take care of them by day, so that she herself could work.

'I love coming to the City.'

'I do, too.'

'I always feed the gulls here, winter and summer.'

His hand had closed over hers. 'I wonder if——'

'Yes?'

'You're free for lunch.'

'Oh, how lovely!'

Lovely, lovely, lovely. Free for lunch, free for dinner, free for cinema, theatre, night club, free for bed and free for laughter; free and yet no threat to freedom. They had made a world of their own, using his bachelor flat in Camberwell, free from observation, prying eyes and her husband; always free. Until Geoffrey Entwhistle had come home.

Greenwood felt drawn towards the river's siren call, as if he could hear it whispering: 'You have only to come to me, and I will give you rest.'

He started, becoming aware of the fact that he had lost count of time. A pleasant-faced young woman was staring at him with some concern. He walked on hurriedly, knowing that she was watching him, well aware of his attractiveness to women. There had been a time when this had been both a satisfaction and an anxiety to him; he had always been afraid of the obligation of love and marriage. With Margaret, he had felt he had everything, then suddenly it had been snatched away from him. He had realised the danger the moment her husband had returned.

At the end of the bridge, Greenwood bought an *Evening News*, and stood staring down at a photograph of Margaret—lovely Margaret. His heart seemed to turn over. God! There was a copy of this very photograph at his flat, standing on the radiogram. Had anyone else seen it? He had no daily help, but—— Panic rose in him again, driving away the remorse and the grief.

He read:

MOTHER OF THREE STRANGLED

Returning to his Lewisham home after a long drive from a business appointment in Leicester, Mr. Geoffrey Entwhistle found his wife's body in the front bedroom.

She had been strangled.

The police are anxious to interview a tall, dark-haired man wearing a light grey suit, who was seen near Number 23, Billitter Street, about eleven-fifteen last night. It is believed that Mrs. Entwhistle was murdered between eleven and one o'clock. The killer did not disturb her three sleeping children—Clive aged 11, Jennifer aged 7, Carol aged 4.

Mr. Entwhistle was with the police at Divisional Headquarters between four o'clock and seven o'clock, helping with inquiries. Mrs. Entwhistle's mother is looking after the children.

Slowly, Greenwood lowered the newspaper.

He was no longer thinking of Margaret, but of his chances of escaping detection. It was ironic that he owed to her the fact that they had always been extremely careful. Almost the only really dangerous move he had made had been that last night at Billitter Street, where he had gone without warning because Margaret had refused to come to him.

34

If he'd only kept his hands off her, he wouldn't be in this predicament.

How many people *had* seen them together?

Percy Golightly, in charge of a case which already greatly attracted him, was in one of his sunniest moods. He sat at his desk at Scotland Yard, with copies of the evening newspapers in front of him. There were excellent pictures of the dead woman, and, in one, of her husband and children.

The door opened and a youthful-looking man with a hooked nose came in, carrying a wire tray with photographs. He put this tray on the end of Golightly's desk.

'Two hundred prints, as per your request,' he stated.

Golightly picked up the top print, of Greenwood's favourite photograph of a most attractive woman; even he found it hard to believe that she was dead.

'That's good,' he said. 'Enough for all the Divisions and to spare. Thanks.' He nodded dismissal to the man from *Photographs*, and picked up a pencil. He wrote on the back of the photograph: *Accurate likeness of Margaret Entwhistle, murdered by strangulation at 23, Billitter Street, Lewisham, between eleven p.m. and one o'clock in the morning, 15–16 of June. M1 Division requests notification if this woman has been seen in the company of any man other than her husband at any time during the past three months (or longer). In emergency also report to Information Room New Scotland Yard or to Chief-Superintendent Golightly.*

He read this through again, then sent for a sergeant to arrange for it to be duplicated, stuck on the back of the photographs and distributed. Gideon knew damned well that he would handle the inquiry from this office. Good old Gee-Gee!

Golightly stood up, and crossed to a table which held a plastic bag containing dust and lint from the woman's clothing. Pinned to a board were plastic envelopes, containing a number of things: a specimen of her lipstick, her face powder, fingernail scraping, hair—anything that might also be found on her murderer.

Of course, each would almost certainly be found on her husband.

Golightly stood up, whistled softly, went out and upstairs to the laboratory, where white-smocked men stood at a long bench dotted with Bunsen burners and pipettes, test tubes and white crucibles, tripods and forceps. There were two microscopes, and all the impedimenta of a reasonably up-to-date chemical laboratory.

'Got something for you,' Golightly said to the elderly Superintendent-in-Charge.

'Never known the time when you hadn't,' the Superintendent said. 'This the Entwhistle job?'

'Yes.'

'It was the husband, wasn't it?' suggested the laboratory man.

'Who knows?' Golightly asked cryptically.

As this was happening at Scotland Yard, Geoffrey Entwhistle was sitting alone in his house at Billitter Street, Lewisham. His mind was in chaos, grieving and raging at the same time, as well as being a little frightened, for he knew that he was under suspicion.

His wife's murderer was at Shalimar's office, discussing a shipment of Tibetan agate. The thief of St. Ludd's was still at Cannon Row Police Station. Gideon was with the Commissioner, discussing Superintendent Alec Hobbs of the C.I.D. At the same time, Superintendent Hugh Rollo was standing in a cellar beneath a house in Fulham, marvelling at a collection of nude photographs which really had to be seen to be believed.

'Only time I've ever seen anything like this is in the frescoes at Pompeii,' he confided to a sergeant. 'The Romans certainly knew how they wanted their lights o' love. My, my. I think I'll bring Gee-Gee along to see this.'

His companion, a detective sergeant of rare temerity, laughed.

'If I know Gee-Gee, it won't be the bods he'll want to see, but the photographer who took them.'

'Could be. I don't underestimate our commander.' Rollo

grinned. 'He has an artistic eye. First things first, though. Are any of our three dead nudes here? Strictly in the line of duty, Sergeant—take a closer look.'

They both laughed, though neither was amused, and began to compare three photographs, each of a murdered girl, with the photographs on the wall. It was a tedious and time-taking business, and during it their jokes were both crude and lewd, yet covered a deadly seriousness.

In his study in an old oak beamed house near St. Ludd's, the Very Reverend Dean Howcroft was saying into the telephone:

'Yes, I'm quite sure we can rely on his discretion. I was most favourably impressed ... No, he hasn't telephoned me yet, but I have a feeling I know who he will assign to the task ... The moment I have any news I will tell you.'

CHAPTER 5

RECOMMENDATIONS

SIR REGINALD SCOTT-MARLE had been the Commissioner of the Metropolitan Police for several years. Those of his officers who knew him well both liked and respected him. For one thing, he did not pretend to be a detective; he was an administrator. For another, he took advice even in recommending senior appointments, which were made officially by the Home Office. He was aloof to the point of arrogance, but even those who found him cold and distant admitted his scrupulous fairness. Gradually he had become accepted as the true representative of the police, and under his guidance a great number of improvements had been made in working conditions, pay and general facilities. Members of the Metropolitan Force now felt that they had a square deal, and Gideon, instrumental in persuading Scott-Marle of the need for the improvements, knew that the efficiency of the force was the greater because of the Commissioner.

He reached the door of the Commissioner's office as Scott-Marle, tall, lean, austere-looking, himself turned a corner from the other direction. He nodded, and gave a faint smile.

'Good morning, George.'

'Good morning, sir.'

'Come in.' They were as tall as each other, but Gideon was broader in comparison with his chief. This was a large office, with a conference room opening out on one side, the secretary's on the other. A telephone bell rang in her room as Scott-Marle motioned to one of two chairs ranged in front of his desk. So only one other was expected.

Hobbs?

One of three telephones on Scott-Marle's desk rang.

'Yes,' he said into it. 'I see—thank you.' He rang off. 'Hobbs has been delayed for ten minutes.'

'Not your morning for punctuality,' Gideon remarked.

'Perhaps that's a good thing, for once. How did Dean Howcraft impress you?'

'Favourably,' answered Gideon promptly.

'Good. You had the same effect on him.'

Gideon's eyebrows rose. 'Has he been in touch with you again?'

'No,' said Scott-Marle. Now his smile was, for him, positively broad. 'I don't often catch you out in bad staff work.'

'Where have I slipped up?' asked Gideon, wary but not embarrassed.

'My wife's brother-in-law is the Bishop,' Scott-Marle said, simply.

'Good God! I had no idea, sir.' Gideon smiled a little ruefully. 'I simply had no idea.' As he stared into the Commissioner's amused eyes, thoughts were flashing through his mind, and he went on almost without a pause: 'If the story's reached the Bishop as quickly as this, the investigation means a lot to them and the problem isn't as simple as the Dean made out.'

'Did he make you believe it was simple?'

Gideon said slowly: 'I suppose he didn't. He implied that

the trouble itself was comparatively trifling, but the task of finding out what was behind it was too complex for the Church authorities.' Gideon paused, fingering his chin, more perplexed than he liked to admit. 'I didn't press him for details—in fact I discouraged him from saying too much.'

'He does rather go on and on, doesn't he?' said Scott-Marle. 'The trouble is two-fold—minor thefts of the kind which are quite common, and damage which amounts to serious vandalism if it is part of an overall activity. The anxiety is that either or both could become much more serious. One of the more intractable factors is that the offences seem to be committed by someone with a knowledge of what is most sacred to the churches—they damage things which have ritual significance as well as value, though not, so far, the buildings themselves.'

'Hmm,' grunted Gideon.

'Have you decided who is to tackle it?'

Gideon hesitated. Then: 'I think so,' he said.

'Who?'

'Lemaitre.'

He could not recall ever seeing Scott-Marle show so much surprise as he did at that answer. He stared at Gideon for a long time, making Gideon wonder whether he would try to dissuade him, even wonder whether his own judgment had been warped by a desire to give Lemaitre's morale a good boost. He did not move in his chair nor shift his gaze.

At last, Scott-Marle said: 'He's the last man I would have thought of, but I think I see why you're considering him. He will be extremely anxious to succeed, he's a very straight-forward fellow with a simple pattern of ethics, he will be shocked by the sacrilege involved but not be impressed by piety, ritual or humbug.' Scott-Marle paused in the midst of this quite brilliant assessment of Gideon's thinking, some of it quite impromptu, and then went on bluntly: 'Can we trust his discretion?'

'I've never had any worry about his discretion,' Gideon said. 'He might be too impetuous, but I think he'll restrain himself over this.' Gideon allowed himself a small, experimental grin. 'I'll be next door to him all the time, I don't think that will do any harm.'

Scott-Marle shrugged. 'There you go, taking on more responsibility than you really should accept. However—I would certainly like to feel you had this investigation under your eye. You said you thought you'd decided. Why haven't you fully made up your mind?'

'Only considered Lemaitre for ten minutes,' Gideon pointed out. 'I've decided now, sir.'

Scott-Marle said: 'Very well. Keep me in close touch, won't you?' He paused only long enough for Gideon to say: 'I will,' before going on without a change of tone: 'Now to the Deputy Commander's post. Have you had any second thoughts about Hobbs?'

'No,' said Gideon.

'None at all?'

'Nothing new,' answered Gideon quietly. 'He's now had a full year at N.E. It's been a tough year, and very few men with his background would have got through it the way he has. You still get the odd senior officer who sneers about Public School and party influence, and with a man like Hobbs you always will. I feared it might prevent him from getting on top of his job. I don't think so now. I think he'll make a real success of it.'

Slowly, thoughtfully, Scott-Marle said: 'I hope so, George. I most certainly hope so. I'm going to recommend him, of course, and I've no doubt the appointment will be confirmed. But I'm more troubled than I was before.'

'Why, sir?'

Scott-Marle didn't answer at once, and in the pause movements in the other room suggested that Hobbs had come in. When a buzzer sounded, Scott-Marle pressed a button to tell his secretary to wait. For the first time since he had entered the room that day Gideon saw the other man withdraw; sensed a cloak of reserve, almost of aloofness fall upon him, affecting even the brightness of his eyes. The thing which most impressed Gideon was the freedom with which he had talked up to this moment; the change was really a reversion to normal.

'I want you to give me a serious undertaking,' he said very precisely. 'If at any time in the next six months you have reason to wonder if the appointment is a success, tell me so. Don't keep it to yourself. I know you take a patriarchal interest in your staff. Don't, please, allow that to influence you about Hobbs. I think he will either be exceptionally good, or an unmistakable failure.'

Gideon, wondering at the nature of this confidence yet not sharing the doubt, had the sense to say:

'I'll keep you informed all along the line, sir.'

'Good. Then we'll have him in.' In spite of the words his forefinger hovered over the bell-push and there was an almost unfathomable expression in his eyes. 'George, I have often wanted to say this to you. I have come to recognise and understand you as a dedicated man. I have known soldiers and sailors, airmen and even politicians with a similar feeling of dedication, but I didn't expect to find it in a policeman. I came to this appointment as an administrator, seeing the Force as another kind of army. In a way it is. I have come to see it as an instrument in the age-old struggle between good and evil. You have made me regard it so. Try to make Hobbs see it in the same way. He is a very fine detective and an astute man. Intellectually and academically he is in a class by himself at the Yard. I am not really convinced yet that he has that sense of dedication.'

Scott-Marle stopped.

Slowly, almost painfully, Gideon said:

'I see what you mean.'

He not only saw what the Commissioner meant, he could see why he had doubts about Hobbs. There was another factor which, in other circumstances, might have made him feel selfconscious, but it did not now. He would not have been aware of any sense of dedication in himself. If he had such a sense, it was as natural as breathing, and he didn't think it could be acquired.

If Hobbs hadn't got it, he would probably never have it.

Scott-Marle said: 'All right, George,' and he pressed the bell push.

Chief-Superintendent Alec Hobbs was almost too short for a policeman, barely above the regulation 5 feet 8 inches. There was something curiously controlled about him—the way he dressed, the way he spoke and looked, the way he moved. His clothes, impeccably tailored, were a shade too formal, and every suit he wore appeared to be an exact replica of the last. His dark hair, greying slightly at the temples, was always exactly the same; he had it trimmed every ten days. He had been educated at Repton and King's College, Cambridge, and had spent a year at one of the major American universities, Gideon could never remember which. There had at one time been a certain amount of prejudice against him as being Old School Tie, but as Gideon knew, this intense jealousy had mostly vanished.

He had a private income, but no one knew how much. He lived expensively but without ostentation in a flat overlooking the river at Chelsea, with his invalid wife, to whom he was devoted, and with whom he spent all of his spare time. She was—or she had been—a very beautiful woman, but in recent months her looks had faded, as if her illness were eating them away.

This was the man whom Gideon, a product of a London elementary and secondary school education, had recommended as his deputy; and almost certainly the man who would one day step into Gideon's shoes.

That morning he moved towards the Commissioner's office, guessing, without being absolutely sure, the reason for his summons. Gideon shifted in his seat without rising; Scott-Marle motioned to the one empty chair. Hobbs knew instinctively that they had been discussing him: well, why not? Scott-Marle's expression gave nothing away and Gideon looked a little preoccupied. Hobbs believed he understood Gideon more, in fact, than he understood Scott-Marle, who was first and last a soldier as Hobbs understood soldiers.

'I hope you weren't delayed by anything serious,' Scott-Marle said. Reproof was implicit in his words.

'Traffic, sir,' Hobbs said, half-truthfully. He had never been able to talk freely about his wife and could not bring himself to say that it was a specialist who had been delayed on a visit to her, not he himself.

Scott-Marle made no comment, but continued smoothly:

'I would like to recommend your appointment as Deputy Commander of the Criminal Investigation Department, Hobbs. Can I do so with the certainty of your acceptance should the post be offered?'

Outwardly, Hobbs was unmoved. Inwardly, he exulted.

'Yes, sir, you can. Thank you.'

'You have Gideon to thank as much if not more than I,' Scott-Marle declared.

He glanced at Gideon, who felt a sudden sense of need to put Hobbs at his ease. Scott-Marle, having let himself go so much this morning, was instinctively stiffening again, and the familiar cold exterior was already very faintly hostile. If the conversation could not be lightened, it could at least be changed.

He said adroitly: 'Have you heard about the trouble at St. Ludd's?'

'An old lag has been arrested, hasn't he?' There was very little that missed Hobbs.

'Yes, but there's more to it than that. The Dean——'

'Howcroft?'

'Yes. Do you know him?'

'Yes. Socially.'

'He's worried about what he calls minor offences in a lot of churches and cathedrals,' Gideon said. 'He wants us to probe, without making it obvious what we're doing.'

'Using the thief as the ostensible reason for the St. Ludd's investigation,' Hobbs divined. 'It must be serious, or he wouldn't come to us.' He broke off, obviously waiting for some further comment. Scott-Marle was simply watching them, taking all this in but being no help at all. Gideon pondered before saying almost sententiously: 'Who would you put in charge of that, Alec?'

He hoped the 'Alec' would lighten the atmosphere, yet was uneasy because if Hobbs was socially a friend of the Dean, he might have some reservations about Lemaitre. These *bloody* politics! Gideon had no time for them at all and almost resented Scott-Marle's decision to consult him. Hobbs, frowning very slightly, still determined not to show any feeling, was thinking fast. At last, he shifted his position slightly, and said:

'Lemaitre, I think, if you can spare him from his desk.'

Thank God for that! thought Gideon.

If anything was calculated to show that Hobbs had a heart as well as a head, this was it. He chuckled and Scott-Marle visibly relaxed. Hobbs knew that he had said the right thing.

Sally Dalby was a long way from sure that she was right; in fact, she was afraid she had both spoken and acted unwisely, but she did not see how she could get out of it now. She sat alone in a cubicle in a cellar in North London, half-undressed, nervous and ashamed. She heard Toni Bottelli moving about in the main part of the cellar, and she could hear the background music of a radio. Everything seemed so ordinary and normal, yet here she was, actually undressing so that a man she hardly knew could take her photograph.

'I'm just a prude,' she muttered to herself; then almost at once, she thought: 'What would Dad say?' She unrolled one stocking as far as the beautifully soft and rounded calf of her leg, but stopped suddenly. '*I can't do it!*' She spoke very clearly and precisely. On impulse she rolled the stocking up, snatched her skirt from a hook and drew it on, zipped it with an almost feverish motion and stretched out for her blouse. She had it half on, arms thrust backwards into the sleeves, bosom thrust forward, when the man she hardly knew pulled the curtain aside roughly and demanded:

'How long are you going to be?'

It was the expression on his handsome face far more than his words or his manner, which touched her with fear.

CHAPTER 6

CHILD IN TERROR

TONI BOTTELLI stood glaring at Sally, and suddenly she felt worse than naked; she felt besmirched. His expression changed from impatience and anger to lustful gloating; she could not mistake that for an instant. She backed away but there was very little space, and her hands knocked painfully against the wall.

Bottelli raised his eyebrows: 'Take your time.'

'Toni, go away.'

'What a hope!'

'Leave me alone, I want to get dressed!'

'You've got the wrong idea, Sally old gel. You want to get undressed.'

'No, I—I won't! I can't!'

'You *can't*?' mocked Toni, and there was a harsher note in his voice. 'I'll help you, if you like.'

'Get away from me!'

As she stood there in terror, she had no idea how beautiful she looked, with her honey-brown eyes shining with that fear, the long lashes curling against her fair skin, stained now with a defiant flush. Her lips were parted, and her teeth just showed; she was on the verge of shivering. All she knew was that she was desperately afraid of him. She was seventeen, and although she had known the exploring fingers of youths of her own age, she was a virgin, with all a virgin's dread of violence; yet this man's will to violence showed in his very face, in the tautness of his body. An older woman or an experienced one would have taken one glance at him and warned: 'Don't trust him an inch.'

If he lays a hand on me, she thought, I'll die.

She did not, she could not, know how true that might be.

She simply sensed some horrible and impending danger. Her shallow breathing reached a climax and she began to

45

gulp and gasp. She was aware of it and was now frightened by the feeling of suffocation, knowing that she had to move away, that her body was going limp, her legs beginning to tremble. She thought hysterically: why doesn't he *do* something, why does he just stand there?

Being so young, she did not notice the almost imperceptible change in his expression, the way the glitter in his eyes began to fade, or the way the taut muscles at his lips relaxed. Now the screaming of her nerves and the choking difficulty of her breathing brought her to the verge of collapse. Her lips began to quiver, her teeth to chatter, quite beyond control.

Suddenly, Bottelli said:

'Relax, baby.'

She hardly heard him.

'Relax,' he repeated, and moved to take a robe of gay towelling from a peg on the wall. 'Put that on. I'm not going to touch you.'

She could hardly believe what he was saying.

'Take it easy.' He backed away a pace, holding the gown out for her to put on. When she did not move, baffled by the change in him, he tossed it at her and moved away. 'What you need is a drink,' he said over his shoulder.

A tremendous sense of gratitude flowed through her, of release, as if some drug had been injected into her veins and was moving through her bloodstream, warming, soothing. His back was towards her. She shrugged the shirt-blouse on, the buttons defeating her unsteady hands, pulling the robe tight, tying the sash. There was a couch against one wall, the only one not covered with photographs. As she moved towards it, her legs still weak, she heard the chink of glasses. When she dropped down, Bottelli turned round, holding two glasses. Walking towards her, he was the man she had first met, and thought so handsome, with his beautiful black hair and his olive skin, his luminous dark eyes set against black lashes and brows. He was rather small, but beautifully formed, which was particularly obvious because he wore only a dark, short-sleeved shirt and faded jeans.

He stood over her, holding out a glass.

'Here's to you,' he said.

She took the glass and sipped. It was whisky. Suddenly it flashed through her mind that drinking whisky so early in the day was a very dashing, grown-up thing to do, and she felt a little giggle rising within her.

'Here's to *you*,' she said.

'That's my Sally!'

They both drank, more deeply.

'What got into you?' he asked, and his manner, his tone of voice, everything about him had changed; she was aware of it without even beginning to understand.

'I—I don't know, Toni.'

'Scared of me?'

' 'Course I wasn't!'

'You don't have to be.'

'I know I don't.'

He lowered himself to the edge of the couch, beside her.

'You never will have to be scared of me.'

'I know,' she repeated.

'Not now, or ever.' He sipped, and gave a little quirk of a smile, a most attractive one, the kind which would have lulled the suspicions of many an experienced woman, and melted the resistance of most others.

Sally looked puzzled, in her naïve and simple way.

'What do you mean—not *now*?'

'What I say, Sally.'

'You mean'—her eyes looked enormous—'I did have reason to be scared of you?'

'You certainly did.'

'I—I don't understand you.'

His smile, so attractive and winsome, became much wider.

'Take a look in the mirror,' he said.

After a moment's pause she caught the meaning of the compliment, and gave a pleased little laugh.

'Don't give me that!'

'Go on, look in the mirror. There's one on the wall.'

She looked round at the array of photographs, which had shocked her when she had first come in, making her nervous and starting the tension which had brought her to revolt.

There was no sign of a mirror, although she knew there was a small one in the cubicle.

'What wall?' she asked.

'Don't believe me, eh?' Toni scoffed.

In the nicest possible way he patted her knee, got up and crossed to the wall opposite the cubicle. It appeared to be a solid mass of photographs and she coloured a little, because some of them were in peculiar poses. There was one of a girl, naked, back to the camera, legs apart, bending down and peering between them, long hair falling almost to the floor. Sally did not want to look too closely at this or any of the others, deciding comfortably that most of them were no worse than the coloured photographs one could see on the bookstalls in the West End, remarkable for outsized breasts and tiny waists.

'Here you are,' Toni said brightly.

He put out a hand, pulled at a small knob which she hadn't noticed, and a section of the wall folded back revealing a full length mirror. With a start of surprise she saw herself in the colourful gown, fair hair a little untidy, even the fringe out of place, eyes starry and cheeks flushed.

'Now you have to admit, that's something,' Toni Bottelli said.

'Oh, go on!'

'I knew you had something the first moment I set eyes on you,' he declared. 'I'm more than a photographer, *they're* two-a-penny. I'm an artist, too. Got an artist's eye for a figure, and it takes more than a blouse and skirt to fool me. You want to know something? I've been an artist photographer for nine years, and in my considered opinion I've never seen *anyone* with a better figure than yours.'

That pleased her greatly, but she protested.

'You've never even *seen* it.'

'I can tell.'

'You're just flattering me.'

'What's wrong with a bit of flattery, Sal?' He slid his arm round her waist and squeezed, then moved away towards a camera which stood on a tripod at one end of the room. Opposite this was a raised platform, draped in black, and two silken cushions, beautifully coloured; beyond it a low stool with an iridescent cover of pale sea-greens. 'I know I'm right, though.'

'I'll bet you say the same thing to every girl who comes in here.'

'Oh, well,' said Toni, offhandedly, 'if you don't want to believe that I think you've got the most beautiful body I've ever come across, I can't make you. And I certainly don't want to take your photograph if you don't want me to. Get dressed and buzz, baby! I've got to get myself another model.'

He began to whistle a beat tune.

Sally went into the cubicle and stood very still for a few seconds, piqued and even annoyed at the sudden change in Toni's manner, yet still intrigued and flattered by his compliments. Near her were several photographs in black and white, of quite lovely girls; there was no doubt of the artistry in the pose and the shadows; they *were* beautiful. If she was better than they were, it was really something. Toni ought to know if he had taken all of these pictures. Why, there must be thousands! And he *was* an artist, everyone knew that artists were used to seeing models in the nude; what was it her mother sometimes said? In the altogether. Funny old Mum! And Toni couldn't have been nicer; once he had realised that she was worried, he had been ever so understanding. She must have been quite wrong about him.

Her eyes lit up as decision came upon her. She stripped off the robe, then her blouse and bra, then her stockings and belt. Soon she stood naked, except that a tiny gold chain and cross were about her neck—a gift from her mother, two birthdays ago.

She hesitated; then unfastened the chain, slipped it off and put it in her handbag. Excitement had bubbled out of her fear. She moved back and studied the photographs in the cubicle, to select a pose which seemed to set the model's body off best; one hand on her hip, one just covering the nipple of her breast, head tilted backward. She practised several times, aware of movements in the studio, another *ting* of a telephone. Suddenly she realised that Toni might really be sending for another model. Thrusting the curtains aside cautiously, she stepped out. He was still busy on the telephone, sideways to her, talking in earnest undertones. She crept towards the platform, watching him, but he seemed not to notice. She stepped on to it, and struck the pose, with only a momentary qualm.

That did not strike her as strange. Her heart was light, and she felt quite exhilarated as she gave what she hoped was a professional model's smile. Toni replaced the telephone and glanced up.

He gaped.

The effect was exactly what she had hoped for—staggering. My, how handsome he was! Sitting there, looking upwards across the room, lips parted, eyes rounded. After what seemed a long time, he let out a long, slow breath.

'Was I right,' he breathed, so that she could just hear. '*Was* I.'

He began to stand up, slowly.

She felt wonderful; wonderful.

'Am I all right?'

'*Are* you! I knew it—the moment I set eyes on you I knew it, you've got the most beautiful body I've ever seen in a woman.' He moved slowly forward, his gaze raking her, and finally coming to rest in the valley between her breasts—where the cross had rested. 'You're going to be the most famous model in London,' he promised her. 'Now, I know exactly the right pose for you. Not that one, you want one made especially for you. Posing a model is like being a choreographer, you know—arranging a ballet. That's what you are, really, a ballet of the body.' He climbed up on to the platform and put his hands on her arms. 'Now, let's see. I think I'd like you reclining. That's right, reclining.' He exerted sufficient pressure to make her lean backwards, but he supported her. 'I've got to get you in a dozen positions, first, to make sure which is the best.'

The strange thing was, she did not mind his hands.

Soon, she was reclining. He left her, fetched a camera with a close-up lens and began to take pictures from all angles, all positions. Now and again he would pause to adjust her position, and she held whatever pose he made for her. Finally, he allowed her to relax on her back, the cushions arching her body slightly . . .

When he came to her, she was nearly asleep; drowsy, happy, aware of what was happening and yet oblivious, too.

In the cellar at Fulham, on the other side of London, Hugh Rollo was saying to the knowing sergeant:

'None of the three we're after, then. That's a pity.'

'Can't have all the luck,' remarked the sergeant.

'No reason why we shouldn't hope for it,' said Rollo. He spoke absently as he moved about the studio, glancing at the photographs as a mass, now, not individually. 'We counted over a thousand. How many different faces?'

'Thirty-two.'

'Thirty-two,' echoed Rollo. 'And two out of three taken in a pose that would get anyone who published them locked up for obscenity.'

'*Or* exhibited them for profit,' remarked the sergeant smugly.

'Notice anything else?' asked Rollo.

'They're good photographs.'

'Not that. A common factor.'

The sergeant grinned. 'Female form divine,' he suggested.

'Age,' prompted Rollo.

'Age?'

'Late teens, middle teens.'

The sergeant frowned and began to look again; after a few seconds, he said: 'Now you come to mention it, yes. There aren't any older women here—all young girls.' He scowled suddenly, angrily. '*I've* got two teenage daughters.'

Slowly, Rollo said: 'I don't know whether I have, but Gee——' he paused and corrected: 'Gideon has. Just about make him mad, this will.'

'What will?'

Rollo said: 'I'll tell the Commander what I think, you work it out for yourself. There are two things,' the Superintendent went on. 'They're right under your nose. Don't miss 'em.'

CHAPTER 7

GIDEON PROPOSES...

GIDEON was in a much livelier and more normal frame of mind that afternoon. Some of his problems had been re-solved, several decisions had been made, leaving his mind free to cope with the new cases which were going through. So that he could have time to concentrate, he did not tell Lemaitre all that had been decided when he came from the Commissioner's office, but simply said: 'It's Hobbs,' and went into his own office. He had some slight misgivings about Hobbs's motive in recommending Lemaitre; it *could* have been out of a sense of humanity and goodwill, it might have been because he genuinely felt Lemaitre to be the right man, and it could possibly be that Hobbs thought it would please him, Gideon.

Gideon turned to the reports on his desk. Two more had come in, and there was a request from Golightly.

Spare me ten minutes this afternoon, if you can.

Gideon made a note to send for him at half-past three. Then he lost himself in the cases that were being investi-gated, the ever-increasing volume and the ever-increasing variety of crime. Discounting those induced by new and irritating laws which were not his to question, most of the increase seemed to him to be due to three causes, at least one of them seldom considered in the sociological surveys and reports.

There were more people; the same crime ratio for a popu-lation figure of forty million inevitably meant more actual crimes in a population of over fifty million. A five per cent increase in crime in ten years was hardly an increase at all.

There were too few police; the establishment of every force in the country was below strength, some of them seri-ously. Here at the Yard the Criminal Investigation Depart-ment establishment wasn't too bad; they could use more, but were no longer seriously undermanned. The uniformed branch was, however, and the deterrent and preventive effect of the policeman on his beat or in a patrol car still could not be calculated, although it was very important indeed.

There was the third major factor which only a fool could ignore: the actual increase in crime because more and more people were prepared to rob their neighbours. Even if one made every allowance for the first two factors, this third was the most significant and the most ominous. More people were cold-bloodedly prepared to break the law and while by far the greater proportion of criminals were the old lags and the professionals who were mostly unintelligent and habitual, there was this new breed to contend with: the clever criminal who planned not only his crimes but the disposal of his loot and his way of life, so that capturing him was extremely difficult. There were not a great number of these, but they took up the time of the police out of all proportion to their numbers. Below this intellectual level of criminals there were still many more prepared to live a life of crime for its own sake. The majority of these appeared to be the products of a welfare state which had created living standards the lack of which the social pundits had once believed to be the basic causes of crime.

In the old days, when the Bow Street Runners had been formed and Fielding had wielded both influence and power, most crimes had been committed out of desperate need. In the present time, most were committed out of greed and the desire for an easy life, or out of some neurotic or psychopathic factor that finds in crime the thrill of excitement, or a sadistic pleasure in violence and pain. This was the ugliest aspect, and one against which Gideon had steadfastly fought; he simply did not want to believe that some of the worst instincts of man asserted themselves in a modern society.

But they did; no one could dispute that there was much more evil in crime than there had been.

Now, going through the reports, he found himself seeing each case in the light of this new thinking, aware that Scott-Marle was largely responsible for it. There was a week-old murder investigation—a girl, raped, mutilated, strangled. Beastly but not new, commonplace in many parts of the world long before Jack the Ripper had frightened half the women of London. So far, there was no clue to the killer. Next, a post office hold-up in which a woman had been attacked when trying to call the police; not uncommon, either. Third, a case of an old man, quite penniless, set upon by half-a-dozen youths and beaten to the point of death. Ugh! Savagery. One of the 'new' types of crime. The three young girls, poisoned. No one knew why, no one had any idea by whom, but Gideon, highly sensitive, was afraid that before long the body of a fourth might be found—perhaps tomorrow, which meant that tomorrow's corpse would be today's living, vital body. Of all the cases, Gideon was most troubled by this. There was the murder of Mrs. Entwhistle, a commonplace enough crime. And there were the church 'offences'.

It was time he told Lemaitre about that assignment.

He made a few notes, and pushed the pile of reports away from him; as he did so, the inter-office telephone bell rang.

'Gideon.'

'Can you see Golightly soon?' asked Lemaitre.

'Yes. Where is he?'

'In my office.'

'Send him in,' ordered Gideon. 'Wait a minute, though, make a note of this while I think of it. We could do with a consultant on freak or fringe religious sects—there must be some specialists about. Find one.'

'Okay, George,' Lemaitre promised.

Gideon put down the receiver as another telephone bell rang. He picked up the receiver again impatiently.

'Gideon.'

'Will you speak to Superintendent Rollo, sir?'

'Yes.' Gideon saw Golightly come in, and waved to a chair. He was opening the Entwhistle murder file as Hugh Rollo's voice sounded in his ear.

'Can you spare me twenty minutes, Commander?'

'When?'

'Any time you like.'

'Four o'clock,' Gideon said. 'We'll have a cup of tea in my office.' He rang off and gave his familiar half-rueful smile to Golightly. 'Made an arrest yet, Percy?'

'Not yet,' said Golightly, in a slightly guarded voice.

'Anywhere near?'

'I wouldn't be surprised'—the Superintendent's tone conveyed an ambiguity that might be hiding a tenuous but jealously held clue, or might, on the other hand, merely cover a cunning hope that Gideon would think so—'if the husband isn't our man.'

Gideon made no comment, but remembered Lemaitre jumping to the same easy belief in the husband's guilt. He would be elated if it did indeed prove to be the answer.

'Geoffrey Entwhistle has been away for three years—only home for a couple of weeks each Christmas. A neighbour told him that his wife was often out in the evenings. Wifey——'

'The dead woman?'

'Yes,' said Golightly, taking the implied rebuke in his stride. 'She left home two or three times a week, looking radiant——'

'Whose word?' asked Gideon.

'A neighbour's.'

'The neighbour?'

'The original talebearer, plus three others we've questioned today. Moreover Margaret Entwhistle was seen in night clubs with a man—the same man—fairly frequently. Entwhistle received an anonymous letter just before coming home, telling him about this. He *says* he didn't tackle his wife about it; that he was no saint himself when away from home, and that he was as much in love with her as ever.'

'Any evidence?' Gideon asked.

'At least one terrific quarrel with her, two days ago.'

'Who told you?'

'Two neighbours and the eldest child, a boy of eleven. George,' went on Golightly, his lips curving, 'I am not doing a Lem on you.' Gideon grunted. 'Entwhistle went home at eleven o'clock last night. He left Leicester at half-past seven, came down on the M1 motorway and reached Lewisham

55

just before eleven. His Jaguar $2\frac{1}{2}$ litre was seen by a Divisional policeman. Two neighbours saw him go into the house, then come out very agitated a little before twelve o'clock. He drove off from the car park at the end of Billitter Street, and didn't get in touch with us until after three o'clock. All of these things can be proved to the hilt. In a way, I wish they couldn't.'

Gideon pursed his lips.

'Then why haven't you charged Entwhistle?'

'I wanted to see what you thought. I know you don't like circumstantial evidence.'

'From what you say,' temporised Gideon, 'this is the strongest circumstantial evidence we'll ever get.'

'I think it is.'

'But you're still doubtful,' Gideon said. 'You want to pass the buck.'

Golightly frowned a little; his voice softened disarmingly.

'You really do know me, George, don't you?' It was the second time that day that Golightly had dropped into the familiar 'George', although there was an unwritten law that familiarity should not be encouraged on duty. 'I'm far from sure about Entwhistle. It looks black, but——' He broke off.

'You have a feeling,' Gideon said drily. From any other senior policeman the remark would have been derisory.

Golightly looked faintly like a boy caught out in a misdemeanour.

'Yes. I have a feeling. It looks right, it feels wrong.'

It would be easy to ask why, but impossible for Golightly to explain. It would be a grave mistake to ridicule the feeling, too; many a good detective had a nose for the truth. Gideon contemplated the rather blank-looking Superintendent for some time before saying:

'Bring Entwhistle here for questioning, and I'll have a look at him. If he doesn't want to come, charge him. Tell the Press——' He broke off, suddenly shocked, for the word 'Press' reminded him that he had promised a statement to the newspapermen about the cathedral robbery, but had forgotten. He made a pencilled note, grunted: 'Reminded me of something,' and went on: 'Tell the Press he's being held, and encourage them to think we suspect him. Then if there *is* a lover——'

'No doubt about that,' interpolated Golightly.

'Well, in that case the lover might—if he is guilty—give himself up,' Gideon said. 'It's one thing to commit a murder and quite another to let an innocent man swing for it.'

'But they don't swing these days,' Golightly corrected.

'Metaphorically they do,' said Gideon crisply. He wondered if it was expecting too much, or not enough, of the murderer. A practised criminal, a professional, might stand by and allow another man to be charged for a crime he had committed, but an ordinary citizen who had committed a crime was not likely to. The tension of waiting, the burden of guilt, usually impelled such a man to make some admission—sometimes by giving himself up and confessing, as often by writing or telephoning anonymously to the police or a newspaper. But it was by no means automatic. Gideon ruminated over what had been said. In any case, he would soon be able to form an opinion of Entwhistle himself.

'What about the children?' he asked.

'Still with grandma.'

'Seen them?' asked Gideon.

'Yes. That's how I heard about the quarrel. The eleven-year-old had told his grandmother and she told me.'

'The wife's mother?' Gideon inquired.

'Yes. And she can't wait to see the son-in-law who deserted her daughter for three years, charged with the murder. No love there, George.'

Gideon said wryly: 'So I see.'

Golightly, reading dismissal in the air, pushed his chair back and stood up. Gideon watched him go, then lifted the telephone and asked for the Back Room Inspector. When the man came on the line, Gideon said: 'There's nothing special about the St. Ludd's theft for the Press. Tell 'em so, will you?'

'Yes, sir.'

Gideon rang off, and crossed to the window, looking out on to a troubled Thames. The sun had gone, clouds were low, the wind was high. It looked almost wintry. He pushed up a window as Big Ben began to strike four, and thought regretfully that when they were in the new building, he would miss Big Ben. He heard the door open, knew it was Rollo, but did not look round immediately. The door closed. Rollo did not call out, but moved to the desk rather stealthily; he was in some ways the most self-confident man at the Yard, and no respecter of persons. What was he up to? When Gideon turned, Rollo was swivelling round at the desk, smiling.

'Good afternoon,' he said.

'What's it all about?' asked Gideon.

'A kind of guessing game,' said Rollo.

'I don't much like guessing.'

'I'd be glad if you would have a look at these, though.' Rollo motioned to a dozen or so photographs which he had laid out on the desk and Gideon went across; there was no particular reason for discouraging him.

Each photograph was of the head, shoulders and bosom of a girl. Each girl, in her way, was attractive; some were beautiful. Some were dark, some fair. All were quite remarkably well-developed, all posed so as to show their breasts to fullest advantage. As far as Gideon could judge the nipples had not been touched up; these were natural.

'What's the question?' he asked.

'The common denominator,' Rollo said.

It would not be the obvious one—sex; but nor would it be particularly subtle, being posed by Rollo. He, smothering a laugh, produced a dozen more photographs, laying them out with great precision. Except that each was of a different girl, they were almost identical. Size, he wondered? Bust measurement? Age? *Age.* They were all very young, very well-developed for their age, which was probably in the middle-teens.

'Age,' he said. 'Sixteen, seventeen? And the same dark background.'

Rollo almost guffawed.

'Trust you,' he said. 'Right on the spot. Commander, I found one thousand and ten photographs round the walls of that cellar, and these are the nicest of them. Some of the others are obscene by almost any standard. There were thirty-two different models in all, each one young, no known professional models or prostitutes among them. Our three dead nudes would fit in the pattern easily. Their photographs weren't included, but could well have been. What's more these are all prints. I couldn't find a single plate or negative—and I couldn't find any duplicates, either. See what I'm driving at?'

'Other cellars, full of them,' hazarded Gideon.

Rollo was startled. 'Er—well, yes. I was really thinking of the original cellar or studio, where these were taken. You've noticed the little speck in the corner of each background and there's a good chance they were all taken at the same place. I'd like to charge the chemist's assistant, who developed these, under the Obscene Publications Act, and talk to him.'

'What's stopping you?' asked Gideon, momentarily exasperated; had every senior officer chosen today to evade his responsibility?

'He's packed up and left his lodgings,' Rollo said simply. 'This wouldn't normally be a charge with a general call, but I'd like to see him as soon as I can.'

'Put out the call and the description,' Gideon ordered, abruptly. He went on almost as if talking to himself: 'A lot of young girls, a lot of nasty poses, good pay or some kind of inducement or persuasion—they all seem happy enough—in fact, they look very dreamy, don't they?'

'George,' said Chief-Superintendent Rollo, the second man to break the unwritten law of names and titles that day, 'I really do hand it to you. Dreamy is the word. So you see the common denominator and why I want that chap pulled in.'

'You're afraid that drugs are being used.'

'Could be.'

'Get him,' said Gideon. 'I don't like that possibility at all.' He moved to the desk, sorted through some of the files, took out those on the Photo-nude murders, and read through the summary: *Clear indications of barbiturates in each blood*

59

sample. Dose not large. Probably taken within an hour of death. 'Yes,' he went on. 'Get these devils quickly.'

He thought again of the dread possibility that some young girl, lovely and full of life and as beautiful as any of these, might be the next victim of the same murderer.

Such as Sally Dalby.

CHAPTER 8

FRIGHTENED MAN

GEOFFREY ENTWHISTLE was a very frightened man.

He recognised himself as being in the grip of a web of circumstantial evidence which already almost precluded a chance of escape. Fighting for his life, he was shocked to discover that in his deep concern for himself there was hardly a thought in his mind for Meg or his children. Meg was dead and the children were in the care of a woman who disliked him but would do her duty by them—whereas his own problem was terribly urgent and pressing.

He sat in a bleak, bare room at Scotland Yard, where he had been for over half-an-hour. Standing by the door was a youthful-looking man in plain clothes, outside was a policeman in uniform. There was a table, two hard wood chairs, and a Bible; that was peculiar, a Bible. No one spoke to him, but on the desk was a newspaper, the *Evening Echo*, with a photograph of Meg.

The door opened sharply enough to make him jump. The detective who had already questioned him twice, came in, alone. He was a little too smooth, a little too honey-tongued. In this gloomy room, his eyes seemed full of menacing shadows. He closed the door behind him as Entwhistle stood up.

'You may sit down.'

Entwhistle dropped back into his chair. It was too small for him, for he was a tall, bony man, his cheeks pale with the pallor of the tropics, his aquiline features sharpened by anxiety. His eyes were tired, and the lids drooped.

'I want to ask you some questions,' Golightly said.

Entwhistle said wearily: '*More* questions? I tell you I know nothing about my wife's death.'

'If you don't, you have nothing to fear,' said Golightly.

'The bloody fool!' thought Entwhistle, that ivory pallor flushing in powerless anger. 'I know nothing about it and yet there's a hell of a risk that I'll be found guilty of murder. Isn't *that* enough cause for fear?'

Golightly, seeing the colour suffuse his cheeks, made a mental note: that Entwhistle was truly frightened.

'This time,' said Golightly, 'we are going to take questions and answers down in shorthand. Have you any objection?'

'No.' 'Get on with it,' thought Entwhistle.

'Did you kill your wife?'

'No.'

'Did you return home at about eleven-fifteen last night?'

'Yes.'

'Did you leave again about an hour later?'

'Yes.'

'Did you report the death of your wife at three o'clock this morning?'

'Yes.'

'Did you untruthfully state that you had returned home at three o'clock, found her dead and then telephoned the police?'

'Yes.'

'Why did you lie?'

'I—I don't know.'

Without a change of tone, without the slightest hint of impatience, Golightly asked again:

'Why did you lie?'

'I still don't know.'

'Was your wife alive when you arrived home at eleven o'clock?'

'No.'

'Are you sure?'

'Yes.'

'How can you be sure?'

'I held a mirror in front of her lips, tried her pulse and felt for her heart. There was no sign of life. I gave her the kiss of life, without success.'

'Are you a qualified physician?'

'No, but I am fully trained in first aid.'

'When and where were you trained?'

'In London, before taking up my appointment in Thailand. Becoming fully proficient in first aid was a condition of the appointment.' Entwhistle answered almost automatically. 'I took a twelve months' part-time course with the St. John Ambulance Brigade and have their certificate.'

'Thank you. And you are quite sure your wife was dead?'

Entwhistle drew a deep breath.

'*Yes.*'

'Did you telephone for a doctor?'

'No.'

'Why not?'

'I saw no point in doing so.'

'Why didn't you notify the police?'

Wearily, Entwhistle answered: 'I *still* don't know. I suppose I was in a state of shock. I couldn't really believe it.'

'What precisely do you mean by "it"?'

'That my wife was dead.'

'Thank you. What *did* you do on making this tragic discovery?'

'I went to see my children. They were all asleep, and obviously they didn't know anything was wrong.'

'Thank you. What did you do after seeing if the children were all right?'

'I wanted to think. I just went out.'

'Leaving the children to wake and find their mother dead?'

Entwhistle did not answer the question, but stared intently at Golightly, as if at some new kind of anatomical specimen; and the detective kept silent, perhaps because Entwhistle's expression affected him.

'Let *me* ask a question,' Entwhistle said. 'Have you any children?'

'No, but the question is immaterial.'

'I think not,' said Entwhistle brusquely. 'If you had children, you would know that little short of an earthquake would wake them at dead of night, once they were asleep. There wasn't a chance of them finding their mother.'

'So when you left you intended to return before long.'

Entwhistle said gruffly: 'I suppose I took it for granted that I would. I just walked. I couldn't even tell you where I went—I just had to keep on the move.'

'Mr. Entwhistle, saying that you suppose you took your return for granted _is_ hardly an answer to the question,' Golightly observed. 'Did you intend to return or not?'

'I—I suppose so.'

'Why did you leave at all?'

'I was so—so shocked. I wanted to think.'

'Do you think it normal for a man who comes in and finds his wife murdered to need to go out and *think* before deciding that he should telephone the police, send for a doctor and also send for someone to look after his children?'

Entwhistle said bleakly: 'I should think normality hardly came into it. In such a situation a man does not have much practice. You must take it from me that *I* needed to think.'

'Why?'

'The whole thing knocked me cold.'

'Mr. Entwhistle,' Golightly said, 'it is not unknown for a husband to have good reason to be jealous of his wife, to have cause for bitterness and resentment. Did *you* have any reason to be jealous of your wife?'

Entwhistle's forehead was shiny with sweat, and there was a fractional pause before he answered:

'I've told you already! I'm not the jealous type!'

'I would like you to tell me again, for the record,' said Golightly, glancing at the plainclothes man, who was making his notes with effortless ease, hardly pausing except when there was a much longer gap than usual between question and answer. 'Had you reason to be jealous?'

'I had a filthy letter from some damned busybody, probably a woman who didn't know what she was talking about. It made all kinds of accusations. I knew where to put *that*.'

'Did you believe the accusations, Mr. Entwhistle?'

'I've told you before—I don't give a damn what people say. I'm no plaster saint myself. My wife was on her own for three years, with the kids to look after, and if she had some companionship, male, *I* wouldn't blame her. In fact, I'd rather she was happy with someone else than sitting miserable at home by herself, wishing she were dead.'

'What makes you think she would have wished she were dead?' flashed Golightly.

'That was a figure of speech.'

'In the circumstances, a very sinister one,' Golightly rasped.

As he spoke, the door opened and another, much bigger man came in. Entwhistle had the feeling that he had seen him before, but couldn't place him. Golightly jumped up and the plainclothes man sprang to attention, so this was a V.I.P. There was something about the rugged face and the penetrating grey eyes beneath rather shaggy eyebrows which impressed Entwhistle.

'Good evening, Commander,' said Golightly. 'This is Mr. Geoffrey Entwhistle. Mr. Entwhistle, this is Commander Gideon.'

Ah! Gideon.

Gideon, to Entwhistle's surprise, shook hands; his grip was very powerful. His gaze was searching, even disconcerting, and against him Golightly faded into insignificance. The sergeant brought another chair for Gideon, who sat down. When they were all seated, he said drily:

'I heard that unfortunate figure of speech. Go on from there, Superintendent.'

'That's all it was,' Entwhistle said sharply, his voice slightly higher than normal.

'So you said,' murmured Gideon.

That was the moment when Entwhistle's spirits dropped, when he felt the net really closing in. There was no justification at all for their suspicions of him; but who would believe it? It was his own fault, his innocent folly, the way he had behaved last night with never a thought to safeguard his position. Didn't these coppers understand what could happen to a man who came in and found his wife dead; murdered? What harm had the delay in reporting her death done to *her*?

Golightly said in a subdued voice: 'Mr. Entwhistle has somewhat unconventional attitudes towards marital fidelity, Commander. He was told anonymously that his wife had a lover, but (*a*) refused to believe it, and (*b*) said that he himself being no saint, had no right to do other than expect her to amuse herself in her own way. Is that correct, Mr. Entwhistle?'

'I think I'll have the question and answer verbatim,' Gideon said.

There was a pause as he looked expectantly at the shorthand notes. The plainclothes man flipped over a page, collected himself, and began to read in a heavy, expressionless voice of deadly monotony. Every word was enunciated carefully, everything was verbatim, but as Entwhistle heard, his heart went cold within him. He knew exactly how his words, without his own inflections, struck Gideon; how heartless and improbable they sounded. He watched Gideon's face and saw the way his expression hardened and bleakness touched his eyes.

The stenographer finished.

Gideon nodded, and said: 'Was your wife aware of your attitude towards such matters, Mr. Entwhistle?'

'I doubt it.'

'Don't you know?'

'It's hardly a subject I would discuss with her, is it?' asked Entwhistle. Try as he might, he could not keep a cold, half-sneering tone out of his voice, and knew that almost every word strengthened the bad impression he was making. The worst thing was his inability to explain what had driven him away from the house last night. How could he explain what he could not explain to himself? It had been like coming home to a nightmare, going off had been a kind of effort

65

to wake himself up... And yet in another way, he had simply run from the hideous reality, not wanting to admit the truth.

'Did you know your wife's lover?' Golightly demanded.

'I've told you, I don't even know that she had one!'

'Did you have any reason to suspect she had a lover before you left England three years ago?' Golightly's merciless voice did not change tone or expression as his questions went on and on.

'What do you make of him?' Golightly asked Gideon.

'Not much, but that doesn't mean he's a murderer,' Gideon said. 'I'd let him go home and see what happens in the next day or two, before charging him. Meanwhile you'll want the name of the neighbour who wrote that letter, and——'

Golightly ventured to interrupt.

'It's all under control, Commander.'

'Good,' grunted Gideon.

That evening, Eric Greenwood bought a later edition of the *Evening Globe*, found the story of his murder on an inside page, and read:

Mr. Geoffrey Entwhistle, the dead woman's husband, was at Scotland Yard for several hours this afternoon, helping the police in their inquiries.

'That means they suspect him!' Greenwood muttered, and the expression in his eyes was not far short of exultation.

Entwhistle, alone in that house of evil memory, read the same paragraph, recalled the interrogation vividly and gave a sudden, uncontrollable shiver.

Sally Dalby shivered, too. She was just coming round from a long, long sleep in that room of a thousand photographs, and she did not yet feel the horror, the shame nor even the first onset of the longing for whatever had given her that glow of exhilaration.

66

The office day was over for Gideon and he felt the usual mixture of satisfaction with work done, dissatisfaction with all that had been left undone, and a slight gloom because there were matters he was a long way from being happy about. The Entwhistle murder, for one; he had not taken to the suspected man, but that didn't make him a murderer, and he wondered whether anyone burdened with a sense of guilt could talk so carelessly. He hoped Golightly's efforts with the dead woman's photographs would soon bring results; if there had been a lover, he wanted to check the man's movements closely and talk to him before any arrest was made. There was obviously a possibility that Entwhistle, if scared, would do something silly; that would go a long way to removing any doubts about him.

The nude photographs and the drug murder possibility was an even greater worry; because of his own daughters he was always sensitive to danger involving young girls. Almost guiltily, he realised that he hadn't given Penelope more than an occasional thought during the day.

There was another thing, which made Gideon angry with himself. He hadn't yet briefed Lemaitre about the church and cathedral problem. But surely there couldn't be any urgency about that.

CHAPTER 9

THE VANDAL

LONDON'S crime lay hidden under a mask of peace and quietude, the church of St. Denys, tucked away in Kensington behind the great museums, standing dark and still—except in the Lady Chapel, where a single dim bulb glowed. The south door stood open as it always had, for the Vicar of St. Denys' believed that souls could be saved at any hour of the day or night and that the best place for saving them was the church. There were many like him, but few had earned his reputation, gained in two world wars and since consolidated. In some ways he was regarded as a Fighting Parson, although nowadays there were few who could be called more truly men of peace.

His vicarage was a street away, for St. Denys was sandwiched between two massive blocks of offices, built on sites cleared by bombing. No one lived next to the church except their caretakers.

The south door led from a dark, narrow lane between the church and one of the dimly lit office buildings. A man appeared from the direction of a car park near the Albert Hall, walking on rubber-soled shoes. His advance was not furtive, nor could it be called bold. He glanced over his shoulder as he neared the church, clearly visible had anyone been there to see, noticed no one, and turned into the lane.

A moment or two later, he pushed wider the south door and stepped inside. He did not hesitate but stepped straight to the altar, which apparently he knew well. He went behind it, a shadowy figure, pale-faced, a man of medium build and height. He knelt down. At first it looked as if he were praying with his back to the cross, but in fact his hands were busy. He took out an object which looked like a candle with a very long wick, pushed this beneath the altar, tucking it close against the marble. He withdrew, bent down on one knee, took a lighter from his pocket and snapped it on.

Flame flickered.

He picked up the end of the fuse, held the flame to it and kept his hand steady as the strands slowly caught. He carried this, the flame gaining rapidly in strength, close to the steps leading to the nave, put it down, and without a backward glance walked out of the south door. Outside in the alley he waited only long enough to see if anyone was in the street, then walked briskly towards the car park. He was near it when he heard a muffled explosion. It had no outward effect on him, and he stepped into a pale blue Morris 1000, one of the most common cars in England, and drove off.

His thin, austere face was quite relaxed. It showed no sign of vindication or rejoicing, of pleasure or of gloating; only the rather arid satisfaction of a man whose task is done.

Several people heard the explosion, one of them a young policeman in Princess Way, one a taxi-driver waiting for a fare to come out of a block of flats near the Albert Hall, one a young woman at a window on the third floor of a house nearly opposite the car park—the only house within sight of the church. She was restless, and for no particular reason walked to the window. She saw the man, heard the explosion, heard a car engine start up and, a few minutes afterwards, saw a shabby Morris appear from the car park and nose its way along the street.

The policeman was very alert.

In his experience an explosion was followed up by some kind of flurry. If a gas- or an oil-heater had burst, as they sometimes did, the alarm was quickly raised; but he saw and heard no one, although he was quite sure it had been no small matter.

The thing which sprang to his mind immediately was: someone's blown a safe. No one would create a flurry after that.

Should he call for help? Or should he first find out what had happened? If he brought a patrol car for nothing he would look a proper fool; on the other hand, if he didn't and a burglary were reported next morning, he would never forgive himself. He quickened his pace, sure of the direction from which the sound of the explosion had come. One of the two big office blocks, more likely—there must be dozens of safes in each of them.

All was still and silent.

Across the road was a telephone kiosk, and making a swift decision he went into it and dialled 999.

'Wait there,' the Information Room Inspector ordered.

Less than two minutes later a car pulled up at the corner, and the police constable recognised men from his own Division. The driver leaned out.

'What's on, Charley?'

'I heard a bang.'

'Getting nervous out here on your own?'

'No, seriously. It came from along here.' The constable

69

looked towards St. Denys', without giving the church a thought. 'Might have been in one of the offices.'

'We'll find out,' the driver said. 'See anyone?'

'I heard a car, that's all. It must have gone the other way.'

'Let's check,' said the man next to the driver. They climbed out of the car, three big, matter-of-fact detectives whose job was simply to seek out bad men, and walked with long strides towards the buildings—and incidentally towards St. Denys'. As they passed the end of the lane, the uniformed man saw a flicker of raw, undisciplined light.

'Look!' he exclaimed.

'The church!' breathed the driver. 'Come on!'

They turned hurriedly into the lane, and as they neared the door, flames showed vividly at a small window. One man spun round, ejaculating: 'Fire!' and ran back to the car. The others thrust their way into the church, and as they did so the red and yellow of leaping flames shone on their faces, on the pillars, on the choir stalls. Regimental standards, hanging in tatters, were already alight, a magnificent seventeenth-century tapestry was smouldering, the altar cloth and the rich Persian runner in front of and behind the altar, were in flames. The altar itself had been smashed to smithereens, and pieces of marble had been flung about the nave, striking walls and wood but, strangely, missing the windows.

The three policemen tore at the standards, then the tapestry, stamping out what they could, until the fire-brigade bell sounded and a fire engine roared up.

Gideon did not hear about the latest sacrilegious vandalism until half-past eight next morning, when he was about to leave for the office. Kate was in the kitchen, looking through a daily newspaper. All the children were out, including Penelope, who had appeared quite bright and cheerful. Gideon answered the telephone, which was in the hall of this high-ceilinged Victorian house, and leaned against the side of the staircase as he did so.

'George?' It was Hobbs.

'Hello.'

'Are you on your way?'

'Nearly.'

'Good,' said Hobbs. 'I've put my foot in it.'

'What's "it"?' asked Gideon, covering his surprise at such an admission.

'I thought you'd told Lemaitre about the church investigation, but he doesn't seem to know anything about it.'

'My fault,' said Gideon promptly. He felt sure this wasn't the sole reason for the call, 'I was pushed for time and wanted to brief him properly. What brought the question up?'

'There was an explosion in St. Denys' Church, Kensington, last night,' answered Hobbs. 'I found Lemaitre here and asked him why he wasn't at Kensington. The remark wasn't appreciated.'

'I can imagine,' Gideon said. It was a thousand pities that Hobbs *had* got off on the wrong foot with Lemaitre, but that wasn't the pre-eminent worry: the church affair was. 'Where's Lemaitre now?' he asked.

'Here. Says he'll go to St. Denys' on your instructions or not at all.'

There was, as always, something reserved about Hobbs, and it would be easy to infer a kind of criticism—that he, Gideon, should not have allowed this situation to develop. Gideon pushed the thought aside.

'Have me transferred to him,' he said. 'And I'll be late, I'll go to St. Denys' first.'

'Very well,' said Hobbs.

Lemaitre was soon on the line.

'Lemait*re*,' he announced with an excessive precision which indicated that he was standing on his dignity.

'Meet me at St. Denys' as soon as you can get there,' Gideon ordered. 'Bring a driver, and look through the papers which the Dean brought me yesterday while you're on your way.'

'Er——' said Lemaitre, his tone softening; and then it hardened again. 'Right!'

Twenty minutes later, Gideon drew up near the church and saw Lemaitre getting out of a car a hundred yards away. A police car and a builder's van were parked near by, there was a small crowd of people, mostly young, two policemen and several newspaper reporters and photographers. One of the reporters came up to Gideon, a sandy-haired man whose round face was peppered with freckles.

'Taking this seriously then, Commander?' He had a faint Scottish accent.

'We always take crime seriously,' Gideon replied gravely.

Another, older, hard-faced man spoke, and two cameras clicked, one flashing bright against the dark buildings and an overcast sky.

'Do you think there is a campaign against the Church, Mr. Gideon?'

Gideon's reaction was swift as light, but he did not make the mistake of answering too quickly.

'Good Lord, no! What makes you ask such a question?'

'There was a break-in at St. Ludd's Cathedral, remember?'

'There have been thefts from churches since there were churches,' Gideon said drily. 'Gold and silver still have a good value whether it comes from a private house, a museum *or* a church.' He looked up at Lemaitre, who had a way of walking which seemed to use up a lot of energy, knees slightly knocking, arms swinging with unnecessary vigour. He was smiling his official smile.

'Good morning, Commander.'

'Good morning, Superintendent.'

'Commander,' the sandy-haired man asked, 'is it true that Chief-Superintendent Hobbs is to be the next Deputy Commander?'

All the Press men were looking at Lemaitre, not at Gideon, and Gideon half-feared a sharp reaction from Lemaitre. Instead, his grin broadened and he said bluffly:

'Couldn't be a better man if he is.'

'Can I quote you?' the hard-faced man asked.

'There's nothing to quote,' Gideon said. 'No appointment's been made. You *can* quote me as saying that we'd be glad to hear from anyone who knows about the trouble here last night—if any man or woman was seen, on foot or in a car, if anything was heard—the usual things. That way you'll be helping us.' He moved towards the lane, and Lemaitre followed. A policeman moved aside, nodding, inarticulate. Two or three big pieces of marble stood outside the south door, another policeman by them. 'Lem,' Gideon said, 'it looks as if there's something very ugly brewing, and this may be part of it. It was on my agenda for this morning.'

'I know,' Lemaitre said, grinning broadly. 'You'd made a note and clipped it to the envelope the Dean left. I took it home to read, because you'd put *Lem to read* on it.' He was very pleased with himself, with reason, and Gideon repressed an obvious query: why had he put on an act with Hobbs?

'Then you know more about the trouble than I do,' Gideon said. 'We won't talk about it here, but does this crime fit the pattern?'

'Haven't seen any pattern yet.'

'It's what we're looking for.' Gideon stepped inside the church, the door of which was blocked open.

The first glimpse was enough to appal both Yard men. In the daylight which filtered through one stained glass and four plain glass windows, the damage was shown up vividly. Pieces of marble had been violently hurled about, cracking pews, seriously damaging some beautifully painted heraldry on the choir stalls. The lectern, with its magnificent brass eagle, had been smashed, a dozen oil paintings had been ruined, the old medieval font had a big piece out of it. The aisles were littered with debris. At the wall near the altar were the charred remains of the standards, and the blackened end of the big tapestry showed how nearly that, too, had been destroyed. Of the altar itself, only a few broken pieces remained in position.

On his knees a Fire Service officer whom Gideon knew slightly as an expert on arson, was minutely examining the heart of the explosion. Police photographers from the Division, as well as detectives from Fingerprints, were going about their jobs with a disciplined application which Gideon liked to see.

Watching them all was the Reverend Miles Chaplin.

He was a man whom Gideon had met when taking part in the British Legion March Past at the Cenotaph, and on other occasions when the Church and the Army shared some ceremonial or memorial service. Almost completely bald, he was a remarkable man to look at.

His cheeks were lean, his nose finely curved, while his hooded eyes, deeply sunken beneath a wide forehead, held the sharp alertness of a predatory bird. He stood in his black cassock, arms folded across his chest; it was impossible even to guess what he was thinking.

Gideon went up to him.

'I couldn't be more sorry, Vicar.'

Chaplin glanced at him without recognition, and replied in a clipped, high-pitched voice:

'Nor could I.'

'I am Commander Gideon of Scotland Yard,' Gideon said, and received a brief glance of interest. 'This is Chief-Super-intendent Lemaitre.'

'Lemaitre!' Chaplin said sharply, his interest now fully aroused. He stared into Lemaitre's equally bony but far less interesting face.

''Morning, Padre,' Lemaitre said, in the tone of an old familiar, if not a friend.

CHAPTER 10

OLD FRIENDS

GIDEON saw the real pleasure in the vicar's eyes, matching the glow in Lemaitre's. The two men gripped hands for what seemed a long time, as if this were a true reunion. No one else seemed to notice. Their hands dropped as Lemaitre said:

'Bloody bad business this—sorry, Padre! I forgot where I was. Any idea who did it?'

'I most certainly have not.'

'We've got to find the basket,' Lemaitre said. 'Any hate campaign, threats or that kind of thing?'

'None whatsoever,' said Chaplin. 'Except, of course, that this is a declaration of hate in itself. It is a very terrible thing, a shocking thing.' The eyes were very bright beneath those heavy lids. 'Do you believe in evil, Commander?'

Gideon answered: 'In a way.'

'Don't you think this is an evil act?'

'Yes.'

'Carried out by an evil man?'

'Or a sick one,' Gideon said.

'Please, please,' protested Chaplin in a sharp voice. 'I hardly expect a senior officer of Scotland Yard to pay even lip service to this modern psychiatric jargon. Evil is evil, sin is sin, a man possessed of the devil is not sick. It may be possible—it *is* possible, to my certain knowledge—to cast the devil out, but it is not sickness.'

'I know exactly how you feel, sir,' Gideon said. 'You must forgive me if I see this simply as a crime committed—it is no part of my job to say why it was done, only who did it. Is this the first act of vandalism carried out here?'

'*Van*dalism? Sacrilege, you mean.'

'Is it the first crime?' demanded Gideon. He was troubled by the old man's manner and disappointed, because his reputation was that of a tolerant and broad-minded cleric. Had he changed? Or had the attack so angered him that it had temporarily blocked a cooler judgment?

'No,' said Chaplin. 'It is not the first crime in this house of God. There have been others. Three times in the past few weeks the offertory boxes have been broken open and the contents stolen. Hymn books and books of Common Prayer are often despoiled by tearing, or by offensive words scribbled across the pages. It is an outrage I find it hard, even impossible, to forgive.'

'Have you reported this to the police?'

'The thefts, yes. It seems quite beyond your capacity to prevent such crimes, which are now commonplace throughout London. There was a day when an offertory box was considered sacred, when a church was truly a sanctuary. The

75

attitude in this so-called civilised age is quite different. There is no respect for the law, none for the Church.'

At these impassioned words everyone looked at the old man, whose voice was rising steadily to a crescendo of denunciation. Anger flashed from his eyes as if preaching a sermon which would soon lead to a general threat of hell-fire and damnation.

Abruptly, he stopped.

A girl of about eighteen had entered. She looked young and fresh and quite purposeful in this scene of destruction and defeat as she came forward. Every eye turned towards her. Chaplin seemed to draw within himself as if, the words now said, he was prepared to don again a mask of humility and forgiveness.

'I've just heard what a beastly thing has happened,' she murmured, going up to him. 'I *am* sorry. Mummy would have come herself, but she was not feeling up to it. Are you all right, grandfather? It must have been a dreadful shock.'

She spoke as if she were humouring a child.

'I'm perfectly all right, Elspeth,' Chaplin said testily. 'Why shouldn't I be?' He drew a deep breath, and went on: 'But I am a little tired. If you will excuse me, gentlemen, I will go along to the Vicarage. You will find me there if you need any more information.' Head high, he led the way, with the girl a step behind him.

Gideon entered his office just before eleven o'clock that morning, two hours later than usual. A detective inspector was stand-in for Lemaitre, and it was immediately evident that Lemaitre had been away; the reports were in the wrong order, explanatory notes were much more prolix; Gideon had a feeling that things could misfire. Instead, it was he who was wrong. The internal telephone rang five minutes after he arrived; it was Hobbs.

'How did things go?'

'There won't be anything to worry about with Lem,' Gideon answered. 'Humour him a bit, that's all.'

'I'll try,' Hobbs said, quietly. 'Was there much damage?'

'Far too much,' said Gideon. 'I want to settle down for an

hour with the Dean's papers as soon as I can. Have you seen anyone?'

'Yes. Rollo, with nothing to report. Golightly says he hasn't had any response at all to his photograph inquiry. We've turned the St. Ludd's burglar over to the City Police, he's up for a hearing any time now. Simmons wants another week before he can brief us thoroughly on that Hobjoy Fraud Case, and won't commit himself beyond that. There's nothing much in, this morning—the usual crop from burglary to breaking and entering, shop-lifting to bag-snatching. Two men raided a post office out at Eltham, but were scared off by a dog who tore a patch out of a pair of trousers. Seventeen cars were stolen in the Metropolitan area last night. West Central raided a strip club, which provided cubicles for the members to have private shows. The manager and two of the strippers will be up this morning for running a disorderly house——'

'Are they known?' Gideon interrupted.

'Guy Mason's the manager.'

'Oh, that mob,' Gideon said. 'Close 'em down in one place and they bob up in another. Yes?'

'A hit-and-run in Brompton Road, Knightsbridge,' Hobbs went on in his precise way. 'A light grey Jaguar was involved. Alleged rape on Wimbledon Common, a truck-load of cigarettes stolen from the Goods Yard at Paddington. The Newcastle police are worried about the death of the man found sitting in his car, they think it was murder—can we send someone to check on some rather suspicious details? Brighton aren't happy about that child's body found in the sea and they're asking for information from other seaside resorts. The lungs contained sea-water all right, but also some particles of seaweed not commonly found in the Channel.'

'What did you do?' interrupted Gideon.

'I recommended getting a few specimens and the autopsy report and sending them round to other resorts,' Hobbs said.

'Do that, will you?'

'Yes. Apart from all this, nothing,' Hobbs added.

Gideon said: 'Good,' and rang off without considering the irony of Hobbs's final words. *Good.* It was a catalogue of crimes of nearly every conceivable variety, and yet it posed no new major problems. The important ones remained the Entwhistle murder, the nude photographs case, and the church crimes. Although he still felt a sense of disquiet about the murdered girls and the missing photographer, he did not dwell on it but sat at his desk to study the report that Dean Howcroft had brought and which Lemaitre had read ahead of time. Hobbs's recital, so lucid and comprehensive, left him with a feeling of satisfaction, that the new Deputy Commander-to-be was the right man.

Soon, he was absorbed in the Dean's report, which covered incidents in the Southern and Home Counties.

He began to feel worried, for the second page showed that the total number of 'offences' in the past twelve months was over a thousand, only a few of which had been reported to the police. The major items on the list were:

Damage to hymn and prayer books	107 instances affecting 2,501 books
Damage to fonts	18
Defilement of fonts	18
Damage to altar and dossal cloths	142
Slashing of vestments	41
Damage to missals	375
Forced and rifled alms boxes	36
Damage to heat and light systems	48
Damage to stained-glass windows	40

Each one in itself was hardly a serious crime, and it was understandable that the Church authorities, aware of the current attitude of almost morbid tolerance towards criminals, should be nervous of risking an indignant outcry at so-called unchristian behaviour if they appealed to the police. It wasn't surprising that they had taken action to tardily.

A cautious note in the memorandum followed:

The nature of these instances gives some reason to

suspect wilful and malicious damage by a church member or other person associated with the church, but the number and frequency of the offences now make it appear possible that the offences were caused by outside interference. As so many of the offences were similar it seems possible that the perpetrators were in collusion. No Baptist or Quaker premises have been affected, and very few Congregationalist or Methodist.

Gideon thought: Why, oh why didn't they come to us earlier?

Almost at that very moment a young commercial photographer, named Henry Rhodes, was entering the cellar in which Sally Dalby had been photographed, and was saying to himself: '*Why the hell didn't I come here earlier?*' He was frightened because he knew that the police wanted to interview him and he was fairly certain that once they questioned him it would lead to his arrest. For one thing, he had sold a great number of those 'artistic' photographs to customers at the shops; for another, he had employed a number of agents to sell them to workers in big stores, offices and factories. There was little doubt that he would be charged and found guilty under one section or another of the *Obscene Publications Act*, resulting in a sentence of at least six months' imprisonment. Since a friend at the chemist's shop where he worked had tipped him off about a police inquiry, he had been in hiding with a girl-friend who had been happy to share her bed and board without asking questions.

But he was nearly broke and needed money. This cellar in Tottenham was the obvious place to come, for Toni Bottelli worked here, and Toni was close to Mr. Big, if he wasn't Mr. Big himself.

Rhodes, until two years ago an unworldly young man from a small provincial city in the Midlands, felt excitement stirring at the thought of 'Mr. Big'. There was great drama in it for him, as there had been drama and excitement at being on the fringe of crime. He had drifted into it, selling a few nasty pictures for a joke among friends, and had been paid well for running off a few prints in the dark-room at the shop. Now, eighteen months afterwards, he earned over £2,000 a year from this 'spare-time' occupation—and spent up to the hilt, on girls, on the dogs and on casino gambling. He had always been fond of showing-off, and had always been a success with 'the ladies'. He had a natural, easy manner, and he was a curiously forthright individual, who would tell a girl that he liked her legs, her face or her bosom without thinking there was anything over-bold in it. That was the way they were made, wasn't it? Consequently, he had fallen naturally into this job. Persuading girls to pose had seldom been difficult; nor had selling the pictures. He saw no harm in either, and would hold forth indignantly if challenged.

'All the great artists paint nudes, don't they?'

'Take all the nudes off a museum wall and you wouldn't have much left, would you?'

'And what about statues? Haven't you ever heard of Michelangelo? Look at some of his, men *and* women. *He* didn't hide much.'

'Lot of prudes, that's what people are.'

This, then, was his honest conviction.

Now, he went through the small tobacconist's shop above the cellar where Toni Bottelli worked. An elderly woman in the shop, a *madame* to the girls who came here, knew him and allowed him through. The cellar was approached by a concealed door in the wall of a staircase, Bottelli knowing very well that a police raid could be very awkward.

Rhodes pressed a warning bell, slid the door open and went downstairs. As he stepped into the cellar he heard a flurry of movement, saw Bottelli throw a towelling robe over a girl on the cushions on the dais.

'Okay, okay, I'm used to it,' Rhodes sang out.

Bottelli stood with his back to the girl, glaring.

'What the hell do you want?'

'Just a little bit of lolly, Toni.'

'Who told you to come here?'

'I told myself,' said Rhodes, jauntily.

'Well, get to hell out of it and don't come back unless I send for you!'

Rhodes caught his breath.

'Now take it easy,' he protested. 'That's no way to talk.'

'It's the way I'm talking to you! Get the hell out of it!'

Rhodes spoke more angrily.

'Don't you talk to me like that.'

'Get out, or I'll throw you out!'

'Oh, will you?' Rhodes said. Inwardly he was feeling scared, but nothing in his voice or manner showed it. 'I'd like to see you try.'

They stood facing each other, Rhodes appalled, Bottelli viciously angry. Gradually Rhodes's anger began to fade into anxiety. He needed help, and needed somewhere to hide, and this man had introduced him to the business; there was no one else to go to.

'Get *out*,' Bottelli growled.

'Listen, Toni, you don't understand——'

'I don't have to understand. *You* have to.'

'Toni, I need some money! I'm on the run!'

The last words came out as Bottelli began to move forward, his hands outstretched, his eyes shimmering with anger. At first the phrase 'I'm on the run' had no effect, but suddenly he stopped short, caught his breath and ejaculated:

'You're *what*?'

'I'm on the run. The cops are after me! You always said you'd see me right if I ran into trouble. How about proving it?'

As he spoke, Rhodes stared at the handsome man in front of him, wondering what lay behind the inscrutability of his eyes. Nothing in them gave Rhodes the slightest inkling of the truth.

'If the cops catch him,' Bottelli was thinking, 'he'll talk. And he's not going to talk.' Without consciously putting it in so many words, his mind went smoothly on: 'I wonder which way I'd better get rid of him.'

CHAPTER 11

ONCE A KILLER

HENRY RHODES'S lips and mouth felt dry as he stared at Bottelli, who had hardly moved since hearing the other say: 'I'm on the run.' The girl on the couch didn't stir, but he was not concerned with her; had he given her a thought he would have assumed that she was lying doggo. Bottelli's eyes began to narrow, and suddenly he smiled, showing his vivid white teeth.

Rhodes's heart leapt with relief.

'So you're on the run,' Bottelli said. 'How come, Henry?'

'The cops got hold of some of the pictures, some blabber-mouth at the Bowling Lanes told them where he'd got them from.'

'When did this happen?'

'Monday.'

'Monday! God! It's Thursday now.'

'I've been lying low.'

Bottelli said very softly: 'So you've been lying low, have you? Where?'

'Katey Lyle's place.'

'You've been laying while you've been lying low, have you? She's quite a doll.'

'She's a doll all right.'

'But you let her go.'

'I ran out of the lolly, Toni.'

'So you ran out on the cops and you ran out of the dough and after that you ran out on Katey Lyle.'

'You make it sound like I was always running out,' Rhodes protested peevishly. 'I thought I was doing the right thing.'

'And so you were, Harry,' Bottelli said. 'You've got to keep away from the cops and there's only one way of doing that—get out of the country until they cool off you.'

Rhodes's eyes lit up.

'Then that's what I'll do!'

'You'll certainly need some lolly,' Bottelli said. 'And a plane ride—how about luggage and things?'

'I've got some over at Katey's.' Rhodes could hardly conceal his pleasure.

'That's fine,' said Bottelli. 'Now I know a man who can fix you a cheap flight to France—you got a passport?'

'Why, sure!'

'At Katey's?'

'That's right.'

'You thought of everything, didn't you,' Bottelli said smoothly. 'Okay, Harry. You go back to Katey's and stay there until after dark. I'll arrange for a Honda motor-cycle to be parked outside her place, and I'll drop an ignition key through the letter box, with directions as to the place to go. It will be in a field near Ashford, Kent, or near Southend— I'm not sure yet. You'll find the two-seater plane and a pilot waiting for you, and you'll be dropped in France with the motor-bike and some dough. Right?'

'It sounds wonderful!' Rhodes's voice was high-pitched. 'I knew you'd see me through, Toni. I can't tell you how grateful I am.'

'Think nothing of it,' Toni Bottelli said.

As far as Henry Rhodes could judge, everything went according to plan, and fair-haired, plump-bodied Katey Lyle could not have been sweeter nor more compliant. He rode to Southend with directions in his pocket, helmet on his head, wind whistling past his goggles, happy as a young man could be. Even when he turned into the field, indicated by a white circle on the bark of a tree close to the gate, and found no sign of an aircraft, he was unperturbed; it had been delayed, that was all.

He waited by the gate, on a bright starlit evening.

He heard a rustling, but did not suspect danger. He had not the slightest sense of impending death, and in fact was whistling softly, looking up into the sky for the aircraft which was never to come.

He felt a sudden, sharp, bruising blow between his shoulder blades, heard the muffled roar of a shot—and died.

He was Toni Bottelli's fourth victim, and the first one whom Bottelli had murdered by shooting.

He had arrived on a B.S.A. motor-cycle which he had stolen and was now heading back on the Honda for London and for Sally Dalby, who was probably still asleep on the dais in the cellar of photographs.

About the time that Henry Rhodes died, Gideon was sitting at the table in the kitchen at his home, watching amateur boxing on a small television set. The volume was turned low and he listened with half an ear to the cascade of the piano, as Penelope played in the living-room. The rest of the family was out. Penelope went on playing with a fury of abandon which gradually pierced Gideon's consciousness and he got up slowly and went to her. She was playing a Grieg concerto, and he had never known her play with such fire and such virtuosity; even he, the unmusical member of the family, was impressed and admiring. He stepped just inside the room. The piano, a Bechstein grand bought years ago when the Gideons had realised that they had two gifted daughters, was in the far corner, and Penelope's back was towards him. Her fair hair rippled down past her shoulders. Her slender body moved with the concentrated tension of the playing. Her fingers seemed to dance over the keys as if she had four hands, not two. As she reached the final crescendo her very life seemed to be part of the wonderful sound.

When she stopped, she sat motionless, fingers still poised.

Gideon, remembering how dreadfully she had been disappointed only yesterday morning, wondered what was going through her mind now—would despair surge over her again? When she sprang to her feet he was taken by surprise, and had no time to back out of sight.

Her eyes were glowing, and her radiant young face lit up even more when she saw him.

'Daddy!' she cried. 'I *am* good, I know I am!'

'My God you're good!' Gideon said fervently.

'*You* could tell?'

'If that examiner were here now——'

'I know, but it was my fault, I gave it the wrong interpretation, I tried to be too clever. There *will* be another chance and next time I'm going to play this, and I'll pass. I *know* I will.'

'You'll pass,' said Gideon. 'Penny——'

'Daddy, you're wonderful!' she cried, and threw her arms about him. As he felt the strength of her young body and saw the glow in her eyes, he felt a moment of sheer exultation—that she was his daughter; his, and Kate's. She was still hugging him in her new-found delight, when the telephone bell rang. She gave him a final hug, and broke away.

'I expect it will be for you.'

'Probably.' Gideon stepped back into the hall, lifted the receiver, and said: 'George Gideon.'

'George.' He recognised Rollo's voice on the instant, and a pang went through him, because this was probably to do with the three dead girls. 'Sorry to worry you so late, but I've got a nasty one.'

'Another body?' Gideon pictured the photographs he had seen the previous afternoon and heard Penelope playing, very subdued this time, so that he could hear what was being said.

'Different sex,' said Rollo. 'That photographer I was looking for, Henry Rhodes. He's turned up dead. Freak chance we found him so soon. A courting couple, going into a field, nearly fell over the body.'

'How was he killed?' Gideon demanded.

'Shot in the back.'

'Where?'

'Five miles from Southend. They had his photograph—I'd sent it out—and called me. I'd like to go down there with a couple of our own chaps, and get cracking under floodlights. Those three girls could have been killed by the same man, and he could have killed Rhodes to keep him quiet—sorry George, I know I'm doing a Lemaitre on you. All right for me to go?'

Gideon said: 'Yes. You don't need an official request for help from the Essex people, as we want him for the London jobs.'

'Put a call in to square things for me, will you?' asked Rollo.

Gideon said: 'All right.' He was about to ring off when a thought flashed through his mind. 'Hugh!'

'I'm still here.'

'Have you been checking closely on any other girls who are missing?'

'You bet I have.'

'How many have been reported?'

'This week, six,' answered Rollo. 'Last week, three. Multiply by at least five and you've got the number of those who are really missing. If parents would only make sure we knew in good time . . .' This was Rollo's hobby-horse, which, once started, must never be allowed free rein.

'Quite, quite,' interrupted Gideon soothingly, 'I'm absolutely with you. But, let me see, *how* many girls did you say have the statistics we're looking for?'

'Two,' answered Rollo.

'Names?'

'A Doris Manning, of Salisbury, and a Sally Dalby, who comes from Guildford. She's the latest—her father reported her missing only yesterday. Apparently she told a friend that she was going to pose in the nude for a photographer.'

'Did she, by George!' Gideon's voice rose. 'Get her photograph out and a general call for her.'

'First thing in the morning,' Rollo promised.

'Tonight,' ordered Gideon, and then remembered. 'You want to get down to Essex, of course. I'll see to the other thing, then.'

'Why not Golightly?' suggested Rollo, with a chuckle in his voice. 'He's had an easy one over the Entwhistle case and he's at the Yard now.'

After a moment's pause, Gideon said:

'Put me through to him, will you?'

Geoffrey Entwhistle lay back in an armchair, a whisky bottle by his side, a nearly empty glass in his hand. He wasn't drunk, but at least he was not remembering the past so vividly, not regretting his decision to leave home for three years so much. He had left because he had seen his marriage breaking up, and had thought desperately that a long parting would help. He had come back, believing that he could settle down to a new life.

If things went on as they were, it would be a new life all right—a life sentence in prison for a murder he hadn't committed.

The whisky created a hazy kind of resignation and the ability to face facts without alarm. Fact: he was under suspicion of the murder of Margaret, his wife. Fact: he hadn't felt any grief at her death. Fact: he had been away from his children for so long that they were strangers to him and he to them. Fact: his mother-in-law hated him, believed he had killed Margaret and was busily making sure the children believed it, too. Fact: he had not killed Margaret.

Probability: by tomorrow he would be charged with the murder.

He gave a snort that was half-laugh, half-groan, gulped down the whisky in the glass and picked up the bottle.

Eric Greenwood stood looking at the photograph of Margaret, whom he had murdered, for a long time. Slowly and deliberately he picked it up, and carried it to the empty fireplace in his living-room. He put the photograph in this and set light to a corner; the flame caught tardily, gradually crinkling the face and then devouring the print bit by bit. Before the last flicker, he turned to a desk, full of his private papers, and began to search through it for letters and notes which Margaret had sent him. He made a pile of these in the grate and burned them also.

Watching these higher, consuming flames and not knowing the strange light they cast upon his eyes, he said aloud:

'It's a good thing I never wrote to her.'

He had always been very careful about this, so anxious had he been to avoid any involvement in divorce.

He did not believe in divorce.

'Percy,' Gideon said, 'I've an urgent job for you.'

'I'll buy it,' Percy Golightly said.

'A girl named Sally Dalby is reported missing. I want her photograph and description sent out on a general call. To-night.'

'Don't remind me of photographs,' Golightly protested. 'There hasn't been a single bite about Margaret Ent-whistle's.'

'How is that shaping?'

'Looks more and more like the husband,' answered Go-lightly. 'The mother-in-law let her hair down tonight. According to her the Entwhistles quarrelled like hell before he left for Thailand. She was too flighty for his liking. Looks more and more as if he came back, goaded by that anony-mous letter, and let his wife have it.'

'We'll talk about that in the morning,' Gideon said. 'Fix the call for Sally Dalby.'

There was something about the name which attracted him; Sally Dalby. He was sensitive about young women to-night, of course, but that kind of over-sensitiveness did no harm. He tried to put all the Yard's cases out of mind and picked up the newspaper, but inside ten minutes he was reading the *Police Gazette*. It was late before he heard a key in the front door, and got up to greet Kate, who was bright-eyed and tired after a visit to the cinema with a neighbour.

'Oh, put that thing away, George!' She flicked a hand towards the *Police Gazette*. 'You should have come with me tonight, you would have enjoyed it almost as much as if it had been a Western. Some of that South African country is beautiful and the photography was absolutely breath-taking...'

Drinking tea and eating biscuits, listening to Kate's en-thusiastic chatter, seeing the children as they came home one after the other, four of them living at home these days, Gideon forgot all the problems of the Yard. It was when he was in bed, Kate by his side, that he thought: 'I hope there's no more trouble in the churches tonight.'

CHAPTER 12

FIVE-IN-ONE

POLICE CONSTABLE EDMUND DAVIES was a man in his middle-thirties, keen on his job but unambitious, a contented family man who took it for granted that one day he would be promoted sergeant, that he would retire at fifty-five and take on a part-time job. He had one hobby: gardening; one sport: boxing. It was two years since he had last been to church—at the christening of his third-born.

Like every other policeman in the London area, he was on the *qui vive* that night whenever he neared one of the three churches on his beat. There had been a special instruction during the day, that every church should be watched, door handles tried, vergers and clergymen, where possible, asked what precautions were normally taken. This was a routine commonly applied to cinemas, theatres, banks and post offices, but it was new and comparatively exciting where churches were concerned.

Davies's favourite church was St. Ethelreda's.

He liked the weathered grey stone and the smooth, beautifully kept grass and the hill it was on. Once it had over-looked farm and meadow land; now masses of red roofs and chimney pots, ribbon-roads, factories clustering the reservoir, lay beneath it. In this part of the outskirts of London, the countryside which Davies loved was still within easy distance, and he liked to stand by day near the church gate and look north-west. One, in that myriad mass of houses, was his own; one of the little green patches was the one where he laboured so lovingly.

Tonight there was a slight drizzle, misting the lights in windows and creating halos about the bright street lamps. Over the doorway of the church was a single electric lamp in a wire shade, for the vicar of St. Ethelreda's liked the church to be available for prayer by night as well as day.

Davies plodded up the hill. A car passed, wheels slithering on the damp macadam. A cyclist wobbled by; two couples passed on the other side of the road, oblivious of the rain. The misted light glowing outside the church porch burnt steadily.

'No one would ever do anything there,' Davies thought, but the reflection did not make him careless. He opened the gate, noted its creak, and walked slowly up the tarred path. Only the sounds of night were about him, and he was so used to this lonely job that he did not give a moment's thought to danger.

He put a hand on the wrought-iron latch, and pushed the door open.

As he did so, a dark figure leapt out of the faint yellow light which filled the church. Taken completely by surprise, Davies had no time to protect himself. The man launched his body forward, and an outflung boot caught Davies in the groin. Agony shot through him as he staggered to one side.

His assailant dashed through the door and was lost to sight.

Davies was so pain-racked that for seconds he almost forgot where he was. Flung up against the wall, he saved himself from falling, then bent down, jack-knifing his body to stave off the worst of the pain.

He was aware of the flickering, spitting light, but not yet of its significance. He forced his head between his knees until gradually the waves of pain eased. Slowly he became increasingly conscious of the unusual quality of the light. Straightening up, he saw a tiny spot of bright flame on the floor at the far end of the nave, and a word ripped into his head.

'Dynamite!'

Fighting waves of pain and of fear, he staggered towards the altar, understanding at last exactly what was causing the spitting and spluttering: a lighted fuse. He must put it out. Once he fell against the end of a pew, the jarring blow bringing on a wave of excruciating pain. It held him back for precious seconds, but he was driven by the desperate urgency of the situation: he *must* put that fuse out.

Not once did the thought of personal danger occur to him.

He actually managed to quicken his pace, until he saw the flame close to the side of the altar and sensed that there was little time. The fire was now spitting more wildly, and he scrambled down on his hands and knees, able to see the two sticks of dynamite to which the fuse was attached. There was only an inch unburned. He had nothing with which to douse the flame, and unhesitatingly thrust his hand forward, to press his palm on to it.

There was a sudden, blinding flash, a roar, and awful pain in his eyes and in his right hand; then he lost consciousness.

In the churchyard were two lovers, sheltering beneath a yew tree, dry and secure and satisfied, lying close but still, as they looked into each other's eyes. Suddenly, a flash lit up the entire scene. There was a roar and the sound of crashing glass. The man started up, and a sliver of glass stabbed into his cheek.

'God!' he gasped.

'Jock!' cried the girl. 'What is it?'

'It's in the church.' He leapt up. 'Go and telephone the police. Go on, hurry!' When she bent down, scrambling for her shoes, he screamed again: 'Hurry! *Hurry.*'

Sobbing, bewildered, she moved uncertainly away as he ran towards the front of the church, oblivious of a dribble of blood splashing down his cheek.

In north-east London, near Charlton; in South London, in Camberwell; and in south-west London, close to Putney Bridge, other churches suffered the same kind of damage, but no one was hurt.

Gideon woke to a morning of bright sunshine, and was cheerful because of it. Kate was still sleeping, and he left her undisturbed. Creeping downstairs, he made some tea and toast, and was out of the house by seven-forty-five. He kept his car garaged round the corner and was nearly out of earshot when his telephone began to ring; he went back, muttering.

It was Lemaitre.

'Okay, I'll see him at the office,' Gideon said.

The Embankment road was clear and Gideon was at the Yard in twenty minutes. He saw Lemaitre's car; Lem was really making sure he kept on top of this job. A constable fresh on duty saluted Gideon, but no one else was about. He opened the door of his office and as it closed Lemaitre's door opened; Lemaitre's eyes had the glassy look which follows a sleepless night; he hadn't shaved, his collar and bow tie had a crumpled look.

Gideon's heart dropped.

'More?'

'Five more—making six in all.'

'Why didn't you call me?'

'You've got enough on your plate.'

Gideon let that pass.

'Where did they happen?'

'Different parts of London. There's worse.'

'What?'

'One of our chaps had a hand blown off, and was blinded. He was trying to stop the explosion.'

Quite suddenly, Gideon went cold. Few things were more precious to him than the security and safety of his men, and this news came so unexpectedly that it hurt badly. It was several seconds before he asked:

'Where did that happen?'

'St. Ethelreda's, Wembley.'

'On the hill?'

'Yes.'

'When?'

'About eleven o'clock.'

Just after Kate had come in, Gideon remembered.

'A couple canoodling in the churchyard heard it, and sent for our chaps. They found Davies——'

'The injured constable?'

'Yes. Got him into hospital within twenty minutes.'

'Isn't there any doubt about the injury to his eyes?'

Lemaitre answered wearily: 'No, George.' He sat down on the arm of a chair opposite the desk. 'I've just come from the hospital. Saw his wife there—plucky woman. I promised her we'd see she's all right.'

'All right,' Gideon echoed bitterly.

'You know what I mean.'

'Sure I do. Anything to help us find who did it?'

'Nothing to help with any one of the six,' Lemaitre said. 'George, I could do with a cuppa.'

'Sorry,' Gideon said. He lifted a telephone. 'Tea, in a pot, and some breakfast for Mr. Lemaitre. Make it snappy.' He rang off before there was time for an answer, and picked up a box of cigarettes kept for visitors. Lemaitre took one, and lit up. 'Five or six separate crimes. Timing?'

'Two were undoubtedly short-time fuses, as in all probability were the others. The explosions were all within ten or fifteen minutes of eleven o'clock, so we must assume there were as many different men.' When Gideon hesitated, Lemaitre drew deeply on the cigarette, and said: 'Okay, okay, or women.'

'None of them seen?'

'A car was heard to start off after each explosion, but that doesn't mean much,' Lemaitre said. 'No one's come forward to say they saw prowlers about. There's one thing, though. We found a girl who saw a man walk away from St. Denys' the night before last. He was a small fellow wearing a bowler hat and carrying an umbrella. She thinks he drove off in a pale-coloured Morris 1000. A pale-coloured Morris 1000 was seen parked in St. Ethelreda's Road last night. I'm following that up.'

Gideon said heavily: 'Several different churches at the same time. Lem, what have we struck? I hope to God——' He broke off.

Lemaitre frowned. 'Now what?'

'Was it a mistake for me to go to St. Denys' yesterday morning?'

'When it was on your route to the Yard? Been damned fishy if you hadn't.'

Gideon said: 'Something seems to have quickened the pace and worsened the nature of the crimes.' Frowning, concentrating, he was irritated when Lemaitre grinned.

'Jumping to conclusions, aren't you?' Lemaitre quipped. '*What?*'

'How do you know this is the same series of crimes? Could be imitative—these are much worse than any of the crimes on the Dean's list.'

Gideon stared, and then began to smile.

'You win,' he said. 'We need to check a lot of things.' Before he could go on, the door opened and an elderly messenger brought in Lemaitre's breakfast and an extra cup. Gideon motioned to a table beneath one wall and the messenger put the tray down. 'Tuck in,' Gideon said, feeling hungry at the sight of bacon and eggs, sausages and fried bread. He poured himself a cup of tea and went to his own chair. 'Morris 1000, and a man in a bowler hat carrying an umbrella. There must be thousands of the first and tens of thousands of the second. We need——' He broke off. 'What do you recommend, Lem?'

'Double watch on all churches tonight,' Lemaitre said. 'Can't keep anything quiet any longer. If the Dean had come to us weeks ago, we might have stopped this kind of nonsense. As it is we must keep a special look-out for light-coloured Morrises, a check on every man who goes into or out of a church after dark tonight, and make an examination of the residual ash of the dynamite and of the container. As a matter of fact that was made by Hecht and Hecht, of Watford.'

Gideon said: 'Sure?'

'Certainly I'm sure. Quarry and demolition blasting dynamite, available quite freely. They've got several hundred customers in the London and the Home Counties, *and* a couple of dozen wholesalers.'

'We want every stockist checked.'

'I started that last night,' Lemaitre mumbled through a mouthful of food.

Gideon said: 'Good. Had any sleep at all?'

'Nope.'

'Get home as soon as you can.'

Lemaitre said: 'I hope that's not an order, Commander. I want to be busy this morning.'

Gideon smiled at him faintly, and said at last:

'Not an order, Lem.'

'Ta,' said Lemaitre, and after a pause, he went on: 'How's Mr. Acting New Deputy Commander Mr. Basket Alec Bloody Hobbs getting on?'

'I'll find out when he comes in.'

'He's been in for an hour,' said Lemaitre. 'Your henchmen really work these days, George. *You* can take it easy.'

Gideon didn't answer, but thought bleakly that he did not see any likelihood of taking anything easy until the church crimes were solved. If five men had been involved, why not fifteen? Or fifty? That seemed to him the most significant question, and against it, all other investigations seemed negligible, for there was no telling where the sacrilege would stop.

So far, only the smaller churches had been seriously damaged; there was no guarantee that cathedrals were immune.

At that moment, a man of medium height and build was sitting at a knee-hole desk in a large room in a flat overlooking Westminster Cathedral. There was coffee and toast on a tray at his left hand, and a book open in front of him. The book, entitled: *The Churches of London,* was open at the E section. In red ink, he placed a tick against *St. Ethelreda's,* Wembley, and then turned the pages to the G section, and ticked off: *St. Giles',* Camberwell. Next he marked *St. Olave's,* Charlton and finally *St. Colomb's,* Putney. He was a pale, thin-faced man, with bony hands and anaemic-looking fingernails; the ink showed up darkly against an almost transparent colourlessness.

In all, there were 2,000 churches, chapels and synagogues listed, under the headings:

> Church of England.
> Roman Catholic.
> Free Churches.
> Foreign Churches.
> Synagogues.

Of the 2,000, only those now marked off, and *St. Denys'*,

Kensington, were ticked. He ran his eye down each list, until his pen came to rest at *St. Paul's Cathedral*. The pen hovered, then moved down a line to *St. Paul's*, Clapham, and he wrote the name of this on a slip of paper, then seven more church names, each on a separate slip. He took eight plain envelopes from a drawer in the desk, and addressed each to a different man, at an address in London. He slipped the names of the churches in these envelopes, sealed and stamped them.

Not once did he smile; not once did he pause on his way to a post box opposite the tall red tower of the cathedral.

CHAPTER 13

ANXIETY

GIDEON knew that it would not be long before Scott-Marle wanted to know more about the raids on the churches, and expected an urgent call from the Dean of St. Ludd's. He ran through the reports which had accumulated during the night and that morning, then called Hobbs, who was still in his office on the floor above.

'Come down, Alec, will you.'

'Yes, at once.' Hobbs never wasted a word.

He was in Gideon's office less than five minutes later, alert-looking, immaculate as ever, somehow very different from any other detective Gideon had known. He managed to make Gideon feel momentarily ill-at-ease.

'I'd like you to do the briefing again,' Gideon said, and handed three files across his desk. 'Seen Rollo's latest?'

'No.'

'Henry Rhodes was shot in the back. There'll be a post-mortem this morning, but Rollo says the wound was the cause of death. Signs of a heavy motor-cycle which had stood in a hedge near the gate where the body was found are the only clue. A little oil had leaked—*Castrol* 30. Rollo's down at Southend, and Golightly's handling the London end. The most important thing is to find out whether Sally Dalby visited Rhodes and whether hers is one of the photographs on the cellar walls. Also, we want to interview the girl-friend in whom Sally Dalby confided that she was going to model for a photographer.' Gideon paused, Hobbs nodded, and Gideon said: 'All the rest speak for themselves.'

'One thing,' Hobbs said.

'Yes?'

'Golightly wants to know whether you want Entwhistle pulled in yet, or let him sweat.'

'Nothing else in?'

'No.'

'Let him sweat,' Gideon said.

In fact, Entwhistle was sleeping off the whisky.

Eric Greenwood, in a much brighter frame of mind, reached the office of Cox and Shielding earlier than usual, even before Bessie Smith. He dealt with a lot of shipments which he had neglected the day before, from Persian and Indian carpets to Chinese jade and rose quartz, ivory from Hong Kong and opals from Australia. When Bessie came in, nose and cheeks an innocent glow, he dictated at twice his usual speed. Twenty-five minutes later, he said:

'That's the lot, Bessie.'

'I must say it's plenty,' she said complainingly. 'And I'm not at my brightest this morning.'

'You look fine,' Greenwood said heartily. 'What's the trouble?'

'I was up half the night, with——'

'I didn't think it of you,' Greenwood interrupted with pretended shock.

Bessie sniggered dutifully. 'As a matter of fact, the church opposite me was one of the four which was damaged last night—you know, St. Ethelreda's. Didn't you read about it?'

Greenwood said: 'No, I've hardly looked at my newspaper.' He opened it, and read the headlines:

He scowled, his lips set tightly, and there was righteous anger in his eyes.

'The sons of Satan,' he said hotly.

'They're devils, that's what they are,' muttered Bessie. 'Why on earth would anyone want to do such a thing? And where will they strike next, that's what *I* want to know. The police don't seem to have a clue.'

'The police?—they're no damned good,' Greenwood said.

He did not even look to see if there was anything new in the paper about Margaret Entwhistle's death; it was almost as if he felt that he had received absolution, and the burden and the fear of his crime had been taken from him.

In the course of the morning, most of the department managers spoke about the church explosions...

In fact, during that morning, most of London mentioned them. Overnight, it seemed, Londoners had become more church conscious than they had been for fifty years. The blinding of P.C. Davies was mentioned with horrified sympathy, while the sacrilege at the churches was discussed with shock, shame or anger. Vergers, priests and churchwardens found their aisles thronged, the clink and rustle of money going into the offertory boxes was trebled and quadrupled, and churches which seldom saw a visitor had many throughout the day. The damaged churches were besieged with newspapermen and tourists.

At Wembley Hospital, Mrs. Davies sat and waited for news of the operation which would mean life or death to her husband. Her children were with their grandmother.

At Lewisham, Entwhistle's mother-in-law had her grandchildren with her.

At their small suburban house, Sally Dalby's mother and father were answering the questions which Golightly put to them.

All over London, the work of the police went on; and at Scotland Yard, Gideon, Lemaitre and Dean Howcroft met together in Gideon's room.

Howcroft looked older and more frail.

Lemaitre, his eyes glassy and red-rimmed, had shaved and changed his shirt, and put on a blue-and-white-spotted bowtie. He managed to look almost fresh.

Gideon, direct from Scott-Marle's office, was at his grimmest.

'We do feel that some degree of priority is required for these crimes,' the Dean said, a note of reproof in his voice. 'Unless we are assured you can give that we shall be very anxious indeed.'

'If you'd come to us weeks ago we might have found out enough to have stopped it,' Gideon remarked. 'As it is, I think we've a major crisis on our hands. It will certainly get priority.'

The Dean, rebuked, spread his pale, brown-spotted hands.

'The obvious question is—which church or churches next?' Gideon went on. 'Lemaitre is organising the closest possible watch, but every church can't be protected all the time without a lot of help.'

Lemaitre put in:

'All the church authorities are being co-operative.'

Gideon nodded, and waited.

'What we can't find is a common factor which might help us to anticipate the next churches likely to suffer,' Lemaitre said. 'We've had a high church, two low church Anglicans, a Roman Catholic and a Wesleyan. They've nothing in common in antiquity, one was built three hundred years ago, one only twenty-two years. They don't seem to have a thing in common except that they're churches.'

'Christian churches,' amended Dean Howcroft mildly.

'Of course they're Christian, what else ——' Lemaitre began, and then stopped abruptly.

Gideon asked sharply: 'What do you mean, Dean Howcroft?'

Again the old man spread his hands.

'I was simply being specific,' he said. 'The churches you mentioned are Christian.'

'Meaning, they're not Jewish Synagogues?'

'As you say, yes.'

'Nor are they Moslem mosques or Hindu temples,' Gideon went on; he looked forbidding, almost menacing. 'I hope you won't make a remark like that in the hearing of the Press.'

'My dear Commander, I stated a fact.'

'In a way which could be construed to carry an implication against the Jews or other religions,' said Gideon. 'We've had far too much anti-Semitism in London. It's died down a lot, and we don't want it revived.'

Lemaitre fidgeted uncomfortably, sensing a conflict, but unable to do a thing about it. Gideon, huge compared with the Dean, florid against the other's pinkish pallor and silky white halo, sat glowering. The Dean met his gaze squarely, sternly unrepentant. Utterly at a loss, Lemaitre said tentatively:

'Everyone's talking about it.'

'Of course they are,' said Gideon. 'That is why we don't want the wrong kind of slant.'

The Dean drew a long, slow breath.

'Commander, I hope you are not refusing to consider every possibility?'

'All we can see are being considered.'

'I'm very glad to hear it. There *is* such a thing as anti-Semitism. And there are among the Jews young and fanatical individuals who hate the Christian Church for it, just as there are fanatical, anti-Semitic Christians. We are not yet in an age of full religious tolerance.'

Gideon said: 'There's a lot of bitterness between High Church and Low in the Church of England. There are extremists in the Church of England as well as in the Roman Catholic Church. One group is no more suspect than another. If the Press gets hold of a remark like yours they may twist and distort it. Even a whisper could start a wave of religious hatred that could do great harm. Surely you can see *that*.'

Lemaitre had never seen Gideon so plainly angry, and now kept silent, knowing that there was nothing he could usefully do.

The Dean said: 'Yes, Commander, I can indeed.'

'Then why——' Gideon began.

'Forgive me,' interrupted the Dean in a voice in which Gideon's forgiveness seemed the very last thing for which he craved. 'Perhaps my remark may be easier to accept if I explain at once that it was, in fact, a quotation from one of your own officers, heard this morning.'

Gideon felt as if he had been flung against a wall, the impact of that statement was so great. Lemaitre pressed his hands against his damp forehead. For a few seconds, no one spoke. Eventually, the Dean broke the silence:

'Commander, if we cannot solve this mystery quickly, there will be no stopping rumour of every kind. I am only too keenly aware that you should have been informed before, and deplore the fact that you were not. But—forgive me again—we have to deal with the situation as it is, not as it should be. Is there any clue?'

'None yet,' Gideon said, gruffly.

'I wouldn't say that,' protested Lemaitre. 'We know where the dynamite's made. We're on the ball there all right. We simply lack the motive.'

'Superintendent,' said the Dean, 'there is no fanatic more dangerous than the religious fanatic. As Mr. Gideon has reminded us, there has been a long period of quiet on the issue of religious tolerance. This could bring that period abruptly to an end.'

Gideon said: 'Dean Howcroft, are you being wholly frank?'

'In what way?'

'Do you have any reason to believe this is being done to stir up religious fanaticism?'

'I have no reason to believe it at all. It is an obvious possibility, however. The newspapers won't fail to point it out, and gossip and rumour are no doubt already busy with it. If this were not enough, our churches, perhaps some of our most historic churches, are in danger of serious damage.' He paused, leaned forward, and asked earnestly: 'Are you *sure* that nothing more can be done to find the perpetrators? Watching and guarding the churches is essential, of course, and invaluable—but the real preventative will be to remove the danger.'

When the Dean had gone, Lemaitre looked at Gideon's set face and said uneasily:

'The old man talks a lot, but he's no fool.'

'No,' agreed Gideon drily. 'And no one's going to agree with the last half of your sentence more heartily than he will. But we've got to pull out all the stops, Lem. Not being a fool isn't enough to produce the culprits. I saw the Commissioner this morning, and the Lords Spiritual are beginning to chase the Home Secretary who is beginning to chase us. We've got a really ugly situation on our hands. If you can solve this one quickly——'

'I'll solve it,' Lemaitre interrupted, with a confidence he could not justify. 'Don't you worry, George. I'll solve it.'

When he had gone, in turn, Gideon wondered for the first time whether it had been a mistake to give this case to Lemaitre. Over-confidence could be disastrous.

Toni Bottelli was over-confident, too.

He felt quite sure that he had not been seen and recognised. He had travelled to Southend from London on a heavy B.S.A. motor-cycle, left that in a village parking place and returned from the rendezvous on the Honda, wearing helmet and goggles. The B.S.A. could not be connected with him or the murder; someone would come and collect it in a few days. There was nothing to worry about, no direct association between his photographic studio cellar in Tottenham and the one in Fulham from which Rhodes had been driven.

So he could go back to Sally Dalby.

He did not know himself really well, but there were things he did recognise; among them, the fact that certain girls had a fascination for him. He wanted to dominate them absolutely, wanted to make them do everything and anything he desired. He did not know why he felt that way about one girl in twenty or so, he was only very sure that was the way he felt. Twenty would look more or less alike, their measurements wouldn't greatly vary, but one of them would have the quality that mesmerised him. Until she was virtually his slave, he could not look at anyone else. Once he had a girl completely under his thumb, she lost her attraction. Three of them had been so appalled and horrified at the lengths to which he had gone that they had threatened to tell the police.

So he had given them an overdose of sleeping tablets— and they had died.

Now he was going back to his latest 'slave'; Sally. Sally was still attractive to him; he had brilliantly circumvented any danger which might have spread from Harry Rhodes and could concentrate with an easy mind on the girl.

CHAPTER 14

'I WANT TO GO HOME'

'I WANT to go home,' Sally said.

'What's the matter with this place?' Bottelli asked. 'Isn't it grand enough?'

'It's lovely, but I want to go home.'

'Why can't you be at home here?'

'It isn't the same,' insisted Sally.

She sat up in a big bed, looking almost incredibly attractive, her hair falling in golden strands to her shoulders, her eyes only just touched with eye-shadow, her naturally curling lashes very slightly darkened, her complexion wholly without blemish. She wore a frilly bed-jacket, high at the neck, and the pillows behind her were downy and luxurious. The bedspread was of a very pale pink. Opposite her and on each wall, were huge mirrors, from which one could see reflections at every conceivable angle.

Toni sat on the side of the bed, very handsome in a dark and swarthy way. He was not annoyed or angry but in a teasing mood, knowing exactly what he wanted. He knew, too, that the drugs would gradually weaken her resistance, until a moment would come when she would be wholly compliant.

'I should think it's not the same,' he said. 'This is luxury, you live in the slums.'

'Oh, I don't!' she protested.

'Not far off,' he said. 'Have you got a room of your own?'

'Well, no, but——'

'You share it with little sister Mary,' he reminded her. 'She's a school kid who throws her clothes all over the place, uses your lipstick and powder and borrows your stockings. Remember?'

'Well, she *is* my sister.'

'And she gets under your feet all the time.'

Sally looked at him steadily and soberly, and then said: 'I don't care what you say, I want to go home.'

'Okay, so you shall—one of these days.'

'No—today.'

He stood up, half-frowning, half-smiling. Looking up at him Sally was a little frightened, and at the same time a little admiring; he *was* so good-looking. She wondered if she had made him angry, while in rather a vague way she associated him with pain.

'I'll see what I can do,' he promised. He moved towards the door, then hesitated, came back to the bed and selected a chocolate from a rich-looking box at the bedside. He bit into it appreciatively. 'Like one?'

'They're lovely.'

'They're the best—only the best is good enough for you!'

She chose one with a nut on top, as he knew she would; and she would eat several more, now she had started. In each was a quantity of hashish which would make her forget all about that tiresome desire to go home. Her fears and tensions would relax and she would do whatever he wanted.

He knew, because she already had.

He knew, also, because there were three other girls to remember, all of whom had become compliant after eating those chocolates while reclining in that bed.

Golightly entered the Food Supermarket where a girl named Daphne Arnold worked, walked past the bright stacks of tinned and packet foods, of bread and of cheese in great variety, past meat and pies displayed at the delicatessen counter, and finally reached the office marked: *Manager*. A surprisingly youthful man looked up with irritable preoccupation and demanded:

'What can I do for you?'

'I'd like to see Miss Arnold,' Golightly said.

'The staff can't be spared for private matters in business hours.'

Golightly simply took out and proffered his card. The young man's manner changed at once. He sprang up, and with a murmured apology hurried out, calling sharply: 'Miss Arnold—wanted at the office, please.'

A girl approached from one of the counters. She had an exaggerated mop of black hair, a snub nose and a figure which managed to overcome the disadvantage of a mass-cut, dark blue smock. She looked at Golightly demurely.

'Yes, Mr. Smith?'

'This gentleman would like a word with you. I'll be in the store-room.' The manager went out abruptly, while Golightly waited for the girl to drop her gaze.

'You're a friend of Sally Dalby,' Golightly said at last.

'Yes, that's right.'

'She told you she was going to pose as a photographer's model.'

'Yes, that's right.'

'Do you know where she was going to pose for him?'

'No, I don't.'

'Did she say anything more about it?'

'No, she didn't.'

'Would you like to come along to the police station for a few hours, until you've recovered your memory?'

The girl's eyes rounded with alarm.

'No! *I* haven't done anything!'

'Sure about that?' asked Golightly. He let his gaze move about the Supermarket, at the cash desks and the crowded shelves, looked back at her, and went on: 'What else did Sally tell you about this photographer?'

'Not much,' Daphne Arnold said.

'How much? Let's stop wasting time.'

'All I know is that she said his name was Toni,' answered Daphne with a rush. 'But she made me promise not to tell anyone, because if her father knew, he would be hopping mad. That's the truth—I *promised* her.'

'What else did you promise not to tell anyone?' Golightly demanded.

'Nothing, really. She'd been to see this feller once, and she told me what the place was like.' Boldness crept back into the girl's eyes and manner and confidence returned with it. 'She said there were hundreds and hundreds of photographs around the walls, she wasn't the only one to be photographed without any clothes. There was nothing to be ashamed of, she said. Her figure was as good as anyone's there.'

'Did you ever see this Toni?'

'No. I swear I didn't.'

'Did she ever talk about meeting other people with him?'

'No, she wanted to keep him to herself.'

'Why?'

'He was ever so handsome, she told me,' Daphne said. Her expression changed again and her voice rose. 'He was an Italian, or a Spaniard, or something like that.'

Golightly felt that he had made quite a step forward.

There being nothing else that the girl could tell him, he went straight from the Supermarket to the street of small terraced houses where Sally Dalby lived. Her father was a sign-writer who worked in a shed in the backyard. Her mother was a grey, fluffy, vague individual, on whom nothing seemed to make an impression.

'Oh, it's another policeman ... Come about Sally, I daresay ... You haven't found her, I suppose? ... No, well, I expect she'll turn up one day, like a bad penny ... Yes, my hubby's in, will you come through?'

He followed her through the house to a shed which smelled of potatoes, paint and varnish. The whole of one wall was of glass, and crowding the others were half-finished paintings in vivid and striking colours. A stack of gilt picture framing was piled in one corner beside a bench crammed with pots of paint and half-filled jars of brushes. On another bench were some inn signs and notices, all boldly and effectively done.

Dalby was a short, stubby-haired man; a hedgehog of a man.

'Where's the detective who usually comes to see me?' he demanded suspiciously.

'Following another angle,' Golightly told him smoothly. 'Mr. Dalby, has your daughter ever talked to you about a man named Toni?'

'No.'

'Did you know she was interested in posing for a photographer?'

'If I'd known, I'd have had the hide off her.'

'I see,' said Golightly. Rollo had told him that talking to Dalby was like talking to a brick wall, and he began to understand what his colleague meant. 'Have you had any message at all from or about her?'

'If I had, I would have told you,' Dalby stated.

Golightly looked at him steadily, nodded and turned away. As he reached the door he heard a movement behind him, but he did not turn round until he was halfway to the back door of the little house.

'Superintendent,' Dalby called.

'Yes?'

'Find her, for God's sake find her,' Dalby pleaded in a desperate voice. 'And tell her she can come back. What ever she's done. I won't take it out of her. You must make her believe that.'

Golightly thought; but is it true? and turned to face this man squarely, the question on the tip of his tongue. He did not say it, however; he needed no telling at all that at the moment Dalby's whole being was in the words he had uttered, that he was flagellating himself because of a sense of guilt at having driven his daughter away.

'We will do everything we can,' Golightly promised.

As he drove off, he wondered what would happen in this strange household if he had to report that the girl had been murdered.

About the time that Golightly drove away from the Dalby house, Rollo entered the laboratory at Southend Police Headquarters to talk to the pathologist who had finished the autopsy on Rhodes. Eric Greenwood was walking up the gangway of a ship which had brought a special cargo of llama wool from South America. Entwhistle was making himself some strong coffee. Mrs. Davies was waiting for the verdict as two surgeons fought to save her husband's life. The Dean of St. Ludd's was entering the main gates of Lambeth Palace to report to the Bishop; while Elspeth Chaplin watched her grandfather's pale face and pain-racked eyes, sharing his distress at the damage to the church he loved.

While all these things took place, part of the surging, throbbing vitality of London's life, while the police and the transport men and, in fact, all of London's eight million human beings went about their business, Lemaitre stepped out of his car outside the last of the churches to be damaged. Along the road there was a branch post office, and letters were being left there for sorting before the next morning's delivery.

Among the letters being carried in a big sack was one posted by the man whose flat overlooked Westminster Cathedral. Oblivious of this, as the police must be of so many crimes in their incipient stage, Lemaitre went into the Roman Catholic Church of St. Augustine, Maida Vale, which had been damaged the previous night. The routine work was finished and much tidying up had already been done. Eight or nine women and a priest were busy among the litter caused by the explosion, and the priest turned and limped towards Lemaitre. This was Father Devan, a priest well known because of his television appeals for charity. He was a round, chubby-faced man, with merry eyes, bald, rather portly and distinctly rubicund. His voice was clear and beautifully modulated.

'Hello, sir. How can I help you?'

'I'm Superintendent Lemaitre, from Scotland Yard.'

'Oh, I heard you would be coming, Superintendent. May I say how appreciative we are of the consideration of the police.'

'We do what we can,' Lemaitre said. 'Can you spare me ten minutes?'

'Of course. My study will be the best place.' Father Devan led the way towards the side of the church. Passing the workers he went out to a house almost adjoining, and took Lemaitre into a small room, with a table, two chairs, a crucifix, some books and, on one side, some manuscript paper and a quill pen. Lemaitre noticed that there were illuminations on the manuscript pages. Following his glance, Father Devan said: 'I've a great love for illustrated manuscripts, and it's always been my hope to transcribe the Bible in my own hand.' He motioned to a chair. 'Please sit down.'

Lemaitre could not resist picking up a sheet of the paper, scrutinising the immaculate old English lettering, and the red, green and gilt scroll at the top. 'That's really good,' he said with feeling. 'If I weren't a flat-foot I'd like to be an etcher. Like to see what I mean?' He took out his wallet, selected a slip of paper and handed it across the desk, grinning broadly. Father Devan unfolded it, his eyes widening. 'How about that!'

'It's a five-pound note,' the parish priest observed.

'All my own work,' Lemaitre boasted. 'Good job I was born on the right side of the law, isn't it?' He waited for a few moments while the other pored over his forgery, then went on: 'Did it for a joke.' He took it back, shedding humour, becoming at once deeply grave. 'The truth is, Padre, I'm worried stiff over these explosions. Never know what'll go next—look had if they blew up Poet's Corner in the Abbey, or the Nelson catafalque in the Crypt at St. Paul's, wouldn't it?'

'It would be a disaster,' agreed Father Devan.

'Be a disaster for me, too,' said Lemaitre. 'This is one job I mustn't fall down on.'

'How can I help?' asked Devan.

'What I'm looking for is a common denominator,' Lemaitre explained. 'Anything in common with all the damaged churches in this part of London, past and present. I've got a list here—seven R.C. churches and twenty-three Anglican——'

'As many as that!' exclaimed Devan.

'Yes, for a start.' Lemaitre opened his brief-case and put a sheet of paper in front of the priest. 'There's the list, and I want to find out if *you* have anything in common with them. Apart from Christianity, I mean, and that's not the point. Do *you* know of anything you have in common?'

Devan ran his eye down the lists, then slowly shook his head.

'I can think of nothing.'

'Tell you what I want you to do,' said Lemaitre, as if confiding in a bosom friend. 'Go through that list with a toothcomb and put down if you've ever visited them— whether you know the priest-in-charge, anything at all to show a connection. And then I'd like you to make out a list of all your associated groups, clubs, societies, mission stations—every possible bit of information you have. I'm going to get a list from every church and try to find that connection. Tell you one possibility.'

'Oh. What is it?' inquired Devan.

'Someone who hates the ecumenical idea. You or anyone at the church have anything special to do with that?'

'Not as far as I know. There are, of course, my television appeals, but the causes are too widely divergent to be the reason of a specific animosity. However, I will certainly do what you ask to find out any association, any activity—such as service on charity committees and community efforts— which we might share with these other churches.'

'And let me know when you've finished: I'll get it collected,' Lemaitre said. He stood up, and the priest followed suit, rather awkwardly. 'Hurt your leg?' asked Lemaitre commiseratingly.

Devan smiled. 'I left a piece of one behind in Normandy, on D-Day.'

'Oh. Bloody bad luck,' said Lemaitre, and added hastily: 'Sorry, Padre. Forgot where I was.'

He strode out, cheered up by the interview. Though he had gained little, there was something about Devan's personality which appealed to him. As he settled into his car, he began to calculate how long it was likely to be before hearing from all the priests concerned.

'A couple of weeks, and we need results in a couple of days. What the hell's the use? If only those so-and-so parsons had let us know before.'

That night, eight more churches were severely damaged.

CHAPTER 15

THE BISHOP'S PALACE

ON the other side of the River Thames from New Scotland Yard, between the bridges of Westminster and Lambeth, lay Lambeth Palace, the Archbishop of Canterbury's official residence, where the business of much of the Church of England was carried out. Far less known than the Abbey, which lay between the two buildings, or the Roman Catholic Cathedral of Westminster, which was only a few hundred yards away, it nestled near the river bank, ancient and venerable as buildings go, under the shadow of the Houses of Parliament. Great decisions had been taken in the palace during the Lambeth Conferences of all the Anglican Bishops throughout the world. Almost exactly a hundred years ago the first of the convocations had been held, with some dissidents and some heart-searching. During the intervening years a host of subjects had been discussed, many of them controversial, and many recommendations had been made to the Privy Council of the Church. In those early days the recommendations had been cautious and had seldom carried great weight. Today, decisions of the Conferences were of key importance in Anglican affairs.

Every conceivable subject which might affect the welfare of the church and the health of Christianity had been discussed. Here were taken the first steps towards reunion with those churches which had broken away centuries before. Here successive Archbishops of Canterbury, their London home at the Palace, made historic pronouncements on ecumenical affairs, on marriage, divorce, or ritual, creed and dogma. No change of any significance had ever occurred until it had been discussed and deliberated upon in this place.

Not once in the history of the Palace, however, had an issue been discussed involving Scotland Yard and actual crime.

There was an air almost of unreality among the five men who gathered there on the afternoon when Lemaitre had been boasting of his skill in forgery. The Archbishop of Canterbury was not in residence but had delegated his powers to another Bishop, whose forbidding air was tempered by the homeliness of steel-framed bifocal spectacles worn well down on the bridge of his nose. Howcroft, Dean of St. Ludd's, and the group's liaison officer with the police, was at his right hand. The Dean of the Abbey was next to him, a gentle-looking ascetic with a mind known to be as decisive as a trap. There was also a representative from the Free Church Council, William Steel, a well-known broadcaster and writer who looked not unlike a popular actor of the times. The fifth man was the Roman Catholic, Jonathan Northwick; the Administrator for the Cardinal, tall and patriarchal-looking. These five were gathered about an oval table in a book-lined room overlooking a lawn so vividly green and velvet smooth that it seemed more like baize than grass.

'Gentlemen,' said the Bishop, 'we all feel that the urgency of the situation is so great that we should take emergency measures—distressing though the situation is. As we have met so often to discuss ways and means in which we can work more closely together, I thought it advisable to meet, briefly, before we are joined by others, seldom in our councils. Seldom indeed.'

He paused, looking over his lenses at everyone present.

'I have, at the request of the Commissioner of the Metropolitan Police, invited the Chief Rabbi or his chosen representative, and also the Commander of the Criminal Investigation Department, whom some of you may know.'

'Gideon,' remarked Northwick. 'A very sound man.'

'I've met him,' said Steel, briskly.

'Do we—ah—seriously fear that synagogues might also be affected?' asked the Bishop.

'The police think so,' said Howcroft, as if that clinched the matter. 'The only essential preliminary, as far as I can see, is that we should all be aware of the possibility of a worsening situation and the very real probability that the number of churches affected might increase quite alarmingly.' He peered at the Dean of the Abbey, and paused.

'*Are* there any grounds for such theories?' the Dean wanted to know. 'I am not being an obstructionist, you understand, but neither do I feel the need to be an alarmist.'

'Do we know what Gideon will expect us to do?' asked Steel.

'Expect?' Northwick's eyebrows raised in surprise rather than disapproval.

The Bishop looked interrogatively at Dean Howcroft.

'I'm quite satisfied that Commander Gideon takes the matter very seriously and has it in proper perspective,' the Dean declared. 'I think we shall be well advised to be guided by him.'

Before anyone could comment, there was a tap at the door. Dean Howcroft stood up and moved towards it as it opened. A very broad, thickset man, Daniel Cohen, the Secretary of the London United Synagogues, came in; Gideon, much the same build but a head taller, following. Howcroft led them to the table, and the Bishop introduced them amid a general shuffling of chairs and murmuring.

Gideon found himself next to Dean Howcroft.

'Now that we are all here,' said the Bishop, 'I'm sure I voice the sentiments of everyone present when I say how grateful we are to the police for their swift and ready co-operation.'

There was more murmuring.

'Commander,' went on the Bishop, 'I wonder if you would care to make a statement on the situation as you see it at this moment?'

Gideon, seldom in the slightest degree self-conscious, was a little embarrassed. He had never before been in Lambeth Palace, and there was something a little awesome—not about the building itself but about its history and its traditions. He had a confusion of ideas, partly that this was rather like a prayer meeting, partly that he was very out of place. Even the other layman present habitually moved in a more rarefied religious atmosphere. Gideon was acutely conscious of his lack of knowledge of ecclesiastical modes and affairs. In a way he was glad that he was called on so quickly; he did not have time to worry.

'The situation as I see it now,' he echoed, a little hoarsely. He coughed. 'That needn't take much time, sir. I will say at once that the position appears to me to be of the utmost gravity. The incidents last night really alarmed us at the Yard. If I had my way, every church of every denomination would be placed under police guard until the problem is solved—but we haven't enough men to do it even in the Metropolitan area. So—we need your help.'

'Ah,' said the Abbey Dean.

'In what way?' demanded Northwick.

'Each church must have a watchman every hour of the day and night,' said Gideon. 'Something like the fireguards and the wardens during the war. You had then a team of over two hundred at St. Ludd's, and the Abbey had as many. You wouldn't, of course, need that amount now, but every door needs watching. The churches and cathedrals will have to be kept under close surveillance during services to make sure no one stays behind. It has to be done quickly and thoroughly. I can make sure that there is at least one policeman on call all the time, and at the bigger churches I'll have a regular patrol. Flying Squad and patrol cars will be available at all hours. It will mean stretching our forces to their limit, and if we get a rush of other crimes we'll be in trouble, but this case has priority. We'll do our share—but our effort may well be wasted if you can't help substantially.'

When he stopped speaking, the silence seemed to come from a group of men utterly appalled.

'*Can* it be so bad?' asked the Abbey Dean, obviously shocked, but prepared to minimise the shock of others.

'I think so, sir.'

'You mean you think that if we institute this guard, these —ah—vandals will exert themselves to circumvent it?'

'Yes, sir.'

'It is quite easy to get round guards,' Cohen said, almost dejectedly. 'One man, one tiny object, little bigger than a matchstick—and a whole church can be destroyed, sacred objects ruined, the very sanctity of our beliefs violated. It can be done. The problem is constantly with us, and our congregations already form patrols. The Board of Directors of British Jews has the problem continually under review.'

He gave a grim smile. 'Ask any Hindu what can happen to his gods, and any Muslim what can happen to the Koran.'

'So you are accustomed to these attacks,' Northwick said uncomfortably. 'I hadn't realised it was so bad in the Synagogues.'

'Few people do, except the police,' said Cohen.

'The point is, can you all do what I ask?' Gideon said authoritatively.

'Not immediately, I fear,' answered the Bishop. 'It certainly cannot be done tonight. A start might be made, but no more. By tomorrow night we could have a greater number of churches protected.'

Gideon looked at Northwick. 'And you, sir?'

'The same applies, although perhaps on a slightly quicker scale. The Catholic Police Guild——'

'You won't get much help from them, sir,' Gideon interspersed bluntly. 'All the members will be on overtime or standing by for extra duty.'

Northwick said: 'Oh, of course. All the same, we can call

on the St. Vincent de Paul Brothers, or the Legion of Mary. Yes, you can rely on us.'

'I'm very glad. And you, Mr. Steel?'

'The big churches, yes,' answered the Free Churchman promptly. 'The smaller ones—membership and workers are so pathetically small, but—yes, we can make a start.' He rubbed his chin. 'The mechanics of the situation are difficult in themselves. How can we get messages——' He broke off, forcing a laugh, and went on: 'I am sorry. This has put me off my stroke. I will arrange for an Action Committee to start telephoning our clergy at once. That is'—he glanced sharply round at the others—'if we all agree that it is necessary.'

Northwick said: 'It seems we have no choice.'

'Yes, I suppose it is inevitable,' said the Abbey Dean reluctantly.

'The wording of our message—I wonder if we are underrating the difficulties,' Dean Howcroft murmured, the lines of his face falling into folds of age and barely tolerated resignation.

Gideon, deeply relieved, opened a small brief-case and took out some typewritten pages. He passed these round from hand to hand, so that everyone had a copy, and there were several left over.

'We had this memorandum prepared today, gentlemen. If you care to approve or amend it, we can have sufficient copies printed for one or two to go to every church secretary —or leader, or vicar, or priest,' he added hurriedly, conscious of the sensitivity of dogmatic toes. 'Anyone who has authority to act, that is. And we can distribute them to our divisional stations and sub-stations and have them delivered from there. Each Division knows the person to consult about each local church.'

The Bishop said with rare warmth: 'We are indeed indebted to you.'

Gideon felt almost triumphant, as the silence settled after the murmur of assent, and all fell to reading the memorandum he had prepared early that afternoon:

Wilful damage to churches and church property is being carried out with obvious malice by a number of persons. The Metropolitan Police have reason to believe that every place of worship in the London area may be in danger.

Small but highly dangerous charges of high explosive can easily be left in pews, fonts, carvings, candlesticks or holders, and elsewhere. They can be left behind by individuals in the guise of worshippers or tourists.

For the safety of your church, we strongly recommend that you institute an exhaustive search as soon as possible. The local police will assist you in this but the manpower necessary must be mainly from church members and officials.

It is strongly recommended that *all* doors are locked at dusk until this period of emergency is over. A night watch, on the lines of fire-watching during the Second World War, is also strongly recommended. Police officers will always be near at hand and police reinforcements will be readily available.

It is impossible to stress the importance of these precautions too strongly. Eleven churches have now suffered serious damage.

Signed:

The Dean of St. Paul's—*For the City of London.*
The Dean of the Abbey—*For the City of Westminster.*
Jonathan Northwick—*For the Cardinal Archbishop of Westminster.*
The Dean of St. Ludd's—*For Anglican Church in Greater London.*
William Steel—*For the Free Church Council.*
Daniel Cohen—*For the London United Synagogues.*

Within two hours of Gideon's return to the Yard, the notices were speeding on their way.

At the same time, church members and church workers

were homeward-bound from shops and offices, factories and warehouses, from the countless little businesses which make up commercial London. Office managers and typists, sales girls and models, directors and janitors, commissionaires and salesmen—all of these and many others, on reaching home, were called out by their church and asked to serve.

Almost without exception, they agreed; men and women, shocked and angry, ready to defend that which was of paramount importance to their way of life.

As darkness fell, half the churches of London were fully protected.

That night, not a single church was attacked.

CHAPTER 16

A PROBLEM IN FRAUD

LEMAITRE, looking much fresher after a full and undisturbed night's sleep, breezed into Gideon's office with a perfunctory tap, and spoke even before Gideon looked up. It was a perfect morning. The blue of the sky was clear and vivid and the shimmering of the sun's reflection on the river touched the windows of the office and played like a shadow dancing on the glass of a photograph of the cricket XI of the Metropolitan Police taken twenty years before.

'Good morning, George! We've stopped the baskets.'

Gideon went on writing, merely grunting:

'What's that?'

'I said we've stopped the baskets.' Lemaitre, conscious of an implied rebuff, hovered in front of the desk. He was so smooth shaven that his skin was shining, his hair so pomaded that it looked like the painted head of a Dutch doll.

Gideon, studying the latest reports on the Photo-Nudes Murder Case and glum because Sally Dalby had not been found, felt a flash of exasperation which was not far from annoyance at Lemaitre's facile optimism, but checked the expression of it as he looked up.

'Or they stopped themselves.'

'Doesn't make much difference, so long as they've stopped,' said Lemaitre, and then went on earnestly: 'I didn't mean we'd finished altogether, George, even I'm not such a silly beggar as to think that. I mean we stopped 'em for last night, and that's given us a breathing space.' He paused, obviously hoping that his words carried conviction.

Gideon had a peculiar flash of thought: that for all these years he might have been taking Lemaitre's over-optimism too seriously. The flash died away in the realisation that in fact Lemaitre was at last trying to correct this deeply implanted habit.

'Yes, and we can use the breathing space,' Gideon said. 'What we need to know is how many churches are properly guarded.'

'I've got a system,' Lemaitre declared.

Gideon suppressed a snort of amusement; it was too frivolous for the occasion.

'I can't get out to all the Divisions,' Lemaitre continued importantly. 'I'd need to cut myself in pieces to see the lot. But they can come *here*. So if you'll call all the Divisional Supers in for two-thirty, say, I could brief 'em. *They* can check how the churches are being protected, what kind of response the memo's had, and they can tell me—us I mean —of any weak spots. We can then get to work on the bloody Bishops.'

Gideon found himself laughing.

'Call the Divisional Superintendents in if you wish,' he said, glancing at his watch. 'It's only nine-fifteen. No reason why they shouldn't be here by half-past eleven. Send out a teletype request, sign it for me. Use the main lecture room. Let 'em know what it's about so that they will bring all the information we need.'

Lemaitre's eyes were glowing.

'Right away, George!' He strode out, let the door slam,

opened it again and said: 'Sorry!' breezily, and went out with hardly a sound.

Gideon sat thinking for a few moments, and formed one obvious conclusion. Lemaitre's very heart was in this job; he saw it as a way to justify himself completely in his own eyes because he had been passed over for Hobbs. His enthusiasm and his eagerness were infectious, but if he should fail he would find it a bitter, and, in its way, a killing blow.

Was he, Gideon, exaggerating?

He pushed the thought aside, and rang for the Chief-Inspector who was standing in for Lemaitre.

'Who's waiting to see me?'

'Mr. Rollo, sir, Mr. Golightly and Mr. Simmons.'

'I'll see Mr. Simmons first, then the others together.'

'Right, sir!'

'Is Mr. Hobbs in?'

'No, sir. There was a message. I didn't take it myself, but I heard about it. His wife's very ill, sir.'

'Oh. Yes.' Gideon nodded, and added: 'Ask Mr. Simmons to come in five minutes.' He picked up the outside telephone. 'Get my wife for me, please.' He rang off, and almost immediately the internal telephone rang, and he plucked up the receiver. 'Gideon.'

'Commander,' said Scott-Marle, abruptly, 'I have the Governor of the Bank of England in my office.'

Gideon thought quickly: 'Should I know what this is about?' He could recall nothing.

The Commissioner went on: 'He has some reason for anxiety about gold losses—very serious gold losses—in shipments between here and South Africa and Australia, as well as international shipments between several countries.'

This was absolutely new to Gideon and thought of it made everything else fade from his mind—even the attacks on the churches. Such losses must be on a big scale if the Governor of the Bank of England was at the Yard in person.

'How long has he known about this?' Gideon asked.

'A day or two. It has to be kept quiet for the time being, but there will have to be a conference of senior police officers and senior customs officers of the countries concerned. I would like you and the Commander of the Special Branch to attend the conference which will be held in Paris on Tuesday and Wednesday next. I know you are deeply involved in current affairs, but this is unavoidable.'

Gideon said: 'I can see that, sir.'

'Officially the conference will be on drugs,' the Commissioner went on. 'In fact, the only subject will be the gold bullion problem. Will you arrange to go and see the Governor some time today or tomorrow and discuss it with him?'

'Certainly,' promised Gideon. 'Do you say he's with you now?'

'Yes.'

'Would this afternoon be convenient for him?'

There was a murmur in the background before Scott-Marle spoke again.

'Half-past three, at the Athenæum Club. He will be in the Library.'

'I'll be there,' said Gideon.

As he rang off, the door opened and Chief-Superintendent Simmons came in. Simmons looked a little like a lecherous Punch, and the fact that he was the cleanest-living man imaginable did not lessen that impression. Behind a jocund leeriness, however, lay one of the keenest minds at the Yard. He was a mathematician and an accountant, and no one in England knew more about company law. For over five weeks now, he had been investigating the activities of a company which controlled dozens of subsidiary companies, among all of which there was reason to suspect enormous tax evasion; there was also reason to suspect a major case of share-pushing.

'Sit down,' Gideon said.

'Thanks.' Simmons looked at Gideon searchingly, and then said in a rather grating voice: 'Heard any good sermons lately?'

Gideon chuckled.

'Any ideas about that job?'

'Haven't given it a thought,' said Simmons. 'Hope the beggars don't have a go at St. Paul's or the Abbey, that's all.' He paused.

'So do I. What have you got?'

'Trouble and worry,' answered Simmons. 'I'm not sure there's a case for the Public Prosecutor—certainly there isn't yet, and finding out for sure whether it's a civil or a criminal case will take another four weeks of solid going.'

'Think it's worth four weeks?'

'It is to me. It is to Inland Revenue—their Investigation Branch really thinks it's on to outsize evasion. It's border-line, mind you—very clever accountants on the other side, but there may be a share-pushing angle as well as tax evasion. The thing is——' He paused.

'What other job have I got for you?' suggested Gideon.

'That, and—should we leave it to the Inland Revenue and only come in if they can hand us share-pushing on a plate?'

'How long will the Inland Revenue chaps take?'

'Another year, at the present rate of progress. They'd like us to keep on too, of course.'

'I daresay they would,' remarked Gideon drily. 'That way they would get half their work done for them.' He watched the faint reflection from river and window play on the back of his hand, then looked straight at Simmons. 'If the parent company promotes any more smaller companies, it could fleece a lot of people in a year, couldn't it?'

'It certainly could.' Simmons's corrugated forehead looked almost smooth for a moment. 'Do we want to risk it?'

'No. Keep at it. If it looks like keeping you busy for more than a month, let me know. Have you got all the help you need?'

'Yes, thanks.'

'That's something,' said Gideon.

When the door had closed on Simmons, he opened the Fraud Case file, made a note, pondered for a few moments, then closed it. He brought out an empty manilla folder, and made some pencilled notes on the inside of the cover. They ran:

B. of E. Bullion.

What countries besides G.B., S.A. and Aust'a?

Athenæum, 3.30, today.

Check flights to Paris after seeing Gov. He may have something planned.

He closed the folder, knowing that there was a real possibility of a major investigation over the gold, wishing he knew more about it and also wishing that it hadn't come at this juncture. There could be ugly developments at the churches by Monday or Tuesday, and he would have preferred to stay in England. Hobbs would have to take over, and he wasn't too keen on Hobbs and Lemaitre working together on this particular investigation—Lemaitre might be far too sensitive. Then he thought: Dammit, I asked for Kate. He lifted the outside telephone as the door opened to admit Rollo and Golightly. He waved to chairs as he said: 'What happened to that call to my wife? ... Yes, keep trying.' He rang off, and looked into the faces of these two officers who were so different and yet could work together as an excellent team. Rollo looked as vigorous and healthy as ever, ten years younger than his age; Golightly had an air which suggested that butter wouldn't melt in his mouth.

Neither looked particularly pleased, yet Rollo never found it easy to hide elation.

'Who's going to start?' asked Gideon.

'There isn't another clue in the Rhodes murder,' Rollo announced. 'We haven't found the motor-cycle, haven't discovered where Rhodes holed up, haven't found any of his associates. He did this job at the chemist's, and was competent enough. The cellar was a spare-time and evening occupation. Percy did spot one thing which I missed.'

Gideon turned his gaze on Golightly.

'The photographs on the wall of Rhodes's cellar were all printed off the same kind of negative,' he said, 'and printed on the same kind of paper and in the same type of solution. We're checking photographic suppliers.'

'Couldn't Rhodes have obtained the stuff?'

'The paper he used in the printing at the chemists is a poorer quality than that of the cellar photographs,' Golightly stated. 'The cellar ones are all printed on Kodak *Bromesko*, a white, smooth, glossy paper, and all developed

123

by a good high-definition developer from a fine-grain film. I'd say a very good camera was used, German or Japanese. All of the prints were obviously handled by someone wearing rubber gloves—quite common in the developing process —and there are no prints except Rhodes's.'

Gideon said: 'And the Dalby girl?'

'Vanished without a trace.'

'This Italian or Spaniard whom the girl at the Super-market talked about?'

'No line on him yet.'

Gideon glanced down again at the flickering on the back of his hand.

'Has the time come to try to get in touch with all girls who pose for photographers and see if they know about this man?'

'That's the rub,' said Rollo.

'No need to be obscure,' rebuked Gideon.

'Sorry. These aren't regular models. I've been to twenty photographers who specialise in nudes and none of them admits to recognising any of the girls. I've tried every art and model agency in London, too. Rhodes and this good-looking Toni used amateurs—and so far we haven't found any of the girls he used.'

Gideon said: 'Dammit. How many have been reported missing and still haven't turned up? Thirty?'

'Thirty-two.'

'And we can't even find one of those?'

'We've found the three dead ones,' Rollo reminded him. 'Rhodes had their photographs all right.'

There was a moment of absolute silence, so acute, so profound and searching that it was almost as if all three men had stopped breathing at the same moment; after a few seconds, all of them began to breathe again, a little stiffly, and with an effort.

Gideon said: 'Are you seriously telling me you think *all* the other girls have been murdered?'

Rollo shifted in his chair, and began to speak at the same moment as Golightly.

'I know it sounds crazy——'

'It may seem ludicrous——'

They both came to an abrupt halt.

'When did you start thinking like this?' demanded Gideon.

'Idea struck me last night,' said Rollo. 'Percy and I had a talk on the telephone.'

'It hit me like a sledgehammer,' Golightly put in.

'It's hit me like a piledriver,' said Gideon gruffly. 'Get all thirty-odd photographs out to all the Press, television, anyone who can use them. If these girls aren't in England it seems to me they're more likely to have been shipped abroad than to have been murdered. Whichever way it is, it's very bad. We want news of any of them—and we want it urgently.'

Both men were already getting up from their chairs, and in a few moments they had gone, leaving Gideon in a mood not far removed from tension and alarm.

Thirty-two girls——

He muttered to himself: 'What a morning!' and glanced at the reports. The church problem, the gold problem, the photo-nudes problem. A new thought came, relaxing him for the first time since the shock of the silence when he had realised the full significance of what the Superintendents had implied. Religion—money—sex; the three motives which controlled most human behaviour now demanded the attention of the Yard more than they had ever done before.

Gideon felt a heavy burden of responsibility far beyond one man's due.

If he failed in any one of these investigations, how deep would the effect of such failure be?

CHAPTER 17

BRIEFING

THE lecture room at the Yard was neither large nor impressive. It was pleasant to know that when the new building down the river was ready there would be at least two lecture halls for instruction and for briefing. Meanwhile they must make do with what they had, and that morning, just after half-past eleven, the largest available room was crowded to overflowing with Divisional Superintendents, Seconds-in-Command, the Commander of each of the districts into which the Force was divided, the Commander of the Uniformed Branch and a few other key officers. As Gideon stepped inside the room which was already thick with smoke, there was a pause in the hum of conversation. Lemaitre, at a table which stood on a small dais, waved to him.

'Be a bit of a mess if someone blew up this lot, wouldn't it?' He grinned, obviously delighted with himself. 'Going to take the chair, George?'

'I can't stay long,' Gideon told him.

'Pity,' said Lemaitre, trying hard to disguise his pleasure. 'I asked Hobbs. He hasn't come in at all yet.'

Gideon said: 'I know. Are you ready?'

'Yes—I've the plan of campaign.'

'Right.' Gideon went to the front of the dais, his right hand raised. Silence fell immediately. It was a long time since he had seen so many senior officials together, and by the nature of things, most of those present were in his own age group—the middle-forties to the middle-fifties. There were at least a dozen with whom he had walked the beat, when superintendency had been a far-off dream. He had a warmth of affection for most of them, and knew that it was returned; but he wondered how many, if any, would have the faintest idea what he was talking about if he attempted to describe to them the overwhelming feeling of responsibility which lay so heavily on him.

They fell silent. Usually he would have been ready with a joke, but this wasn't the morning for any kind of light-heartedness.

'Glad you could all make it,' he said in a carrying voice. 'But I'm sorry it was necessary. Our biggest worry, as you must have realised, is the church outrages. There *is* a danger that we might think, because we had a quiet time last night, we're over the worst. I don't believe it for a moment. Whether we like it or not we've got to gear ourselves for a continuing effort until we find out who's behind it. Lemaitre will tell you how we think it can best be done. I want to tell you that it's just about the gravest problem I've ever had to deal with at the Yard.'

'*And that's saying something,*' Lemaitre interpolated in a loud aside.

'There's another case in which I need your help,' Gideon went on, 'but before I mention what it is—do any of you have any ideas about the motivation of the church crimes?'

For a moment no one spoke, then a man with a north-country voice suggested from the back of the room:

'Religious persecution, maybe.'

'Intolerance, I was going to say,' put in a Welshman.

'Plain bloody hate,' a Cockney piped up.

'Insanity,' suggested another.

'There are probably quite a number of these vandals,' Gideon remarked. 'Madmen don't normally get together and plan a campaign like this. Let's cut out insanity.'

'Fanatical hatred of the Church,' the Welshman suggested.

Two or three others began to speak at the same time, but stopped when Gideon raised his voice:

'All right, so no one has any ideas we haven't tossed around ourselves. When Lemaitre's briefed you, it would be a good idea to have a discussion, something might come out of it. There is one important point to consider, for instance, and that is that instructions for the last crop of outrages must, in all probability, have been sent out the day before the incidents. How? At a meeting like this? By telephone? By letter? By personal messenger? But I needn't elaborate.'

Gideon paused, until he was sure they all realised he had finished with the church crimes, and then went on: 'Now about another matter. We're gravely worried over the Photo-Nudes.' Only two or three men grinned, a clear indication that most of these took the Photo-Nude Murders very seriously. 'Golightly and Rollo will see you all get a set of thirty-two photographs. We want any line at all on any one of them. If you get even a whisper of information, send it through to us at once.'

There was a murmur of understanding, and several men echoed: '*Thirty-two.*'

'Over to you, Lem,' Gideon said.

On this kind of assignment, Lemaitre was good; anything which assured him of the limelight and fed his ego, also assured his effectiveness. Gideon left him with feet planted firmly, head and shoulders thrust slightly forward in a form of restrained aggressiveness. As he entered his own office the outside telephone bell rang.

'Yes.'

'Mrs. Gideon, sir.'

At last!

'Put her through ... Hello, Kate, I've been trying to get you,' Gideon infused a little lightheartedness into his voice, which was always easy for him to do with Kate. 'Been buying up London?'

'George,' Kate said, 'did you know Helen Hobbs was in a very bad way?'

Gideon caught his breath.

'No. But I had an idea she was not too good. In fact, that's what I was ringing about—to ask you to go and see her.'

'She isn't likely to last the day,' Kate said quietly.

Again Gideon caught his breath, and this time it hurt. Kate would not say such a thing unless she were sure.

'I've just been there,' Kate told him. 'Alec was with her.'

'Oh,' said Gideon. 'He—I hope he doesn't feel he must come into the office.'

'He does. He wants to.'

'He mustn't. He——'

'George,' interrupted Kate, 'he can't do any good. She's in

128

a coma, and the doctors say there's no chance that she will come out of it. That's what I wanted to ask you. Is there something he can really concentrate on?'

The church outrages—the gold—the Photo-Nudes.

'Dozens,' Gideon said.

'He mustn't have time to think.'

'I know.'

'George,' Kate said with a sob in her voice, 'she still looks so beautiful.'

Alec Hobbs stood with his back to the window, studying his wife's face. In the coma she looked peaceful, as if she were indeed asleep. Although the illness had wasted her body, it had never touched her face; thin she was, but not gaunt. She still had some colour, and her beautiful black hair shone with its early lustre. She did not appear to be breathing. When she had first been seized with the respiratory onslaught she had been in pain, but there was no pain now. Then, in between spasms, she had liked to be able to look out of the window which overlooked the river which she loved. Now her bed was raised at the head, so that a reflection like the one which played about Gideon's face and hands, only a mile along the river, played on the eyes which were closed for ever.

Hobbs had stood there for a long time.

Slowly, he moved, and turned his back on his wife, looking out on to the river's sparkling bosom, seeing tugs and barges and some pleasure craft, trivial against the might of the Battersea Power Station. He had come home and found her sitting here so often, so patiently, and love for her and grief for her had had to be lightened to a gentle gaiety. Now all that was over.

He turned away, unable to face the ebbing of her life.

In the next room, a middle-aged nurse put down a magazine.

'I'm going to the Yard,' Hobbs said. 'You can get in touch with me there.'

'Certainly, sir.'

He nodded, and went out, turned left along Chelsea

Reach and walked stoically, agony held off a handsbreadth away, towards Westminster and Scotland Yard. Passing a new church close to the Embankment, which served a host of flats and houses built on the sites of others destroyed by bombing two or more decades ago, he thought of the outrages; then he noticed a uniformed constable. He paused.

'Keeping an eye open?' he asked.

'Yes, sir.' The man drew himself up almost to attention. 'We're being *very* careful here, sir. There's a lot of gold in some of the altar plate and the candlesticks and chalices—very valuable, as well as sacred.' The officer was an earnest man of middle age.

'What's the co-operation like?'

'Excellent, sir. Couldn't be better. There are at least four church members on duty there day *and* night. Not much chance of trouble here, I'm glad to say.'

'Good,' Hobbs said. 'Keep your eyes open.'

He walked on.

A spasm of pain shot through him. Keep your eyes open, open, open, open—but Helen's eyes were closed. Eyes open, keep them open—my God, wouldn't he like to catch the devils who were doing this. If only Lemaitre had some other job . . .

The leader of the 'devils' who was organising the outrages on the churches sat at his desk, brooding over the great tower of the cathedral. In front of him were the daily papers with their varying stories about what was being done to save the churches. Each gave it the main front page headline as well as a continuation inside; and each newspaper had a leading article.

The *Daily View* said:

It is quite incomprehensible that any man or woman, or group of men or women, should set out to commit not only crime but sacrilege. We do not believe that any crime committed in London—in fact, in the whole of the British Commonwealth—has shocked the public so deeply. Nor do we believe that the conscience of the

British people has ever been stirred so much as it has been by this abominable campaign of destruction.

It is conceivable, we believe, that good can come out of even so great an evil as this. The people *are* stirred—and perhaps this will awaken them to an awareness of their own shortcomings. Never has church membership been at so low an ebb. If these crimes should give birth to a great revival in religion, who can deny that good will once again triumph over evil?

Already, there are signs that this may be happening. Hosts of ordinary people, our fellow men, are forming their own vigilance committees to guard their churches, the places where they worship. Such spontaneous action is admirable. The only danger is that in their determination to stop the outrages, the authorities might overlook the first essential—which is to find the evil men who are committing these crimes against God and Man.

The more popular *Globe* said:

The public is shocked, and the public conscience is shocked. These are good things. So is the immediate re-action of the police and the official bodies of the Church, in preparing and carrying out a plan of defence. Time may have been lost in the past; none is being lost now.

No outrage was committed last night, but this must not persuade anyone concerned to relax vigilance for a single moment. Until the perpetrators of the outrages are caught, no church can be safe.

And when we say this we are fully aware that we can envisage danger to our great historic churches and cathedrals, part of the British as well as the Christian heritage. Imagine the cry of horror that would rise if the ancient Coronation Chair were damaged at Westminster Abbey; or the portions of the Bayeux Tapestry were burned. The bones of Edward the Confessor, the Abbey's founder, would lie uneasily indeed.

Or imagine the fine mosaic decorations of the ceilings of the Choir at St. Paul's being ruined; or the noise which would reverberate round the world if there were an explosion in the whispering gallery in St. Christopher Wren's noble edifice.

The danger to these, and to every sacred building in the nation, will remain until the criminals are caught.

The organiser of those criminals read through these and other leading articles until he had as clear a picture as a man could have of the defences and forces ranged against him. He showed no triumph, no egotistical delight at being the root and cause of a nation-wide attention. Indeed, there were minutes when his face seemed so still that it was hard to see whether he was breathing.

Presently he put all the papers aside and placed his elbows on the desk, the tips of his fingers together in an attitude almost of prayer. No one could deny that he had the face of an ascetic, even if the expression was touched with a chilling arrogance. No warmth, no troubled doubt emanated from him, and in this statuesque pose he stayed for some time. When eventually he broke it, it was with a sharp intake of breath, which heralded a change in his manner. He became alert and quick-moving. Animation returned to his face, expression to his eyes. He lifted a telephone, dialled, and when he was answered, said crisply:

'I wish to see the Committee of Three in half-an-hour.'

A man said with the quietness of humility:

'We shall be here, sir.'

CHAPTER 18

THE COMMITTEE OF THREE

THE man who had telephoned the curt message was Hector Marriott, who described himself as a Professor of Languages, and as such had once given private tuition. That was some time ago, before he had inherited his father's money. He was in fact a millionaire, although few were aware of it; so many of his stocks were managed by trusts, so many of his proper ties were owned under different names. He had for many years managed his affairs skilfully and successfully, making more and more money, although its amassing appeared to give him little pleasure.

He was an ascetic.

He was also a man with a mission.

And he was a man who had visions.

A great many men have visions; only those who believe them to be inspired are likely to be dangerous. Marriott was absolutely convinced of the inspiration, and that no vision would ever direct him along the wrong path.

For many years he had worshipped in an ordinary Anglican church, a member but not active in his membership, nor one of whom much notice was taken; Mr. Marriott, it was said, preferred to keep himself to himself. He did not resent this, but it did nothing to endear him to his fellow members.

During the war, the church received a direct hit and was utterly destroyed. The parishioners, such as were left at home, built a wooden shack by their own endeavours, made a wooden altar, fashioned a wooden cross and worshipped there. The simplicity of the place of worship and the friendliness of the people did a thing which was unique in Marriott's experience. Together, they warmed him. He actually began to like people, and to stop thinking that all they wanted was his money. He had never known happiness in the true sense of the word—he had never been in love, although he had had the normal, occasional relationships of the average man—but during the wooden hut period he had been nearer to happiness and contentment than ever before. After a while, however, some of the other church members had become restless, wanting something more materially worthy in which to worship, and a rebuilding fund had been launched.

Marriott had subscribed cautiously; had even agreed to serve on the Rebuilding Fund Committee.

Before long, arguments had started, the target crept higher, more and more expense was incurred on gold, on silver, on rich embroideries, on rare woods. Gradually, the fund drove away all thought of worship. There were quarrels. There were jealousies. There were refusals to give to deserving charities. There was even quarrelling about ritual.

Hector Marriott resigned, simply, and without verbal protest.

The time came when the new church was built and the first service was held, and in spite of his doubts, Marriott had attended. That was the day when, in a church notice, these words, under the name of the vicar, appeared:

> I have good news for all of us, especially for those who have laboured so long in preparation for this beautiful new House of God. The site on which our old church stood and where our hut now stands, has been sold to very great advantage. We shall now be able to adorn the altar and the pulpit, the choir stalls and the windows, in a way which is worthy of their high purpose.

Hector Marriott, unaware that he was already mad, left the church determined never to set foot in it or in any other so-called place of worship again. Next day, passing the end of the street, he saw a cloud of dust or smoke, and went to see what it was. The little hut which he had so loved, not knowing that it was love, was a smoke-filled ruin, the sides split, the roof off, the door torn from its hinges. The demolition contractors on the site simply stated:

'It wasn't worth saving—we had to blow it up.'

Hatred had overflown in Hector Marriott's heart.

Still not knowing—to his last day not knowing—that he was insane, he had gone home and sunk to his knees, calling upon God to strike down the destroyers. And that night, in his dreams, he had had a vision: that the new church itself should be destroyed in the pride of its idolatry. At first he had believed that the church would destroy itself, and his dream would be fulfilled in that way, but he had other dreams—that he himself should be the instrument of such destruction.

He began to daydream.

He was an ascetic, and he hated war, and he did not know

the love of a woman or love for a woman, and he was a psychopath, and he had millions of pounds to do what he liked with, but the only desire he felt was to desecrate and eventually destroy what others, in the name of worship, had built up.

How?

He waited for a 'vision' and one came: in a dream, he saw himself and other men standing amid the smoke-rimmed debris of a church. So, he must not do this alone. He did not feel any sense of urgency, simply one of purpose, and so he studied books and records of other religious rebels, especially those who had rebelled against the pomp and ceremony of the Church, from Luther to Billy Graham, across the centuries and across the world. A study of strange and out-of-the-way religions began to fascinate him and he went to services of little-known sects, even crossing the Atlantic in his search for information that would nourish his vision.

There he found the sex sects, the worshippers of Baal and of Osiris. He found the Doukhobors who wrestled—as he wrestled—with the spirit, so as to purify its doctrines, and who flagellated themselves and each other in their lust for purification. He felt drawn towards the Shakers in their belief in a celibacy which would destroy themselves, the Amanas who had the same horror of sex. He was revolted by the cult of voodoo, half-Christian, half-Black Magic, with its awful rituals and terrifying superstitions. He visited the hills of Tennessee where the snake-worshippers prayed in the name of Christ; he traversed the high mountains of Utah into the hinterland where some still practised polygamy, convinced it was the will of God because the Prophet, George Smith, had seen a vision—as he, Hector Marriott, had seen visions.

But *his* were true.

In the course of these travels and the meetings he met other men who had the same ascetic tendencies as himself, and the same resentment against the wealth of the Churches, the finery, the jewellery, the *objéts d'art*. In time he found himself their leader, for he possessed those two

135

great things which move mountains: wealth and faith in his destiny.

Their sect evolved slowly. A chance phrase which Marriott himself used, led to their adoption of the name: *The Simple Brethren*. The main differences between them and other Christian sects was the fact that they were a secret society and that they were all pledged to desecrate and destroy idolatry, pomp and show, and all but the simplest of altars and buildings. In the beginning, the word 'destroy' was not used literally, although in Marriott's mind there was always a vision of the ultimate destruction he and others were to bring about one day, and for that day he felt an inexorable lust and yearning; but there was no hurry, no sense of urgency; the time must be ripe, and the perpetrators prepared.

The membership of *The Simple Brethren* was strictly controlled. Before one could become an associate, papers of extreme erudition in matters of idolatry and rare and strange religions had to be read and approved. Cromwell became a hero, almost a godhead. All Christian sects which worshipped with an absolute minimum of ritual won approval, but none of this was enough. Marriott and his closer associates began to practise more and more rigorous forms of asceticism and self-denial. They had fast days, and days of silence, days of flagellation, days of penitence. More and more was demanded of them. They eschewed the pleasures of life almost entirely, even the pleasures of eating and drinking. They denied themselves all forms of sexual indulgence. They eschewed theatres, cinemas; all games, all activities but those of earning their daily living, and of worshipping.

Those who were married left their wives and families, though not without support; for Hector Marriott supplied each family's needs, except that of the husband and the father.

Those who had been engaged to marry broke their engagements.

There was no love but their love for one another and, they said and believed, the love of God.

Gradually, the weaker Brethren dropped out of the circle, only those who could withstand the rigour of such self-discipline and such abnegation before the Lord and before themselves stayed. Over the years, there were nearly five hundred who quit for one reason or another, but a hundred and two remained. Now and again a new Brother was admitted to the sect and there were times when some, deeply awed by Marriott, saw him as the Father of the movement.

To designate him Father Marriott was too reminiscent of the Roman Catholic Church, so they called him Elder Brother.

These were strange men, each clever and competent in his way, each with his own particular gifts, each with the deep conviction that the worship of God should be in the simplest form and in the barest of houses, that the heirlooms of the Churches were gifts from the Devil, and that all outward signs of wealth, all insignia, all holy objects which were bejewelled, or of gold, should be destroyed. They saw the Church as an enemy of God, and they believed that the enemies of God should be utterly annihilated.

Slowly, painfully, Marriott the Elder Brother trained these men, converting them to his own beliefs, his own visions, almost to believe in his own divinity. They did not worship him but they worshipped through him, and so they worshipped through his madness, becoming one with it.

He had taken to himself three advisers; these were the Committee of Three. But it was Marriott who made the decisions; and he had timed the explosions to coincide with the tenth anniversary of the destruction of the little wooden shed. And it was he who had decided that on each night of action the number of churches attacked would double those of the previous attack. It was a purely arbitrary decision, and inherent in it was the realisation that, once launched, the campaign of destruction must quickly reach crescendo, to ensure the maximum amount of damage being done before successful methods were put in train to stop them.

The Committee of Three met in an office in Victoria Street, only five minutes' walk from Marriott's flat. On the hall staircase there was a painted notice: *The Brothers' Bible Society—Third Floor*. Marriott owned the building, letting it off in offices. He himself occupied three rooms in all, in which he ran a Bible and tract distributing business, with a genuine trade. The Committee met, as always, in a room at the back, quietly, and unobserved.

When Marriott arrived, the others were waiting, standing by their places at a round table. One, Joliffe, was tall, lean, melancholy. The second, Abbotsbury, was of medium height, thin, sad-looking. The third, Dennison, was sturdier and actually had a little colour in his cheeks.

Each was dressed in clerical grey.

Each stood silent until at last the Elder Brother said: 'Amen.'

All of them sat down.

'You will have seen the effect of what we have done already,' said the Elder Brother. 'It has been highly successful, the hand of God aiding our endeavours. It will not be so easy in future, however, and so our preparations must be well considered. Do we all agree?'

There were three murmurs of assent, sounding as one.

'These houses of idolatry are being closely guarded and as closely searched but we shall be blessed if we overcome our difficulties and cursed if we fail to rise to the opportunities. As you well know, we contemplated the possibility that the police would aid the Churches and so we made our plans. Are we all aware of those plans?'

Again a single murmur of unified assent hummed through the room.

'As we are aware, yesterday I sent to sixteen of our Brethren the directive; each knows which house is to be visited next. None must fail.'

Assent greeted him.

'If one is apprehended by the police it is possible that he will betray, wittingly or unwittingly, the existence and the dedicated purpose of *The Simple Brethren*.. Since no one knows where I live, and since this office is unknown except to us, we have nothing to fear.'

'Nothing to fear.'

'Nothing to fear.'

'Nothing to fear.'

'Nevertheless, we will not come here and we will not meet again until I summon you. I will send the directives out as they become necessary. If our efforts are blessed, none of the Brethren will be detected and we shall strike again the night after tomorrow. If, on the other hand, the forces of evil should assert themselves and we cannot foregather, each of us knows the final task.'

'I know.'

'I know.'

'I know.'

'Each of us has sworn to accomplish that task, at the risk of his life.'

'Each of us has.'

'Each of us has.'

'Each of us has.'

'I will ask each of you to remind himself of his obligation, and to repeat it, under solemn oath. Brother Joliffe.'

The tall, lean man said in a frail but steady voice:

'I hereby swear by solemn oath of allegiance to *The Simple Brethren* and to God that at risk to myself, even unto death, I will destroy the house of idolatry known in this land as the Cathedral of Westminster.'

'*Ah-men.*'

'Brother Abbotsbury.'

'I hereby swear by solemn oath of allegiance to *The Simple Brethren* and to God that at risk to myself, even unto death, I will destroy the house of idolatry known in this land as the Synagogue of London.'

'*Ah-men.*'

'Brother Dennison.'

In a firm, clear voice, the third member of the Committee declared:

'I hereby swear by solemn oath of allegiance to *The Simple Brethren* and to God that at risk to myself, even unto death, I will destroy the house of idolatry known in this land as the Abbey of Westminster.'

'*Ah-men.*'

There was a pause, which became prolonged. Tension crept stealthily round the room, to be broken by the voice of the Elder Brother, speaking with the slow and frightening clarity of the utterly possessed:

'I hereby swear in solemn oath of allegiance to *The Simple Brethren* and to God that at risk to myself even unto death I will destroy the house of idolatry known in this land as St. Paul's Cathedral.'

'*Ah-men.*'

'*Ah-men.*'

'*Ah-men.*'

CHAPTER 19

HOBBS *v.* LEMAITRE

'EVERYONE thought the same,' said Lemaitre to Gideon. 'They all think we're dealing with a lot of cranks and crackpots. Ordinary methods won't do any good, we've got to out-think a bunch of weirdies. What a hope!'

In a quiet voice, Alec Hobbs asked: 'You don't view our chances very favourably, then?'

'I view our chances of stopping most of the baskets very favourably indeed, but not those of finding out who they are,' Lemaitre said. He was still a little awkward in Hobbs's company, and rather dogmatic. He did not know about Hobbs's wife, but he could see the glassy-eyed look and the evidence of strain in the other's manner, and wondered what it was all about. When Hobbs gave no answer, Lemaitre took silence for implied criticism, and went on almost stridently: 'If they have another go tonight at several churches we ought to catch one or two of them, and *if* we can make them talk, then Bob's your uncle.'

'Don't you think we can make them talk?' asked Hobbs.

Again Lemaitre took this to imply criticism: *you* can't, I can, but not in so many words. He became wary, even more conscious of his position. He was still Hobb's equal in rank, but the official promotion to Deputy Commander was due in a matter of days; from then on Hobbs's superiority would be established. Lemaitre thought, if this so-and-so expects me to call him 'sir', he's got another think coming.

'I've been at this game a long time,' Lemaitre said, picking his words very carefully. 'The most difficult ones are the fanatics, the I'll-die-for-a-cause type. If we're dealing with that type, none of us will make 'em talk. Not even the gestapo could make 'em. You'll see.'

'Probably,' Hobbs conceded.

They were in his office across the passage from Lemaitre's and Gideon's, with a view of the courtyard, the parked cars, and a corner of Cannon Row police station. It was a small, carpeted office, with a photograph of Hobbs's wife on top of a bookcase, and a clock over the mantelpiece. There were no pictures although the C.I.D. chart showing the 'family tree' of the Department from the Commissioner and Assistant Commissioner down, was centred on one wall. There was more than a touch of austerity, and nothing about the room, excepting the one photograph, was homely or personal.

Lemaitre drew a deep breath.

'You got any ideas?' he demanded.

'Not at the moment,' Hobbs said. 'If anything occurs to me, I'll have a word with you.'

'Do that.' Lemaitre put a hand on the door. 'I'll be out most of the afternoon. Going over to West Central, then up into the City. Gee-Gee's worried about the Abbey and St. Paul's.' He opened the door. 'See you,' he said, and stepped out.

He stood in the wide corridor for several seconds, watched curiously by a constable on duty in the hall and noticed by several inspectors and detective sergeants who passed. At last, he went across to his own office and sat down. On his desk was a note: *Look in, Lem—G.* For once, Lemaitre did not jump to a virtual command but stood at the window, glooming. He was becoming more and more worried about the undertone of criticism, or disapproval that he sensed in Hobbs.

'Be a bloody sight better if he'd come straight out with it and say he thinks I'm a clot,' he muttered.

There was more to his mood than that. He knew that he was doing everything within his capacity on the church job, but he was beginning to feel out of his depths. He had a sense of impending crisis, a presentiment of danger. When he said that you could not make fanatics talk, he knew what he was talking about, and the alarming growth of the sacrilege, the extremes to which its perpetrators were prepared to go, had all the indications of the worst kind of fanaticism. On the crest of a wave of optimism and achievement that morning, now that the Divisional Superintendents had dispersed and he was on his own, Lemaitre felt thoroughly depressed.

Hobbs hadn't helped.

Hobbs never would. The fear of what would happen once he was a superior officer was deep in Lemaitre's mind.

'Better retire early, I suppose,' he muttered.

There was a tap at the door. He spun round, as Golightly looked in.

'Where's Gee-Gee, Lem?'

'Isn't he in his office?'

'No. I want a word before I finally pull Entwhistle in.'

'Well, I don't know where the great man is.'

'Hobbs says go ahead without Gee-Gee. What do you think?'

Lemaitre muttered: 'Won't do any harm. If you ask me, Entwhistle ought to have been charged a couple of days ago. Any special hurry?'

'We had a tip-off that he's planning to leave the country.'

'Go get him then,' said Lemaitre.

Golightly, obviously satisfied, went out. Lemaitre tapped perfunctorily on Gideon's communicating door and looked in; the office was empty. He fingered the *Look in* note, said *sotto voce*, 'It couldn't have been very serious,' wrote across the note: *Back six-ish* in his fine copperplate hand, and went out.

Soon, he was talking to church officials at St. Paul's and the Superintendent-in-Charge from the City Police, checking the security plans. North and west doors, all the chapels, all the altars, the pulpit, the font, the Whispering Gallery and the crypt where so many had worshipped, were under constant supervision and his spirits rose. He left in better heart, reached Westminster Abbey, where he found the Superintendent from the Westminster Division. They made a slow, comprehensive tour, mingling unnoticed with parties of sight-seers and their guides. Starting at the north entrance, they moved along the Statesmen's Aisle, across to the south transept, passing the High Altar, with its magnificent mosaic of the Last Supper, and the great carved stone screen. Wherever there was a thing of beauty or of antiquity, there were people, English and American, German and Japanese, travellers from all over the world, their guide-books open, their cameras swinging. Past the poppy-framed tomb of the Unknown Warrior, past the memorial to Winston Churchill, beneath the great west window with its warrior figures, Lemaitre and his little party trod their vigilant way.

The farther they went, the more troubled Lemaitre became.

'It's going to be a heck of a job,' he remarked.

'We understand that, Superintendent,' said the gentle-voiced official with him, 'but *every* spot is watched. We have a constant patrol going over the exact route we have taken, day and night. And we have watchers in the galleries, two men in the Henry VII's chapel, two at St. Edward's Shrine, four in the nave and the choir stalls; we also have a man in the Muniment Room and two in the Triforium Gallery. The watchers are in the guise of tourists, but each can be identified by the guide-book he carries in his right hand— the only one with a green cover.'

Lemaitre said to the Divisional man:

'And our chaps?'

'Eight dotted about inside, two at the north and west entrances. It couldn't be covered more fully.'

Lemaitre forced himself to give a satisfied and congratulatory smile. 'Good. That'll foil the beggars.'

He thought: 'One stick of dynamite could do a hell of a

lot of damage, though. My God, I wish I hadn't taken this job on.'

It was twenty minutes to six when he left the Abbey, walked across to the Houses of Parliament and then along to the Yard.

At twenty minutes to six, Chief-Superintendent Percy Golightly looked into the face of Geoffrey Entwhistle, and said with great precision:

'It is my duty to charge you with the wilful murder of your wife, Margaret Entwhistle, and to warn you that anything you say may be taken down and later used in evidence.'

Entwhistle said bitterly: 'Okay, use it.'

The sergeant with Golightly wrote swiftly in his shorthand notebook.

'What do you mean?' Golightly demanded.

'Use what I say. I didn't kill her.'

'That will be recorded.'

'I don't know who did kill her.'

'That will be recorded.'

'There's a man wandering around London, laughing like hell at you and at me. *He* killed her.'

'Your remark will be recorded.'

'Oh, to hell with you,' rasped Entwhistle. 'Let's get going.'

'You are at liberty at any time to call your solicitor,' Golightly said.

As Entwhistle stepped into the police car which was to take him to Cannon Row police station, where he would spend the night before appearing in court next morning, Eric Greenwood walked briskly along Lower Thames Street. He passed the Custom House and Billingsgate Market, where only a few porters, wearing their solid-topped hats and their striped aprons, worked on opening crates of frozen fish. He noticed the blueness of their hands, the harshness of their voices as their mallets smacked the marble slabs. Greenwood walked on, up a steep cobbled hill, to an odd-shaped church with threefold steeple. This was the Church of St. James, Garlickhythe. Across the road stood a policeman, who appeared to take no notice of him; but Greenwood was past worrying about policemen, he felt completely safe. He slipped inside the unusually light and lofty church, with its tall columns panelled as high as the gallery. He was looking up at the vaulted ceiling when a man in a dark suit came towards him.

'Good evening, sir.'

'Good evening.'

'Haven't I seen you here before?'

'I've certainly been here before—to the lunch-time service, usually.'

'And in the evenings, I believe.'

'Yes,' said Greenwood. 'I like to look in.'

'You are very welcome, sir. Do you know anything about the history of the church?'

Greenwood smiled faintly.

'I was here when it was bombed. I used to fire-watch.'

'Good gracious! I had no idea. I was overseas at the time.'

'I often wished I was,' said Greenwood. 'I came and had a look most days when the rebuilding was going on.'

'I remember, sir.'

'It took a long time.'

'It did indeed. Excuse me—aren't you Mr. Greenwood? from Cox and Shieldings?'

'That's right,' said Greenwood, both pleased and surprised.

'I was a seaman on the British–India line—I saw you come aboard occasionally.'

'It's a small world.'

'It is indeed. Mr. Greenwood, I wonder if you could help us?'

'If it's possible, of course I will. What's the trouble?'

'We have some difficulty in the city in getting the evening volunteers we need to watch the churches,' the other said. 'We are trying to establish a rota of fire-watchers again.'

'You mean you think St. James's might be attacked?'

'There is no way of making sure,' said the verger. 'The police have warned us of the danger, and so have the church authorities. The police are giving us as much help as possible, but they can't neglect their ordinary duties, can they?'

'I suppose not,' said Greenwood. For the first time since entering the church he remembered the policeman he had seen outside St. Ludd's; and he thought of Margaret. 'It'd be dreadful if this place were damaged again,' he went on.

'It would indeed,' agreed the verger. '*Can* you help?'

'I'll be glad to,' promised Greenwood. His heart swelled with a sense of righteousness he had not known for a long time. 'What are the hours?'

'If you will come along with me to the vestry, sir, I will show you the rota as far as we have completed it. We have all the help we need by day, thanks to the quick response, but between six o'clock in the evening and six in the morning we are in *very* great need.'

'I wouldn't mind one night, right through,' said Greenwood. 'With time off for meals, of course.'

The verger's eyes lit up, and the warmth of his thanks made Eric Greenwood, murderer of his mistress, feel a very fine fellow.

'I don't know, dear,' Mrs. Dalby said. 'I really can't imagine where she's gone. She's very naughty, isn't she?'

Dalby said in a taut voice: 'Yes, very.'

'It's such a worry, isn't it?'

'Yes, a great worry.'

'How long has she been gone now?'

'Six days,' Dalby answered.

'That's too long, isn't it?'

'Much too long.'

'Dear,' said Mrs. Dalby vaguely, her voice still sweet, her smile untroubled, 'you don't think anything could have happened to her, do you?'

'I should hope not, Sarah.'

'I've been thinking.'

'Have you, then?'

'Yes, dear. You know that policeman who came to see you this morning?'

'I know.'

'Why don't you ask him if *he* can find Sally?'

Dalby nearly choked as he turned away from her.

'That's a very good idea, Sarah,' he said. 'I'll do that.'

'I thought perhaps you would,' said Sarah Dalby with satisfaction.

As they talked in their strange and unreal way, their daughter lay in the huge double bed, surrounded by mirrors, possessed by a strange tempest of desire which the man with her could not satisfy. This was one of the moods in which she had no fear, no sense of shame or decency, no thought of home.

In the cellar, two stories below, were the photographs of thirty-two missing girls, and three known to be dead.

CHAPTER 20

NIGHT OF ALARM

GIDEON thought he heard a movement in Lemaitre's room, and opened the door. Lemaitre had just come in from the passage, and for a moment both men stood with fingers on the handle. Gideon saw at once that Lemaitre was worried, but he made no comment. This hour of the day was one for relaxation and as far as possible they would take advantage of it.

'Come in and have a whisky, Lem.'

'Oh, thanks. Don't mind if I do.'

'Did you know Entwhistle is across at Cannon Row?'

'Denying it right and left,' Lemaitre said.

'He was bound to.' Gideon went to a cupboard in his desk, and took out a bottle, two glasses and a siphon of soda water. 'Have you heard about Hobbs?'

Lemaitre's lips tightened. He gulped down half his drink, and stared at the glass, avoiding Gideon's eye.

'What about him?'

147

'His wife died this afternoon. She'd been in a coma for several days.'

Lemaitre, startled almost beyond belief, jerked his head and his glass up, spilling whisky over his hand. He did not appear to notice it. He stared, unseeing, at Gideon, who was gazing out of the window at the dark clouds behind which the sun was slowly sinking.

'*Dead*,' breathed Lemaitre. '*Dying* for *days?*'

'Yes.'

'And he didn't say a word to us—to *me*—about it.'

'He didn't tell me until he had to. Kate found out, and I heard about it from her.'

'Good God. What does he have for a heart?'

Gideon said heavily:

'Is that how it affects you, Lem?'

'He certainly doesn't wear it on his sleeve.'

'Is he any the worse for that?'

'I see what you mean,' muttered Lemaitre. 'My God, if anything happened to Chloë—or if anything happened to Kate—we'd be off our heads.'

'Think I would wear my heart on my sleeve?' Gideon asked.

Lemaitre said: 'I'd be able to see it, anyhow. The poor sod.'

Gideon glanced out of the window.

'And I nearly let fly at him this afternoon,' Lemaitre went on. 'I thought he was being Mr. Flicking Hobbs, Deputy Commander before his time.' Lemaitre began to walk about the office. 'Never talked about her, did he? I only saw her once, in that wheel-chair—most beautiful woman I've ever seen. Been paralysed most of their married life, I remember Kate telling me. Cor blinking strewth. I *am* sorry. I really am, George.'

'We all are.'

'Am I glad I didn't let rip!'

'Why did you come so near it?'

'He was being supercilious, as I thought—hinting at things without coming out into the open. I began to wonder what the hell it would be like when he was officially promoted.'

Gideon looked back from the river. Lemaitre finished his drink and Gideon waved to the bottle, in a silent 'help yourself'. Lemaitre did so, drank again, moving restlessly, as if he could not meet Gideon's gaze.

'Lem, I have to go to Paris for two or three days, starting on Sunday night,' Gideon told him. 'There's a police conference over drugs, and the Customs and Excise people will be there, too. I've been out, checking.' In fact, he had talked to the Governor of the Bank of England at the club and was convinced of the man's anxiety and insistence on secrecy. 'Scott-Marle is bringing Hobbs's promotion forward a couple of weeks, so he will be in charge while I'm gone. It will be a good opportunity for him to find his feet, although a lot of things will be strange to him. They won't be to you.'

Lemaitre stopped pacing, and stared.

'I get you,' he said.

'I know you do.'

'Don't worry, George.'

'I'm worried only about one thing.'

'What's that?'

'That you won't talk to Hobbs about any problems as freely as you would to me.'

Lemaitre drew in a deep breath.

'Hobbs will be your deputy, you know, which means a second best, only a second best.' He tossed the last of the whisky down. 'But you can trust us not to come to blows.' He stretched his arms dramatically. 'Well, I want to visit half-a-dozen more churches tonight, George. I was saying to Hobbs, these people are cranks and even if we catch some they won't talk.' When Gideon didn't answer, Lemaitre forced a smile and went on: 'Here I go, jumping to conclusions again. You mark my words, though. They won't talk.' He went to the communicating door. 'I'll see you. Er— think there'll be trouble tonight?'

Gideon shrugged.

'I hope not. Any idea how P.C. Davies is?'

'Off the danger list,' Lemaitre said. 'I looked in at the

hospital. No doubt of the blindness, though. What a hell of a thing to happen in a church!'

London was shrouded in lowering skies and battered by a squally wind which made church-watching a more than usually unpleasant duty. All over London the police and the volunteers were alert, from the heart of Mayfair and from Westminster to the slums of the East End, from the sprawling suburbs with their houses cheek-by-jowl to the residential areas where houses stood in their own grounds, from Camberwell to London Bridge, from Trafalgar Square to Hounslow Heath, from Oxford Circus to St. John's Wood, to Hampstead and beyond, from St. Paul's and the city to Whitechapel and Wapping, Bethnal Green to Rotherhithe—the police stood shoulder to shoulder with Christians and believers as they watched over their churches, some built at the time of the Norman Conquest, some built in the last few years.

The sages shook their heads.

'There won't be any trouble tonight. The weather's too bad.'

At the Synagogue in Marylebone a careful watch was kept on the Ark and a policeman paced his beat, never out of sight of the watchers at the entrance for more than ten minutes. The precautions came easily to those who had long been in danger of vandalism, and to whom the methods of defence were second nature. None of the watchers seriously expected trouble, for they did not really believe it would come from members of their own faith, and surely no gentile could get in by night.

When a small car turned into the street, everyone was aware of it—even the police constable, who had just passed the Synagogue and heard the car behind him. As he turned, it slowed down and a moment later, stopped. At once the policeman's steps quickened. A man got out of the car as a gust of wind swept along the street at almost gale force. Rain spattered over the car and its windscreen, shimmering in the light of the street lamps. Presently the car moved off,

eaving the man behind. The policeman slackened his pace
while continuing to advance.

The watcher at the door spoke mildly.

'Can I help you, sir?'

'Yes.' The voice was authoritative. 'I have a message for
Rabbi Perlutt.'

'He is inside,' the watcher said.

'Can I see him, please?'

'I'm afraid you'll have to give me a little more information, sir.'

The stranger said: 'I have come to warn him.'

The policeman, now very close, caught the last words, and
the watcher echoed:

'*Warn* him? What about?'

'I am here to tell him that before the sun rises there will
be an attack on your House of Worship,' the stranger declared, and he looked up into the face of the policeman.
'Did you hear that, constable?'

'I did, sir. Have you warned Scotland Yard?'

'No, I have not,' the man said. 'I will give details only to
the rabbi.'

'As a police officer, sir——'

'I am prepared to give a message of great importance to
the rabbi,' the stranger said impatiently. 'If he wishes to
inform the police that is entirely his affair.' He stood still
and aloof, as doubt chased suspicion across the policeman's
face.

'I think, sir,' said the watcher, 'that you should come in.
Please be careful to observe silence, and remember to keep
your head covered. Constable, if you will be good enough to
stay by the door in case the rabbi wishes to speak to you. I
will be very grateful.'

'I'll be here, sir,' the constable assured him.

The other led the way to the big hall, in which stood the
Ark, the marriage canopy some distance in front of it, and
the Reader's desk. There were only a few lights showing,
and the empty spaces seemed full of menace.

As they stepped forward, the stranger put his hand to his
pocket, took out an egg-shaped object and hurled it at the

Ark. As it struck, it exploded in a violent yellow flash. A fierce blast swept along the pews, smashing the windows, blowing the canopy to smithereens. The policeman heard the roar and sprang forward, but as he reached the doors the stranger appeared, thrust him aside and ran into the street. Coming along was the little car, which slowed down only long enough for the stranger to scramble inside.

Fire and smoke and awful debris filled the Synagogue, and as men recovered from the shock, they raised the alarm which would bring help.

But the vandal got away.

The same methods were used all over London, against Anglican Church and Roman Catholic, some Methodists and one Presbyterian.

All but two of the destroyers escaped.

Gideon's telephone bell began to ring at dead of night, and he stirred in bed, protesting silently, until he felt Kate move and was suddenly conscious of the fact that the ringing would wake her. He stretched out mechanically and put the receiver to his ear. Still half-asleep, he said:

'Gideon.'

'George, there have been sixteen!' Lemaitre burst out.

Gideon echoed: 'Sixteen? Sixteen what?' As soon as the question was uttered he realised the absurdity of it, but Lemaitre cried:

'Sixteen outrages! *Sixteen churches damaged.*'

Gideon could sense the anguish in the other's voice. He could tell from Kate's stillness that she was awake, but perhaps not fully, yet. He pushed the bedclothes back, whispering tersely into the receiver: 'I'll come over. Any of them caught?'

'Only two.'

Gideon's heart leapt.

'We've got two?'

'Yes. They're on their way to the Yard.'

'Where are you?'

'At West Central.'

'Meet me at the Yard,' and then a fearful thought flashed through Gideon's mind, and he asked sharply: 'Any cathedrals damaged?'

'They got the altar at St. Martin's in the Furrows,' Lemaitre said. 'That's the biggest. Er—think I ought to tell Hobbs?'

'No.'

'So long as you agree,' said Lemaitre.

Gideon got out of bed and flicked on a light faint enough not to disturb Kate. He began to dress, seeing from the illuminated dial of the bedside clock that it was twenty minutes to two; well, he'd had two hours' sleep.

'Is it serious?' Kate asked, suddenly.

'Nothing desperate yet. Just some more church damage.'

'It's wicked,' Kate said.

'Downright evil,' Gideon agreed. 'You stop worrying about it.'

'How many were damaged?'

'Sixteen.'

'*Sixteen.* Why, that's twice as many as the last time!'

'They seem to be doubling after each outrage,' Gideon remarked. 'Don't worry about me if I don't come back. I'll probably bed down at the Yard.'

In fact, he was not likely to get any more sleep tonight. As he made his way to his garage, through the chill of a now dry but blustery morning, he yawned, and was aware of being tired; he needed more sleep than he used to. No—he needed to sleep more regularly; he could not throw off the effect of late or broken nights as easily as he had done when younger. But what did it matter? He drove along the Embankment, passed Millbank House, and saw the vague outline of Lambeth Palace across the river. At least eight uniformed policemen were in sight of St. Margaret's Church and the Abbey. What a thing to come to pass—the churches, guarded by the law! They would have to call the military out if the situation got much worse, and so history would repeat itself. He turned into the Yard, and found more than the usual bustle. Up in the C.I.D. offices, lights blazed, men walked and talked noisily, there was a great wave of activity.

He opened Lemaitre's door, but the room was empty, went into his own room and found the lights on, coffee on a tray, all the signs that it had been used within the past few minutes. Smoke rose straight from the stub of a cigarette in the ash-tray. Lemaitre didn't smoke cigarettes these days. He was at the door when it opened and Scott-Marle appeared, gaunt and aloof.

'Hello, sir!'

'Hello, Commander.' The Commissioner was always formal when others were present, and Lemaitre and another Chief-Superintendent were just behind him. 'I want you to interrogate the two prisoners yourself.'

'I will, sir.'

'I've asked Lemaitre to prepare a detailed plan of the locations of tonight's outrages, and to assess the total extent of the damage.'

'I'll get on to it at once, sir,' Lemaitre promised.

'Thank you.'

'One thing,' Gideon said. 'Has anyone been hurt tonight?'

'Not seriously,' Lemaitre said, 'that's one relief, anyhow. A few cuts and bruises. One of the so-and-so's has damaged his arm pretty badly; he's the worst as far as I know.' He glanced at Scott-Marle. 'I'll get down to the plan, sir.' He hurried into his office, then bobbed back: 'They're over at Cannon Row, Geo—Commander.'

The door closed on him.

Gideon looked at the other Chief-Superintendent and said: 'Bring the two prisoners up and stay with them in Mr. Hobbs's room until I send for them.' When the man had gone he studied Scott-Marle's drawn and troubled face, and went on: 'Do you wish to be present at the interrogation, sir?'

'Do you think it would be wise?'

Gideon hesitated, deliberating the matter, then answered with a diffidence that barely sounded in his voice:

'No, sir.'

'Very well,' Scott-Marle said. 'I will be in my office. Don't rush the interrogation on my account, Commander.'

CHAPTER 21

CANNON ROW

IN Cannon Row police station, awaiting the Magistrate's Court hearing of the charge, was Geoffrey Entwhistle, pale and haggard and unshaven, feeling weak and helpless one moment, enraged the next. During the past week he had relied on whisky to keep up his morale, and he had not had a drink for hours. He sat on the narrow bed, head in his hands, hardly able to believe that such a thing had happened to him. He had not yet named a solicitor because, so far, he had had very little need of one. At the same time he felt the situation to be so hopeless, that to fight it would be a waste of effort. They had him; they would convict him.

Suddenly, he jumped up and cried: 'And they won't even hang me.'

The police sergeant on duty in the cells heard him, went along, listened, heard a repetition and noted it down.

Two cells along the corridor, out of earshot, was one of the two men caught raiding a church. He was short, compact, in the late forties, clean-shaven, rather austere-looking. He had refused to give his name. He had been searched, but nothing in his pockets or on his clothes gave any clue to his identity. Next to him was another man, taller, equally silent, equally good mannered. Next to this tall man was the thief whom Eric Greenwood had disturbed at St. Ludd's. He was here because the second hearing was due early the next morning, and Lemaitre wanted to question him again and make quite sure he was not connected with the vandalism.

This man was sleeping.

In other cells there were two prostitutes and a woman who had tried to kill herself and her illegitimate infant. A welfare officer was with her, soothing the hysteria of despair.

A plainclothes sergeant came hurrying down from the station above.

'The two men are wanted,' he said. 'Have they shown any sign of violence?'

'Mild as milk,' the sergeant answered, and then two more officers came, each carrying handcuffs. 'You won't need those,' the sergeant declared.

'We aren't taking any chances.'

The two vandals were removed from the cells without fuss, handcuffed and taken up to the Yard. Four uniformed and two more plainclothes men were there. A photographer at the gates let out a yell and rushed forward into the forbidden territory of the Yard, his light flashing. Two officers closed on him. The contingent of big men, towering above the prisoners and watched by dozens of night-duty men and Flying Squad officers, went in the back way and up in the big, iron-gated lift. At the first-floor level, three men stood waiting.

Throughout all this, the two prisoners had not changed their expression or uttered a word. Now, with a guard in front and one behind, they were taken to Hobbs's office, and escorted inside. They were kept waiting for five minutes before a sergeant came in.

'The first accused, please,' he said.

There was a moment's hesitation before the taller of the two men stepped forward. As he crossed the passage, he saw the door with the name: *Commander Gideon*. One man tapped on this door, and then opened it.

Gideon stood with his back to the window. The prisoner stepped inside.

'Take off the handcuffs,' Gideon ordered. 'And wait outside.'

Gideon, who had become a student of men the hard way from the bitter experience of trial and error, of betrayed trust, of honesty and dishonesty concealed by the most unlikely faces, studied this prisoner as closely as he had ever studied anyone. The first impression never left him; the man was an ascetic. The face was lined, but not deeply, the lips were set, but not tightly. His features were clean-cut and his skin had the clearness which some devotees of extreme physical fitness show; an almost aggressive purity. There was no spare flesh on him, no hint of plumpness. He was dressed in a clerical grey suit, well-cut but not in any particularly modish way. His greying hair was cut quite short.

Gideon knew that he had not uttered a word since his arrest outside St. Botolph's, in the Strand.

Gideon held his own peace for at least two minutes, before saying casually:

'Good evening.'

The man was surprised into opening his mouth, actually forming the letter 'g' and in that moment Gideon felt a flare of triumph; once start him talking and he might go on and on.

But no sound came; the thin lips closed again. Gideon kept silent for a few seconds, and then remarked:

'So you've taken a vow of silence.'

The reaction was sufficient to convince him that the guess was right. The pale eyes narrowed, a gleam of surprise flickered in them but soon died away. Now Gideon felt no flare of triumph, rather one of dismay. If the prisoner *had* taken a vow of silence he would almost certainly keep it, and what was true of him would probably prove true of any others who were caught. Lemaitre had known what he was talking about.

Gideon said: 'Presumably you are aware that you have committed a very grave crime, not only against the Church, but against the laws of the country.'

There was no answer.

'The maximum penalty for sacrilege is imprisonment for life. Do you realise that?'

The man showed no flicker of interest.

'Life imprisonment is no joke, Mr.——'

There was no response.

'Your wife and family may have plenty to say,' remarked Gideon.

No answer.

'You know, all you are doing is wasted effort,' Gideon said, as if to himself. 'A good try, but bound to fail. If you'd simply been seen we might have had trouble in identifying you, but when we put your photograph in the newspapers

157

and on television, someone is bound to come forward and identify you. After that, it will be simply a question of routine questioning of your relations, your friends and your acquaintances. Failure to identify you, and through you your associates in these crimes, is out of the question. You haven't a chance.'

The man standing so still in front of him did not flicker an eyelid.

Ten minutes later, Gideon gave up.

Half-an-hour later, he gave up the smaller prisoner, too.

Immediately afterwards he went across to see Scott-Marle, who was alone in his office, poring over a map of London in which the churches were marked with crosses. He glanced up, hopeful for a moment, then settled back in his chair.

'I'm as nearly sure as I can be that they've taken a vow of silence,' Gideon told him. 'Both men reacted in exactly the same way to the same questions. I should say they've not only taken a vow, they've also practised living up to it. And if we catch any more they'll be the same.'

Scott-Marle, his eyes very red-rimmed, said gruffly: 'You're not often pessimistic.'

'I am about making these men talk. But we can have their photographs in tomorrow's—I mean today's—evening papers and on television. By the day after tomorrow we're bound to get some form of identification. From then on we should be on the way to finding who they are and what they're up to, but—I'll be in Paris.'

Scott-Marle said: 'Yes. You must be.'

'And it may be too late,' Gideon warned. 'These men aren't fools. They know that from tonight on, their number's up. But they've taken some pretty big risks tonight, and they might take bigger ones for bigger objectives.'

'Then before you go, make sure everything is tied up so that nothing avoidable can go wrong,' Scott-Marle ordered. When Gideon made no comment, he went on with a faint smile: 'I know; I'm tired, George.' After another pause, he went on: 'It's a thousand pities Hobbs can't be on duty. How do you think Lemaitre is going to make out?'

Gideon said with forced confidence: 'He's missed nothing, so far.'

Before Scott-Marle could comment, there was a tap at the door, and at Scott-Marle's 'Come in,' Lemaitre entered, carrying a long roll of paper.

'All finished, sir.'

'Good. Let me see.' There was a high table at one side of the room, rather like a drawing-board, and Scott-Marle held the paper flat while Lemaitre, with fingers fluttering with eagerness, pinned it at the corners. There was an outline map of London with every major road marked, and a criss-cross of thin lines, like rivers on an ordinary map, showing the minor streets. There were different-coloured crosses in a spreading rash over the whole area.

'The black are for Anglican churches, the blue for R.C. . . .' Lemaitre's voice was quick with suppressed pride, the words tumbling over each other. 'And the red stars show where we've had the trouble—one star, the first night of attack, two the second, three last night——'

Not wishing to detract from Lemaitre's brief hour of importance Gideon said quietly: 'Do you need me any more now, sir?'

'No, Commander. Lemaitre can tell me all I need to know.'

Gideon went out, and along to his office, pleased for Lemaitre, but deeply worried over the matter as a whole. There was now no shadow of doubt that they had to deal with religious fanatics, and should start concentrating on the known off-beat sects. Time was the problem; he had a sense of urgency which Scott-Marle shared, but what hope was there of getting this investigation put through quickly? They needed weeks.

He turned into his office and found Rollo by his desk, drawing fiercely at a cigarette. In spite of the pressure of the church crimes Gideon's thoughts flashed immediately to the Photo-Nude Murders and to the missing girls.

'Heard you were in,' Rollo said.

'Got anything?' demanded Gideon.

'I think we know the man—a Toni Bottelli.'

'Where is he?'

'Owns a tobacconist and newspaper shop in Tottenham,' said Rollo. 'He's got a cellar on the same scale as Rhodes's. Often has girls down there to photograph—we've found one of the girls.'

'One of those we're looking for?'

'No. One who went down to the cellar and didn't like what she saw,' Rollo said. 'She came forward because she recognised some of the photographs we've had in the papers. She'd seen the same photos in the cellar before.'

Gideon said gruffly: 'Thank God for this much. What have you done?'

'Thrown a cordon round the place.'

'Not too close, I hope.'

'Complete coverage, but it can't arouse suspicions,' Rollo assured him. 'Look.' He picked up a sectional map of North London, drawn on a much larger scale than the one Lemaitre had taken to Scott-Marle, and pointed. 'There's the shop—in the High Street. It's halfway along the block. There's a service road behind it, there.' The service road was marked clearly. 'There's the back of the shop and the living quarters above. Follow?'

'Yes.'

'We've men in parked cars in the High Street, and they took up their posts one at a time. We've men in the side-streets, which Bottelli can't see.' He paused. 'We've four men in the service road covered by garages and outhouses so that they can't be seen, either. At a signal they can all converge on the backyard. The service alley can then be sealed off.'

'Roof?' Gideon asked.

'There's a roof-light. We've also planted men on the roof at the end buildings of the block.'

'What do you plan to do?'

'A straight move in, from the front,' said Rollo. 'Provided Bottelli isn't given any warning, I don't see that he can do much. Golightly's over there, in charge. He agrees with me.'

Gideon didn't speak.

'I can't see Bottelli putting up much of a fight,' Rollo

went on. 'It's one thing to play around with a camera and a lot of girls in the altogether, but when he realises what he's up against, he'll just cave in.'

'Sure he's there?' asked Gideon.

'Yes.'

'Sure the girl's there?'

'*A* girl's there, all right.'

'How do you know?'

'I'll tell you,' Rollo said, with a funny kind of smile, perhaps one of distaste. 'There's a Peeping Tom in a room opposite. A few weeks ago he got an eyeful—he says there's a room of mirrors over Bottelli's shop and he thought he was seeing a nude beauty contest, but he wasn't. There was a man, too, and our Peeping Tom tumbled to the fact that he was seeing what's what. Ever since then, he's watched hopefully. The curtains are usually drawn by day and by night, but they're open occasionally and he's seen a girl in bed in the mirror room today.'

Gideon said slowly: 'It looks good enough.' He paused, but Rollo didn't interrupt. 'Better do as you say,' he agreed at last, 'but take a couple of women officers along, have a doctor handy and don't take any chances.'

'I tell you the swab will give in the moment he realises that he's up against us,' Rollo said.

Gideon thought, 'I hope you're right.' He didn't say it aloud, because it would serve no purpose, and he was sure Rollo would be as thorough as any man in the Force. He and Golightly between them were almost unbeatable, and to adjure them to be careful or to be thorough would be to treat them like children.

He was a little uneasy, but not worried—not to say worried.

Sally was crying.

They were not deep sobs, yet they were more than a grizzle. She was unhappy and afraid, although she did not know why. The reason was simple; she did not yet know that Toni was drugging her, that she was becoming more and more dependent on the drugs and was happy only when she was under their influence. Now she felt as if she were going to die; she had never known despair like it. It was an hour or more since Toni had been with her. In one way she longed to see him again, in another, she shrank from it.

Sometimes he hurt her so.

Sometimes——

Tears flooded her eyes, stinging them, and her sobbing became louder. She did not hear Toni come in, and so did not see his expression, until suddenly he slapped her across the face, and rasped:

'Be quiet!'

She gasped, and shrank back on the pillows.

'Get up and get dressed,' he ordered.

She was trembling with pain and fear, and did not move.

'Get a move on!' he shouted at her, and slapped her again. 'Get your clothes on, we're going away.'

'But—but—but Toni——'

He snatched the bedclothes off her, grabbed her wrists and pulled her out of bed, naked but for a bed-jacket which barely reached her waist.

'Get dressed!' he roared. 'If you don't, I swear I'll leave you dead.'

As he spoke, he drew an automatic pistol from his pocket.

CHAPTER 22

THE PISTOL

SALLY DALBY saw the gun, squat and ugly in Toni's hand, and she screamed. For a moment she thought he was going to shoot her, then she was afraid that he would strike her with the weapon. She staggered towards a cupboard, pulled open the door and dragged out her clothes. As she did so, there was the sharp ring of a bell.

She gasped: 'What's that?'

'Shut up!' Toni kept the gun in his right hand, and motioned to her with his left. 'Put the light out.'

'What——'

'Put it out!'

She scurried across the room to the door and pushed the switch up as he reached the window. The sudden darkness frightened her still more. Her breathing was laboured, and so was his. She heard a rustle of sound, and faint light came into the room; he had pulled the curtains back and was looking out. She could see the outline of his head and shoulders, as he pressed close to the window. Suddenly there was another ring, and Sally jumped wildly.

Toni muttered something, but her teeth were chattering and she did not hear him. The curtains were drawn again, and he called:

'Put the light on.'

Light? What light? What——

'Put the light on!' he screeched at her. She remembered where she was standing and touched the switch. The light, dazzling, showed him nearly halfway across the room, his gun still in his hand. *'Get your clothes on!'* he yelled. 'The cops are here.'

Cops?

As his face twisted in rage and alarm, she had never been more afraid of him. Suddenly she began to scramble into her clothes, hardly knowing what she was doing. Bra, panties, slacks, jumper——

'Get a move on!' He flung a pair of moccasin shoes at her and she thrust her feet into them.

'What—what do the police want?'

'You, you silly bitch!'

'I—I don't know anything, *I* can't help the police.'

'Can't you?' he said, sneeringly, and then, his voice suddenly sharpening: 'Well, you can help *me.*'

'Toni, *how?*'

'You're going to find out. Come on.'

He pulled open the door, and as he did so sounds travelled freely up from the passage alongside the side entrance. Banging, hammering and voices in a demanding medley. Once, a sentence sounded clearly:

'Open in the name of the law.'

'—— fools,' Toni muttered.

Still holding her, he reached a spot on the landing beneath a hatch, and she saw a ladder against the wall. He drew this forward, and thrust her towards it.

'Get up, quickly.'

'No! I can't stand heights, I——'

'Get up!' He gripped her roughly and she began to climb, holding desperately to the side of the ladder. He followed, half-lifting, half-shoving her whenever she flagged. As her head touched the hatch, he pushed her furiously upwards.

'Lever that hatch up.'

Terrified to defy him, terrified to let go even with one hand, and trembling violently, Sally eased the hatch open. There were thudding noises and heavy blows downstairs. Toni stretched past her, pressing hard as he flung the hatch back. Cold air swirled round them, snatching at Sally's hair.

'Climb out,' Toni ordered. She obeyed blindly, scrambling on to a flat section of the roof, then on to a slanting section. Twice, she slipped; each time he stopped her from falling back.

Along the side of the roof, overlooking the street, was a narrow ledge. One slip from it would send them crashing to the ground a hundred feet below. Almost paralysed with terror, teeth chattering, body quivering, Sally edged along it, crouching, hand touching the slates on one side, Toni holding her other hand behind her. Through her terror she tried to speak.

'What are you doing this for? What——'

'Shut up and keep going.' After a moment, Toni went on: 'I've got another shop along here, we——'

As he spoke, a beam of light shot out from a roof on the other side of the street, shining steadily on him and the girl.

Down on the pavement, opposite the tobacconist's shop, a sergeant was talking to Rollo. Above, lights were flashing. Inside, Golightly was leading the raid. Rollo, the younger and more powerful man, was out here to cover any escape. He heard a man call out with strident urgency, glanced up, and saw what looked like a moving ball of light, waving about. Then he realised that it was a beam of light shining on a girl's head. Once he knew that, he could see that she was crouching low and that there was the dark figure of a man behind her. Along the street, a policeman called:

'Look!'

'See that?' shouted another.

'There's a girl!'

'See that man?'

Rollo thought: 'Now we could be in for trouble.' Aloud, he said to the sergeant: 'We need a fire-escape and a catching net—fix it, quick.' He stepped farther into the road, put his hands to his mouth to make a megaphone and bellowed: 'Don't go any farther! Give yourself up!'

The girl's hair was swept back in the fierce wind; from the ground she looked quite beautiful.

'You haven't a chance!' Rollo bellowed. 'Give yourself up.'

He saw a movement without realising its significance. He heard a screeching sound which might be coming from the girl—and the next moment he saw a flash, and almost simultaneously heard a bullet crack against the window behind him. The plate glass broke with a roar like an explosion. Apples and oranges and other fruit rolled about his feet, toppled by the falling glass. At the same time, detectives appeared on the ledge some distance from the couple. The man with the girl must have seen them at the same time, for in the high voice of desperation, he cried:

'Don't come any nearer, or I'll push her off!'

Sally was crouching with her mouth open, trying to utter screams which would not come. This was a nightmare; she was helpless *in* a nightmare—and yet she knew it was real, knew that Toni meant what he said. If the men came any nearer he would push her off. And if she fell, she would die.

Rollo thought: 'He means it.'

There was that sixth sense, or presentiment; an instantaneous recognition of a situation, which made the difference between being a good policeman and a brilliant one; a good officer or a born leader. This man would push the girl off if he thought he was about to be attacked. There would be no reasoning with him; he had acted on impulse, driven by fear, and he would again. Almost without thinking, Rollo weighed up the situation, knowing that the only hope lay in speed. He moved a pace, squashing fruit beneath his feet, realising that the entire pavement and kerb were covered with fruit of all kinds.

The girl's only hope lay in the speed with which the police could act.

He stared up, able to pick out the man and the girl clearly. Two or three of the Divisional men came hurrying, and on the instant, Rollo thought: it might work. The couple were within easy aiming distance.

'Listen,' he said in a whisper. 'Get more men, have everyone pick up apples and oranges, anything heavy enough to throw, and let him have it. *Hurry!*' Aloud, he bellowed: '*You up there!*'

'Don't come any nearer or I'll push her over!' Bottelli screamed.

'*Let her go, and we'll let you go!*'

'*You can't fool me. Call your men off! Call 'em off the roof!*'

'*I tell you we'll let you go if you let her go!*' Rollo shouted. He had half-a-dozen apples in his pockets and more cradled in one arm, and other men were also armed with fruit. In a whisper, he ordered: '*Throw now.*' On the 'now' a hail of hard and soft fruit hurtled upwards, smashing and spattering on the roof, on Sally, on Bottelli. The policemen below grabbed and hurled, grabbed and hurled, in a furious fusillade.

Up on the ledge, Bottelli suddenly felt something soft splash against his cheeks, then something hard strike him on the chin, next a lucky shot struck the hand holding the gun. He snatched his free hand away from Sally, to protect his face. The fruit struck her, terrifyingly, and, crouching against the attack, she sprawled, spread-eagled, against the sloping tiles. Golightly and two others who had climbed on to the roof, realising their chance, scrambled forward. Held fast in the beams of torches from the opposite houses, Toni Bottelli fired two shots wildly into the street, then watched helplessly as the gun was struck from his hand.

A detective officer grabbed him.

Ten minutes later, Bottelli was being taken off in a Black Maria to the Divisional Station, and the girl, in sobbing hysteria, was being put into an ambulance for the nearest hospital. The policemen, newspapermen, firemen and the people from the houses near by heard the tyres crunching over the rolling oranges and apples. Rollo, reaction setting in, began to laugh; once he had started, he couldn't stop.

Gideon heard the news at seven-thirty, when he was called by a detective sergeant, on instructions, from the dormitory bed he had slept on since five-thirty. He listened to a running commentary on what had happened during the night from the sergeant while he showered, then shaved with an electric razor—a method he disliked—and drank very hot tea. The funny side of the fusillade of fruit did not occur to him until later, but in a written report from Golightly there was a generous tribute: *But for Rollo's spontaneous action I doubt if we would have saved the girl's life.* Gideon went down to his office and put in a call to the Division, to inquire about the girl.

'She's under sedation at the hospital,' he was told.

'The prisoner?'

'He'll be charged today, sir. Mr. Rollo said he would report to you by nine o'clock.'

'All right,' said Gideon.

No reports had come in yet from the night's crimes. There would be the usual crop and he would have to get through them as best he could. The only case he really worried about was the campaign against the Churches. It had become an obsession. Subconsciously, he knew, he was fighting against the Paris mission, but he doubted whether he could persuade Scott-Marle to send anyone else in his place—unless

167

he would agree to send Hobbs, which might be a good thing for the new Deputy Commander. Gideon's heart quite leapt at the thought. He was still deliberating whether to ask Scott-Marle, when there was a tap at his door and Hobbs came in. Gideon had no time to hide his surprise.

Hobbs smiled faintly.

'I'm not a ghost, George.'

'Er—no. Sorry. I didn't think. Well anyway, I'm glad to see you.'

'So I imagine. It's been a rough night.'

Gideon said gently: 'Alec, you know how desperately sorry I am about Helen. If there's a thing I can do, it's as good as done. If you need to be busy for a few days with formalities and family affairs, forget the Yard.'

Hobbs's smile deepened. There was a quiet humour in it, a touch of irony, perhaps, in the twist of his lips.

'Helen's brother is looking after the formalities, such as they are.' He paused. 'There *is* something you can do for me.' He stopped.

Gideon looked at him steadily, but Hobbs did not go on. Gideon rounded his desk and said quietly:

'Did Scott-Marle tell you I have to go to Paris on Sunday night?'

Hobbs looked surprised. 'No.'

'Well, I have. A hush-hush conference. Would you like to go?'

Hobbs said flatly: 'No. But you're on the right track.'

'You must keep busy—yes.' Gideon brooded. 'I think the next two or three days are going to be as busy and as harassing as I've ever known. But I won't be here.'

Hobbs didn't speak.

'Alec,' Gideon said, 'if you're under such severe emotional strain, can you stand the added burden of this as well?'

Hobbs answered quickly: 'Yes, I think so. What you can do for me, George, is to let me sit in on all this morning's briefings, so that I can get an indication of all that's going through. Then let me know your ideas about the cases. After that I'd like to plunge in deep.'

Without a moment's hesitation, Gideon said: 'Right.

Let's get started.' He shifted his chair to one side, Hobbs
pulled up another, and Gideon drew the reports to him and
began to go through them, one by one. By the time they had
finished, it was nearly nine o'clock. Hobbs asked few questions and made few notes, but Gideon had no doubt that he
had absorbed almost all there was to know about the cases.
The arrest of Geoffrey Entwhistle was touched on, but not
discussed. The quality of Hobbs the detective was not in
doubt, and Hobbs the executive officer was as established;
but Hobbs the humanitarian—that was still a big question.

He said: 'We've only the one great anxiety then: the
church crimes.'

'Yes,' agreed Gideon.

'I'd like to interrogate the two prisoners.'

'Go ahead.'

'And if they won't say anything to me, I think they should
be questioned by different officers, each officer with a different personality and approach. Lemaitre after me, perhaps,
then Golightly, then Rollo. They shouldn't be allowed to
rest or to take it easy.'

Gideon frowned. 'No,' he said dubiously. 'There's no
need to have them in court today, of course, so we can keep
at them, but they must have a chance to send for a lawyer.
We certainly can't overdo the pressure. You know that as
well as I do.'

'They won't send for a lawyer, for fear it would help us to
identify them,' Hobbs reasoned. 'And you're too senti-
mental, George. They've got to be made to talk, and we
have to bend every rule in the book to make them. Bend,'
repeated Hobbs, looking very steadily at Gideon. 'Not
break.'

Gideon returned the challenging gaze levelly.

'I don't think we're going to get results by subjecting
these two men to any particular kind of pressure. I think
we've got to increase the effort in other ways.' He paused for
a long moment and added: 'Talk to Lem about it, will
you? I think we should concentrate a lot more on out-of-the-
way and little-known sects—what might be called the religious lunatic fringe.'

'Only don't say that in public,' cautioned Hobbs.

That was so characteristic of a remark Gideon himself might make that it was like hearing himself speak. Gideon had not fully recovered when there was a tap at the door, and Lemaitre strode in.

CHAPTER 23

SEARCH FOR SIMPLICITY

LEMAITRE was obviously pleased with himself, so much so that even seeing Hobbs did not put him out of his stride. He slapped his hands together loudly, boomed 'Good morning, all!' and then his expression changed ludicrously and he stared open-mouthed at Hobbs.

'What a clot I am,' he gasped.

Quickly, quietly, Hobbs said: 'Let's take some things as said, Lem.' He smiled quite freely. 'And I don't mean that you're a clot! The Commander and I have come to the un-original conclusion that our only pressing problem is the church outrages. We feel a desperate need for a new approach.'

Lemaitre swallowed hard, gave Hobbs a sidelong glance, then rubbed his knuckly hands together.

'New or old, what does it matter? I'm on to something.'

Gideon felt a surge of excitement, rare in him. Hobbs stiffened.

'I've been following an angle you mentioned earlier, George. Cranky religious sects, and these chaps are cranks if ever I've known one. You know that old boy we saw over at St. Denys' in Kensington?' Gideon recalled the almost skeletal face of the old man in the damaged church, and remembered the girl Elspeth who had come to him, so soothingly. 'Well, I happened to know he's a bit of a crank himself, very interested in out-of-the-way religions, made a proper study of it. I happened to notice the books on his shelves. That set me thinking. So I went over to see him the next day, and asked him to make out a list of all the off-beat sects in London—England, really, but most of them are in London.'

Gideon thought, 'Why didn't he tell me?' He said: 'Nice work, Lem.'

'I'll say it was nice work,' Lemaitre crowed. 'There are dozens in London, and they range from West Indian voodoo-worshippers and Tennessee snake-worshippers to the Black Mass boys. We'd find some sun-worshippers if we looked hard enough, I daresay. And then we were on the lookout for buyers of dynamite, remember?' He did not pause for comment, but careered on: 'Funny thing about that dyna-mite. I couldn't understand it. Why *dynamite*?'

He paused, not for an answer from the others but in a kind of artistic triumph. Hobbs glanced at Gideon, who was watching Lemaitre intently, and thinking: he had to justify himself, that's why he's been keeping all this back. He was astonished that Lemaitre, always bursting to talk, could have been going ahead like this and keeping his own coun-sel.

'I mean, why not nitro? Or cellulose nitrate? Or any of a dozen things easier to conceal. Why *dynamite*? Because it was easy to get hold of, or because it had some kind of sig-nificance? Remember the man *Bishop*, George? He tried to burn London down because his wife and kids were burned to death in a slum fire.'

'I remember.' It was like being asked if one remembered the Battle of Britain.

'Anyway, the Vicar of St. Denys', Kensington—old Miles Chaplin, you saw him—gave me these lists of sects and their leaders, some of them so obscure hardly anybody knows about them. I had every one checked—just as you said—and had a special eye kept open for one of them who could get hold of dynamite easily. *And*,' brayed Lemaitre, 'I found it.'

Very softly, Gideon said: 'Well done, Lem.'

'Sect called *The Simple Brethren*,' Lemaitre said. '*Very* strict, they even think the Quakers are ritualists. Run by a man named Marriott, Hector Marriott. They call him the Elder Brother. He's got pots of money, and owns a lot of businesses, and—here's the significant fact—one of them is for the manufacture of fireworks!'

'My God!' Hobbs was shaken right out of his usual calm.

'And they also manufacture dynamite sticks for quarry blasting,' said Lemaitre. 'They use the same cardboard, the same paper, the same packing that's been used in the bits and pieces we've found. No doubt about it—look!'

He took a plastic bag out of his pocket. In this were some tattered scraps of paper, torn cardboard and a piece of fuse. All of these were blackened and burned. He shook them out on to a sheet of paper on Gideon's desk, then drew out another plastic bag containing the same kind of thing in an unburned state.

'They're identical. I've had 'em up in the lab.' He rubbed his hands together as he went on: 'Enough to justify a search at the offices of *The Simple Brethren*, George? They don't call themselves that to the public. Marriott runs a Bible Society—sells Bibles to underdeveloped countries for next to nothing, but old Chaplin says he holds meetings there. He has a flat in Victoria, too, opposite the R.C. Cathedral. How about a search warrant for both places?'

'The quicker the better,' Gideon agreed. 'We want the offices closely watched, too.'

'I've had 'em covered since yesterday morning,' Lemaitre told him jubilantly. 'Everyone who goes there is watched and followed—but don't worry, they don't know they're under surveillance.'

That was the first time Gideon had any real misgivings about Lemaitre's over-confidence. Nothing would be served by saying so; he could only pray.

'We want to raid both places at the same time,' he said. 'Which one do you want, Lem?' He was already at the telephone, dialling Scott-Marle's office.

'The offices.'

'Right. Alec, you take the other—hello, sir. Gideon. I'd like search warrants sworn for two places in Victoria, the offices of . . .'

As he talked, Lemaitre and Hobbs went out together to make arrangements for the raids. There seemed to be a briskness in Hobbs's movements which hadn't been evident for weeks.

Scott-Marle said: 'I'll see to these at once, Commander.'

To hear him, one would think that he was promising action on some matter of routine.

At his desk in the flat, Hector Marriott was reading some tracts which he himself had written, when his telephone bell rang. He did not answer it immediately, but finished reading before slowly lifting the instrument.

'This is Hector Marriott.'

'Brother Marriott,' a man said, and Marriott recognised Joliffe's voice. 'We are being watched and followed by the police. I have no doubt of it. There are watchers in the street outside your flat now. Will you consider leaving at once?' There was a breathlessness in the usually calm voice.

Marriott said calmly: 'If you are right, yes.'

'There is no doubt, Brother Marriott,' Joliffe asserted. 'Go to the window and see for yourself. There are two men at a manhole; they are police officers.'

'Your word is enough for me,' Marriott said calmly. 'You will also leave, making sure that the names and addresses of the Brothers are not left intact.'

'I will see to that.'

'Then we will meet after our final acts of atonement,' Marriott said.

When he replaced the receiver he stepped to the window and looked out. Two men were at a manhole, exactly as Joliffe had said. One of them was looking up at the flat, as if casually. Marriott made no attempt to conceal himself, glancing up and down the street, then drawing back. He picked up a black brief-case, hooked an umbrella over his arm and put his bowler hat on, very straight. He went out, but not towards the lift, towards the stairs. He walked through a doorway marked *Emergency Exit*, crossed a landing where the stairs led up and down, crossed to another door, and was now in a different wing of the building. He walked along to the nearest lift, and pressed the UP button. In two minutes he was in another flat which overlooked the street from a very different angle. He took off his hat, hung it up with his umbrella and sat at a table on which there was only an inkstand and a writing-pad.

Lemaitre stepped out of his car in Victoria Street and took a quick look round. Several Yard and Divisional men were in sight; everything was going as planned. With two Inspectors, a sergeant and a detective officer, he went into the building where *The Simple Brethren* had their office. A man in painter's overalls carrying a brush and paint pot said:

'Still up there, sir.'

'Good.' Lemaitre climbed the stairs two at a time, and reached a door marked *Bibles for Simple Folk*. He did not waste a second in trying the handle, found the door locked, beckoned another, heavier man, and whispered: 'Let's get it down. Try it with our shoulders first.' They put their shoulders to the flimsy-looking door, drew back, and launched their full weight.

The door gave way.

As they staggered in, a sheet of flame shot out from a steel filing cabinet in a corner where a man was standing, working furiously. In another room, two men were ripping paper across and across.

'Stop 'em!' Lemaitre roared. He rushed to the filing cabinet, pushed the man aside, pulled out the drawer in which papers were burning, and emptied it with quick deliberation on to the floor. Fire licked at his hands and face, but he took no notice, methodically treading the flames out. Other policemen had come in and the two men from the inner room were already handcuffed.

An Inspector said: 'I'll do that, sir.'

Lemaitre nodded gratefully and rushed to the other room. Here papers had been taken out of drawers and piled up for burning, others had been torn to shreds. Lemaitre went to one filing cabinet which was untouched so far, and began to go through it. Suddenly he sprang round, snatched up a telephone and dialled the Yard.

'Gimme Commander Gideon!' He was almost exulting. 'Hurry, hurry, hurry! ... Hello, George! ... We've got their names and addresses and a marked list of churches——'

'*And some dynamite sticks,*' a man whispered in his ear.

'And dynamite!' Lemaitre roared. 'If Alec's got *his* man we're home and dry.'

Hobbs, less ostentatious in every way, was just as decisive. He examined the lock of the door at Marriott's flat, a Yale which would take the time they did not have to force. He stood aside and beckoned to men who held jemmies. They started on the door, levering at it vigorously, as Hobbs pressed the bell. He heard nothing except the crunching wood and the occasional sound of metal on metal. As the door swung open he was the first to step inside, and he moved very quickly. It took him less than thirty seconds to discover that the flat was empty.

Within an hour, arrests were being made all over London.

From their homes, their offices, their shops, *The Simple Brethren* were taken by the police, and all premises were searched. In each there was a quantity of dynamite. In some were cards bearing the name of a church, apparently the next to be attacked. In three there were marked lists of churches, and the police set the three men who had these lists aside for special interrogation—men named Joliffe, Abbotsbury and Dennison.

Nowhere was there any mention of Marriott, or of The Committee of Three, nothing more leading than tracts and instructions declaring the purpose of *The Simple Brethren* —worship without ritual and without dogma of any kind.

By mid-afternoon, Gideon's desk was piled high with papers.

'If only *one* of them would talk,' Lemaitre said helplessly.

Gideon was at his most forbidding. 'And if only we hadn't let Marriott get away.'

'We can't expect everything,' Lemaitre protested.

'We need this man because of what he might do,' Gideon said ponderously.

'Can't do more than we are doing.' Lemaitre, secure in the greatness of his triumph, was sitting on a corner of the desk. 'There's a general call out, every paper and every television channel will carry his photograph. We can't be long finding him.'

Gideon, inwardly more disturbed than he allowed Lemaitre to see, turned over some papers, as a telephone bell rang. He picked it up.

'Gideon ... Oh, yes ... Yes, Brixton ... Who? ... Yes, I don't see why not.' He put down the receiver, and said: 'Entwhistle's changed his tune up to a point. He's asked if he can get in touch with his employers, to get them to fix legal aid for him.'

'Suits us if it suits him,' Lemaitre agreed. 'Can't be much of a firm if they haven't already done something about it off their own bat. Pity we can't hang all murdering baskets,' he added. 'Well, I'll see what else I can do.'

He went out.

Gideon made a note in the Entwhistle case file.

Geoffrey Entwhistle, quite sober and very frightened now, told a middle-aged, obviously sceptical solicitor the simple truth, as they sat in his remand cell at Brixton Jail. At that very moment, Eric Greenwood was standing by Bessie Smith's desk, saying that it looked as if the police had caught the sacrilegious devils. In the hospital at Tottenham, Dalby was standing over his daughter, who looked pale and drawn, her eyes darkly shadowed.

'I understand, Sally, I understand, and everything will be all right. We'll let your mother go on thinking that you've been away for a holiday.'

A policewoman sitting in a corner said quietly: 'The important thing is that your daughter should remember everything she can, Mr. Dalby. There are so many other girls we have not yet traced.'

'I am sure she will help in every way,' Dalby said. He bent down and kissed his daughter's forehead.

At Scotland Yard, Rollo was trying to make Toni Bottelli talk, but Bottelli had sunk into a sullen silence. Golightly was looking through the photographs in the cellar at Tottenham, and all the papers found on the premises, but no trace of the other missing girls had yet been found.

Golightly began to go through the stock of the shop itself, while the old crone who looked after it protested sibilantly. He found a section under one counter filled with envelopes marked:

Cigarettes Direct from the Manufacturers
Best Virginian and Turkish Tobacco only used

He opened one of these, to see what literature was enclosed—and found some of the most obscene photographs he had ever come across. Staring at these, even his cheeks became tinged with red.

'My God, what a swine,' he muttered. He tossed them across to another man who was taking sample packets of branded as well as 'privately manufactured' cigarettes; these were going for analysis to the Yard, and if any contained drugs, there would be another charge against Bottelli.

'We might find something from the suppliers of the tobacco, or drugs if there are any,' Golightly remarked. 'Keep at it.'

While all this was going on, bands of voluntary workers were clearing up the debris in the churches, newspapers had more photographs than they could hope to cope with, headlines screamed news of *The Simple Brethren* and the mass of arrests, and every newspaper seemed to heave a sigh of relief, as if the worst were over.

Gideon did not feel so sanguine. Lemaitre did, with ample excuse. Hobbs preferred not to commit himself.

That evening, Hector Marriott sat studying photographs of St. Paul's Cathedral, and at the same time made frequent references to a detailed plan of the main body of the church, the transepts, the galleries and, particularly, the Whispering

177

Gallery. He concentrated more and more on the Whispering Gallery and the various parts of the church which could be seen from it, including the inner dome with the Thornhill cartoons, the high altar and the baldachin. After a while he marked a spot on the Gallery with an X. Standing there, the choir stalls and the High Altar would be clearly visible.

Finished, he moved into an adjacent bedroom and, kneeling, prayed silently for a few minutes before rising and opening a drawer. He took out what looked like a camera, removed the lenses and examined them. They were not in fact lenses, but containers of a particular kind of firework— nor was it a camera, but a light type of pistol.

He fitted in two cartridges. They would be fired simultaneously, and would explode on contact with any hard object. He put the 'camera' down on a table, and took a suit out of the wardrobe. It was very different from the suits he usually wore, being of greeny-red tweed, the jacket belted over bulky knickerbockers. There was also a Tyrolean hat with a feather tucked in the narrow band, and a pair of brown shoes with thick rubber soles.

He contemplated these sartorial aberrations with a satisfied eye before again sinking to his knees in an attitude of prayer. After a long, long silence, his voice rose in supplication:

'When shall it be, O Lord? Grant me the vision that I may do Thy will on the appointed day.'

CHAPTER 24

THE WHISPERING GALLERY

On the Sunday evening, with no further progress made, Gideon flew to Paris.

On the Monday morning, there was a message from Dean Howcroft; would Commander Gideon be good enough to attend an emergency meeting of the Council of Advisers? The message reached Hobbs, who had come in after an early morning cremation service at the Hampstead Crematorium. He rang for Lemaitre, who came in as promptly as he would have had Gideon been there.

'What's on?' he asked.

Hobbs said: 'Dean Howcroft wants one of us at a Council of Advisers. Are you free to go?'

Lemaitre stared.

'I'm *free* enough, but you're Gee-Gee's stand-in.'

Hobbs said stiffly: 'Do you want to go, or don't you?'

Lemaitre, still over-sensitive, drew himself up and answered sharply:

'Naturally I want to go. Any idea what they're after?'

'No,' Hobbs said. 'It's for three o'clock this afternoon.'

'Right. I'll be there.' Lemaitre went off, and Hobbs stared out of the window, wondering whether it was wise to send Lemaitre to such a meeting. He was not thinking as clearly as he liked; in at least one way he had sent Lemaitre because he himself did not feel able to cope.

Helen's death hurt more, infinitely more, than he had expected; the anguish of his loss, the emptiness of wasted years, was almost greater than he could bear.

Lemaitre, very self-conscious and for once unable to cover nervousness with an air of boisterous bonhomie and cock-sureness, entered the room where the Council of Advisers was already waiting. He recognised all of them. There was something almost forbidding about each as they sat together round the table. They made him welcome and yet he had the feeling that they were acutely disappointed at Gideon's absence.

At last, the Chairman Bishop said:

'Mr. Lemaitre, we have two decisions to make and in one of them we shall be guided by your advice.' He paused, to cough. 'Simply this: there is a certain amount of evidence to suggest that the emergency is over, and that the police have made so many arrests that there is little more to fear. It has been suggested that we should not continue with our precautions; at the same time, we do not want to take any grave risk. What is your opinion?'

'Shouldn't think there's any risk for the smaller places,' Lemaitre answered promptly. 'Wouldn't like to say the same about the cathedrals and the Abbey while this chap Marriott is about. He's liable to try anything.'

'But you think we can safely relax the vigilance at the smaller churches? It will be a great relief to many people who are freely giving time they can ill afford to spare.'

'Relax it slowly,' advised Lemaitre. 'You can't be absolutely sure Marriott hasn't got a special hate. He was a member of the C. of E. once.' He sat back, satisfied and pleased with himself, now quite at home. 'What's the other problem?'

'That is one of a rather more delicate nature,' the Bishop said. 'We are, all of us, concerned for the men who have been arrested. We know they have committed grievous offences, against the law and against the Churches we represent, but nevertheless they are human beings. There are rumours of very undue pressure being brought to bear on them, so as to make them talk ...'

Lemaitre slapped his hand on the table, loudly enough to betray his anger.

'I soon told them where to get off,' he reported to Hobbs, an hour later. 'Undue pressure, with Gideon in control! I let 'em have it, I can tell you.'

'They don't know Gideon as well as you do,' Hobbs said drily. 'How about the cathedrals and the Abbey? Have you doubled our patrols on them?'

'Yep! Every place of vantage is covered, there's no need to worry about that.'

'Good,' said Hobbs, trying to force enthusiasm into his voice. 'Now, why don't you go and get some sleep? You've been at it night and day too long.'

'Like an echo of Gee-Gee, you are,' remonstrated Lemaitre. 'If it's okay by you, that's what I'll do.'

He went off a few minutes later, and as soon as he had

gone, Hobbs pulled the telephone towards him and told the operator:

'I will be out for the rest of the day. Don't try to find me. I'll call in from time to time.'

'Yes, sir, but——'

'I'm in a hurry,' Hobbs said irritably.

'There's a call from Paris coming through for you now, sir. From Mr. Gideon. Will you take it?'

Hobbs sat down heavily.

'Yes. Put him through.' Almost immediately there came a voice speaking in almost incomprehensible French, followed by Gideon, saying:

'Are you there, Scotland Yard? Are you——'

'No one's blown us up yet,' Hobbs said mildly.

'Who—oh, Alec. Alec,' repeated Gideon, 'I've been looking through one of the catalogues put out by Marriott's pyrotechnics firm. They make warning lights, miniature Very lights as well as fireworks, and some of them are very small. They've two or three varieties which expel a pellet which only catches alight on contact. That's the kind of thing Marriott might use if he can't get close enough to the place he wants to damage. So all points of vantage from galleries at any height want close watching.'

'I'm going to have them checked personally,' Hobbs said.

In a few minutes, he was on his way.

He went first to Westminster Abbey, up into all the galleries where plainclothes men as well as churchmen were on duty twenty-four hours a day. He was accompanied by the Dean himself, for once untouched by the transcending beauty of the church, as he pointed out every likely place from which great damage could be done. It seemed to Hobbs that the greatest harm would be caused from the Muniment Room, from which the High Altar and the Sanctuary could be seen, and he stationed two more men there. He went to the Roman Catholic cathedral, doubled the police guard at the gallery entrances, and was assured by the Head Sacristan that every possible precaution was being taken. Satisfied, Hobbs drove to St. Paul's.

It was crowded with tourists.

He went first to the higher galleries, and then to the Whispering Gallery, the most obvious place from which to attack the High Altar at a distance. The whole length seemed to be alive with murmurings as of the waves of the sea. Hundreds of people were there, young and old, English and European, American and Asian, most of them apparently intent on the wonder of the great dome and intrigued by the way in which every sound reverberated. There was a German party at the main entrance.

Hobbs went to the outdoor gallery where men stood on duty, making sure no one could climb the columns supporting the dome, or approach from the roof of the nave. It was a pleasant day. No one seemed to notice the plainclothes men. He went back into the gallery and walked about it, peering through the intricate wrought-iron work, deciding that the view immediately opposite the High Altar was likely to be the danger spot.

From here, so much of the cathedral was vulnerable.

Then he saw a weakness in their defence.

The plainclothes men were always on the move, mixing with tourists while paying particular attention to any man on his own. Yet it would take Marriott only a second to point an ejector such as Gideon had mentioned, and aim from the gallery opposite the altar. If a man were so to aim, he would undoubtedly want to be as central as he could, to make sure he caused the greatest possible damage. Hobbs checked this position, doubled back, and went up to the Chief-Inspector in charge of the police on duty.

He said in an aloof way: 'Why aren't you carrying out Mr. Lemaitre's instructions accurately?'

The man was Detective Inspector Goodways of the City Police, under the Yard's authority for this particular task. He was big, middle-aged, experienced and well-trained, and he replied at once:

'I thought we were, sir.'

'Two men ought to be over there,' Hobbs pointed to the central vantage point. 'Didn't Mr. Lemaitre give those precise instructions? I'm sure he did.'

'Er——'

'All right, if you forgot, you forgot,' Hobbs said. 'Make sure the men are there from now on. And watch out for any man who appears to be taking a photograph through the railings, or for anyone who puts his hands to his pocket—or inside his jacket—where he might keep something to throw.'

'Very good, sir.' Goodways showed no sign of his resentment.

Hobbs went off, knowing he had left the man fuming inwardly, but considering it worth while. It might be hard on this man, but it would do him no harm, whereas if anything were to go wrong because of a glaring oversight by Lemaitre, it would have very grave repercussions on Gideon's chief assistant and Lemaitre would never forgive himself. Hobbs had already glimpsed something of the way Gideon got the best out of his men, and had a feeling that Gideon would approve of what he had done today.

Hobbs left the cathedral, still worried, but unable to see anything more he could do.

As he went down the steps opposite the Great West Door, a touring party of Germans or Austrians came up. One of them moved from one side to join the main group, but Hobbs saw nothing strange in that, and flagged down a taxi.

Hector Marriott went in with the crowd of tourists.

Marriott waited until the group were dispersing after being shown the American Roll of Honour and the Tijou Sanctuary Screens, then made his way towards the entrance to the winding staircase leading to the Whispering Gallery. He looked about him all the time, knowing that many of the people nearby were police and cathedral guards, fully aware that he would have only a second or two in which to carry out his mission. He did not hurry even when he reached the gallery, but went round to the section above the choir, bent down to look through the railings, pointed his camera and pretended to take pictures. Then he strolled round towards the spot where Hobbs had stationed the two men. Near by was Detective Inspector Goodways, still smarting, still not sure whether he had indeed misunderstood Lemaitre—or whether Lemaitre had forgotten to tell him.

He watched the solitary tourist who had both hands on the camera with the very long lens attachments. He noticed, with his extra sensitiveness acquired in the past fifteen minutes, that this man seemed to be particularly intent. It was unusual for a German or an Austrian to break away from his group. Alerted, Goodways stepped forward as the man reached a spot exactly opposite the High Altar. The two detectives stationed at the rail moved forward, too. None of them really suspected this man; they were simply taking precautions.

He bent down.

'Excuse me, sir,' Detective Inspector Goodways said.

As he spoke, he saw the other's body tense, saw that instead of straightening up—as would normally have been the case—he bent lower, thrusting the lens with determined calculation through the wrought-iron. On that instant, Goodways realised the awful truth. He let out a great bellow, and leapt forward. At the same moment, an eerie booming filled the gallery and the great dome, echoing and echoing to the clamour of the oncoming police. Goodways grabbed the strap of the 'camera', jolting the man backwards, saw the lens pointing to the roof, and waited breathlessly for the roar he feared would come.

The 'camera' dropped from Marriott's hands. He twisted round, glaring at his assailant. Goodways pulled again at the strap, but Marriott suddenly ducked, put his head through the loop and raced for the exit. He thrust one policeman aside, dodging and turning from others blocking his path. People were shouting, children screaming, there was pandemonium in the gallery and down in the great nave.

Marriott saw one chance; the outer gallery. He ran towards it with police pounding after him. He got through. Beyond was the mighty panorama of London, the shimmering Thames, the great new buildings, the countless spires; in the distance far beyond the great bridges of Blackfriars,

Waterloo and Hungerford, was the outline of Big Ben, the Houses of Parliament and the Abbey.

Footsteps thudded behind him.

Without a moment's hesitation he climbed on to the stone balustrade, poised and dived downwards.

CHAPTER 25

GIDEON'S HOPE

GIDEON stepped off the plane at London Airport on the Wednesday evening, was given all facilities in a perfunctory passage through Customs, and saw Lemaitre among the crowd at the rail beyond the Customs' bay. Lemaitre, looking thoroughly pleased with himself, pumped Gideon's arm and led him away.

'How are the ladies of Paris these days? ... Okay, don't tell me, don't tell me ... Had a good trip? ... Things have gone just right here, George. Had a bit of trouble with the hashish. Golightly's on to something there ... Found where those girls go to, too ... Yes, fact. They get drugs in tobacco from a little spot in the Middle East, can't say where in public or it would start a war ... Excuse me, madam ... In return, our White Slave hero, Bottelli, shipped girls over for the enjoyment and edification of European *gentlemen* who can't get all they want in Europe ... Fact, George. They sign an agreement, and go over as chorus girls. Yes, we've talked to some of them ... First of all Bottelli made a selection, then, after doping the kids, he took his pictures, after which he did his deal with them ... Eh?'

They were getting into his car.

Gideon said: 'What about the Dalby girl?'

'She's okay now. Needs time to recover, but the medicos say she won't remember much.'

'The three dead girls?'

'They threatened to talk, so he gave 'em an overdose of sleeping tablets—young Rhodes got the drugs for him.'

'Does Bottelli admit that?'

'Yes. Rollo worked a miracle on him.'

Gideon grunted as he sat back in the car.

'Anything else?'

'Entwhistle was committed for trial this morning, at the Old Bailey. He did it all right.'

'Looks like it,' Gideon said slowly, conscious of a stirring within him, faint but persistent.

'The hashish and the tobacco have been coming in by air, so I've just been talking to the Airport Police and Customs ... No problem. The church trouble's a thing of the past,' Lemaitre rattled on airily. 'And we're the white-haired boys of the ecclesiastical pundits. Makes a nice change!'

Gideon said: 'Did Marriott say anything?'

'Didn't have time. He broke his neck.'

Gideon said gravely, 'You did a very neat job, Lem.'

'Not so bad, was I?' said Lemaitre, not attempting to assume humility. 'I'll tell you one thing, George.'

'What?'

'Alec Hobbs isn't such a bad old basket.'

Gideon glanced round quickly.

'Getting on all right?'

'Better than I expected. Everyone seems to like him, after all. Doesn't throw his weight about as much as we expected he would, and he's on the ball, believe me he's on the ball. Know what I think, George?'

'Go on.'

'In a funny way, his wife's death helped. Everyone felt sorry about it and if you ask me, it's made him a bit more human.'

'I daresay you're right,' said Gideon slowly. 'Anything new come along?'

'Nothing to worry about,' said Lemaitre. 'The Old Man wants to see you at ten o'clock in the morning, I can tell you that.'

Sir Reginald Scott-Marle was at his desk when Gideon

went to the office next morning. He stood up at once to shake hands, then motioned to a chair.

'How did the gold affair go, George?'

'As far as I can judge it's a storm in a teacup,' Gideon reported. 'Nothing that each country can't handle for itself with a bit of help from Interpol. Most of the others seemed to agree by the time the conference was over.'

'Oh,' said Scott-Marle. 'Pity you went, then.'

'Not a bit,' said Gideon. 'It cleared the air—and it enabled Hobbs and Lemaitre to get to know each other better.'

'That's most encouraging,' said Scott-Marle. 'I'm very glad.'

Gideon went down to his own office, and found the usual pile of reports on his desk, including a request for him to telephone his opposite number in the City of London Police. He put a call in at once.

'Hello, George,' the other man said. 'Bring any Paris lovelies back with you? ... Sly old devil ... I wanted a word about one of our chaps, Detective Inspector Goodways, the man who stopped Marriott shooting in St. Paul's.'

'What about him?' asked Gideon.

'I'd like to recommend him for the George Medal—he took a hell of a risk. But he seems to think you chaps at the Yard have a down on him ... Eh? ... Well, apparently Hobbs tore a strip off him because he'd forgotten something Lemaitre *didn't* tell him to do ... Yes, I said didn't ...'

The City man explained in some detail and in the course of the recital, the obvious truth dawned on Gideon: that Hobbs had chosen this way to cover up the one essential thing which Lemaitre had overlooked. He was smiling broadly by the time the City man had finished.

Then: 'Put through the commendation. We'll gladly support it.'

'Splendid!' the City man enthused. 'I didn't think you would disappoint our Dean.'

Gideon said, puzzled: 'Dean? What Dean?'

'Howcroft,' said the other. 'He seems to have formed a high opinion of you; and he's very pro-Goodways. By the way, he's coming to see you this afternoon.'

'Goodways?'

'No. Dean Howcroft.'

'Oh,' said Gideon.

Howcroft arrived, by appointment, in the middle of the afternoon. His white hair was silkier and more pure-looking than ever, his face had acquired, or resumed, a kind of gentleness, as of peace after storm. He sat down opposite Gideon, studied him closely, and then said:

'Commander, the Council of Advisers would be most grateful for more advice from you.'

'Anything I can do,' said Gideon, warily.

'We are quite sure of that,' said Howcroft. 'We have all the warmest appreciation of your attitude and your good counsel. It is simply this. Since Marriott died as he did—I cannot help feeling that it was a merciful deliverance, for his trial would have been a most distressing *cause célèbre*—the members of his sect are, for the most part, without funds. We have discovered that most of them served God in their own way, however dreadfully mistaken that way was, and lived on a very modest stipend—paid by Marriott.'

Gideon said: 'I gathered he was rich.'

'He was indeed. However, he left nothing to them in a will, having died intestate. At a very lengthy session this morning, all members of the Council of Advisers felt that we should contribute towards the cost of their defence. They were shamefully misguided, but——' He broke off, and shrugged his shoulders. 'Do you have any opinion about this proposal?'

Gideon sat back in his chair, contemplating the old man intently, before he said:

'Yes, Dean Howcroft, I have. I think it's very warming indeed. I only hope the day will come when all people of all religions will feel the way you and the Council do now. Then the world will really be a place to live in.'

The old man's smile was both gentle and serene.

'And you would be out of a job! But I felt sure you would feel like that,' the Dean went on. 'What a remarkably understanding man you are.'

Gideon shuffled uncomfortably, as he was apt to do in the igh moments of his life.

Late that evening, he tried to find the words to tell Kate hat Howcroft had said; she was the only person in the orld whom he could possibly tell. The words wouldn't ome—but Penelope did, bright-eyed and excited. There as to be a special mid-term examination for the near-misses nd she was to sit for it. She was sure she would pass this ime.

Soon, Gideon's home resounded to the joyousness of her laying.

THE END